Testosterone, Dublin 8

First published in 2020 by
Liberties Press
1 Terenure Place | Terenure | Dublin 6W | Ireland
www.libertiespress.com

Distributed in the United States and Canada by
Casemate IPM | 1950 Lawrence Rd | Havertown | Pennsylvania 19083 | USA
Tel: 001 610 853 9131
www.casemateipm.com

Copyright © Gerry Mullins, 2020
The author asserts his moral rights.
ISBN (print): 978-1-912589-13-5
ISBN (e-book): 978-1-912589-14-2

2 4 6 8 10 9 7 5 3 1
A CIP record for this title is available from the British Library.
Cover design by Roudy Design
Printed in Dublin by Sprint Print

Testosterone, Dublin 8

Gerry Mullins

For Ella and Vinny

'Testosterone makes stuff happen. That's what it's for.

'Testosterone is the life-force that enables everyone – male and female – impose their will. It helped us kill other animals for food and defend ourselves when attacked. Without it, our species wouldn't have survived.

'Every act of lust; every baby that was ever conceived outside of a test tube happened because of testosterone. But also every rape. Every murder. Every violent robbery. Every war. Every despicable act of war – testosterone was the enabler.

'Every big business deal: testosterone was at the centre of it. Every race that was ever won; every goal ever scored; every target ever hit - testosterone made it happen.

'You have taken the most powerful substance known to our species, and injected it into your body. You shouldn't be surprised that stuff happened.'

Brother Amos to Jimmy, chapter 24

1

⋺⋺⋺

The Redeemables

At an industrial estate in Dublin 8, on the southern side of Dublin city on a dark, damp night, two men furtively approached a broken fence.

'It's clear,' said Davey nervously. His fair hair was covered by a dark hat that could be pulled down into a balaclava when necessary. His nervousness showed. He didn't like these jobs, but he wouldn't see a friend stuck.

'OK, I'll go,' said Joey. He enjoyed these jobs, but was clearly nervous too. 'You stay here. Whistle, or just shout, if anyone arrives. Or bang a rock off that gate.' He missed the days when a mobile phone didn't track his movements.

Joey scurried over the fence. He kept his body low as he darted across the car park towards the door of the main warehouse. It was locked, but conveniently, a window was open in the floor above. Even more conveniently, a ladder lay on the ground not far away. He couldn't believe his luck.

Moments later, the ladder was against the wall, and he went up. He forced the window open further, but not wide enough to climb through. He produced a short metal bar from his pocket and used it to lever the frame. He scraped at the hinges, hoping to remove some old paint. It helped, but not enough.

Inside, he could see boxes, neatly stacked from floor to ceiling. There was an office desk, and on it, a laptop. There was also a cashbox. He smiled: *This could be a very good night.*

Joey decided to remove the actual window by putting sideward pressure on the hinges. It worked, but a little too quickly. The window slipped quickly off its hinges, flew out of his grip, and smashed on the ground below. He froze, his eyes darting around to see if anyone had been alerted. But no alarm sounded. No lights suddenly illuminated in nearby buildings. No throaty barks from security dogs. Nothing.

In the shadows, he could make out Davey's figure. He whistled over once: a quick, high-pitched peep. Davey replied with two quick toots, as if to say 'OK'. The coast remained clear.

With the window removed, a sizeable space gaped in the window-frame. Joey heaved himself up, transferring his weight gently from the ladder onto the frame, and hurled himself head-first onto the dark floor inside.

He lay still on the ground, listening for any sound that would indicate that his presence had been detected. His eyes adjusted to the room, which was darker than the car park outside.

Suddenly he felt something hard wrap itself around his left ankle. Then the same feeling was on his right ankle. In the moment when he was trying to figure out what was going on, he felt something grab his left wrist. 'What the hell?' he shouted.

*

Joey Watt was blinded by the sudden illumination of two quartz lights and a spotlight. From behind the boxes appeared several people, wearing headphones and sporting clipboards. Two people operated cameras: one on a tripod, the other hand-held. He looked around, to see that three of his limbs were chained to the wall.

'What the fuck?' he bellowed. 'What the fuck? What the fuck is going on?'

A man approached Joey, and said calmly: 'Hi, I'm Jimmy Fyffe, the producer of *The Redeemables* on TV Ireland. This is a citizen's arrest, under the Criminal Law Act, 1997. I believe you to be in flagrante, having committed, and about to commit, arrestable offences.'

'Get the fuck away from me, you bollix!' Joey roared. 'Let me go, or I'll fucking kill you!'

Jimmy continued: 'We will surrender you to Garda custody as soon as practicable, but first we must ask you an important question.'

'Ask my fucking hole!'

'You may avoid surrender to An Garda Síochána if you agree to be our guest on *The Redeemables*, and abide by our terms and conditions.'

Joey lunged at Jimmy, but was restrained by the chains. 'Get the fuck away from me, you prick! Get the fuck away, or I'll fucking kill you!'

Jimmy remained calm and out of range of Joey's feet and fists. 'I must warn you that this is being recorded for broadcast. Everything you do and say, including death-threats, may also be used by An Garda Síochána as part of their criminal investigations.'

'I don't give a fuck, you fucking prick!' shouted Joey, his voice rising to a hysterical level. 'I will waste you! I will waste the lot of you. I will find out where yiz all live!'

With his free hand, Joey reached into his jacket and grabbed his metal bar. With one swift and strong back-handed movement, he flung the bar hard. Jimmy saw it too late, and was struck on the side of the head. He fell backwards on the floor, stunned. He was unsure how bad his injury was, but he could feel blood trickle from his eyebrow down into his ear.

Jimmy was dragged along the carpet from the lighted office into a larger room down the hall that had been used by his team earlier. People shouted questions at him: 'Jimmy, are you OK?' 'Jimmy, do you want us to call an ambulance?' 'How many fingers am I holding up?'

Back under the TV lights, Joey roared out the open window: 'Davey, it's a trap! Don't come up here, Davey! Get outta here!'

A well-dressed woman approached Joey, and bent over to speak to him. 'My name is Linda Carroll from Carroll and Wakeman Solicitors. I have been assigned to provide you with legal assistance.'

'Fuck off, bitch!'

The solicitor held out two documents, and continued: 'You have two choices. You are invited to take part in *The Redeemables*, agreeing to work with our advisers to identify and tackle the issues that have led you to commit crimes tonight, and appear on the show in the coming weeks. Or the evidence of your crimes that we recorded tonight will be given to the police and may be used as evidence in a court of law.'

'It won't work, bitch,' snarled Joey. 'That's entrapment. You haven't a fucking hope.'

Linda remained cool: 'Thanks for your advice, but I'm the lawyer here, not you. Entrapment is when someone is tricked into breaking the law. In your case, there was no deception. You weren't tricked into committing crimes tonight; you were intercepted *while* committing them.'

She looked down at her notes. 'Your crimes tonight include aggravated burglary, causing criminal damage, threatening to kill, and assault. You need to decide if you are ready to face these charges in court, or if you will accept the invitation to appear on *The Redeemables*.'

Joey lowered his tone. 'I'll get you, you fucking bitch! Me and me mates!'

Linda smiled. 'You're really not helping yourself.' Turning to the crew, she said: 'Why don't we give this gentleman a few minutes to think about his options?'

In the other room, Jimmy's wound was being treated. It looked worse than it seemed; the only real damage was to his pride. 'How're you feeling, Jimmy?' Danny, his assistant producer, asked. 'I don't think you'll need a stitch.'

'I . . . I didn't see it coming,' said Jimmy, examining the back of his hands. 'Look, I'm shaking.'

'You *do* look a bit shook, all right,' said Danny.

The rest of the crew began pouring into the room, to see how their injured producer was. Jimmy looked pale and confused. 'I should have been ready, I suppose . . . . I . . . I . . . He caught me by surprise.'

As he spoke, the edges of his mouth tugged downwards and his facial muscles contorted. His eyes welled up.

Danny was surprised to see Jimmy start to cry, and moved quickly to spare his boss any embarrassment. 'Out, out! Everyone out,' he said, as he shooed the crew from the room. 'Give the man a bit of space.'

'I'm sorry,' said Jimmy, composing himself. 'I don't know what that was all about. I'll be fine.'

'That's all right,' said Danny. 'It's probably a bit of shock setting in.'

*

Four weeks later, Jimmy was a hero again.

Joey Watt was TV gold. He was already on a suspended sentence – which meant that any evidence supplied to the Gardaí by the television station would automatically land him back in prison to finish off a previous six-year sentence. He had no option but to co-operate fully with the show. Many of *The Redeemables'* reluctant stars were serving suspended sentences at the time they were invited to take part in the show.

Joey's life-story made grim, but compelling, viewing: a violent home; an addicted mother; the first forays into crime as a teenager; the drugs; and the ultimate descent into serious crime. The hour-long programme also showed his earnest efforts to engage with a psychologist and a career counsellor the show had provided. In the editing studio, Jimmy made use of photographs provided by Joey's family, press photographs from his many court appearances, and interviews with Joey's friends and family. Short interview clips with psychologists and criminologists carried stern warnings of the dangers of drugs, and getting involved in criminal behaviour. Jimmy illustrated these warnings with slow-motion footage of a raging Joey on the night of the break-in.

Jimmy edited out much of the bad language, but the violence and anger of a trapped animal remained. The episode started with this hard edge but gradually gave way to softness as the viewer learned more about 'the boy within the man'. The dramatic arc was completed when a tearful Joey held his daughter and promised to turn away from crime and be a better father.

TV Ireland knew that the ratings would be high, just as they had been in the previous edition, when Jimmy's team had intercepted a car thief in a similar manner. *The Redeemables* was making money, and the credit was mostly due to one man: Jimmy Fyffe, the show's creator and producer. Jimmy felt good.

There was a snag, however. Danny took Jimmy to one side as the show ended, and out of earshot of the crew whispered: 'I thought we were going to bleep out the name "Davey".'

'Yes, we were,' said Jimmy.

'Well what happened?' asked Danny.

Jimmy took a deep breath, before continuing, quietly: 'I dunno. It was on my list of last-minute edits, but I must have let it slip.'

'Why were you editing?' asked Danny. 'That's not your job.'

Jimmy was at pains to explain: 'It would have meant bringing in Kevin at the weekend, and I just couldn't deal with the pain of asking him.'

'That's his job, Jimmy. And it's your job to tell him when to edit, no matter what day it is.'

Jimmy was clearly disappointed in himself: 'I know, I know, but I couldn't deal with another confrontation. I decided I'd be better off doing it myself.'

'And why didn't you?' asked Danny.

Jimmy took another deep breath. 'I dunno, man. It was on a list of about ten edits, and I just overlooked it. I don't know what happened. Between yourself and myself, I forgot. OK?'

'OK,' said a worried-looking Danny.

'But say nothing,' said Jimmy. 'There are lots of Daveys out there. We don't know if there was a Davey there that night, or if it was an alias, or a code-word, or whatever. Let's just say nothing, and hope nobody notices.'

Monica Jenkins, chair of TV Ireland, smiled coldly at Jimmy as he left the set. She enjoyed the authority that came with being head of the station, almost as much as Jimmy resented it.

'Well done,' she said. 'Though it was a bit risky leaving in the part where the guy shouts out "Davey".'

Monica always knew how to take the joy out of a screening night for Jimmy. 'There are lots of Daveys out there, Monica,' he said, feigning indifference. 'He wasn't identified. The lawyer wasn't concerned. It reminds the audience that for each redeemed person, there are others still out there, committing crimes.'

'Mmm, I wouldn't be so sure,' mused Monica in an offhand way. 'You need to be more careful,' she said, as she glided away.

Inspector 'Squeezy' McClean ambled over to Jimmy, holding some Oreos in a napkin. He was the most senior Garda in the Kilmainham district – which meant that the warehouse, the TV station, and Jimmy's home were on his beat.

'Well done, Jimmy boy,' said McClean. 'Entertaining, at least.'

McClean was of a generation of men who believed a comb-over could conceal baldness, and a generation of policemen who thought a cream raincoat would enable them 'blend in'.

McClean irritated Jimmy. He liked to play the cute country Guard, and slink around saying as little as possible, but observing everything.

Worse, in Jimmy's eyes, McClean liked to play the cute country Guard *from Cork*. Despite having lived in Dublin for more than thirty years, McClean had neglected to transfer his accent from his native Doneraile. He still punctuated his sentences with 'boy', and often expressed a view that suggested that Dublin would be a lot better if it only tried harder to be like Cork.

'Do you think, boy, you'll be doing many more of these ol' programmes?' asked McClean, as if attending *The Redeemables* was a chore for him.

'Hopefully, Squeezy, hopefully,' said Jimmy. 'We're just trying to help you out with the business of law and order.'

The relationship between An Garda Síochána and the TV show was always strained. The police didn't enjoy the ease with which Jimmy's team could catch people in the act of committing crimes. It led to questions in the media, and in the Dáil, about the Gardaí's competence in this important aspect of police-work. Despite this, a Garda presence was necessary on the night of a live-screening, and McClean was always eager to mooch around the studio, picking up titbits of food – and information.

Jimmy was eager to wish Joey well before he left. They both lived in Dublin 8, so there was every chance they would bump into each other on the street. It was important for Jimmy to end the evening on good terms.

He saw Joey heading for the door with a man who looked out of place: too nerdy to be a criminal, and too conservative-looking to work in TV. He wore a long old coat that reminded Jimmy of student union marches in the 1980s, and a pair of boot-runners that were only partially laced. He had acne, and stubble of the non-designer kind. His hair needed a trim and a wash.

'Who's yer man with Joey?' Jimmy asked Squeezy.

'That, I am told, is Joey's "medical advisor",' replied the inspector, in a sceptical tone. 'He came in case Joey had an asthma attack. He's the GP of choice for Dublin's criminal class: the doctor of last resort.'

Jimmy crossed the room quickly. 'Joey, I just wanted to say: you were great tonight,' he said, extending a hand. 'I bet you inspired thousands of young people who might otherwise – '

'Go fuck yourself, you pompous prick,' replied Joey sternly. 'You got your fucking show, now fuck off out of my life.'

'Right,' said Jimmy, unsure of what to say next. He turned to the man beside Joey, and stretched out his hand again. 'I'm Jimmy, the show's producer. Thank you for coming tonight.'

'I'm Malcolm, Joey's medical advisor,' said the other man, in a mid-Atlantic accent.

'Oh, do you practise locally?' asked Jimmy, hoping to get an address, or the name of a clinic.

'Yes,' he replied, unhelpfully. 'I practise wherever and whenever my patients need me.' He reached into his pocket and produced a business card. 'Here, you might need to call me sometime.'

As they left, Jimmy examined the card. It read simply: 'Malcolm, Medical Advisor', and gave a mobile number.

Danny appeared again at Jimmy's shoulder: 'Hey, the team is heading out to a party. Wanna come? I'd say it will be a good one.'

Jimmy laughed at the impossibility of the idea. 'Danny, you know . . . I have no doubt it will be a good party, but . . . you know the way it is. TV attracts beautiful people. Beautiful people attract cocaine. So it's not the kind of party a boss should attend.'

'Come for one,' said Danny. 'Let's celebrate another great show.'

Jimmy looked wistfully at the happy studio. Pretty girls laughed with gay men, and nobody had to work for three more days. It was a tempting prospect for a single man. But he wasn't single. It was a forbidding prospect for a married man. But he wasn't really married either. The sadness of his home-life entered his mind momentarily. He was unsure of his social position; unsure of his own boundaries. He wondered if he dared enjoy himself.

'Come on, Jimmy,' said Danny. 'Let yourself go.'

Jimmy shrugged. 'Thanks, I'd best go home.'

*

'There are lots of Daveys out there, Gunner,' pleaded Joey. 'Our Davey wasn't identified.'

Joey's hands were tied behind his back. Blood, sweat, tears, saliva and mucus oozed from different parts of his head, and mingled on the table that his face was being bashed against.

'You stupid arsehole!' roared Gunner as he lifted Joey's head by the hair at the back of his head. 'You don't . . . ' – smacking Joey's head off the table – 'shout out . . . ' – *smack* – 'your partner's name . . . ' – *smack* – 'in the middle of a fucking job!' *Smack.*

'Gunner, honest to God, I wouldn't rat out my friend . . . . I was trying to save him! He's my mate. There's no point in us both gettin' trapped,' pleaded Joey.

Davey stepped towards the table. 'He didn't mean any harm, Gunner. He was just trying to look out for me, he was.'

Gunner wasn't much taller than Davey, but he was considerably broader, and far more aggressive. His small red head was set on a short thick neck, and whenever he got angry, it looked like it might pop off. His arms, tattooed and muscular, ended with two large fists, one of which he raised to Davy's face and bellowed: 'Fuck off, ye little faggot! Youse little fuckers have to learn how this business works. Yiz don't do yiz'er own jobs without telling me first! Righ'? Ye don't go on the telly making a fuckin' arse of yourself, crying about your sad life in crime! Righ'? And ye don't go on the telly shoutin' out your mate's name! Do yiz understand?'

Davey nodded in fearful agreement, and returned to his seat beside another young gang member, Midget.

'Now, what are we going to do with our teammate here?' roared Gunner.

Before anyone could answer, Hank Savage entered the room. Davey and Midget stood, in deference to their boss.

'Hank, I didn't do nothing wrong!' roared Joey. 'There's a million and one Daveys out there, there is. He wasn't identified.'

'Shut the fuck up,' said Gunner, giving him a box in the ribs.

'Enough,' said Hank. 'What's going on?'

Gunner started: 'These young lads need discipline, Hank. They've no fucking idea what they're at – making trouble for themselves and everyone else.'

'We weren't making trouble,' shouted Joey. 'We wuz just doing a little bit of our own work . . . .'

'Shut the fuck up!' shouted Gunner.

'Enough, I said,' countered Hank. 'Gunner, let's talk outside.'

The two senior men went into the next room of the garage, which served as the gang's base.

'Gunner, he didn't identify Davey,' said Hank. 'He just – '

'Boss, these are your rules. You made them up years ago, and that's what made us strong,' said Gunner emphatically. 'You always said "Zero tolerance." "Zero fucking tolerance." "Ye don't tolerate fuckin' messers." That's the way it was before you went into prison, and that's the way I ran things while you were inside.'

The older man tried to calm the conversation: 'I know, Gunner, but he didn't identify anyone.'

'He fucking did! He identified himself by going on the telly. Everyone – cops, mee-ja, and other gangs . . . they all know his best mate is Davey. So everyone knows Davey was out that night doing a warehouse. Everyone knows they are our men, even if it wasn't official business. That compromises us.'

'But there's been no charges, Gunner. The TV company isn't going to pass on any evidence.'

'You always said, "Nip it in the bud!" Ye get rid of the bad apple before it contaminates everything. These lads have to be taught a serious lesson.'

'Like what, Gunner?'

'Like, you know what,' said Gunner, in a lowered tone.

'Boss, don't kill him,' said Davey, who had been listening at the doorway. 'Just teach him a lesson, like, cut one of his fingers off, or something.'

'I'll cut one of your balls off, you little prick, if you don't fuck off back inside!' roared Gunner.

Davey returned to the other room – and his seat beside Midget. Both looked defeated.

'Gunner, I don't think it's right to kill the lad,' said Hank. 'He's a kid. They're all kids.'

'You always said – '

'I know what I always said, for Christ's sake!' said Hank, in an irritated tone.

'Hank, you're the boss. You have to decide: do ye want these lads to respect ye, or do ye want them to fear ye? Or do ye just want them to like ye?' asked Gunner dismissively. 'You have to set the example here.'

'I know I do, Gunner. I . . . I . . . I . . . I just don't think it's right.'

'You're the boss. I'm only carrying out orders,' said Gunner. 'You make the decision, and I'll just do what I'm told.'

Hank was silent for a while, then swore under his breath: 'All right, do what you have to do.' He left the building without saying anything more to his employees.

Two days later, a farmer in County Meath made the grim discovery of Joey Watt's body in a ditch.

*

Morning radio broke the news that a man's body had been found. The usual coded message was used to assure the good people of Middle Ireland that it wasn't one of their own who had been murdered. 'The victim was "known to Gardaí",' said the newsreader, with an almost-audible wink.

Jimmy heard the news as he drove to work, and thought nothing of it until he got to the office. There, the journalists already had the victim's name, and they remembered that he had been on *The Redeemables*.

Jimmy's heart sank. He had grown to know Joey well, having conducted the interviews with him, and then spending hours editing them. He knew when and where Joey was born, his siblings' names, and all about his nasty parents. He had interviewed his girlfriend, and met his daughter. He knew where they lived – which was just ten minutes' walk from his own house in Dublin 8. He also knew that if the murder could be linked to *The Redeemables*, the show could be in jeopardy.

The following day, *News Ireland* cited 'well-placed sources in Dublin's criminal underworld' who linked the murder of Joey Watt with his appearance on *The Redeemables*. A meeting was called for Monica Jenkins' office at 11AM. Jimmy and Danny, as well as a few senior station officials, were summoned. When Jimmy saw that the head of HR was present, he sensed trouble.

Monica avoided eye-contact with Jimmy as she started the meeting: 'OK everyone, thank you for coming. I don't need to tell you why we're here. Suffice to say, we are in a crisis. And the best way to limit the damage is for the station to distance itself from the show.'

'What do you mean, Monica?' asked Jimmy.

Monica looked at him glumly, and said: 'We're cutting the show.'

'What?' gasped Danny, almost rising to his feet. 'What the hell? You can't do that!'

'Easy, easy, Danny,' said Jimmy calmly. 'Let's hear what Monica has to say.'

Monica continued: 'Cathy is here from HR, and I have asked her to meet with each of the team individually to go over the . . . erm . . . procedure.'

'What procedure?' asked Jimmy.

Monica took a deep breath, and spoke to Jimmy as if she was explaining something Jimmy already knew: 'Jimmy, you and the others are on specific-purpose contracts. If there's no show, there's no contract.'

'No way!' shouted Danny. 'You can't just terminate us. I've a mortgage to pay!'

'Easy, Danny,' said Jimmy again. 'Monica, let's just go over the options before we jump to any conclusions. We haven't even talked through the controversy yet. Let's discuss it, and then make informed decisions.'

'*We* have discussed it,' said Monica, glancing at the other officials. 'And we *have* made informed decisions.'

Jimmy felt belittled. He tried hard to think of a retort, but nothing came to mind.

Danny could think of plenty to say: 'I'm not fucking happy about this. This is my fucking job you're talking about! Myself and Jimmy, and the others: we've all got families, and mortgages to pay.'

'I'm aware of that,' said Monica, 'and I'm very sorry about it all. Nobody was expecting this to happen. Nobody thought somebody was going to get killed.'

'We can work through it,' said Jimmy. 'Crims shoot crims all the time. It's not necessarily our fault.'

'If the public says it's our fault, then it *is* our fault,' said Monica.

'The public hasn't spoken on the matter, so all the more reason for us to keep our own voices out there,' said Danny.

'Don't you look at social media?' shouted Monica. 'Twitter is in meltdown over this.'

Jimmy frowned in disbelief at Monica: 'There's no such thing as Twitter going into meltdown.'

'The public is saying very clearly that *The Redeemables* should be shut down,' said Monica.

Danny leaned forward. 'Monica, we have a viewership of over 300,000. There were less than a hundred comments on Twitter. What's that? A bit of a percent? You want to make an important decision based on the comments of a few people who have too much time on their hands?'

'The comments are unanimous,' she retorted.

'So what?' said Danny. 'They're hardly a representative sample. Would you say "Nobody in my local pub liked the show, so we're shutting it down"? Or "Nobody on my bus home liked the show, so we're letting you all go"? Of course not.'

'Monica, we can work through this,' said Jimmy, trying to think fast. 'We can have a special programme in memory of Joey. Show previously unseen footage. The whole thing emphasises the bravery of our team, and the importance of our work. We might evoke a degree of sympathy for' – he used his fingers to indicate quote marks – "the unfortunate individuals who try to escape the vice-grip of crime".'

He remembered how to influence Monica. 'The viewership will be the biggest ever. Massive.'

Monica had already considered this. 'I know it would be massive, Jimmy, but we wouldn't make a cent. The advertisers won't touch the show.'

'It's not all about money,' shouted Danny. 'It's about people too.'

Monica responded calmly: 'Gentlemen, you are in the business of crafting TV. I am in the business of getting someone to pay for it. Nothing happens unless someone pays for it, so it *is* all about money.'

Monica closed her notebook and put her pen down, to indicate that the meeting was over. 'Gentlemen, this station has a potential buyer coming in from America next week, and I can't have this crisis hanging around like a bad smell as we go into negotiations. So I'm sorry, but *The Redeemables* is finished.'

After the meeting, Danny tackled Jimmy: 'Why didn't you stand up for us in there?'

'You heard her: the decision had been made,' replied Jimmy, weakly.

'You're our producer: our leader. You're the one we look to to protect our jobs,' said Danny.

'What did you expect me to do?' demanded Jimmy.

'I expected you to fight. At least fight for your own job, if not ours!'

'How?' demanded Jimmy.

'I don't know. It's your job to figure that out, not mine,' said Danny. 'Why didn't you tell her that you'll take legal advice, and that you'll sue her arse off if she terminates our contracts? Huh?'

'Well, I'm not sure if we have a case legally – '

'So what?' shouted Danny. 'You used to be able to bluff your way out of things. You used to be good at issuing credible threats! It doesn't matter if you've a legal case or not: you would have put doubt in her mind. It would have bought us time. Why didn't you tell her that if she touches our jobs, we'll go to the newspapers and tell them how she encouraged us to take risks, but then cut us off when one backfired?'

Jimmy was flustered. 'I'm not sure that that would be a wise approach, considering – '

'Wise approach!' repeated Danny, disdainfully. 'We've lost our jobs! How wise was your approach?'

'Danny, I ah . . . I think you're assuming I could just magic up a solution . . . .'

'I'll tell you this, Jimmy,' said Danny. 'There was a time when you figured things out very quickly, and that witch wouldn't have dared fire you, because you would have bitten her fucking head off. But you've changed, Jimmy. You're not the man you used to be.'

*

At home, Jimmy broke the news to his wife Milfoth.

'You let her do that? You didn't even put up a fight!' she roared.

'I didn't have a choice,' he said despondently.

'Well, do you have a choice about paying the mortgage? Huh?'

'I'll get severance,' said Jimmy wearily. He had hoped for support, not another rebuke.

'You'd better get good severance,' shouted Milfoth. 'And you'd better get up tomorrow and get yourself another job. Wash dishes, or whatever it takes. It might toughen you up.'

'Look, it was not in my control to save the show, but it *was* in my control to leave on the best possible terms, so that when another opportunity arises, they'll bring me back in.'

'Well, you'd better hope that other opportunity arises tomorrow, because we have bills to pay,' she said, as she turned away from the conversation. 'You're too soft – in more ways than one.'

Jimmy watched his wife go up the stairs, and raised a middle finger in her direction. It happened often.

2

❧❧❧

Dublin 8

Nobody from Jimmy's background aspires to living in Dublin 8. Children in the area where Jimmy was raised didn't dream of owning an artisan cottage in Dolphin's Barn, or a flat in The Coombe, or anything in the Liberties.

Their parents didn't encourage playdates in Inchicore, or making friends with the girls and boys of nearby Crumlin or Drimnagh. Maybe some people who grew up in Dublin 8 were content to live there, but they weren't from Jimmy's tribe.

He had aspired to a life in the cleaner, more affluent suburbs of one of the three 'Rs': Ranelagh, Rathgar and Rathmines. He hadn't considered a fourth 'R', Rialto, until the booming economy pushed house prices in 'nice' areas beyond his reach.

Jimmy and Milfoth first met on a beach in Paros when island-hopping in Greece was at its most popular. She later told a friend that she was attracted instantly to Jimmy because he was engaging and funny. He told a friend that he was attracted to her because she was nearly naked.

They first got together a week later, at a party on Ios. And when they both showed up at Santorini on the same day, it seemed that fate had determined they would be together. They returned to Ireland as a couple, but only stayed long enough to save for a backpacking trip around South America.

They were good travelling companions, and created a lot of happy memories. Jimmy enjoyed finding interesting destinations and reading up on the history and geography of an area in advance. Milfoth enjoyed the logistics: making sure they arrived at the right place, and at the right time, with passports and other necessary documents.

Three years after their Greek adventure, the couple made love under a full moon after a day of surfing at Australia's Byron Bay. Their daughter was conceived that night and they would name her Byron. It was time to come home and settle down.

With little savings or employment records, Jimmy and Milfoth found that the Dublin 2, 4 and 6 postcodes were gone from their list of possibilities. They had to settle for the unfamiliar postcode of Dublin 8. Jimmy's father, who funded their deposit, openly resented their choice of neighbourhood, and rarely visited.

They bought in a cul-de-sac of terrace houses built by the Irish state fifty years earlier. The area had served as the bellwether of the wider Dublin 8 economy: originally a poor local-authority district; then a stable community as locals purchased their homes from the council; and now a somewhat prosperous district as new owners remodelled their homes to capture light and space in ways that had not been envisioned by the original architects.

Jimmy and Milfoth weren't alone. Hundreds of other couples had also bought in Dublin 8, all thinking it was 'only for a few years'. But no sooner had they unloaded their furniture when a great iron door slammed shut behind them. The economy crashed; they owed more than their houses were worth; so they were stuck. They just had to accept that their temporary housing solution was now their permanent home.

But there were silver linings in the dark Dublin 8 cloud. The Luas arrived, connecting the area with the courts service – which made it an attractive location for legal practitioners. And the new children's hospital attracted medical professionals and other higher-paid workers to the area.

The council made it easier for blow-ins by removing some of the housing projects that had brought infamy to their postcode. It demolished the notorious St Michael's Estate in Inchicore, leaving only a field. It pulled down the St Teresa's Gardens complex, with a promise of regeneration. It removed the former Weaver Park and Chamber Court flat complexes, and replaced them with a playground and a skate-park. The Dolphin House complex was upgraded with balconies and other features that made them look, in Jimmy's opinion, 'respectable – almost desirable'.

The most notorious of all the estates, Fatima Mansions, was expunged; not even its name survived. The former centre of Ireland's heroin trade was replaced by new, mixed-use, pleasant buildings called 'Herberton'. The area was now so acceptable that people of Jimmy's demographic went there to use the gym. It was one of the few places in Dublin 8 where the different tribes – natives, blow-ins and foreigners – mingled.

Jimmy wondered sometimes what had happened to the people who had lived in the neighbourhoods that had been demolished – but not for very long. Such is the process of gentrification all over the world that the new arrivals have little knowledge of, or interest in, the people they have replaced. Their focus is on what they see as improvements: new coffee shops and restaurants; and remodelled pubs.

Consciously or otherwise, Jimmy's tribe of blow-ins differentiated themselves from their native neighbours. They dressed differently, had different social outlets, and spoke with accents derived from outside Dublin's inner city. The newcomers had more liberal political views too – so much so that Jimmy sometimes referred to his area as 'fast becoming a hotbed of organic foods, mindfulness and lesbianism'.

He could identify fellow blow-ins by the cars they drove. They tended to be more expensive brands, but old models – indicative of high aspirations tempered by high mortgages. Jimmy himself drove an eleven-year-old Mercedes, saying 'It's the only marque that looks better with age'.

Blow-ins lived independently of their native neighbours in most aspects of their lives, but the two tribes were funnelled towards each other in certain areas. These included the pleasant walks along the Grand Canal, where Jimmy used to jog until it brought him into conflict with dog-owners and what he termed their 'four-legged shitting machines'. On one occasion, he almost came to blows with a 'real Dub' who was walking a Doberman that was not on a lead.

'Put a fucking lead on your dog!' shouted Jimmy.

'Ara, would you relax, it's only a pup,' insisted the man. 'Come over here and pet her yourself.' The dog rolled over and the man rubbed its belly.

'I'm not touching your mange-bag!' shouted Jimmy.

'It would do ye good to pet a dog,' said the other man. 'It would help ye get rid of all that stress.'

On another occasion, Jimmy was startled by a teenager who sped along the footpath on a bicycle. Jimmy stopped him and, while holding the handlebars, lectured the boy on bike safety and etiquette.

The boy said very little, except the customary 'Would you ever fuck off?' Then suddenly, he stood high on the pedals and headbutted Jimmy.

Jimmy drew back his fist, but realised quickly that this was a fight he could not win. Could he really stand the embarrassment of being arrested for assaulting a teenager? It occurred to him also that he had never thrown a punch before and couldn't be confident that it would connect. He felt that he had no choice but to let the youth go. He continued his jog – cursing the kind of people who made up his community.

In recent years, he lacked the energy either to jog or to fight with his neighbours, so he retreated to the relative calm of the gym. He pushed weights for a few years, but with no noticeable benefit. Increasingly he made straight for the hot tub, where he hoped that the heated bubbles would dissolve the layers of fat that had gathered around his abdomen. It didn't seem to work, though.

Children's education was the area where tribal separation required the most vigilance. Native families were comfortable in the bosom of Roman Catholic schools. That pushed blow-in parents to seek out alternative school patronage.

The Educate Together system was the preferred choice for Dublin 8 blow-ins – an option sometimes referred to by Jimmy as 'Educate Apart'. And the local Protestant school was at capacity, even though Jimmy was not aware of any families in the area that were practising Protestants.

Irish-language schools were also popular for blow-ins, even though the Irish language itself wasn't. Jimmy and Milfoth sent Byron to an Irish-language school. All three of them refused to speak the language in their home.

And then there was the defining badge of Dublin 8 blow-in-ness: Ennis Butchers in Rialto. It reminded Jimmy's tribe that even if they couldn't afford to live in middle-class Dublin, a little bit of middle-class Dublin dwelt amongst them. Jimmy described it as 'a good place to get your quail eggs'.

It was here, in the socio-economic mixing bowl of Dublin 8, that Jimmy first got the idea for *The Redeemables*. He was standing in his local shop beside a pregnant woman who was buying cigarettes, and a young man who was behaving so aggressively that Jimmy was afraid to make eye-contact with him. Catching sight of the young man's neck tattoos, Jimmy wondered if, with the right supports, he could ever be 'redeemed'. He wrote a proposal that was accepted, and he created the show that had sustained the family for several years.

3

⊷⊷⊷

Jimmy and Milfoth

Of course, 'Milfoth' wasn't her real name. It was derived from the acronym for 'Mother I'd Like to Fuck', which had been applied to her more than once. Jimmy had often taken pride in being married to a MILF.

But in recent years, as their hostilities intensified, Jimmy lengthened the acronym to MILFOTH: Mother I'd Like to Fuck Outta The House. Jimmy ceased addressing his wife by any name, and Milfoth was a moniker he only ever used silently.

He worried that Byron would turn out to be argumentative, like her mother. He mused that if he could afford boarding school, he would send them both there.

Losing his job didn't just present Jimmy with a financial challenge, it stirred up a long-felt feeling that he had under-achieved in his life. He had reached four and a half decades without a job that was permanent, or savings that would sustain him in his retirement years. He was married to someone he didn't like, was father to someone he couldn't connect with, and lived in a district his old friends didn't like to visit. He didn't have many new friends.

He felt he had been raised for finer things: a lifestyle best described as 'middle-class'. His school friends had achieved this, as had his siblings. But he hadn't, and he was reminded of this every time his family got together. He felt the burden of competition, or, more to the point, the burden of defeat in a never-ending competition.

His late father, known widely as 'Jacko', had written Jimmy off as early as his teenage years. Like many men of his era, Jacko's ambition for his son was influenced by Tony O'Reilly whose success in international business had its roots in relationships he formed while playing rugby.

With such ambitions for Jimmy, Jacko sent his slightly-built boy to Blackrock College and it was a failure. Jimmy joined the ranks of that pitiful category of privileged Irish teenagers: the boys who went to Blackrock but didn't play rugby. This gave licence to Jacko to openly question the merits of funding Jimmy's education, as well as his sexuality.

'Not good enough' was his mantra when dealing with his sensitive boy. 'Not good enough.'

Even Jimmy's successes in television in later life were minimised by a cruel jibe: 'It isn't RTÉ, never mind the BBC.'

And now, as Jimmy lay in bed the morning after his show had been cut, the wounds returned. For a moment it seemed that his father was in the room with him, mocking him from the seat in the corner. 'Not good enough, James,' he said caustically. 'You wouldn't listen to me, and now look at you.' Even in death, Jacko had the ability to hurt his son.

Jimmy had intended going into the office to tie up the last of the loose ends, but he couldn't. He had showered, and started to dress for work, but a wave of despair and anxiety rolled over him with such force that he returned to bed, still wearing his work-shirt.

Fortunately, Milfoth and Byron had left the house early, and weren't there to witness his crash. He cried, at first quietly, but then he howled. His sobbing was so loud that he feared that his neighbours might hear him. He pulled a pillow over his face and bawled into it.

He looked at himself in the mirror, almost to verify that it was him who was crying. He saw red eyes and wet cheeks, and a sad crumpled man looking back at him. 'What the fuck are you going to do?' he asked himself over and over again. 'Oh Jesus Christ, what the fuck are you going to do now?

4

Out in the Cold

The social welfare system wasn't designed for Jimmy's tribe. First, they made him queue to get a weekly payment, and then that payment was far too small for someone who was paying a mortgage. It came from the Department of Social Protection, but he didn't feel socially protected.

At his local welfare office on Cork Street, Jimmy pleaded with the deciding officer to deliver his payment directly to his bank account, rather than him having to queue at a post office. But she wouldn't budge.

'Why? Are you planning on not being in the country?' she enquired, with a suspicious tone.

'No, I'm just trying to . . . maintain my dignity,' replied Jimmy wearily.

'Our other clients are happy to get their payments in the post office,' countered the lady behind the desk. 'Do you think you're better than them?'

Jimmy didn't answer.

At the nearby post office, Jimmy queued for his money. In front of him, a man was shouting into a phone in a broad Dublin accent – something about money owed or not owed. Someone else in front of him stank of piss. The lady in the welfare office was right: he *did* think he was better than the people around him.

Jimmy kept his eyes on the door, in case someone he knew walked in. He had taken the precaution of carrying a package, so that, if he was seen, it might look like he was in the post office for reasons other than collecting his dole.

He despaired because he knew that his value in the job market was diminishing. Most of his skills lay in television, and there was only a very small number of television stations that might be hiring. There were many TV production companies, but they tended to be small, hand-to-mouth operations. The collapse in domestic advertising revenue, and the rise of foreign streaming services, had put a further squeeze on the available opportunities.

He was called for an interview for a music radio station. One of the interviewers asked if he had experience in radio production. Jimmy said that he hadn't, but that if he could produce TV successfully, then he could probably produce radio.

The lady persisted, asking: 'How can we be sure you can produce radio, if you've never done it before?'

Jimmy explained that producing television was a more demanding affair, and he had done that for two decades. He noticed that his words made sense, but he had no energy or conviction to put behind them. He thought the woman was too stupid to understand, and he gave up trying to enlighten her.

He found it humiliating to be questioned by people who were considerably younger than him. In an interview at a media production company, three hipsters sat across the table, asking him about cross-platform content development, and some new app he hadn't heard of. To his horror, he realised that one of the interview panel was a daughter of a woman he had dated back in his college days. Her mother had married early and well, and now her daughter was deciding whether Jimmy was good enough to employ, or not. Apparently, she chose the latter.

Jimmy was always suspicious of public sector interview panels. He felt often that the job was already allocated, but in the interest of 'fairness' there was still the pretence of a recruitment process. He felt that a lot of his time and hopes were wasted that way.

In an interview for a state agency, Jimmy noted that the panel was older, in terms of both how they looked and how they dressed. They seemed bored, as they went through competency-based questions.

'Can you tell us about a time you had to make a difficult decision?' asked one. 'What about a time you had to correct the behaviour of a co-worker?' asked another. Jimmy struggled to find examples: this interview style restricted his opportunities to delve into his variety of achievements. Finally, one of the panellists, in an annoying 'Dort' accent, said: 'Tell us about your weak points.'

Suddenly Jimmy mounted the table and bashed the heads of two panel members together. He roared at them: 'My weak point is that I am good enough to do this job in my sleep, but in order to get it, I have to somehow impress you stupid bunch of clock-watching, unemployable-in-the-real-world twats. My weak point is that I want to rip out your spleens and shove them down your throats! My weak point is *you!*'

At least, that's what he did in his head. In reality, he muttered some answer that he had read in a careers book: something about getting impatient when other people are tardy. He didn't believe it. They didn't believe it. He didn't get the job.

He applied for senior roles, but felt deep down that he wasn't good enough for them. He applied for junior roles, on the basis that it would be better to work at something – anything – rather than nothing. When he didn't even get called for interview at that end of the spectrum, he wondered if he would ever work again.

In despair, he bought far too many Lottery tickets. When he checked each one at his local Centra, the machine read: 'Not a Winner'. Jimmy took this as a comment on his life in general.

He turned down many invitations to lunch and pints. He didn't want friends to see him at this low ebb. He was invited to a wedding, there was a school reunion, and there were two funerals of people he knew. He declined them all: anything to avoid the question 'What are you doing with yourself these days?'

Increasingly, he thought about killing himself. Not that he wanted to do it imminently, but he felt that things were sliding towards that inevitable conclusion.

In previous years, he had imagined a suicidal person as someone in obvious despair; someone whose mind was in such disarray that they made a tragic impulsive decision. But Jimmy didn't feel that way now. His was a slow and reasoned approach.

He had decided upon the means (rope) and the location (a tree along the path linking the War Memorial Park and Chapelizod). He'd even picked the time of day: late evening, when there would be fewer people around.

He was aware of public-information campaigns advising men to talk about their problems, but this seemed pointless to him. He reasoned: 'If I'm distressed because I'm unemployed, and I talk to someone about it, what difference does it make? I'm still unemployed.'

One morning he sat down with a pen and paper to write two lists. The first one was headed 'Reasons I want to die', and beneath it was a long column of words, including: 'Unemployed', 'Broke', 'Fucked off with life', 'Stuck', 'Humiliated' and 'Failure'.

'This shit is not what I'm here for,' he wrote in a flurry. 'I'm better than this.'

The other column was headed 'Reasons I want to live'. He struggled to find anything to write. He thought about Milfoth. He felt that she'd be embarrassed if he hung himself, and inconvenienced for several weeks by the rituals and paperwork. But he felt that there would be minimal emotional impact. Anyway, his insurance policy meant that he was worth more to her dead, than alive.

Other family and friends? Certainly he could expect a large and memorable funeral, but his loss would have no substantial effect on their lives.

The only relationship he couldn't discount was that with Byron. His voluntary departure would be a severe assault on her developing psyche, with incalculable long-term ramifications. It would be a betrayal of her – a reneging on his commitment to serve and protect his child. Despite their difficult interactions of late, he knew that she needed him. He resolved to stay alive for her.

After due consideration, he wrote just one word under the second heading: 'Byron'. Then he ripped up the paper, went back to bed and cried.

*

Jimmy's discipline slid. Most days he got up late, didn't shave, ate breakfast cereal in front of the TV, and caught up on American courtroom sagas. He switched between radio stations, but found himself becoming agitated by people who called or texted shows to say they were offended by comments by politicians or celebrities.

Callers to RTÉ's *Liveline* particularly annoyed him. One person was offended because a well-known journalist had criticised people who had large families. Several others called in, each trying to outdo the other with their level of outrage.

Another caller was offended because an environmentalist had criticised people who used their cars for long commutes. Another complained about co-workers who used the office microwave to cook fish and other foods that create a strong odour. Jimmy found himself shouting at the offended parties on the radio: 'At least you have a fucking job!'

One afternoon, as he sought in vain a soothing broadcast, he got an idea for a TV show to pitch to RTÉ. Suddenly he was energised again. He felt a sense of purpose as he made an appointment with RTÉ's commissioning editors. He asked Danny to help flesh out the idea and join him for the pitch. He had missed Danny's company.

The idea was a variation on RTÉ's former *Live at Three* format, with an afternoon show targeted primarily at senior citizens. There would be a look-back at times gone by through old news reports and interviews, as well as live, gentle music: songs that had been popular during the heyday of the audience.

'Don't you think it's a little old-fashioned?' asked a commissioning editor on the other side of the table.

'Yes,' said Jimmy. 'The whole idea is that it feels old. It's from a previous time. It's tender. It's nostalgic.'

'It also sits comfortably within the terms of RTÉ's public-service remit,' chipped in Danny.

'I'm not feeling it,' said another of the editors – a man who, Jimmy observed, clearly didn't understand the rule against washing white shirts with black jeans.

'Broadcasting to people in old folks' homes?' said his colleague.

'Not only,' said Danny. 'We have a rapidly aging society, but more and more people enjoying active lives into their seventies and eighties while living at home.

'The figures we have outlined in our proposal confirm that the target audience is amongst the most affluent in Irish society,' Jimmy interjected. 'Advertisers are aware that this group has more disposable income than any other group.'

'Yea, but they can't get out to spend it!' joked one of the editors, looking to his colleagues to share the laugh.

Jimmy continued, but he felt his energy draining away. 'Advertisers also know that this is the section of the market that is least likely to switch channels during commercial breaks. Older people are the population group that is most loyal to domestic TV production; they are least likely to use on-demand services.'

Although the station officials promised to give the proposal 'serious consideration', Jimmy and Danny knew that the battle had been lost.

'At least we gave it our best shot,' said Danny as they walked across the car park.

'They're just fucking eejits,' said Jimmy, clearly frustrated. 'Like, they're just *fucking* . . . .' He shook his fists in frustration. Tears welled up in his eyes, and he was unable to finish his sentence.

Danny felt a little embarrassed. 'You OK?' he asked. 'It was just a pitch, like. Nothing lost.'

Jimmy lowered his face into his hands. 'Sorry, it's just . . . . You shouldn't be in a commissioning role if you can't think outside the box! If all you can think of is more of the same . . . and you just can't *think* . . . or *imagine!*'

Danny tugged gently on Jimmy's elbow. 'Come on, let's walk and talk. Don't let them see you like this.'

The two men walked in silence until they were in Danny's car. 'Sorry Danny,' said Jimmy. 'Just, this place has always been a graveyard for ideas.'

Danny felt that this was a diversion, and got to the point: 'What's going on with you, Jimmy?'

'I'd be fucking grand if I didn't have to deal with this . . . fucking . . . endless parade of incompetent . . . pricks!'

'That's not what I meant,' Danny persisted. 'What's going on with you? Tell me.'

'I dunno,' replied Jimmy. 'The whole thing is just . . . y'know . . . . It's like . . . .' Jimmy's head was lowered, and he shook it back and forth in a repetitive 'no' motion. His right hand massaged his forehead, but also served to prevent eye-contact between the two men. 'It's just a fucking . . . . For fuck's sake, I just . . . . Y'know, just fuckin' pricks . . . .'

'How's your mental health, man?'

Jimmy took a long time to answer, then whispered: 'Not good.'

'How not good?' asked Danny. There was silence. 'Like, on a scale of one to ten?'

There was another long silence, punctuated only by Jimmy's sniffles, then: 'Pretty bad.'

Danny stared out of the windscreen, reluctant to start the car. 'You've got a kid, you know.'

'I know.'

'You've got to think of her. She needs you.'

'Do you think I don't know?'

Danny changed tack slightly. 'You talk to your wife about this?'

'No.'

'You talk to your doctor?'

Jimmy suddenly became animated. 'See, there's the thing. I lose my fucking job, and with that I lose my health insurance. Y'know? And I qualify for a shitty dole payment, but I don't qualify for a medical card!'

'For goodness' sake, Jimmy, I will pay for you to go to see a doctor. I will pay, OK. And for whatever meds you need, I will pay. If you want, pay me back when you're strong again. And you will be strong again. I know you will!'

Confronted by Danny's kindness, Jimmy could only sob again – this time burying his face in both hands. 'Just drive, please,' he said, without raising his head.

'Not until you promise me you'll go and see someone,' said Danny sternly.

It took a while before Danny answered. 'OK, I will. And thanks, but I don't need your money.'

*

Jimmy hadn't been to a doctor for many years, so didn't know which one to call. And he couldn't ask Milfoth, because he didn't want her to know about his difficulties. Then he remembered a meeting he had had several months before. He rummaged through a box of work-files until he found the business card. It read: 'Malcolm, Medical Advisor.' He called the number.

'Hello,' came the calm reply.

'Hi,' said Jimmy, surprised. He had expected a receptionist to answer. 'Is that . . . Dr Malcolm?'

'This is Malcolm. How can I help you?'

'My name is Jimmy. I met you after a show we did on TV Ireland a while back.'

'Yes, I remember you. What seems to be the problem?'

Jimmy didn't feel strong enough to discuss his problem over the phone, so he lied: 'I'm . . . I'm worried about my prostate. I would like to have it checked.'

'OK, but why come to me?' asked Malcolm, cautiously.

Jimmy was taken aback. 'Well, why *not* you?'

'Regular doctors are good for that sort of thing.'

'Are you not a regular doctor?' asked Jimmy.

Now it was Malcolm's turn to hesitate. 'I'm . . . a . . . little more specialised.'

'Well, can you help me or not? I don't know who else to call,' said Jimmy, with an air of desperation.

'You sound anxious. Have you symptoms of prostate cancer?'

'No,' said Jimmy. 'No, I don't think so. No.'

'Well, why do you need my help?'

'There may be other things,' said Jimmy, sheepishly.

The voice on the other end of the line softened. 'OK, let me give you the address of my surgery.'

They set a time for the following day. Just before the call ended, Malcolm said: 'Cash only. I don't do medical cards, or give receipts for health insurance.'

'Well, that's convenient,' said Jimmy. 'I'm too rich for one, and too poor for the other.'

Malcolm seemed to lighten. 'You must be new to Dublin 8.'

*

Jimmy found Malcolm's practice above a disused shop near Donore Avenue. He was buzzed through the door and went up a steep staircase into a sparsely furnished, dimly lit room. There, in front of his desk, dressed in scrubs, stood a stern Malcolm.

'Hello,' said Jimmy cheerfully. 'It took me a while to find the place. I – '

'What do you want?' demanded Malcolm.

'Well, I'm at the age when I should get fully checked out, so I thought I'd give you a ring to . . . .'

'Bullshit,' said Malcolm. *'What do you want?'*

'What's going on? Do you not run tests and stuff?'

'Are you recording this?' demanded Malcolm. 'Are you filming?' He peeped through venetian blinds to the street below.

'No,' said Jimmy. 'Why do you ask?'

'Leave your bag outside the room, please. And your phone. And anything else metal in your pockets, like keys, or your belt-buckle. Is that a badge on your jacket? Please leave your jacket outside.'

Jimmy was taken aback. 'S-sure,' he said, trying to calm the situation. He left the items outside the door, and aimed to create a more favourable atmosphere. 'What's up? Does the metal upset the machines, or something?'

'Are you reporting on me?' asked Malcolm.

'What? No? What are you talking about?' said Jimmy.

'You're a journalist, aren't you?'

'Well, yes. Kind of. I lost my job.'

'I know that. What are you doing now?'

'Well . . . nothing,' said Jimmy. 'That's why I'm here. OK, yes, I was bullshitting you. The reason I'm here is that I've lost my job. I think I have, . . . kind of . . . well . . . maybe depression. And I'm hoping you can help.'

The two men stared, each sizing-up the other. Eventually Malcolm took a deep breath, and invited Jimmy to sit down. Jimmy took the offered seat, still hoping to calm the atmosphere in the room. He pointed at some medical equipment in the corner, covered by a sheet: 'It's like you've got your own A&E ward.'

Malcolm remained serious. 'It's not illegal to own medical equipment. And please don't talk to anyone about this place, OK?'

'Right.' There was an awkward silence.

'Anyway,' continued Jimmy, 'I lost my job, and I've been having a very tough time since.'

'You lost your job, but one of my patients lost his life. His family has been having a very tough time since.'

'Well, I'm very sorry about that,' said Jimmy. 'I suppose that puts things in perspective.'

'Yes, it does,' said Malcolm. There was another awkward silence.

Jimmy decided to go on the offensive. 'Well, perhaps some of your other patients killed him? Did you raise your concerns with them?'

Malcolm didn't answer, but began to show Jimmy a little more respect. 'OK, so you're feeling a little depressed?'

'A moment, please,' said Jimmy. 'Are you even a qualified doctor?'

'Have I presented myself as a doctor?'

Jimmy was unsure. 'Well, I assumed – '

'Assumed? You assumed, but have I presented myself as a doctor?' Malcolm didn't wait for an answer. 'No, I haven't. I didn't describe myself as a doctor. I have only presented myself to you as a medical advisor.'

'OK, thank you,' said Jimmy.

'Are you recording this?'

'No,' responded Jimmy, showing his irritation.

'But for your information, I *am* a qualified doctor.'

'Like, registered and licensed to practise?' asked Jimmy.

'Maybe not, but that's nothing to do with my medical knowledge.'

Jimmy was about to ask why he wasn't allowed to practise, but decided against it. 'Are you able to help me, or not?' asked Jimmy.

'Possibly,' said Malcolm. 'What's going on?'

In such an unsympathetic atmosphere, Jimmy wasn't tearful, and gave a succinct account of his recent difficulties.

'When did it all start?' asked Malcolm.

'It's hard to say. I used to be very confident when I was younger. But gradually over the last few years, maybe more – it's hard to be sure – my confidence just ebbed away. Maybe it was the pressure of work. Maybe the rows with my wife. It happened gradually. I can't point to a particular time when I started feeling bad.'

Jimmy summed up his feelings. 'I don't feel like a real man any more. I never thought I'd say this, but I feel vulnerable – especially in a work situation, or anywhere there might be conflict. I feel like I've lost my vitality. I've lost my energy. I've lost my zest for life. I . . . I'm not a proper man any more. It's like I'm fading away. Maybe it's just age, I dunno.'

Malcolm perked up. 'Hey, let me ask you a question. When was the last time you won an argument?'

'When?' asked Jimmy. He couldn't remember. He could barely remember contesting an argument in several years. 'A long time ago. Not in the last year, anyway.'

'You were running a TV show, and you didn't win arguments? When was the last time you imposed your will upon someone; like, got someone to do something they didn't want to do?'

Jimmy shrugged. 'I dunno. I . . . I can't remember.'

Malcolm nodded, as if he had correctly predicted Jimmy's answers.

'So, I wonder if I might need an antidepressant . . . . But I suppose you can't prescribe anything for me, can you?'

Malcolm was non-committal, and replied slowly: 'Maybe. Maybe not.' Then, after a prolonged silence, he said: 'But you don't need antidepressants. They are a long-term solution, and you have a short-term problem. You have reactive depression, not clinical depression. As soon as you get a job, you'll feel better.' He indicated that the meeting was over. 'OK?'

'Is that it? I tell you my life-story, and you tell me to get a job?'

'If you don't accept my advice, I strongly urge you to get a second opinion. There are lots of doctors out there who will be very happy to put you on antidepressants. But I advise that this is not the right solution for you.'

'You want me to pay you for this?' asked Jimmy.

'Don't pay if you don't want to. I'm hardly going to sue you.'

'Right,' said Jimmy, and muttered a dissatisfied 'Thank you'. He started to leave the room.

Malcolm seemed to have second thoughts, and softened. 'You might consider anti-anxiety medication, but on a very short-term basis only. If it helps you get through a job interview, or take on some temporary work, then it might be useful to take a short course of Xanax.'

He handed Jimmy a silver tray of nine tablets: 'Here, this is all I have at the moment.'

'Thank you,' said Jimmy.

'But don't make a habit of using them,' said Malcolm. 'Perhaps also try some cognitive behavioural therapy, to help you make sense of it all. I will be happy to make recommendations.'

'Thanks,' said Jimmy, quietly. 'I'll bear it in mind.'

As he made for the door, Malcolm spoke again. 'OK, there's something else. It would seem that you have another underlying issue.'

Jimmy returned to his seat, prepared for some grim news.

'It seems likely that you have hypogonadism,' said Malcolm.

Jimmy furrowed his brow. That sounded serious.

'Your symptoms are consistent with testosterone deficiency. Your body isn't producing enough of the hormone.'

'What?' said Jimmy, laughing. 'What's that got to do with anything? I'm not as horny as I was as a teenager, but I can live with that.'

'Testosterone governs far more than just libido,' said Malcolm. 'It's what makes you a man. It governs your mood, your drive, your confidence. Your physique. The best sportsmen have higher levels of testosterone than the not-so-great sportsmen. Just like the most successful businessmen have higher levels of testosterone than the less successful ones. If two men suffer a setback, like you losing your job, the one with the lower level of testosterone will be slower to recover. Just like you.'

Jimmy took a moment to absorb this unexpected news. 'And how do you know this applies to me?'

'I just know.'

'Aren't you supposed to do a blood-test, or something?'

'I don't do blood-tests. I don't interact with labs.'

'Then how do you know?' asked Jimmy, impatiently.

'Low testosterone is more a clinical diagnosis than a laboratory one. In other words, symptoms are more important than lab-results. You're not a full man any more; you told me that's how you feel. You're crying in public, lacking concentration. You made mistakes at work. Getting depressed. Rarely having sex. No interest or energy for physical activity. Lacking ambition. Subservient . . . .'

'I never said I was subservient,' said Jimmy, sternly.

'I watched you in the TV studio that night, talking to that boss-woman.'

'Monica Jenkins?' said Jimmy.

'I don't know her name, but your body-language screamed "submissive".'

Jimmy knew that Malcolm was right, and admired his observation skills, reluctantly. 'Y'know, even that relationship, I can't understand. I started in TV at the same time as Monica. She was fun. She was OK at her job; but nothing special. She used to come to me for help all the time. And now look at her. She has the confidence to run a country. And I'm on the dole.'

Malcolm took off his glasses and rubbed his eyes in the way of someone who has something to explain. 'Women have testosterone too, but they spend the first half of their lives governed by the hormone oestrogen. It brings out more caring personality traits – which is probably evolution's way of making them good at child-rearing. And their testosterone is suppressed by oestrogen.

'Later in their lives, around the time of the menopause, their oestrogen levels drop off. So the testosterone in their bodies isn't suppressed any more, and suddenly it's as though they're on a testosterone supplement. They start showing much more ambition, more focus, more assertiveness, and they stop giving a shit about what people think of them. So they have a surge of testosterone around the same time the men in their lives start losing theirs.'

This made sense to Jimmy. He thought about his late mother, and other older women who were submissive in their early adulthood, but appeared to rule their husbands in their later decades. 'Wow,' he said, nodding his head.

Malcolm looked at Jimmy, as if to say: 'I rest my case.'

Malcolm wasn't finished. 'You also need to know that the lack of testosterone in your body is bringing on a touch of gynecomastia,' he said gravely.

Jimmy looked shocked. That sounded like a terminal illness. 'What the hell is that?'

'You're growing a pair of tits!'

*

Malcolm outlined treatment options. 'You can go to a conventional doctor, get referred to a consultant on the public system, and wait a year or two before you even get an appointment. I don't think you can wait that long.

'You can go to a conventional doctor, get referred to a private consultant. They will charge you a lot of money, but I don't think you'll be willing to pay it.'

'What makes you think that?' protested Jimmy.

'I just know,' replied Malcolm, waving his hand as if swatting away the question. 'Either way, the chance of you finding a doctor in this country who will help you boost and sustain your testosterone levels is quite slim.'

'Why would doctors not know about this?' asked Jimmy.

'A lot of them think testosterone for men of your age is just about vanity,' said Malcolm. 'A bit like dentistry in Ireland when you were young: the dentists seemed to think that straight white teeth were just about vanity. Now, they see them as necessary for good health. In the same way, doctors here in years to come will see high testosterone levels in middle-aged men as being necessary for good health, not just vanity.'

'So what should I do?' asked Jimmy.

'There's the unofficial route. Go to your local gym, find the guy with the biggest muscles, and ask him where you can find someone to hook you up with a supplier, and advise you on your bloods.'

'Why my bloods?'

'Testosterone has a very powerful influence on people's lives. You'll need good medical advice, and to have your blood tested regularly to make sure you aren't overdosing. It's cheaper if you draw your own blood and mail it to the UK for testing.'

'Can you hook me up?' asked Jimmy.

Malcolm looked at Jimmy as if he was still sizing him up. 'Why should I trust you?'

*

Jimmy left the surgery with a box of testosterone sachets, and a short list of books on testosterone treatment. He rushed home, and read the instructions. Facing his bedroom mirror, he squeezed the clear gel onto his right fingers and smeared it over his left shoulder and the upper parts of his skinny left arm.

He squeezed the remainder of the sachet onto his left fingers and applied the gel to his right upper arm and shoulder. Then, he rubbed the residue on his abdomen with both hands, and laughed. He wiggled his man-boobs and wondered whether this illicit substance could really get rid of them.

When he thought of people using testosterone illegally, he pictured the flat stomachs of elite athletes, where the blood supply lay just beneath a thin layer of skin. He wondered if the gel would be strong enough to burrow through his thick layer of belly fat.

The instructions also made him laugh. The leaflet warned against having sex after applying the gel, in case it transferred to a partner through skin-on-skin contact. This could cause her to 'show signs of increased testosterone, including hair on her face and on her chest, and a deeper voice'. He pictured Milfoth waking after a night of passion, wearing a beard. Sadly, he knew there was no chance of him contaminating her at this stage of their relationship.

The next day, Jimmy went to his gym to look for advice about steroids. He approached a man-mountain who was surely a user, but he had little English. He went to the next biggest man, but he seemed suspicious of Jimmy's questions. He tried another man, who seemed small compared to the previous two, but who still dwarfed Jimmy. He didn't seem interested in helping.

Finally, Jimmy found a muscular man who was able to offer him some advice. 'Testosterone is an anabolic steroid. It's a controlled substance. So you should educate yourself on the process, and the side-effects.

'And remember, once you start taking testosterone, you can't stop. Your body will stop producing the hormone naturally when you start juicing. So think about it very carefully.'

'Is it worth it?' asked Jimmy.

'Is it worth getting your confidence back? Is it worth feeling better about yourself? Feeling smarter, sharper? Is it worth having a body you can be proud of?'

'Am I going to end up looking . . . like you? Like, a big build, and stuff?'

The man laughed. 'Testosterone doesn't give you free muscles; you have to work for that. But it does increase muscle-mass, so any weight-training you do will be more apparent in your physique. It will also help you lose fat, so the muscle you have will stand out more.'

He directed Jimmy to an online pharmacy in Serbia where, later that day, he ordered two boxes of testosterone: two months' supply. He rose from his computer and stood bare-chested in front of his bedroom mirror. He opened another of the testosterone sachets that Malcolm had given him. He spread the gel on his shoulders and pectorals, and on his belly.

He smiled as he whispered to himself: 'Out with the old Jimmy, in with the new.'

5

࿐࿐࿐

Hank Savage

Jimmy hated medical consultants. He'd never met one who didn't come across as having graduated from the School of Arrogance. Dr Henry Warnock-O'Brien, Endocrinologist, only reinforced his prejudice. Jimmy's brother – the one he liked least – was a consultant.

The endocrinologist was addressing the Rialto Men's Health Group at St Andrew's Hall in Rialto. He had arrived late which, Jimmy assumed, was because of excessive time spent on his perfectly coiffed hair. He wore an immaculately tailored suit, and seemed to glide onto the small stage, his nose tilted upwards.

Jimmy sat in the small audience, with a list of questions about testosterone therapies, but lost faith quickly in the doctor's ability to deliver answers of value.

Warnock-O'Brien started his presentation by making an unfounded assumption about his Dublin 8 audience: 'Many of you are smokers'. Then he opined that 'Many of you enjoy your pint of porter', especially 'after a day on the job' or 'with a game of darts'. He advocated healthier lifestyles and regular GP visits, asking the men if they were 'making the most of your medical cards?'

Jimmy decided to steer the presentation towards something more substantial. 'Excuse me,' he said, raising his hand. 'If a man had depression, would you suggest that he have his testosterone levels checked?'

'Not particularly. If a man is depressed, he should see a psychiatrist, not an endocrinologist.'

This didn't tally with Jimmy's recent reading on the subject.

He was about to ask another question, but an older man who apparently shared Jimmy's interest, got there first. 'Excuse me,' the man said, in a flat Dublin accent, 'what's your view on testosterone optimisation?'

'You mean testosterone replacement therapy? Well, it's a very common – '

'No, no, no,' said the man sternly. 'I said testosterone *optimisation.*'

The doctor appeared to be taken aback, but recovered his air of confidence quickly. 'Endocrinologists have, of course, extensive training in testosterone treatments, and we do prescribe testosterone where there is a medical need. Usually a referral is sent by a man's general practitioner to an endocrine specialist.' He finished his comment with a forced smile, before changing the subject.

'Excuse me,' the older man said again. 'And I'm sorry now to be stopping your flow. It's just that I'm wondering, if a fella comes to you and says he wants to have a higher level of testosterone, so he can live **a** better life, but you say there is no *medical* need, what then?'

Dr Warnock-O'Brien didn't enjoy the interruptions and indicated so with a weak smile. 'We deal with medical needs. If there is a medical need, such as low testosterone, we will help the patient with that problem, often through diet or lifestyle changes. We will also consider medical intervention which may include hormone replacement therapy. Should a patient have a desire for a testosterone level that is beyond his medical need, I will assume it is for vanity reasons: perhaps he is a body-builder, or a young man wanting to improve his appearance for the young ladies. Or indeed, he may have a desire to play on the first fifteen for Lansdowne. It would appear to me that such cases do not merit the attention of a medical doctor; unless it is to deter him. OK?'

He paused just long enough to give the impression that he would welcome another question, but resumed speaking quickly to prevent this from happening. 'Now, I would like to talk for a moment about – '

The older man's hand went up again. 'See, the thing is,' he said slowly, 'how do you know what is a medical need, and what's a – to use your word – vanity need?'

This time, Warnock-O'Brien paused long enough to indicate his irritation. 'We have a scale that defines the normal range of testosterone for a man,' he said quietly. 'The patient has a blood-test, and the results are analysed by an experienced medical professional. If the patient's testosterone reading is outside the normal range, that indicates he has a medical need. Now, I'd really like to move on.'

The older man was unperturbed. He had a quiet confidence, and was unruffled by the medic's superior training and diction. 'Ya, and I wouldn't like to hold you any longer, Doctor,' he said. 'And I'm grateful for your time here, but what is the normal scale? For a man like myself.'

The doctor seemed relieved to be given the opportunity to close off the matter with his uncontradictable scientific knowledge. He blurted: 'The normal scale is around 250 to 1,000 nanograms per decilitre, usually expressed as "ng" over "dL". A nanogram is one billionth of a gram. A decilitre measures fluid volume that is one-tenth of a litre. So you can see, it's a little complicated, and perhaps too technical for this audience.'

Jimmy felt patronised again.

'OK,' said the older man, 'and thank you for the explanation. But tell me this and I'll ask you no more. That's the normal scale for me, who is in me sixties. What's the normal range for a man who is in, say, his thirties?'

The doctor seemed flustered. 'Well, that's an entirely hypothetical question.'

'But is it the same range?'

'Of course it isn't. Well actually, it is,' he continued, correcting himself. 'Remember, it is a range. So the younger man would expect to be at the higher end of the range, and the older man towards the lower end. Actually,' said Warnock-O'Brien, laughing at his own wit, 'perhaps we should consider splitting the range in two.' But he still seemed unsure.

Jimmy, who had been enjoying the doctor's discomfort, suddenly remembered something Malcolm had said that day in his makeshift surgery. He raised his hand and asked: 'Would you agree that, when assessing a patient, the symptoms of low testosterone are more important than blood-tests?'

'Of course not,' retorted Warnock-O'Brien. 'This is science. It is an evidence-based discipline. I am a medical clinician, and I learned a long time ago that if the science tells you something, and the patient tells you that they are *feeling* something else . . . well, it's the science that wins.'

Jimmy suddenly had a feeling that he hadn't experienced in years: the ability to defeat someone. He sensed the doctor's weakness, and his consistent display of hubris suggested that he deserved to be finished off.

Jimmy said: 'And I am a communications professional. I learned a long time ago that, if an audience member asks you a question, and you don't know the answer, you can either *tell* them you don't know the answer, or you can *show* them.'

There was a silence in the room, as each person processed Jimmy's comment. The medic's eyes slowly narrowed in anger, and other members of the audience let out a quiet snigger.

The older man who had spoken earlier let out a thunderous laugh and clapped his hands loudly. 'Ah Jaysus, that's a good one! You got him there, me lad! You got him. Ha-ha!' He stood up and shuffled towards the door. 'I think this is where myself and the good doctor part company. Good night, everyone!'

Jimmy watched as the man left, then glanced towards Warnock-O'Brien, who looked angry. Jimmy felt a surge of energy inside. He had taken on a consultant, in public, and won. It was a victory – a very small victory – but it felt good. He felt breathless with joy.

He wanted Warnock-O'Brien to come back at him, to make a snide remark that he could then react to. But the endocrinologist was defeated, and it wasn't going to get any better. With a wide grin, Jimmy also left the room, and caught up with his fellow deserter as they both stepped out on to South Circular Road.

'I'm telling ye, the doctors in this country know fuck-all about testosterone,' said the older man.

'Do you know much about it yourself?' Jimmy asked, sensing that the answer would be in the affirmative.

'I do, but I had to learn it all by myself. No thanks to them cunts!'

Jimmy was delighted to find someone who had informed himself on the subject. He had so many questions to ask his older companion, but started strategically: 'Wanna go for a pint?'

As the two men walked the short distance to The Bird Flanagan, Jimmy extended a hand of introduction. 'Jimmy's the name, by the way,' he said. 'Jimmy Fyffe.'

'Nice to meet you, Jimmy,' said the older man, grabbing just a couple of Jimmy's fingers.

'And what's the name?' asked Jimmy.

'Oh, sorry, I thought you knew who I was. I thought everyone knew me around here. Ye can call me "Hank". Hank Savage.'

Jimmy's heart missed a beat, but he kept walking as if this was a stroll with an old friend. Hank Savage! The former drugs-lord. Wasn't he supposed to be in prison? Jimmy wanted to turn and leave, but he was already committed to having a pint with the notorious criminal. It was too late to back out.

Everything about Hank seemed to be overly sensitive to gravity. His rotund belly, his sloping shoulders, his jowls, the edges of his mouth, and the bags under his eyes all seemed to point downwards. He would have been taller than Jimmy if he stood upright, but he stooped. His skin was leathery, as if it had had a lifetime of over-exposure to the sun.

Inside The Bird, the two took seats in a corner, out of earshot of other customers. Jimmy felt as though he was being observed. Other customers glanced discreetly in their direction, and then brought their heads closer to their companions for a quiet word. Jimmy wanted to go home, but had no choice but to outline his story – which he did quickly.

'You should see if you can find a doctor in the UK who understands this stuff, if you can't find one in Ireland,' said Hank. 'Your best bet is to get someone online. It'll save ye the bother of going back and forward to meet them. You can do yer own blood-tests with the mail-order kits. No need to be queuing up and payin' the doctors just for drawing yer blood.'

The older man liked to talk. Jimmy started to relax and was happy to listen. Hank had been a body-builder, and through his use of anabolic steroids, his ability to produce testosterone naturally had diminished. 'But I was grand,' he said. 'I never wanted kids, so I didn't care about that. Everything was fine, until they put me in prison, y'see?'

Jimmy nodded, as if talking with a former prisoner was a normal part of his social interactions.

'They put me away, and then they wouldn't let me have the juice, y'see? They wouldn't let me have testosterone in the prison. A smart move on their part,' he said, tapping his temple. 'But it messed me up big-time. I got my solicitor to appeal, but they called in a couple of doctors, who said I didn't have a medical need for me medication. This bullshit about medical need!

'Y'know, the prison guards one time found some testosterone in my cell and took it off me. I sez to them, "I'm not trying to get high, or an'tin'. Why are ye taking away my T?" And d'ye know what one of them says to me?'

'No,' said Jimmy.

'He sez: "For the same reason they cut Samson's hair".'

Jimmy smiled, to show his understanding of the anecdote – but not enough to show sympathy for the prison guard.

'Anyway, they took away my T. And I couldn't produce it naturally. So I started to lose me physique. And then I started to lose me focus, and me drive, and me ambition. And me confidence. Physically and mentally, I went back to some former version of myself. And then my business on the outside started to fall apart, coz I didn't have the ability to keep a grip on it.' He made a grasping shape with his fist.

He looked around, as if checking to see if anyone was listening. 'Between yerself and meself, y'see, some of my lads were juicing. The steroids made them big and strong, but it also made them too aggressive, and reckless. And then they're snorting the white powder as well. That made things even worse. It was enough to give criminals a bad name.' He winked as he spoke, and Jimmy smiled at the wry humour.

'Anyway,' he continued, 'to control them from the inside, I needed to be extra-aggressive, not less aggressive. So I lost control of them. Some of me best lads went off to form their own gang, and I lost a lot of me business.'

'I'm sorry to hear that,' said Jimmy, wanting to ask about Hank's business, but opting not to.

'Yeah, but here's the thing,' said Hank, pointing a finger at Jimmy. 'The juice helped me become successful in business – which was great, but it also cost me the business.'

'How come?' asked Jimmy.

'See, the cops came after me because I was the number one: the top dog. If I had stayed number three or four, they would have left me alone, let me get on with my business. But number one . . . never be number one, I'm telling ye. It attracts the wrong kind of attention.'

Jimmy nodded silently. He didn't want to interrupt Hank's flow.

'So what I'm trying to figure out now is what the right level of testosterone is for me. I've problems with me prostate now so I'm not supposed to be taking any testosterone. But I can't get me business going again without some testosterone in my bloodstream. I can't produce it naturally any more. So how much should I inject? I was hoping to get some answers from that gobshite tonight.'

If what Hank was saying was true, he shouldn't be saying it to a stranger. But he also seemed to be a man in need of company. 'I'm sorry to hear all this,' said Jimmy. 'I wish I had the answers, but I'm new to this whole subject.'

*

Jimmy spent the evening googling *Hank Savage*. Dozens of images appeared of a tanned and toned young Hank, with muscles glistening under stage-lights. He had been a champion body-builder during the 1980s, with a full head of hair and a waist that seemed impossibly narrow, and shoulders that seemed impossibly broad.

Later photos were of a partying Hank, still broad, and often holding a Champagne glass beside some celebrity or pretty woman in a nightclub or beach bar. His preferred style was a well-cut business suit – often pinstriped – with a good shirt – often pink – that was always open at the top, as if to suggest that no garment was strong enough to contain his massive chest. The most recent photos were grainy – perhaps taken from a distance by a hidden photographer, or surreptitiously by a fellow inmate.

The Hank with whom Jimmy had shared drinks did not resemble the Hank in the earlier photographs. The current Hank was tired, and soft around the edges. His body sagged, as if the skin that had stretched to contain his bulked-up muscles had failed to retract when his juicing had stopped.

The many press articles about Hank told the story of a criminal who didn't know when to stop. One profile, under the sub-heading 'The con who didn't know when enough was enough', described how Savage had started by importing illegal steroids for Ireland's small community of body-builders, but had later progressed to importing cannabis and cocaine for far larger markets. He became the top drug importer and distributor in Dublin, but sparked conflict with other gangs by venturing into the Cork, Limerick and Belfast markets.

He fronted his business with a string of gyms and nightclubs around Dublin, as well as a horse-drawn carriage service for tourists. This brought him publicity – which he enjoyed. He cultivated a bad-boy image that attracted thugs, media-types, and women.

The press couldn't resist punning on his last name. 'A Savage Beating' was how one headline described his treatment of a young criminal who crossed him. Other victims of a feud were 'Savaged', and the actions visited upon them were described as 'Savage-ry'.

Despite this, Hank came across as a likeable villain. In several of the articles, the journalists seemed to be in awe of their subject: they reported Hank's anecdotes verbatim, and described his glamorous and comfortable lifestyle.

In one article, Hank announced proudly that he would never have anything to do with heroin. 'It ruins communities,' he said, adding that he had joined marches to drive out drug-pushers from Fatima Mansions and other places.

Another gushing piece described the lavish party he had thrown for his mother on her eightieth birthday. It seemed that everyone in Rialto drank for free in McCauley's that weekend. 'He never forgot his roots,' declared one elderly resident of Rialto Cottages.

Much of the later coverage focused on the loss of Hank's houses and other property to the Criminal Assets Bureau. The articles documented the decline of a once-powerful man: his move from a large house behind a high wall in the Dublin Mountains, to a small house in the Rialto of his childhood. One photograph showed a down-at-heel Hank returning from a supermarket wearing a fake-Burberry tracksuit. The heading: 'Chav-age'.

Jimmy read how Hank was finding his life after prison particularly difficult. Several pieces described how Savage had lost control of the north side of Dublin to his former lieutenants, the Deveney brothers. It said that Hank was now struggling to retain his grip on the drugs trade in the south inner-city.

The final portion of media coverage linked Hank to the murder of Joey Watt, 'shortly after he starred on the TV show *The Redeemables*'. One newspaper, quoting 'informed sources', said that 'remnants of the Savage gang were believed to be behind the abduction, torture and murder of the twenty-three-year-old father-of-one'.

This sent a chill up Jimmy's spine. He walked around the room exhaling loudly, as if the story might have changed by the time he returned to his computer. Jimmy had difficulty linking the genial character in the pub with the gruesome end to Joey Watt's life.

You can't always believe what you read in the papers, he told himself. *It's only speculation. And anyway, why would Hank do such a thing?*

But even if Savage wasn't responsible for Joey's murder, there was plenty of other people's blood on the hand that Jimmy had shaken that evening.

Jimmy pondered the significance of such a chance meeting with the man who had, indirectly, cost him his job. *What are the chances?* he asked himself, as he paced the room. *This town is too small. This postcode is too small.*

He was apprehensive, but he also realised that it had been the most interesting interaction he had had in months. In his soul, which had been so deadened by unemployment and depression, something had come alive.

6

⊰∾⊱∾⊰∾⊱

Taking the medicine

After several weeks of dosing with testosterone, Jimmy noticed improvements in his mood and mental focus. However, he couldn't be sure that this wasn't a placebo effect. In addition to the treatment, he was living a healthier lifestyle, so it was to be expected that he would feel better.

The books he read said that testosterone alone would not benefit him. He should eat better, sleep better, drink less, and start a weight-resistance programme. And so he did: he rose early in the morning, ate a protein-rich diet and went to the gym every day – the weights area, this time, not the jacuzzi.

Milfoth and Byron usually left the house early, so he had time in the morning to stand in his bedroom, looking in his mirror to check for developments. One morning on the radio the subject was 'dad-bods', and the possibility that the belly that develops on a man of parenting age could be sexy. The presenter asked if there were any men listening who had 'turned it around' in their forties; any men who had 'been flabby as they turned forty, but became lean and trim in later years'.

Jimmy held his breath, and turned, so that the dusty finger of sunlight shining between the curtains caught his embryotic contours. He could just about see the body of a virile young man; not that it would be noticeable to other people, but progress in any part of his life was welcome. 'I'm going to turn it around in my forties,' he said to himself, with an air of certainty.

As he smeared another sachet of the testosterone on his torso, he pondered a chicken-and-egg-type question about his life: did the state of his marriage cause stress that diminished his testosterone level, or did low testosterone reduce his interest in his wife, and harm his marriage? He couldn't decide.

He linked many of his marital difficulties to a night four years earlier: the night of Milfoth's staff-appreciation night, to which spouses and partners weren't invited. She had left the house early that evening, saying that she would be home by midnight, but rang later to say that it would be 'one or two' in the morning. This wasn't unusual, however, when he woke at around 4 AM and found the bed beside him empty, he worried for her safety.

He called, but her phone went straight to voicemail. He texted, but got not reply. Then he phoned and texted again, and again. He worried as he visualised his drunken wife walking through their neighbourhood alone in the early hours.

He thought about phoning the Gardaí, but it wasn't exactly a missing-person issue. He thought about driving around the city to look for her, but that would mean leaving Byron in the house on her own. So he sat in his kitchen, drinking tea, until there was a noise in the hallway at around seven.

Milfoth shut the door quietly, and was already tiptoeing up the stairs – stilettos in her hand – when Jimmy emerged from the kitchen.

'Oh, you're up,' she said in a slurred voice, then said, chirpily: 'Good morning!'

Jimmy was in no mood to exchange pleasantries, and demanded an explanation.

'Oh Jaysus, what a night!' she said. 'First it was Champagne as we arrived, then wine with dinner, then someone produced shots of Jägermeister then – '

'Where were you until now?' demanded Jimmy.

Milfoth looked puzzled. 'I'm getting to that. So after the meal, someone said: 'Let's go to Coppers!' I didn't think we'd get in, but Christine . . . you know Christine . . . well, she knew the guy at the door, and – '

'Where were you until now?' demanded Jimmy again.

Milfoth ignored the second interruption. 'Anyway, I wanted to go home. Christine was saying – imitating Christine's high-pitched enthusiasm – "No, stay, you're great craic." And I said "no." And she said, "OK, walk me back to my apartment, and I'll call you a taxi from there." And that's what I intended doing. But the cab took ages, and I must have nodded off, because next thing I knew, I woke up and it was 6.30 AM.'

'Why didn't you call me? Or answer my texts?'

'What? Oh . . . well, this phone . . . . The battery ran out halfway through the night. It's ridiculous. I need a new phone.'

'Why didn't you call me on someone else's phone?'

'Look, I don't know,' she responded angrily. 'I fell asleep. I didn't mean to. What's with all the questions? I didn't think it would matter. I thought you'd be asleep at this time.'

'I thought something bad might have happened to you,' said Jimmy, his anger showing.

'Well, I'm sorry to disappoint you, but it didn't,' said Milfoth. 'It's nice of you to wait up for me, but I must go to bed. I have a headache.'

'I'm not happy about this!' shouted Jimmy after her.

'It's not like you never got drunk and stayed out late!' shouted Milfoth, as she disappeared up the stairs. 'I suppose you think only men are allowed to have fun around here? Don't be so controlling.'

Use of the gender-card shut Jimmy up successfully. He wasn't sure if he had a right to be angry, or if he was being controlling. Or worse: controlling in a one-sided, male-chauvinist way. Yet, he was angry, and he felt he had a right to be angry. And the more he pondered the matter, the more he felt he wasn't being controlling. Surely he had the right to know where his wife was in the middle of the night?

Later that morning, and in the afternoon, he tried to discuss the matter again, but each time he went into the bedroom, Milfoth was either asleep, or pretending to be. When she finally rose, it was night-time. He tried to discuss 'the issue' with her, but she waved away his efforts, saying: 'Oh please, I've a terrible headache.' Actually, it looked to Jimmy more like she had been crying.

The next day, a Sunday, she remained in bed again. When Jimmy entered the room around midday, she spoke to him, but avoided eye-contact. When he asked her why she looked like she'd been crying, she replied: 'I think it was something in the gin. It must have triggered my allergies.'

She didn't go to work on Monday or Tuesday. She called in sick and remained in her room, only venturing into the kitchen when she thought that Jimmy had left the house. She looked tearful and pale.

'Would you like me to call you a doctor?' asked Jimmy when he was in a kinder mood.

'No,' she replied. 'Just a bit of food-poisoning,' she said, shrugging her shoulders, and escaped up the stairs again.

Before her night out, Jimmy and Milfoth had sometimes joked about her boss, who, everyone said, had the hots for her. After that night, the joke was never made again.

Within months, she had left the job where she had worked for nine years. She didn't stay in touch with her former colleagues, even though many of them had visited their home previously. Milfoth shut down any efforts Jimmy ever made to discuss the matter. Eventually he stopped trying.

After that night, their relationship changed. The talking didn't stop, but the laughs that they once had, did. The quarrels, which - before that night - had been seldom, and short, became frequent and lengthy; and the jibes more hurtful. Sex became less frequent, less intimate, and only when induced by alcohol. After many failed attempts to rekindle the physical side of their relationship, Jimmy moved into the guest-room as part of a policy he called 'Separate rooms, separate lives'. 'At least it provides clarity,' he said, with a sigh.

He read a quote in a magazine that said that depression was caused by frozen anger. Certainly, he felt that his anger about this issue had been frozen.

He wanted her to die. He wasn't the violent sort, so he couldn't imagine killing her. But if she happened to pass away, it would be convenient. Her insurance policy would clear the mortgage. He would no longer have to work: the two greatest annoyances of his life would be gone.

He smiled to himself as he made up a joke: 'How would I know if my wife died? The sex would be the same, but the house would be paid for.'

He wanted to leave her, or throw her out, but a rudimentary assessment of their finances told him that this wasn't advisable. They couldn't afford two residences. So they stayed together, making the best of an economic, non-romantic arrangement. He often described their union as 'a typical Irish marriage: shit, but stable'.

One morning, as he admired his reduced paunch and improved biceps, he regretted leaving it so long before starting to work on his body and mind. He asked himself how different things might be if he had started several years earlier.

He felt his testicles. They felt tender and seemed to have shrunk. This may have explained why their contents were particularly eager to escape of late. With no assistance being offered by Milfoth, he had to resort to manual evacuation at an increasing rate. Testosterone made him feel like a teenager again – and not always in a good way.

7

❧❧❧

Men's Health

Several weeks passed before Jimmy felt confident about returning to the Rialto Men's Health Group. There were matters he wanted to discuss with Hank Savage, if he was there, but he would need a degree of courage and conviction that had been absent from his life in recent years.

The topic of this night's presentation interested him. The blurb on the website said: 'Fight depression and anxiety with Cognitive Behavioural Therapist R. R. Giles.'

Jimmy's redundancy payment was depleted, and there was no sign of a job offer. His anxiety levels had been very high in recent days, so he booked himself a place at the talk.

In his introduction, the facilitator of the event said that the night's presenter was 'an international expert on fighting depression and anxiety', that he had been 'an influencer at events all over the world', and that Rialto was 'honoured and privileged to host him this evening'. The small group in attendance offered a round of applause as R. R. Giles moved from the shadows at the back of the hall to the brightly lit stage. Jimmy clapped heartily at first, but then stopped abruptly. He was startled to see a familiar figure accept the applause and mount the stage. The person referred to as 'R. R. Giles' and described as an international influencer and world expert was someone much more familiar. It was Malcolm.

His scraggly hair was now clipped, and his stubbly chin was shaven. He wore a three-piece suit with a bright silk tie, and in his mid-Atlantic accent addressed the attendees with the style and confidence of a Southern Baptist preacher.

'You have three minds,' he announced, and raising one, then two, then three fingers, said: 'your conscious mind, your subconscious mind and your higher-conscious mind. Tonight, I am going to focus on your subconscious mind, because you are what your subconscious mind tells you you are. Think about that: you are what your subconscious mind tells you you are.'

R. R. Giles let silence descend on the room, before continuing. 'But the subconscious mind cannot tell the difference between what is actually happening in our lives, and what we tell it is happening. So if we tell our subconscious that we are depressed or anxious, then we will have depression or anxiety. But if we tell our subconscious that we are happy, and successful, and talented, and brave, then that is what we will be. So tonight I am going to show you techniques to plant the right thoughts in your subconscious mind, so that those thoughts will, in turn, become reality.'

'Oh good Jaysus!' exhaled Jimmy. He had little tolerance for what he termed 'fake medicine bullshit', a catch-all phrase he used to describe aromatherapy, homeopathy, prayer, and anything that involved the word 'holistic'. Now to this list, he would add Emotional Freedom Techniques (EFT). He wanted to leave, but was sitting mid-row at the front, so could not get away without seeming to be making a point.

Giles continued: 'EFT involves tapping the tips of your fingers near the end-points of your energy meridians. We do this while voicing positive affirmations.'

He demonstrated what he meant by using his index and middle fingers to tap rapidly, first his cheekbone area, then his top lip, his chin, an area near his collarbone, an area in his armpit, and an area at the back of his hand. All this time he recited a mantra that sounded like it was in a foreign language, or a made-up language. Jimmy cringed.

Giles turned suddenly to the audience and announced that he needed a volunteer. Before Jimmy had time to look away, he was hauled onto the stage.

'And what's your name, sir?' Giles spoke into the microphone.

'You know my fucking name,' Jimmy said quietly, out of range of the microphone. He wanted to tell the audience that the presenter's real name was Malcolm, but actually, he couldn't be sure if that was the case.

Giles kept smiling – and kept his hand on Jimmy's arm. 'What name would you like to go by tonight?'

'You can call me "Jim".'

'OK, Jim, I assume you came here this evening because you have anxiety or depression. Yes?'

Jimmy fumed at being brought in front of a group to discuss his difficulties. He felt trapped on stage. 'I don't know,' he said quietly. 'I just came out of curiosity.'

'Now try this,' said Giles. 'Let's identify the issue. What is it, Jim?'

Jimmy hesitated, and eventually offered up: 'Lack of confidence.'

'Lack of confidence, great,' enthused the presenter. 'Now let's set up your affirmation. Try this: "Even though I feel I lack confidence, I deeply and completely love and accept myself".'

Jimmy did what he was told. He repeated the phrase several times on instruction, until he had it by heart.

'Now,' said Giles, 'I want you to repeat that phrase while following the tapping sequence.' He showed Jimmy the sequence again, and soon Jimmy was engaged in tapping while repeating the mantra.

It was only then that he saw Hank Savage sitting at the back of the room. Jimmy thought he would be embarrassed, or nervous, about a pending interaction with Savage, but he wasn't. Unexpectedly, he felt calm. He felt that he could rise to the challenge of his situation. He was in control. If he wanted to remain on stage, he could, easily. But he chose not to. Without hesitation, he turned to Giles, and said: 'Thank you very much. Good night!' As Jimmy left the room he caught Hank Savage's eye, and beckoned him to follow him outside.

*

'I know who you are,' said Hank, as the two met in the foyer.

'I know who *you* are,' said Jimmy.

'It took you long enough. I thought you media people knew everyone.'

'Your appearance has changed,' said Jimmy. 'You don't look the same as you did in the papers.'

'I suppose you want to ask me about Joey Watt's death?' said Hank.

'If I asked you about it, would you tell me the truth?'

Hank was quiet for a moment, then offered a defiant: 'Probably not.'

'Then I won't ask,' said Jimmy.

Hank nodded in agreement: 'What do you want, then?'

'I want to talk business,' said Jimmy. 'Not here. Let's go to The Bird.'

The two men retraced the steps they had taken weeks earlier, and settled in the same quiet corner of the pub. Jimmy got straight to the point: 'I want to go into business with you. The cocaine business.'

Hank fixed him with a stern look. 'Are you bullshitting me? *You?*'

Jimmy continued: 'If what I have read in the papers is even partly true, you are looking for ways to re-establish a foothold in the Dublin market. I can help. You source the product, and I'll source customers.'

'Is this some sort of a set-up?' asked Hank, looking around the lounge. 'Are you doing one of your television programmes?'

'If I was, it would be entrapment, so it wouldn't work,' said Jimmy confidently.

'I know nothing about this,' said Hank, rising to his feet. 'I have not taken part in this conversation.' He started for the door. 'Don't follow me!'

Jimmy followed him, and caught him by the arm. 'Look, if it makes you feel better, I will talk, and you only have to listen. There's no law against listening. You don't have to give me an answer tonight.'

Hank slowly returned to his seat, but didn't say anything. Jimmy continued: 'The Dublin coke market is – as it always has been – awash with crap. The coke is cut with novocaine, and baking soda, and speed, and all sorts of shite that you know more about than I ever will. In the short run, that's good for profit, but in the long run, it damages the market. Bad coke is only good for students and young workers who don't have much money. They just want to get off their heads. They don't care much about what they're taking, or where their buzz comes from.

'This product is too unreliable for more mature users: the people who have proper money to spend. They can't trust what they're getting, so they stop using it, and revert to alcohol. They are lost to the coke market, and that's bad for business. So, to borrow a phrase, bad coke drives out good coke.'

Hank remained unresponsive, but listened intently.

'The papers say that, in your heyday, you had that lower end of the market cornered. And also the upper end of the market, where you presumably sold good-quality stuff to the pop stars and film stars, and anyone else who was your friend – or acquaintance.'

Hank smiled at this, as if reminiscing about the good days.

'So here's the challenge,' said Jimmy. 'The bottom end of the market is still being supplied; *over*-supplied. And so is the top end. But who's tapping into the broad middle? Who's supplying the people who can't pay celebrity prices, but who are happy to pay a little bit more than students if the product is of a reasonably good quality? These are the people who can be regular and reliable customers, particularly in a growing economy. Particularly in a more urban and more international society, like the one we're living in. Who's going to supply this new Dublin?'

Hank still wouldn't speak so Jimmy answered his own question: 'I'll supply this new Dublin. You source the product, and I'll create the market.'

'How?' ventured Hank, breaking his silence.

'I worked in TV and advertising for two decades. I know the market – personally.'

Hank shifted in his chair. 'It wouldn't work.'

'Yes it would,' said Jimmy.

Hank countered: 'Your plan is to take premium product and sell it at half price. There's no industry in the world that would do that.'

Jimmy was stern. 'Every industry does it. It's called market segmentation.'

Jimmy sat forward in his seat. 'OK, let's say you need a new white shirt. Where do you go to get it?'

Hank was unresponsive.

'I'll tell you where,' said Jimmy. 'You go to Brown Thomas. You pay €300. You get a nice white shirt: 100 percent cotton. Eight buttons up the front, single cuffs. Nice, huh? Like what you used to wear.'

Hank nodded.

'Or you go to Penneys,' said Jimmy. 'You pay €30, and you get a nice white shirt: probably 60 percent cotton, plus a mix of other materials. But still eight buttons up the front, single cuffs. Nothing wrong with it: a nice white shirt – just not the same as the Brown Thomas one. Some people wouldn't notice the difference.'

Hank agreed.

'And that's your two ends of the cocaine market: Brown Thomas and Penneys. In the past, you supplied both. But I'm saying there's another part of the market.'

Hank raised an eyebrow, as if to say: 'Tell me'.

Jimmy continued: 'Why not get your shirt in Arnotts? It's white. One hundred percent cotton, just like Brown Thomas. Not the same quality of cotton, and the stitching isn't as good, but who would notice? It's far better than what you'd get at Penneys; not quite as good as what you'd get at Brown Thomas, but good value for €120. That's the middle market.'

Jimmy could see he was winning Hank over, so he pressed home his advantage. 'Interestingly, Hank, all three shirts are probably made in the same factory – just like the coke. And here's something else that might interest you: Brown Thomas, Penneys and Arnotts – they're all owned by the same people.'

Hank sat silently, searching for a counter-argument, but none came to mind.

'So in case I wasn't clear,' said Jimmy, 'I'm talking about becoming the Arnotts of the coke business.'

'I figured that part out myself,' said Hank, eventually finding his voice. 'All this is fine in the shirt business, because they stitch little labels on the product, to tell the customer what quality they are buying. But you can't brand a clear bag of white powder: you can't brand an illegal product.'

'Yes you can,' said Jimmy. '*I'm* the brand.'

'*You?*' said Hank, almost annoyed by the suggestion. 'How the fuck can *you* be the brand?'

'I build up a small, but reliable, network, based on personal contacts,' said Jimmy.

'You alone cannot sell enough product,' said Hank, dismissing the idea.

'Enough for what?' asked Jimmy quickly. 'I never said I was going to sell in vast quantities.'

'Well, what's the point if you're not going to sell in vast quantities?' asked Hank.

'Hey, you told me that it was pointless being number one. It's too dangerous. You said you become a target for the cops. I'm taking your advice.'

'But the quantities will be too low to generate worthwhile profits,' said Hank.

'Overheads will be low as well,' countered Jimmy. 'Fewer people in the loop means fewer people to pay off. It means less chance of arrest, and less chance of losing stock in a raid. We'll always deal in small quantities, so even if there's an arrest, it needn't be the end of the world. No lines of credit means no need to pay enforcers. Like Ryanair, you cut your costs, and the profits rise. We can have a steady, low-profile business.'

Hank exhaled heavily. He stared at the carpet and shook his head. Eventually, he ventured: 'How would we work this, you and me?'

'I don't want to meet you, except in exceptional cases,' said Jimmy. 'If trouble arises, you text me about the next meeting of Rialto Men's Health. We meet there. OK?'

'OK,' agreed Hank.

'I only deal with one of your associates. Only one, and the same one every week. No new faces. We keep this really tight. Your guy meets me in my gym every Thursday afternoon – in the jacuzzi.'

'What?' exclaimed Hank. 'Are you a fuckin' queer, or what?'

'I want to see that he's not wearing a wire,' said Jimmy. 'There's no CCTV in the wet area of a gym. And it's very hard to bug a jacuzzi. Believe me: I've tried.'

'I bet you have,' said Hank.

'In the jacuzzi, under the water, I pass your guy a key to a locker in the changing room. There's no CCTV in the changing rooms either, by the way." Hank nodded his approval.

'In the locker, inside a gym bag, there's money for that week's purchases,' continued Jimmy. Your guy inspects it. If he's satisfied, he takes the money and leaves a bag of product in the locker. He returns the key to me in the jacuzzi.'

'What if he does a runner with the money while you're still sitting in the hot-tub, like a fuckin' eejit?'

Jimmy shrugged. 'It's only a week's money. If you want to screw me over for a week's money, good luck to you. You can have it. My bigger concern is that you would screw me on the quality of the product. You can't fuck around with the quality, Hank. This business will be built on quality – you understand? If the quality's not right, the customer gets their money back – which means *I* get my money back. Agreed?'

Hank nodded a weak approval. 'Agreed.'

Hank was pensive for another moment, then fixed Jimmy with a stare and spoke quietly: 'OK, here are some other rules. Sell on the south side of the city only. Don't go onto the north side. The Deveneys have set up there. We have an uneasy relationship, at best . . . . To be honest, they probably want me dead, at this point. But if you start selling on their patch, I can't protect you. It's too dangerous.'

'Sounds reasonable,' said Jimmy. 'Any other rules?'

Hank spoke slowly. 'We might just have a deal.'

8

⊰⊱⊰⊱

Risky Business

Jimmy compiled a list of people who he had worked with, or knew socially, who were users, or potential users, of cocaine. Then he started making calls to arrange quiet chats 'about a confidential matter'.

His first meeting was with a former TV colleague who had formed her own production company. Jimmy explained that he had a pal who had a connection, and that he was able to get her a regular supply of high-quality cocaine at a good price.

She was interested, but in a noncommittal way. Owning her own company, and becoming a mother, had reduced her partying opportunities for the foreseeable future. Jimmy realised that he needed to aim at younger targets.

His next meeting was with a guy he had employed as an intern four years previously, and who had had a chequered career since. Jimmy could see he was delighted to hear about a new supply line. However, it was also clear that he would not be able to afford Jimmy's prices. Jimmy's market was proving more difficult to crack than he had expected.

With his next call, he aimed higher. He met with a friend who had rented out equipment to production companies and bands for twenty years. But, he was already connected, so didn't need Jimmy's services.

As a disappointed Jimmy turned to leave, his friend offered him some advice. 'Target separated or divorced men. They use good coke to attract younger women – and they will always buy enough for two people. I can give you a few names.' Jimmy's business model shifted.

Jimmy's first customer was a middle-aged accountant. Divorced, and living alone in an apartment in Sandyford, Joe had a sizeable income, and was willing to spend large parts of it on anything that would entice young females to spend time in his company.

Joe's senior corporate position told Jimmy that he couldn't be out on the street trying to score drugs, or have thugs calling to his door who might raise the concerns of other residents in the apartment block. He had bought cocaine on the internet using bitcoin, but he was concerned that he might have left a digital trail. He felt vulnerable to a Garda raid. He needed a reliable and well-dressed contact who wouldn't draw the wrong kind of attention; someone such as Jimmy.

Over coffee, Jimmy explained the terms of business: 'You call me Monday, Tuesday or Wednesday, and I deliver to you Thursday or Friday. That means you *never* call me from a party at three o'clock in the morning. OK?'

'OK.'

'You never call me when you're drunk or stoned. OK?

'OK.'

'You never call me when you're in the company of another person. You never accept delivery from me when you're in the company of another person. You never introduce me to another person, or talk about this to another person, unless you've cleared it with me first. OK?'

'OK.'

'You understand, this is to protect you, as well as me?'

'Yes, I do,' said Joe, who seemed reassured by Jimmy's rules.

Jimmy continued: 'It's always cash on delivery. Full payment. There are no credit arrangements, and there's no haggling. OK?'

'OK.'

'Minimum spend is €400. I'm not driving all the way out here for a fiver. And maximum spend is €2,000. I don't like to travel with large quantities, and it's probably not in your interest either to have a large quantity in your home.

'If, for any reason, you are not happy with the product, you tell me. Tell me as soon as you can. And return the remainder to me. I will have it tested, and give you a full refund if it is clear that I have given you inferior product. OK?'

'Sounds reasonable,' said Joe.

'Those are my conditions. In return, I offer you a regular, discreet supply of Grade A cocaine, at a reasonable price. Delivered to your home or office, or some other safe place. Any questions?'

*

Hank told Gunner he was to be the link-person with Jimmy.

'Wha'?' said Gunner. 'The fuckin' fag wants to take a bath with me every week?'

'It's only for a few weeks,' said Hank. 'Let's see if it works. If it doesn't, we'll stop it.'

'He's not one of us,' said Gunner. 'He's a fuckin' blow-in. How do we know we can trust him?'

'I made sure he is very clear about the consequences if he does anything to lose my trust,' said Hank.

'I don't trust them posh cunts,' said Gunner. 'I'm gonna keep an eye on him, Boss.'

*

As Jimmy sat in the jacuzzi the following Thursday afternoon, a short, tough-looking man strutted towards him. Gunner had what Jimmy's father used to describe as a gurrier's swagger: his head jutted forward, as if he had spent his formative years saying 'Are ye startin'?'

Gunner's oversized biceps and pectorals suggested to Jimmy that he was a steroid-user. This was confirmed when Gunner turned his back to climb down the ladder into the bubbling water: a triangle of acne linked his shoulder-blades with the nape of his thick neck.

Gunner's body was adorned with tattoos. A list of people with 'RIP' after their names was on his right shoulder. On his left shoulder was the crest of Arsenal Football Club. A crucifix and rosary beads was inked around his neck.

'Here, did I see you in Arnotts?' asked Gunner. It was the code-phrase that meant 'Are we safe to talk?'

'Yes, I like to shop there,' replied Jimmy – which was code for 'We can talk' or 'The coast is clear'.

'What have you got?' asked Gunner.

Jimmy passed a key to Gunner under the water. 'Locker 176,' he said. 'Four hundred euro for eight grams.'

'You brought me down here for fuckin' €400?' said Gunner.

'I didn't bring you anywhere. Your boss told you to come here,' said Jimmy sternly.

'Yeah, but you talked him into it, ye did,' said Gunner.

Jimmy was taken aback by Gunner's insubordination. 'You're a courier. A messenger. If you have a problem, I suggest you take it up with your boss. Otherwise, please go to the locker, confirm that there is €400 in it, and kindly replace it with eight grams of your finest. Then return the key to me. At your earliest convenience, please.'

Gunner sat looking at Jimmy defiantly.

'Pronto, por favor,' said Jimmy.

Gunner did what he was told, but showed his resentment. He returned a short time later and passed the key to Jimmy under the water, saying: 'Here, I hope you do better next time.'

9

※❦❦※

I'm Offended

The sight of Gunner's impressive arms prompted Jimmy to ask himself why his own were still showing little more than enhanced tone. Whenever he used a gym-machine after another man, he had to offload weights before starting his own exercise. He felt he was the weakest man in the gym, despite his recent progress.

On the advice of a man whose physique resembled that of a gorilla, he went to a supplement shop and bought a large tub of whey protein, in the hope that it would deliver on its promise to help turn his 'fat into muscle'. In addition, he procured a small tub of creatine. 'It will give you extra strength,' the gorilla told him. 'Like, when your body wants to give up after six reps, it will help you get to eight.'

The guy behind the counter, whose biceps were as large as Jimmy's thighs, advised him to consider using an Omega 3 supplement. 'You need more essential fatty acids in your diet, to improve your muscular and neural coordination, as well as your memory.' Jimmy didn't quite believe that the supplement could improve his brain function, but he made the purchase anyway.

The sales assistant saw his opportunity, and recommended a probiotic. Jimmy purchased it, along with a multi-vitamin supplement, and a bottle of Vitamin D capsules because, he was told, 'it will boost your free testosterone'.

'Anything else?' he asked Jimmy.

'Do you have anything for sleep? I find myself waking up in the middle of the night for no apparent reason.'

'That's because your body is buzzing,' said the man behind the counter. 'You are taking testosterone and working out. Your body is making cells; working overtime to transform itself, even when you are asleep. Try this combination of zinc, magnesium and Vitamin B6,' he said, handing another bottle to him. 'It will help you maintain normal nerve function, and keep your heartbeat steady.' Jimmy did as he was told.

He also bought carbohydrate powder 'to nourish his body' before, during and after a workout. Despite the heavy financial outlay, he was proud to become one of those gym-users who walked around shaking, and drinking, a lumpy-looking concoction.

One morning, on the Serbian pharmacy website, he found an interesting article on the advantages of injecting testosterone, instead of applying it to the skin. He added injectable testosterone to his shopping cart and hit 'Buy now', just as Danny phoned. 'You know that the closing date for TV Ireland's commissioning round is tomorrow?' Danny said.

Jimmy hadn't thought about his TV career for several weeks, and hadn't even realised there was a new commissioning round.

'It's not like you to miss an opportunity to pitch,' said Danny. 'Any ideas?'

'I always have ideas,' said Jimmy. 'I just have to tease out one or two.'

'How are you getting on generally? You OK?'

'I'm good, thanks,' said Jimmy reassuringly. 'Much better, actually.'

'You sound preoccupied with other stuff,' said Danny.

'Just stuff around the house,' said Jimmy. 'But thanks for calling. I might have missed this otherwise.'

It usually took Jimmy several weeks to complete a pitch, but on this occasion he had no time to linger. It was a Thursday – which meant that he was delivering cocaine that evening. He would have to get a good start on the proposal immediately, and finish it the following morning, before submitting it at noon.

He settled on an idea called 'I'm Offended'. He planned out the idea, identified the target audience, and worked out the financial requirements before lunchtime. Then he wrote the treatment, and identified any questions that might be raised by a commissioning editor. His focus was intense, and he had it all done by teatime.

Then it was time to do his drop-offs. Several of his clients favoured delivery between 7 and 9 PM. It gave them time to get home from work, and didn't hold them up if they wanted to go for a Thursday-night pint.

Jimmy liked that time-slot too. Visiting apartment blocks at this time didn't arouse suspicion, and he was usually home early enough that Milfoth didn't ask him where he'd been.

On this particular evening, Jimmy felt good. He'd cleared €2,000 in profit from his evening's work – which was far more than he would have made in his TV work in a week.

His number of clients had increased to twelve. They were mostly middle-income single men who hadn't let their advancing years kill their hopes of attracting young women.

One of his Dun Laoghaire clients put him in touch with two colleagues who lived in the Irish Financial Services Centre. This was technically on the north side of the city, but in Jimmy's view it wasn't the *real* north side: it was merely spill-over from the financial centre on the south side. He remembered Hank's warning to stick to the south side, but felt that he was keeping a low enough profile, so it shouldn't matter. He smiled to himself, remembering that he preferred to seek forgiveness than permission.

It was a warm summer evening as he made his way home from a delivery in Sandyford. He decided to detour through Rathmines, and parked in the shade of the trees beside Palmerston Park. He strolled past the pond and the well-tended flower beds, feeling shabby compared to the casually elegant Dublin 6 inhabitants all around him.

He noted that the playground was without a single sign of vandalism; there wasn't even any graffiti. The children in the playground were attended to by women who were so well maintained that he couldn't tell if they were yummy mummies or yummy au pairs.

Down Palmerston Road, he gaped at the wealth displayed in the properties and cars. Splendid red-brick Victorian houses peeped over carefully trimmed hedges, while even the stones in the driveways seemed to glisten in the evening light. An array of late-model BMW, Mercedes and Porsche SUVs stood in the driveways, looking like they'd been positioned there for magazine adverts.

Outside Morton's supermarket, a few teenagers were being loud and mischievous. Jimmy found their antics laughable; their accents and attire meant that they lacked the menace of their Dublin 8 counterparts.

As he drove home that evening with a wallet full of cash, and a plan for a new TV show, he decided that, soon, he too could live in Rathmines. He smiled as he gripped the steering wheel. *And why not? I deserve it.*

10

❧❧❧

Risky Business II

The north-side clients proved lucrative. Jimmy wondered if lower rents meant that they had more money to spend on cocaine. He marvelled at the splendid new district that had taken the place of the warehouses that had lined the quays for centuries.

After several weeks, his two clients introduced him to a third buyer. All three complimented his supply, saying that it was much better than what they had been able to procure locally.

An invitation came to meet yet another new client. He lived in a penthouse on Spencer Dock, a new district that seemed to be inhabited entirely by young financial workers. As Jimmy drove down Mayor Street, he could see only well-dressed and serious-looking office workers. It seemed to him that someone had transported a generation of UCD Commerce students *en masse* to this new and unfamiliar part of Dublin.

He followed directions to an underground car park. He had been given a code and told where to park, and soon found his way to the elevator, and the top floor. Jimmy was met by his potential client's personal security man: an imposing eastern European. He was polite, but asked Jimmy to leave anything metal outside the room. Jimmy obliged by putting his keys, phone and watch on a tray, in much the same manner as a person might do at airport security.

The client's name was Colin. Judging from the man-cave style of the penthouse, Jimmy guessed that he was moneyed and single: an ideal customer for his product.

A large TV dominated the room, which also contained two sofas and a mirror-topped table. Colin muted the TV and rose to meet Jimmy. He was of short stature, but tough-looking. Aged around fifty, he had the gut of a man who enjoyed his pints, but the shoulders of yet another steroid-user.

Once again, Jimmy gave the spiel about his conditions of sale, and Colin smiled approvingly. 'Very good,' he said, in a hard Dublin accent. 'I like your style.'

A noisy machine started up in another room. 'Sorry about the noise,' said Colin. 'Igor is in doing a bit of work. Tell me, where are you getting your stuff?'

'That's not something I discuss,' said Jimmy diplomatically.

'That's grand,' said Colin. 'I understand. And have you some for me now?'

'No,' said Jimmy. 'I deal by advance orders only. Sorry.'

'That's fine. Very professional.' Colin seemed more interested in Jimmy's business model than his product, and that made him feel uncomfortable.

'Would you like a drink?' Colin asked.

'No thanks, I'd best be off,' said Jimmy. 'But make sure to send me a text early next week if you would like to place an order.' He wanted to leave.

'What do you think of the view?' said Colin, rising and pointing towards one of his floor-to-ceiling windows. 'Right over there is the Aviva Stadium. You can see part of the pitch from this angle.'

'It's very nice,' said Jimmy. 'With a good set of binoculars, you could save yourself the price of a match ticket.' Both men chuckled. 'Now, I must be off,' said Jimmy, also rising.

'And over there is Croke Park,' said Colin, pointing in the opposite direction, and ignoring Jimmy's attempt to leave. 'I can't see the pitch, but I've often sat on the balcony and listened to Springsteen and U2, and whoever else was playing.'

Jimmy wasn't sure if Colin was hoping to seduce him, or if he was a lonely person hoping to make a new friend. 'Well, thanks for that. I'll look forward – '

'And there's Dublin Port,' said Colin, pointing towards a large brightly-lit area next to the dark expanse of the Irish Sea. 'It never sleeps. Stuff coming in at all hours of the night and day. Is that where your supply comes in?'

Jimmy evaded the question by recalling his own fact about the area. 'Y'know, Spencer Dock is named after the great-great-grandfather of Diana Spencer.'

'Who's that?' asked Colin.

'The Princess of Wales,' said Jimmy, assuming it was obvious.

'Is that British royalty?' asked Colin with a frown. 'What are they naming places over here for?'

'Well, her ancestor was the boss over here at the time: the Lord Lieutenant,' said Jimmy, slowly realising that history wasn't his host's favourite subject. 'They say he was a big supporter of Home Rule for Ireland.'

Jimmy had unintentionally killed the conversation. There was an awkward silence between the two men, which deepened when the noise in the next room stopped. Colin's security man entered the room and nodded. Colin then turned towards Jimmy and offered his hand: 'Nice to meet you. Thanks for coming up.'

Jimmy collected his keys, phone and watch as he left the apartment, and was shown to the elevator. As he returned to his car, he remained uneasy. Colin seemed like an ideal customer, but he hadn't given any indication that he would purchase anything.

*

A week later, late in the evening, Jimmy returned from a series of lucrative deliveries. His money was hidden in a bag of smelly gym-gear that was slung over his shoulder. As he came in the front door, Milfoth left the sitting room carrying a tray. On it was a teapot and an empty milk-jug. She was wearing only a bra and knickers.

It was rare that Jimmy saw her in such a state of undress, and his mind jumped to the possibility of a suitable end to an already good day. He smiled at her, and said in his best pervy accent: 'Well hello there.'

Milfoth didn't answer. She looked at him and scowled, and proceeded towards the kitchen. Jimmy stared after her in disappointment. Not for the first time, he felt rejected by her, silently.

Jimmy hung his jacket behind the front door and hung his keys on the key hook. He ambled into the sitting room, where, to his sudden and extreme rage, he saw Colin – the man from the penthouse – sitting on a couch sipping a cup of tea.

'Ah, Jimmy, we were wondering when you'd be home,' said Colin. 'Were ye off doing a few sales?'

'What are you doing here?' said Jimmy, immediately in fight mode.

'Now, now, now,' said Colin. 'Let's not get too excited.'

'I'll get excited if I fucking well want to,' shouted Jimmy, and moved towards him. But as he did so, a thick forearm hooked around his neck, catching Jimmy in a stranglehold. It was Igor, who had been behind the door.

Jimmy struggled, but Igor was stronger than him, and clearly more experienced. Jimmy flailed and spluttered. His eyes bulged and he temporarily lost his vision.

He started to pass out, but Colin raised a hand to intervene. 'That'll do, Igor,' he said. 'Let him sit there on the floor beside you.'

Igor relaxed his grip and sat down. Jimmy collapsed on the floor beside him, coughing and breathing heavily. He held his throat and tried to recover his strength.

'Do you know who I am?' asked Colin.

'You're Colin,' panted Jimmy.

'Colin who?'

'I don't know,' said Jimmy.

'I'm Colin Deveney. I'm a businessman with extensive distribution interests on the north side of the city.'

'OK,' panted Jimmy. 'What do you want?'

Milfoth returned to the room, still wearing only her underwear. She put a fresh pot of tea and milk on a small table in front of Colin, and filled his cup.

'Ah, you've a fine missus here, Jimmy,' said Colin. 'She makes a grand cup of tea,' he said, raising it to his lips.

Milfoth tried to sit at the other end of the couch, but Colin grabbed her arm. 'Now, now, now, back here, love. Back here. Like we were before.' He pulled her towards him. Milfoth surrendered and sat on his knee.

The sight of his near-naked wife sitting on another man's knee enraged Jimmy again. He rose and tried to lunge at Deveney, but Igor placed a firm grip on him.

'Let me at him!' roared Jimmy, but the next sound from his mouth was 'Aaaaaahhh!'

Igor performed a swift manoeuvre that involved twisting Jimmy's arm behind his back, and bending his fingers to the point that Jimmy felt they would snap off.

'Aaaaah, my fingers! My fingers! Aaah!' yelled Jimmy. 'Please, please, please . . . stop, stop!'

Jimmy thought the knuckles between his middle and fourth fingers might split apart. An electrical charge of pain shot up his twisted arm and into his shoulder, which was on the verge of dislocating.

'Ah, ah, ah . . . please stop. Please,' Jimmy pleaded, while the rest of his body lay paralysed on the floor.

'All right, Igor, let's all take it easy for a minute,' said Colin.

Igor released Jimmy, who lay on the floor in pain and humiliation, unable to get up.

Colin wrapped his arms around Milfoth's waist, and chuckled. 'Cheer up, Jimmy. You've a grand wife here. I'd say she was a bit of a looker in her day, wha'?'

Colin and Igor laughed out loud. Jimmy's face remained crumpled. He looked at Milfoth. She was rigid, just staring at the carpet.

'If she was a bit younger, I might have given her a lash before ye came home, wha'?' said Colin. 'Sure, it would be rude not to!' He and Igor shared another laugh.

'Fuck you,' said Jimmy, still holding his wounded hand.

'Ah now, Jimmy,' said Colin. 'You should be glad I'm here. At least I have standards.' He raised his voice, as people often do when addressing a person whose first language isn't their own. 'Isn't that right, Igor?'

'Yesh,' said the voice behind Jimmy.

'If Igor was on his own, you'd never know what would happen. He'd ride anything, he would. Anything, I'm telling ye. Isn't that right, Igor?'

'Yesh,' said Igor again, laughing. 'Have the sex.'

'That's right, Igor! He has no morals at all, Jimmy. If I wasn't here, he'd have ridden your missus, and the little girl upstairs.' Jimmy seethed, but he could do nothing other than listen to Colin.

'The thing about Igor, Jimmy, is that when he rides someone, he leaves such an impression, that very often they never want to have sex again – ever again, in their whole lives!' Colin sounded amazed. 'He is that . . . memorable.'

He turned to Igor. 'Igor, I'm just saying, you're a dirty dog.'

Igor laughed loudly. 'Dirty dog. Yes. Woof, woof!' Colin laughed with him.

Jimmy looked around to see the leering grin of his oppressor. He was missing teeth, and the ones which were on display gave no indication that they had been cleaned recently. 'Let us go,' said Jimmy in an angry tone.

'Relax,' said Colin. 'Yer missus is enjoying the attention. Here, watch this.' He ran his index finger along her bra strap, from her shoulder down her chest and inside her bra cup. 'See, I always know they are enjoying it when the nipple gets hard.'

Milfoth grabbed his hand and moved it away from the area of her chest. Colin and Igor laughed loudly.

'Hey Igor,' said Colin. 'Play the piggy game with Jimmy.'

Igor laughed. 'Piggy game, yesh.' He lowered himself and straddled Jimmy. He sat on the small of his back, with his knees on either side of his torso. He forced Jimmy to walk like a pony, or a 'piggy', around the room, with Igor on his back, shouting 'Piggy, piggy!'

Igor slapped Jimmy's backside, and Colin added a kick to his backside also. 'Gerrup there horsey!' shouted Colin, and they both laughed loudly.

Suddenly Byron burst into the room. 'What the hell is going on here?' she shouted. 'I'm trying to get some sleep!'

The four adults in the room were stunned into silence for a moment. They stared at the teenager, and she stared back at her undressed mother sitting on a stranger's knee, and her father being sat upon by another stranger, and saying 'Oink, oink'.

'We're rehearsing for a play,' said Milfoth calmly. 'Your daddy and I have joined a drama society.'

There was a silence as the other three adults nodded in agreement.

'Well, try to do it a little bit quieter!' shouted Byron, and left the room, slamming the door behind her.

Colin and Igor found this hilarious, and released barely stifled laughter – much to the annoyance of their hosts.

'OK, OK,' said Colin, 'let's get to the point. Sit up there on the chair, Jimmy, and let's have a chat.'

Jimmy did as he was told, and even Milfoth was allowed to sit at the opposite end of the sofa to where Colin sat.

Colin fixed Jimmy with a stare. 'You're been selling coke in my backyard, Jimmy,' he said, 'and I don't like that.'

'What are you talking about?' said Milfoth. 'Jimmy?'

'Hush now, missus,' said Colin, 'this is man's talk. I want to hear what yer husband has to say.'

'Yes,' said Jimmy, guiltily.

'What?' yelled Milfoth. *'You?'*

'What I want to know is, did Hank send you over?' asked Colin.

'Who is Hank?' demanded Milfoth.

'He's a business associate of mine,' replied Jimmy.

'You have a business associate?' said Milfoth incredulously.

Jimmy addressed Colin. 'No, Hank warned me not to sell on the north side.'

'Warned you not to, or said go ahead, and deny my involvement if you get caught?' asked Colin.

'He knows nothing about this,' said Jimmy. 'He told me not to cross the river.'

'What are you talking about?' said Milfoth.

'Hush now, missus,' said Colin. He turned to Jimmy with a steely expression. 'Was he using you to provoke a reaction from me?'

'No, he knows nothing about this,' said Jimmy. 'He told me not to go over to your side.'

'Then why did you do it?' asked Colin.

'I dunno,' said Jimmy. 'I thought . . . . It was just a few clients . . . . Just a few yuppie apartments in the financial area.'

'Oooh,' said Colin. 'Like, you're thinking, the north side is Cabra and Finglas and Ballymun, not the posh cunts who work in the banks and insurance companies.'

'Y-yeah, I suppose,' said Jimmy.

'Did you not think to yourself that someone might already have that market covered?'

'I mustn't have,' muttered Jimmy.

'What's that, Jimmy?' asked Colin. 'You need to speak up.'

'Look, I'm new to this, OK,' said Jimmy. 'I made a mistake. I'm sorry. It won't happen again.'

'Oh, I know that,' laughed Colin. 'Usually, by the time I have to visit somebody's house, they are very sorry indeed. They're sorry that it's a bit late to be sorry.'

'Please leave us alone,' said Milfoth.

'Hush now, sweetheart,' said Colin. 'The men are talking.'

'What do you want?' asked Jimmy.

'I want you to tell Hank about this,' said Colin. 'He might have something to say to you. That's between you and Hank. But tell him I know, and I'm not happy.'

'OK, I will,' said Jimmy. 'I'll do that first thing tomorrow.'

'But you owe me, Jimmy. You've taken some of my clients, cost me a bit of money. Cost me time: me and Igor here giving up our night, just to give you a little adult education. Isn't that right, Igor?'

'That's right, yesh,' said Igor, laughing. 'Oink, oink!'

'Time is money, Jimmy. Time is money.'

'I know that,' said Jimmy.

'So I am going to fine you for all this, Jimmy.'

'OK. How much?'

'Twenty thousand euro,' said Colin.

'What?' said Jimmy and Milfoth in unison.

'I haven't got that sort of money,' pleaded Jimmy.

'Oh, I'd say you do, Jimmy. So don't be telling me any pork pies.' Colin suddenly realised his inadvertent pun: 'Hey Igor, pork pies, wha'?'

Igor laughed. 'Oink, oink!'

Colin continued: 'So Jimmy, €20,000 – now!'

'I haven't got that,' Jimmy pleaded. 'Look, let's talk about this.'

Milfoth interjected: 'We haven't got that kind of money. He's unemployed.'

'Sure, we're all unemployed, missus,' said Colin. 'Poor Igor here hasn't worked in years. Have you, Igor?'

Igor didn't understand the question, and Colin continued: 'Now, Jimmy, let's have a look in that sports-bag of yours.'

'Sure,' said Jimmy, 'but you'll see it's not that much.' He spilled the contents onto the floor, unravelled some smelly gear and a towel, and revealed a bag of notes. Jimmy counted out his money, putting them into piles of fifties, twenties and tens. 'There, €7,000,' said Jimmy. 'Take it, please, and go.'

Colin wasn't satisfied. 'Now, Jimmy, it's good to see you're cooperating,' he said. 'I don't know you that well, but I do know drug-dealers, generally. And I'm going to take a guess, Jimmy: somewhere in or around this little house of yours, there's the rest of my €20,000.'

'No,' said Jimmy. 'Search, if you want.'

'Jimmy, I'm too tired for that sort of thing, so I'm going to make you a deal. You search. I'm going to wait here with your missus, and drink my cup of tea. And if you're not back here in five minutes with my money, Igor is going to ride the fuck out of her.'

Milfoth shouted: 'No!'

'And when he's finished with the main course, he might venture upstairs for a little dessert.'

'You're fucking sick,' said Jimmy. 'I told you, I don't have it.'

Colin looked at his watch. 'Four minutes and fifty seconds, Jimmy. Are you still here?'

Milfoth darted for the door, but Colin was too quick, and caught her by the arm and landed her back on the sofa. 'There's nowhere to run, madam.'

'Call the police,' said Milfoth to Jimmy.

'Call the police, go ahead,' said Colin. 'I'm just sitting here having a cup of tea. No sign of a break-in. The missus here took her clothes off. Apparently she likes to do that when her husband's not around. And the money here . . . well, you can explain that to the Gardaí. They can have it. The thing is, Jimmy, if the cops take this money, you'll still owe me €20,000. And I will come looking for it, with interest.

'And to be clear, if I ever have to come and find you again, I will torture you and your wife in front of your little girl. Or maybe the other way around; I'm not sure yet.'

Jimmy looked defeated and confused. Suddenly, he blurted 'Give me five minutes', and ran out the door.

*

Keeping cash or product on his own property was too risky, because of the possibility of a police raid. Instead, Jimmy used Mrs Kennedy's shed as his business premises. The elderly lady lived with her cat, three doors up the street. Jimmy often cut her grass and did odd jobs for her, so it wasn't unusual to see him in her shed. She was too frail to venture into her back garden, and as a result, Jimmy felt that his money was safe there.

Normally, he entered her shed through her house, but that was impossible now, given the late hour. Instead, he jumped his garden wall into his next-door neighbour's, ran across their lawn, and jumped the next wall. The lush foliage on their plants made it impossible for him to do this without noisily breaking some of the branches.

In the next house again, the patio doors were open. Jimmy waited to see if anyone was about to come out. The occupant chatted in the kitchen on her phone. When her back was turned, Jimmy darted across her lawn, and over her wall, into Mrs Kennedy's.

His heart was pounding, not least because of the obstacle course that he had had to negotiate with an injured arm. For a moment he thought he had dropped the key to Mrs Kennedy's shed. 'Shit!' he exclaimed loudly, but then found it.

He knew he had used up at least two minutes so far, and still had to move some items around in the shed in order to get to his hidden stash. *They wouldn't stick to their five-minute deadline, would they?* he wondered. *Maybe they've already started.*

Jimmy shook his fists, and said to himself: 'Don't think about that. Focus, focus, focus!'

He entered Mrs Kennedy's shed. It was fully dark, except for dim light coming through the plastic window. He pushed aside the lawnmower, and moved the box containing her Christmas tree. Underneath were the Christmas decorations, and underneath those was a box of old curtains. Wrapped in the curtains was a metal cashbox. And in there were the proceeds of two months of successful drug-dealing.

It was too dark to count the money, and he had no time anyway. He stuffed his pockets with notes, and when they could take no more, he stuffed his underwear. He tucked his pants legs into his socks so that the notes wouldn't fall out the bottom. He tucked his shirt into his pants and then stuffed his shirt with cash. He wondered if he could get back to his house without leaving a paper-trail.

Back over Mrs Kennedy's wall, and into the bushes of the patio-door neighbour. She was still chatting away on the phone, and he nipped through her garden again. Over another wall, and another, and back into his own house. He arrived into his own living room panting and sweating.

'Ah, Jimmy, I thought you weren't coming back,' said Colin. 'Igor here thought he was on a winner! Or a loser – depends on your point of view, wha'?' He shared a laugh with Igor. 'Now, what have you got for me?'

Jimmy took a while to catch his breath, and then started producing money from every item of his clothing. He threw the cash on the ground. Igor flattened the notes and started arranging them into bundles of €500.

'One thousand, two thousand, three thousand,' said Colin. 'Seven, eight, nine . . . nine thousand five hundred . . . . Ten . . . . Ten thousand five hundred, eleven. I don't think you're going to make it, Jimmy.'

'That's all I have, said Jimmy, still panting. 'I'm telling you, that's all I got.'

'Just over eleven thousand, Jimmy,' said Colin. 'Plus the seven thousand from earlier. That's eighteen thousand, give or take. You're two grand short. What are we going to do? What do you think, Igor?'

'Piggy, piggy,' said an excited Igor.

'I know what he wants,' said Colin, laughing. 'You're a dirty dog, Igor!'

'Yesh,' said Igor.

'Please, Colin,' said Jimmy. 'I'm begging you. Please.'

'I dunno, Jimmy,' said Colin, shaking his head.

'Please, Colin,' said Jimmy again. 'First offence. Be fair.'

'I'll tell you what,' said Colin. 'Since this is your first time. And since your missus here made us feel so welcome, and makes such a nice cup of tea. And she doesn't look too bad in her skimpies. I think it would be bad manners if I didn't cut you a little slack.'

Jimmy muttered 'Thank you' under his breath.

'What's that?' said Colin. 'You'll have to speak up.'

Jimmy paused for a moment, but realised he couldn't avoid repeating it. 'Thank you.'

'Maybe a bit louder again,' said Colin, 'and with a little more enthusiasm.'

'Thank you very much, Colin,' said Jimmy.

'You're welcome, Jimmy. It has been my pleasure to come and enjoy your hospitality this evening. Now, Igor, why don't you gather up the money, and we'll let these good people get back to whatever they would normally be doing on a balmy Friday night.'

Colin and Igor left, and Jimmy locked the front door with a click. He returned to the sitting room, where Milfoth was dressing. 'Are you OK,' he said, stretching out his arms in support.

Milfoth whacked him. She hit him so hard he saw stars. Then she hit him again, and he lost his balance, and fell onto the couch. Milfoth stood over him, and hit him again and again. 'You fuckin' eejit! You fuckin' eejit! You're the greatest fucking arsehole I have ever met! Are you stupid, or what?'

She kept hitting him until she ran out of energy – to either hit or criticise him. She retreated to an armchair and lay down, covering her face. 'What sort of a fuckin' eejit did I marry?'

Jimmy too had his face covered. 'You're the one who told me to start earning, because we had bills to pay.'

'Was there no other line of work you could have picked?' she shouted. 'You could have pulled pints or served coffee!' There was another long silence, as both of them processed the events of the previous hours.

'What were you doing in your underwear?' asked Jimmy, in an accusing tone.

'You think I wanted to be like this?' she screeched at him. 'They threatened me. They scared the hell out of me. They said that I either did what they said, or they'd go up the stairs to Byron. What else could I do?' Milfoth's face was red, and her eyes welled up.

Jimmy crossed the room to her, but Milfoth raised her hand. 'Don't touch me!' she said.

Jimmy retreated to the couch. 'Well, couldn't you have run out the door, or something?' he asked.

'Yeah, like you could have come to my rescue when I was being sexually assaulted by that man in my own living room! But no, you were in too much distress. "Oh, my finger, my poor little finger."' She held her hand up and grimaced in mock pain. 'My wife might be raped, but I'm going to lie here on the floor in case the big man hurts my pinkie again.'

'I tried, OK. I tried,' said Jimmy weakly.

There was another silence, and then Milfoth sniggered. 'My husband, the coke-dealer, huh? How did all this start?'

Jimmy explained it all, including his introduction to testosterone treatment.

'Oh gawd!' said Milfoth. 'My husband is going through the menopause. What's next: hot flashes?' She shook her head again in disbelief. 'Was that the box that arrived in the post a month ago?'

'Yes.'

'You said it was printer cartridges. You lied to me.'

'I thought you might appreciate the effects of the medication,' said Jimmy.

'Yeah, clearly it's been great,' said Milfoth, pointing around the room, as if Colin and Igor were still there. 'I got myself a new man . . . a new macho man to protect me.' She buried her face in her hands again. 'I can't believe you did all this without me noticing.'

'Did you not wonder where I was every Thursday and Friday evening?'

'I thought you were having an affair,' she replied.

'You thought I was having an affair, and you said nothing?' asked Jimmy.

Milfoth shrugged.

'I leave that kind of stuff up to you,' said Jimmy caustically.

Milfoth didn't reply.

Jimmy felt some of his strength return. 'Why did you let them into the house?' asked Jimmy.

'I didn't let them in. They just walked in!' said Milfoth.

'How?' asked Jimmy. 'Was the door unlocked?'

'No, they had a key!' hissed Milfoth. 'How did these people get keys to our home? Did you give them keys?'

'No,' said Jimmy strongly. 'I have no idea where they . . . .' Suddenly he remembered the visit to Colin's penthouse, putting his keys into a tray, and the sound of a machine in the next room during the unnecessarily long meeting. That, it was now clear to Jimmy, was the sound of his keys being copied. 'I don't know.'

He slumped in the sofa again, and covered his face. 'I don't know,' he said to himself. 'I don't know. I'm sorry. I don't know. I don't know anything.'

*

As Colin and Igor left the house, they turned towards a car that was parked nearby, and another man drove them away. Across the street, in his car, sat Gunner. He picked up his phone and dialled a number.

'Hello,' said Hank.

'You'd never guess who I just saw leaving your pal Jimmy's house,' said Gunner, with an air of vindication. 'I told you we couldn't trust him. I told ye. I fuckin' told ye we couldn't trust him.'

11

❧❧❧

Slump

Jimmy hadn't been so depressed in months. After a fitful night's sleep, he awoke to a severe onslaught of dread as he realised the previous evening's events hadn't been a dream.

In one night, he had lost months of income, had his home invaded by thugs, and his wife had been sexually assaulted. His mind searched for someone else to blame, but he could come to no conclusion other than that he was at fault. He buried his head in the pillow and hoped for more sleep, to take away the anguish.

Milfoth had fled the house early in the morning with Byron. Where? She wouldn't tell Jimmy, but he assumed it was either to her mother's home in Kerry, or her sister's in Galway. The symbolism of his family leaving their home in fear hurt him, but he was glad they were away, so that he could think through the situation.

He drifted in and out of sleep, waking at 11 AM. He tried to get up, but hadn't the energy to do so. He wondered if he might be suffering from shock. He fumbled around in the dim light of his bedroom until he found the packet of Xanax he had started months before. He took two pills, and went back to bed.

It was after 1 PM when he awoke again. The dread and fear had lifted somewhat, and he felt the urge to get up and do something. He wondered if his improved mood was because of the Xanax, or the additional sleep, or if it could be because of the testosterone supplements.

Improved recovery from setbacks was one of the benefits that Malcolm had mentioned. However, increased recklessness was also something he had been warned about. They were both in evidence in recent weeks – which was probably a sign of the testosterone working, though he couldn't be sure. If it was the testosterone, then it had been responsible for the most violent incident of his life, the night before. It was a shocking side-effect of his treatment, so it made sense to stop dosing immediately. But then he thought of how close he had been to committing suicide just a few months before. In that context, he felt that the hormone had been beneficial, and he decided to continue using it.

Jimmy remembered his tap therapy, and started tapping while still lying down. His mantra: 'I may have fucked up, but I still love and respect and accept myself.'

He found it easier to tap under his armpit while standing, so he rose, and immediately felt more energetic. He changed his mantra to: 'I have the courage and intelligence to overcome my challenges.' He repeated this many times as he tapped the meridians that Malcolm had shown him.

Slowly the fog in his mind lifted entirely. He opened the curtains, and a warm ray of sunshine poured through the window and warmed his bare torso. It felt good. 'Remember to be grateful,' he said to himself. 'You're alive and it's a beautiful day.'

He turned to the mirror, and saw the body he had had in his early twenties. His stomach was flat, his chest taut. He checked his biceps. They weren't big, but they had definition. His triceps showed a pronounced chevron when he straightened his arms. Physically he was in good shape: he was turning it around in his forties.

He turned to the window again. He stretched out his arms, and closed his eyes. 'Take five deep breaths,' he said to himself softly, and inhaled deeply through his nose. 'Watch your breath,' he said. 'Look inside at how it enters your lungs, circulates, and slowly leaves through your mouth.' He made a loud hissing noise as he pushed his breath through his barely open mouth. He did this five times.

'Now think of five things to be positive about,' he whispered. 'One: I'm still in business. Two: Milfoth, Byron and I are still alive. Three: I am wiser than I was yesterday. Four: I am stronger than I was yesterday. Five: I am great, and I will overcome this.

'Now think of five things I'm going to do today,' he said, with growing confidence. 'One: get the locks on the house changed. Two: tidy up Mrs

Kennedy's shed. Three: tell Hank what happened. No, that can wait. Three: text Milfoth, and say something supportive. Appear contrite. Four: Take your testosterone. Take an extra dose. You need it. Five: go for a run.'

Jimmy hadn't jogged in more than a year, but his months of gym-work had put a spring in his step. He headed for the canal, where he hoped to find a dog off its leash or an errant cyclist whizzing amongst pedestrians. He felt like fighting somebody. When he couldn't find a suitable target, he was disappointed. *That's the problem with gentrification.* He smiled to himself. *The place is losing its character.*

He turned, and ran to his gym, and straight into the martial-arts area. A heavy punch-bag hung from the ceiling, and Jimmy thumped it as hard as he could with his right fist. Pain shot through his wrist and up his arm. He thumped it with his left. The pain wasn't as strong, but neither was his punch. He kicked the bag several times, and thumped it again and again, until he was exhausted. All this time, the bag seemed indifferent to his actions. It barely moved.

Behind him was another punch-bag. It swung, as if trying to avoid the punishing blows of a squat eastern European punching-machine. Like many others in the gym, he had the look of a man who had been thrown out of the Polish army for being too rough with the other soldiers.

Jimmy approached him tentatively. 'Excuse me, can you show me how to punch?' The man ignored him. 'Please. I'll pay you,' ventured Jimmy.

'How much?' he asked, without taking his eyes off the bag.

'I'll give you €100 if you teach me how to punch hard with both fists.'

'That is everything you want to know?'

'Can you show me finger-locks? I want to know how to really hurt someone who might attack me.'

'You give me €200, I show you everything.'

'Done,' said Jimmy.

*

After three days, Milfoth returned.

'Where's Byron?' asked Jimmy.

'She's going to stay with my mother for a while,' she answered.

'Why did you come back?' he asked.

'I forgot my hair-dryer,' said Milfoth, sarcastically.

'I've changed the locks,' said Jimmy. 'I've left your set of keys on the hook.'

'Thanks, I suppose,' she said. 'If they come back, do you think new locks are going to save us?'

'They won't be back,'.

'Is there anything else we need to do?'

'No,' said Jimmy. 'The windows are double-glazed; hard to break.'

'Would they stop a bullet?'

Jimmy shrugged. 'We haven't the money for bulletproof glass.'

'Oh, I forgot,' she said, with an accusatory air.

Jimmy was about to react to her tone, but held back. Milfoth saw the potential for an argument too, and backed off.

'What about a dog?' she said.

'Not sure what good it would do,' said Jimmy.

'I can ask the rescue-people if they have any suitable guard-dogs,' she offered.

'Well, maybe look into it . . . . Just to see what they have.'

'I got you something,' she said, and handed Jimmy a brown padded envelope.

'What's this?' he asked.

'Open it and you'll see.'

Jimmy ripped open the package and removed a heavy object, wrapped in layers of tissue paper. He worked his way through the paper and found a large silver crucifix, wrapped in a heavy silver chain.

'What would I want with this?' he asked.

'My mother gave it to me. She had it blessed in Lourdes. She wants you to wear it. She says it will protect you.'

'Thanks, but I don't need protection.'

'I want you to wear it,' she said firmly.

'Look at the size of it,' said Jimmy. 'Even Madonna wouldn't wear that.'

'Wear it inside your shirt,' insisted Milfoth. 'Nobody will see it. But I want you to wear it.'

'Since when do you believe in this sort of thing?'

'Since I was almost raped in my own home a few nights ago. I'm willing to accept help from any quarter at this point. Now please, put it on. It might save your life.'

'Look, thanks, but it's not for me – '

'Put it on,' she said forcefully. 'Just do it.'

Jimmy felt compelled to put it on, despite his misgivings. He draped the chain around his neck, took a look at the crucifix, and dropped it inside his T-shirt. 'I suppose it's big enough to stop a bullet,' he said.

'Thank you,' said Milfoth.

Jimmy was puzzled. 'Why are you doing this?' he asked.

'You might be a shit husband,' she replied, 'but you're the only one I have.'

'You know,' said Jimmy, 'that's the nicest thing you've said to me in years.'

12

⧽⧽⧽

Detention

Jimmy rose early to go to the gym. As he got into his car, a young, slightly-built man appeared from the side door of a van which was parked nearby. 'Hey, mister, do you know where I'd find a vet around here?' he said.

'Around here?' said Jimmy. 'I don't know. What's up?'

'My dog's after getting hit by a car,' said the younger man, pointing into his van. 'The poor thing doesn't look good.'

'Shit,' said Jimmy, approaching the van. 'How bad is it?'

'He looks really bad. See for yourself,' said the younger man, stepping out of his way. 'I have him under a blanket there.'

Jimmy looked inside the van and carefully pulled back the blanket. But under the blanket, there was no dog, just a coat, rolled into a ball. Jimmy was puzzled.

'There's no dog here,' he said, turning to the young man, but it was too late.

Bang! Jimmy was hit across the head, and simultaneously pushed from the rear, so that he flew head-first into the van. It was Davey who hit him. His accomplice was Midget, and he was already in the van. Midget jumped on Jimmy, and both he and Davey grabbed his hands and feet, and tried to tie them together.

Jimmy was dazed at first, but his body recovered quickly. With no possibility of flight, his mind switched to fight-mode. He felt calm, but aggressive. He rose into a crawling position – so strongly that he threw Midget off his back. Davey tried to restrain him, but Jimmy turned around and flailed at his face.

Jimmy overpowered Davey, landing some blows to his face. He also surprised himself by landing a kick at Midget's head at the same time. His recent training at the gym helped.

'Grab his feet!' shouted a third voice. It was Gunner. He recognised his voice from the jacuzzi deals.

Midget tried to grab Jimmy's feet, but Jimmy managed to kick him in the face. That bought him a moment to tackle Davey, who was attempting to sit on his chest. Jimmy pushed his torso up so quickly and strongly that he threw Davey head-first at the side of the van, making a loud noise. He followed up with an elbow into his face. This blow drew blood instantly.

'For fuck sake, would yiz get him under control!' roared Gunner at his two accomplices.

Jimmy landed two blows into the face of Midget, who was still trying to grab his feet. Then he was grabbed from behind by Davey. He struggled to free himself, and continued to kick at Midget's head and chest.

'Do I have to do it myself?' roared Gunner. He sprang into the van and landed on Jimmy, who felt Gunner's superior strength instantly. Jimmy received two blows to the head, and then one into the chest that winded him.

Jimmy swung at Gunner, but it was difficult while Davey grabbed at him. He pushed a fist into Gunner's face, and blocked a few return blows, but it was an uneven fight.

Gunner flipped Jimmy over onto his face, and put him in a full-nelson hold. Soon the three men were on top of him, and Jimmy could no longer resist. He could barely breathe, and his arms were immobilised. 'Tie his feet,' roared Gunner, 'and take his shoes away.'

The other men did as they were told. Jimmy roared at the top of his voice: 'Help me! Help me!'

'Shut him up!' roared Gunner. One of them put duct-tape over Jimmy's mouth. His hands were tied behind his back. He was pacified.

'Where's his phone?' demanded Gunner. 'Get his phone and fuck it out the door.' Jimmy felt his pockets being rifled, and then heard the sound of plastic skidding across concrete outside the van. They threw his keys out too.

Gunner berated the other men. 'Are yiz fuckin' incompetent, or what? He's a fuckin' oul' fella, and he almost beat the two of ye up.'

'But he's strong, so he is,' said Midget.

'Strong, my hole,' said Gunner, giving a gun to Davey. 'Now take this, and don't let him move.'

Gunner shut the sliding door of the van, and hopped into the driving seat. Midget sat in the passenger seat. The van pulled away quickly.

In the back of the van, Jimmy managed to loosen the duct-tape with his tongue. 'What's this all about?' he panted to Davey.

'Shurrup,' said Davey, putting the duct-tape back on his mouth.

Jimmy loosened it again, and demanded: 'What the hell is going on? Tell me!'

'I said shurrup,' said the younger man, pointing the gun at Jimmy. 'So shurrup!'

'Or what?' said Jimmy. 'You're not gonna shoot me. If you were gonna shoot me, you would have done it already.'

'We're gonna torture you first, and then shoot ya. OK! So shut up now.'

'Who's going to torture me?' demanded Jimmy. 'Gunner? Why? Tell me what's going on.'

'He says you were "cavorting with the enemy".'

'What?' asked Jimmy. 'What enemy? Gunner!' he shouted. 'What's the problem?'

'Shurrup, I'm fuckin' telling ye,' said Davey. 'He'll beat the head off both of us!'

Gunner shouted back from the driving seat: 'What's going on back there, Davey?'

'Nothing, Gunner, I'm just giving him a few digs. He's a mouthy cunt.'

Gunner shouted into the rear-view mirror: 'Jimmy, shut the fuck up, or I'll go in there and bash the head off ye.'

'I just want to know what's going on!' shouted Jimmy.

Gunner slammed on the brakes. 'Don't make me come back there, I'm fucking tellin' ye. I'll put a bullet in both of yizer heads.'

Jimmy's mind was racing. Shouting at Gunner from the floor of the van while he was driving was unlikely to win Jimmy his freedom, or even an explanation. He needed to find another way.

'You're Davey?' said Jimmy quietly. 'Davey . . . Davey.' He thought back to the last time he had been in an editing suite. 'Were you a friend of Joey Watt?'

The younger man's face dropped. He was taken aback, and seemed almost upset at the sound of Joey's name.

This encouraged Jimmy. 'You were Joey's friend, weren't you?' he continued. 'You were there the night of the break-in at the warehouse.'

'Shurrup, I said.'

'He told me about you,' said Jimmy softly. 'You were friends?'

'He was me best mate, he was,' said Davey reluctantly.

'He was only trying to save you on the night, wasn't he?'

Davey went quiet and turned away. 'I know he was. He was me best mate, he was.'

The names of Joey's family came to Jimmy's mind. 'How is Coleen? She is such a beautiful child.'

'She's the spit of Joey,' said Davey. 'She's a great kid. I visit her all the time, so I do.'

'And how's Samantha?'

'She's not good. Kinda depressed, and stuff.'

'He didn't have to die, you know.'

'I know.'

'Who killed him?' asked Jimmy.

Davey shrugged and didn't answer.

'Gunner?' ventured Jimmy.

Davey beckoned to the driver's seat, confirming Jimmy's assumption.

'He killed your best mate, and you're still doing what he tells you?' said Jimmy.

Davey didn't answer, but stared at the floor.

'Hey Davey, I'm asking you a question,' said Jimmy. 'He killed your best mate, and you're still doing what he tells you?'

Davey still didn't answer.

'And you're gonna let him kill me? How long before he decides to kill you?'

'I said shurrup!' said Davey, pointing the gun at Jimmy's head.

Jimmy didn't believe Davey would use the gun, so he persisted: 'What would Joey like you to do now?'

Davey didn't answer the question, so Jimmy answered it for him. 'I'll tell you what he'd like you to do. He'd like you to stop pointing the gun at me, and instead turn around and blow Gunner's fucking head off. That's what Joey *wants* you to do. Do it for Joey.'

'Yeah, but Hank and the others would get me then,' said Davey.

'You don't know that. Hank might be happy to get him out of the way,' said Jimmy. 'Let me go, and I'll kill him. Just give me the gun. I'll do it.'

'Look,' said Davey, 'there's nothing I can do. I can't let you go. Al' righ'?'

'If someone killed my best mate, I'd kill them. Out of honour, and respect for my friend. I'd do time for them. But by the way, the cops would go easy on you. It would be self-defence. I'd be your witness.'

Davey went silent, thinking through the possibilities. 'I dunno, right. I can't . . . . Now, stop talking. I can't trust you anyway.'

'Yes you can,' said Jimmy. 'Untie me, and give me the fucking gun.'

Davey shook his head, and seemed pensive. Finally, he changed the subject: 'Are you afraid of dying?'

Jimmy took a long time to answer. He felt a sudden pang of fear as it became clear to him that his death was a likely outcome that morning. 'If you asked me a few months ago, I would have welcomed it. Things weren't going so well. Dying seemed like a logical conclusion and I didn't fear it. But now . . . I would like to . . . . I want to . . . live.'

'Do you want me to send a message to your missus, or anything? Like, after the funeral, I could do an anonymous call, or something.'

The enormity of the predicament revealed itself to Jimmy in waves, and now it was his turn to become pensive. 'Like what?' he asked quietly.

'Like your last words were that you said you loved your wife and daughter?'

Jimmy thought for a moment, then said wistfully: 'I suppose it would be the politically correct thing to do.'

The van came to a sudden halt. The van door slid open, and Jimmy was hauled into a disused garage, brought up a stairs, and sat on the same seat that Joey Watt had used in his last hours. Jimmy's face lay sideways on a table. Behind him sat Davey and Midget. Gunner was clearly in charge. He seemed to be putting on a performance for the younger men.

'Now, ye prick!' Gunner shouted at Jimmy as he strutted around the table. 'You and I are going to talk.'

'Good,' said Jimmy. 'But if you wanted to talk, why didn't you just call me?'

'Shut up, for fuck's sake!' shouted Gunner. 'I'll do the talking here!'

'Are you going to tell me what this is all about?' shouted Jimmy.

'You were cavorting with the enemy,' said Gunner.

'Cavorting? What do you mean, "cavorting"?' asked a puzzled Jimmy. 'I think the word is "consorting".'

The two younger men sniggered – which only made Gunner angrier. 'Shut up, you prick!' he shouted again.

'What enemy are you talking about?' demanded Jimmy.

'You had Colin Deveney and Igor over at your house the other night,' said Gunner with a smile. 'I seen them, so don't deny it.'

'Jaysus, that's what this is all about,' said Jimmy, almost relieved to know why he had been abducted. 'I can explain that.'

'So you're not denying it,' shouted Gunner.

'Of course I'm not,' shouted Jimmy. 'If I can just explain – '

The interrogation was interrupted by Hank entering the room. The two younger men stood up to show their respect. Gunner turned to Hank. 'He admitted it, Hank. I told ye I'd get him to talk.'

'Hank, you and I need to have a chat,' said Jimmy.

'It's too late for that now, Jimmy,' said Hank.

'Hank, you need to know what's going on here,' shouted Jimmy.

'Shurrup, ye prick,' shouted Gunner, and thumped Jimmy in the stomach.

Jimmy was winded. Tears came to his eyes, and he was unable to draw a proper breath for close to a minute.

Hank beckoned Gunner into the next room. 'What's the plan?' he asked.

'There's some fields just outside Finglas, near where Deveney's mother lives. I'll shoot him there and leave him in a ditch, as a message to Deveney,' said Gunner.

'Just slow down a bit, OK,' said Hank. 'My guy in the Guards says it's already been called in. His wife got suspicious when she saw the car there, and him gone. When the cops came, some aul' wan said she'd heard what sounded like a fight this morning. She says ye made an awful racket, and then a van sped off.'

Gunner couldn't deny it was a messy operation. 'These jobs are never perfect,' he said. 'He left the house earlier than usual.'

'Did you take his phone away?' asked Hank.

'Of course we did. We fucked it out the door before leaving,' said Gunner.

'Are ye sure? The Guard said something about a tracking device. Did you check his pockets, in case he has a second phone?'

Gunner looked blankly at Hank, then turned and shouted in the door to the younger men: 'Here, you two, check his pockets, in case there's a second phone.'

He was about to return to Hank, then turned around again. 'Jimmy, have you a tracking device on you?'

'No.'

'Ye better not have, or I'll fucking kill ye!'

'I thought you were going to kill me anyway.'

'Shut up, ye prick!'

'The woman gave the colour of the van and the reg number,' said Hank to Gunner.

'That's grand,' said Gunner, relieved. 'The reg-plates are false, anyway. They'll be looking for some fella in Waterford.'

'It's not grand,' said Hank. 'The cops will be able to follow the van to here with traffic cameras. We need to get out of here. Wipe anything that Jimmy has touched. If they raid this place, I don't want them to find his DNA.

'Then, I need you to change the plates on the van back to what they were. Get one of the lads to drive it to the farm. Get him to clean it thoroughly: I mean completely! I don't want any of Jimmy's hair found in it.'

'I'll burn it, if ye want,' said Gunner.

'No, it would only attract attention. It would be like an admission of guilt,' said Hank. 'Get the lads to throw a bag of chicken-feed into the back of the van, and then let the chickens live in it for the week. I want the whole place covered in shit. It will keep the cops busy, if they ever send in the forensics team.'

'All right,' said Gunner.

'Now, I need you to move Jimmy to the shed in the Liberties,' said Hank. 'Use your own car, and I'll see you there in a while.'

'What's wrong with Plan A?' asked Gunner. 'Let's just shoot the fucker and dump his arse in Finglas. End of.'

'Because, before you commit a murder, you gotta make sure your tracks are covered,' responded Hank angrily. 'Right now, we have a witness to the abduction, the cops on the case, a getaway vehicle that looks very like ours – and the possibility of a tracking device. This is the shit that happens when you rush stuff, Gunner.'

'You're over-thinking this, Hank,' said Gunner. 'It's just another gangland killing. The cops won't care. Just shoot him. That's the end of the problem. Move on.'

'For fuck's sake, Gunner. It's not as simple as that,' said Hank.

'You're messing with the plans!' said Gunner. 'You're making it too complicated.'

'It's already complicated,' said Hank loudly. 'I'm trying to help you understand that.'

Gunner pointed his finger into Hank's chest. 'Hank, this messing around is why you won't be a top gang-leader again!' Gunner knew this would annoy Hank.

Hank took a deep breath, and spoke slowly. 'Gunner, this messing around is why you will never be a top gang-leader, ever.'

Gunner was stunned by Hank's rebuke. He hadn't expected Hank to respond to his jibe. Hank rarely insulted people; he liked to manage situations in an indirect way. It took a lot for Hank to criticise someone, and that someone had never before been Gunner.

After Gunner returned as a failed footballer from Arsenal aged nineteen, he disappeared into a self-destructive hell of booze, other drugs, and petty crime. It was Hank who had rescued him, Hank who had reminded him of the great athlete he once was, and could be again. He encouraged him to get fit again, and gave him free membership to one of his gyms. Hank became a father-figure for Gunner, and a role-model.

Later, as a member of Hank's gang of enforcers, Gunner made up for his lack of guile and judgement with unshakable loyalty and industry.

When Hank was locked up, his gang disintegrated. The Deveney brothers thought little of forming their own rival group, but Gunner's allegiance to Hank was solid. Despite several tempting offers from the Deveneys, Gunner stood by the man who had stood by him. He ran Hank's operations in his own limited way, until his master returned to resume his rightful position.

Gunner understood that things had been difficult of late between the two of them, but he never regretted his loyalty to Hank, until now. Suddenly he felt disrespected: not only inferior to Hank, but written off by the one he most wanted to impress. Something changed in that moment.

'After all I've done for you,' said Gunner quietly.

'After all *I've* done for *you*,' snapped back Hank.

The two men eyeballed each other, until Hank blinked. Hank could see the hurt in Gunner's face, and saw no benefit in having a dispute with his most trusted employee. 'Come on,' he said, 'take Jimmy to the Liberties. I'll see you there in a while. Call me as soon as you hear or see anything strange.'

The men dragged Jimmy out of the building and threw him face-down on the floor of Gunner's car between the front seats and the back seat. He was too tall for the width of the car, and they had to push his legs into a painful position in order to get the door closed. He found it difficult to breathe in the confined space.

Gunner drove quickly while Davey sat in the passenger seat, occasionally looking back to check that Jimmy wasn't trying to escape.

'Deveney and Igor broke into my house and molested my wife!' shouted Jimmy. 'I wasn't messing around with them. I was trying to stop them attacking my daughter!'

'Shurrup back there,' said Davey, with additional force, as if to impress Gunner.

'Why don't you check with them, if you don't believe me?' shouted Jimmy.

'Shut up, ye fuckin' eejit,' shouted Gunner angrily, and turned on the radio loud enough to drown out any more pleas from Jimmy.

The car got to the narrow streets of the Liberties and slowed down. Jimmy heard a metal gate opening, and then closing. Soon he was dragged into a stable and thrown onto some dirty straw. Amid the smells and paraphernalia of horses, he was ordered to be quiet, and received several thumps from Gunner when he tried to speak.

Hank arrived a short time later, clearly flustered. 'Fuck's sake, lads, my contact says he definitely has a tracking device on him.'

'What?' shrieked Gunner. 'We've already searched him. Here, ya prick, have you a tracking device on you?'

'No, I told you already,' shouted Jimmy.

Gunner was as flustered as Hank by now. Hank looked anxiously out the window, while Gunner and Davey went through Jimmy's pockets and the lining of his jacket, and checked the buttons on his clothes.

'Where are his shoes?' shouted Gunner.

'We left them outside his house. Or we left them in the van,' said Davey. 'I think.'

'Ye *think!*' shouted Gunner. 'If ye left them in the van, that's OK, coz the cops will be on their way to Bray.'

'What about his watch?' asked Gunner.

'He wasn't wearing one.'

Hank was trying anxiously to get through to someone on the phone, saying repeatedly: 'Come on, come on, come on . . . answer the phone!' He turned to Gunner. 'Did you find anything yet?'

'There's nothing, Hank,' said Gunner. 'Your source must be wrong.'

Hank was very tense. 'Strip him! Strip him now!'

Gunner and Davey started to remove Jimmy's clothes, roughly. They had difficulty, because his limbs were tied. Gunner produced a knife, but cutting off Jimmy's jeans proved difficult nonetheless.

'Fuck's sake, lads!' shouted Jimmy. 'If ye just untied me, I could take them off myself.'

Gunner pulled Jimmy's socks off, while Davey performed another examination of the clothes, which were now in a pile. Gunner ripped off Jimmy's T-shirt so forcibly that it hurt Jimmy's raw skin. He was now wearing nothing but his boxer shorts and the crucifix that Milfoth had got him.

Gunner grabbed the cross, and was about to yank it off Jimmy's neck when he hesitated. He looked at the figure of Christ in his hand, and replaced it gently on Jimmy's chest. Jimmy remembered the crucifix tattoo on Gunner's shoulder, and felt that he understood his captor's reasoning .

'Any luck with his clothes, Davey?' Gunner shouted.

'No.'

'Hank, there's nothing here. Your mole is wrong,' shouted Gunner.

Hank was on the phone: 'Come on, come on . . . .' He checked the road outside several more times. He went outside and looked up, to see if there were signs of the Garda helicopter. There weren't.

As he came back into the stable, his phone rang. 'Yes, yes, yes, it's me,' said Hank. 'Fuck it, I've been trying to call you for ages . . . . Yes, I know . . . . OK . . . . Do I need to buy you a charger as well? . . . I know you weren't expecting this. Neither was I. . . . Just tell me what's going on.'

He turned to Gunner to relay the contents of the call. 'Jimmy's wife is talking with the cops . . . . She says he left early this morning to go to the gym . . . . Yes, we know that, we know that already . . . . *What?* . . . You're fucking joking me!' Hank turned to Gunner with a scared look on his face. 'She's told the cops that she got a tracking device for Jimmy a few days ago. It's in the shape of a crucifix!'

The three gang members turned to Jimmy, looking at him in disbelief. 'Ye sneaky bastard!' shouted Gunner.

Jimmy looked back. He couldn't hide his disbelief, but also sensed an opportunity to ingratiate himself with his captors. 'Lads, I knew nothing about this. That's my wife: she's a fuckin' sneaky bitch, I'm telling ye. This is the shit I have to live with. Fuck's sake, I can't believe she was spying on me.'

Gunner ripped the chain away from Jimmy's neck, almost giving him whiplash. 'What do we do with this?'

Hank took it, wiped any fingerprints off it, and gave it to Davey in a handkerchief. 'Take it. Take my car, and drive to the far side of the city. Quickly. Whatever you do, keep moving. Don't get stuck in traffic.

'Then I want you to get on a bus – any bus. At the back seat, on the lower deck, hide this in the gap between the back of the seat and the cushion. That way, it will be driven around the city for the rest of the day, keeping the cops busy. Go now!'

As Davey left, Hank turned to Gunner. 'We have to get Jimmy out of here right now, in case we're raided. Put him in your car. Take him to my sister's place in Rathfarnham. I'll call her, to tell her to take the family away for the day.'

Gunner showed his discontent. 'If you'd only let me plug him in the first place – '

'Shut up, Gunner!' shouted Hank. 'Just shut up and do what you're told to do, please.'

'And what are we going to do in Rathfarnham?' shouted Gunner. 'Make him breakfast?'

'There's a digital trail leading from Jimmy's house to two of our properties,' said Hank. 'If he's murdered, we're in the frame.'

'What do you mean, *if* he's murdered?' shouted Gunner. 'When am I going to shoot him?'

'You're not.'

'Why not?'

'We can't kill him without landing ourselves in big trouble,' said Hank.

'Ah, for fuck's sake!' shouted Gunner.

'Lads, maybe I can have a word here,' said Jimmy. 'Does that mean I can go?'

'Shut up, you!' shouted Hank and Gunner together. Hank took Gunner by the sleeve and brought him outside, out of Jimmy's earshot.

'Well, what then?' said Gunner. 'Just let him go?'

'We're in a spot of bother,' said Hank. 'We can't kill him, or we'll do time for it. And we can't let him go, because he would be an excellent Garda source. He has seen our faces and our premises.'

'I'll tell him in no uncertain terms that if he goes to the cops, I'll break – '

'They've already gone to the cops!' shouted Hank. 'The cops are already all over it. He can't stop them, even if he wanted to.'

'I'll tell him I'll kill him if he tells them anything.'

'You think that would work? His best option would be to tell everything to the cops. And the sooner the better, to get us off the streets.'

'Well what, then?' shouted Gunner. 'What's your bright idea?'

'We can't kill him, and we can't stop him talking to the cops,' said Hank. 'Our best bet is to fix it so that when he talks to the cops, they don't believe a word he says.' He gave Gunner a look, which suggested there was only one possible course of action open to them.

Gunner's face dropped. 'Oh no, not that,' he said.

'Yes,' said Hank.

'No, no. For fuck's sake, *no!'* said Gunner.

'We've no other choice,' said Hank. 'We have to do it. *You* have to do it.'

'Not the Pink Rabbit!'

'Yes, the Pink Rabbit,' said Hank. 'That's why we have it.'

'Not the fucking Pink Rabbit,' said Gunner.

13

⊰⊱⊰⊱⊰⊱

The Pink Rabbit

It was still just mid-morning, and Jimmy was being moved again. He was hungry, thirsty, cold, dirty, scratched, bruised and humiliated. He was also afraid – but less so since Hank had said they couldn't kill him. His limbs ached from being in the same position for several hours. He begged to be untied, but to no avail.

They arrived at a country property; not a farm, but a modern bungalow surrounded by land. Jimmy was dragged into the garage by Gunner – which caused more abrasions, both physical and psychological.

Another car arrived. Hank and Davey joined Gunner in the garage. Jimmy could hear a dog barking outside.

'Fuck's sake, Hank, let me go!' shouted Jimmy. 'I had nothing to do with the Deveneys. They broke into my house and sexually assaulted my wife. Ask them, if you don't believe me.'

Hank approached Jimmy. 'None of that is important now, Jimmy,' he said.

'It's important to *me*, Hank. You and I had an agreement about how to sort out our difficulties. We agreed that we'd meet, and talk as gentlemen.'

Hank walked away, and Gunner gave Jimmy a kick in the shoulder. 'Shut up, or you'll get another one.'

'Don't bruise him,' said Hank. 'Leave as few marks as possible.'

'I'm freezing,' said Jimmy. 'At least throw a coat over me.'

Davey found an anorak hanging on the back of a door, and threw it over Jimmy. Hank and Gunner went to a workbench and started to mix two liquids into one container. Jimmy could see that one liquid was from a whiskey bottle, but the other was an unfamiliar thick brown concoction from an unmarked plastic bottle. They seemed unsure what to do, but eventually ended up with about a cupful of liquid in a plastic bottle – which Hank shook vigorously.

The two men approached Jimmy. He could see that Gunner held the bottle, and also a funnel. 'We need you to hold his legs,' Hank said to Davey. Hank then turned to Jimmy and said: 'Please don't struggle – for your own sake.'

'What's going on?' shouted Jimmy. 'What are you doing? Get away from me!'

'You two need to hold him still,' said Hank. 'Jimmy, it's best if you just remain calm.'

'Hank, what are you doing? I didn't do anything wrong.' Jimmy was terrified, and tried to wriggle away from the men – in vain. 'Please, Hank. Don't. Please, no!'

Gunner sat on Jimmy's chest. He wrapped his arms around Jimmy's head to stop it moving, and trapped Jimmy's arms under his legs to stop them moving too. 'Shut up, ya prick,' he ordered Jimmy, and to Davey: 'Now hold his legs tight. He's going to struggle.'

'Hank,   please!'   pleaded   Jimmy.   'Hankkkkkk   .   .   . Aaaaaaaaaahhhhhhhhhhh!'

Hank put the funnel in Jimmy's mouth, but he spat it out. Hank rammed it back in, with such force that Jimmy felt as though his teeth were nearly dislodged. Still, he managed to force the funnel out of his mouth a second time.

Gunner held Jimmy's nose, so that he'd have to open his mouth to breathe. When he did, Hank rammed the funnel in again. Jimmy wriggled and spat and shouted and struggled, but gradually the three-on-one struggle started to wear him down.

Gunner saw a garden trowel hanging on the shed wall, and it gave him an idea. He pulled Jimmy's head back so violently that Jimmy felt that his neck would break. He let out a shout of pain, and when he did, Gunner shoved the wooden handle of a trowel sideways into his mouth.

The wood prevented Jimmy from closing his mouth, and Hank slipped in the funnel. Then he started to pour in the liquid.

Jimmy's gag reflex was triggered, and liquid bubbled up out of his mouth. It ran down his chin, and spurted onto his attackers, but most of it went down his throat. Because it mostly missed his tastebuds, Jimmy couldn't tell if the liquid tasted as vile as it looked – until it came back up again. And it did taste vile.

He could feel burning along his oesophagus and in his stomach – which seemed to come from the whiskey. He inadvertently inhaled the liquid, which caused him to cough so much that he felt as though he was drowning. This made him panic even more. His eyes bulged and filled with tears, as if he was pleading for mercy.

Eventually the moment was reached when there was no more liquid to pour. The three men stepped away from Jimmy, who lay on the floor in an extended fit of coughing.

Tears seeped from his eyes. He wanted to wipe his face clean, but his hands were still tied. There was a horrible taste in his mouth, which he wanted to wash away. He gagged, as if about to vomit, but not much emerged. 'Water. Water, please,' he pleaded between coughs. 'Please, lads, some water.'

Davey went to the sink and brought a dirty cup of water to Jimmy. He sat beside him, held his head up and helped him sip. Jimmy washed it around in his mouth, and spat it out on the concrete floor. 'Thanks,' he said, still barely able to speak.

'Looks like you got yourself a nice new girlfriend, Davey, wha'?' shouted Gunner.

'What are ye doing? Why are you poisoning me?' panted Jimmy.

'We're doing you a favour, Jimmy,' said Hank.

'My shoulders are very sore,' whispered Jimmy. 'Could you at least tie my hands at the front? Please?'

Davey looked to Hank for approval. 'Is it all right if I do that, boss?'

'Tell him to fuck off,' said Gunner.

Hank stepped forward. 'Jimmy, I'll make a deal with you. We'll tie your hands at the front. If you struggle while we're doing it, we're going to tie your hands behind your back again. Extra tight. OK? Do we have a deal?'

'Yes,' whispered Jimmy.

Davey untied Jimmy's hands, and he didn't struggle. He then retied Jimmy's hands in front of him, allowing him the comfort of burying his face in his hands and assuming a foetal position. 'What was that?' he shouted. 'Have you poisoned me?'

Nobody answered. The men backed away, and watched Jimmy from the other side of the garage.

The concoction raced through his system, and his head started to spin. At first, the sensation was playful, almost gentle, but soon Jimmy felt that he was spinning on a playground roundabout. Instinctively he lay flat, almost as if taking up any other position might cause him to spin out of the garage. He tried to speak, but could only manage indecipherable noises.

The physical sensations gave way to visual ones. Colours and shapes raced into his field of vision, even though his eyes were shut. Endless chains of squares came from all sides. Some stayed as straight as train-tracks, while others turned in circles like rollercoasters. Some started as black-and-white and were then infused with colour; others went from vibrant colour to something akin to monochrome. They danced together, and formed patterns. Single chains split into double chains, which in turn split again. It was like nothing from Jimmy's own imagination; it was as though he was watching a fantastic computer-generated visual display, except that it was more real, and more complete.

Occasionally he opened his eyes to see the three men looking at him. This was real life, and it seemed weird. He shut his eyes again, and the visions returned. He remained tied, but there was no need for him to be. He had no control over his body. Even if they untied him, he wouldn't be able to walk out the door.

Jimmy starting to enjoy the sensation. As his body relaxed into the new sensation, the visions became more welcoming. He noticed that the three men had left the garage, but didn't think much about it.

Sometime later – it was hard to tell exactly when – the three men returned. They had a large dog with them. Even in Jimmy's stupor, he could see that this meant trouble. The dog was a Rottweiler; it was led across the room by Gunner, using a short leash.

Jimmy felt a need to vomit. The concoction in his body wanted to get out. His stomach-muscles went into spasm, and a small volume of liquid shot out of his mouth. 'Oh gawd,' said Jimmy. 'Oh my God!'

'Say hello to Tyson,' said Gunner.

Jimmy shouted 'No!' but to no avail. The dog made a deep guttural bark that sent fear through Jimmy's paralysed body, and lunged at him. He put his front paws on the bare flesh of Jimmy's back, and snarled into the side of Jimmy's face. Saliva from the dog dripped into Jimmy's ear, and he screamed.

Gunner laughed hard, and shouted: 'Go on, Tyson! Get in there! Eat the fucker! Tear him apart!'

Jimmy would have been terrified anyway, but the feeling of vulnerability brought about by the liquid he had been forced to drink made his fear many times greater. He screamed again. His body, tied and paralysed, could do nothing to repel the dog. He leant over on his side to vomit again. He tried to shout, to plead with his tormentors, but nothing would come out, except the word 'Aaaah'.

The vision of beautiful colours that had whizzed through his mind moments earlier was shattered by the vicious animal that was suddenly upon him. He could feel each of the dog's four large paws, and all of the claws on each paw, pounding and tearing at his skin.

His fear was greater than anything he had ever felt before. It was an atavistic fear; something that was present in his earliest ancestors: the fear of being ripped apart by the jaws and claws of another animal. His terror was so great that he thought his heart might fail.

'Go on, Tyson!' shouted Gunner again. 'Get in there!'

Jimmy's bladder had already surrendered, and now he lost control of his bowels. Gunner roared laughing. 'Ye dirty smelly bastard, Jimmy. Yer a fuckin' pig!'

Even the dog seemed to dislike the smell, and it backed off. Hank decided to end Jimmy's torment by Tyson. He pulled the animal off Jimmy and led it towards the door. He told Davey to wash Jimmy down with a hose, and told Gunner to get changed.

The cold water was a punishment in itself for Jimmy, but he took some comfort in seeing his vomit, urine and faeces disappear down a drain in the middle of the floor. He splashed water on his face, which refreshed him momentarily. The drug that he had been given exaggerated all his sensations.

He was still trembling with the cold and fear when a large pink rabbit walked into the garage. Clearly it was a man in a rabbit costume, reminiscent of ones he had seen at children's events at Easter-time. It carried a basket, and in the basket were several carrots.

'Hello, Jimmy baby,' said the rabbit with Gunner's voice. 'Would you like to play with me?'

'Fuck off and leave me alone, Gunner!' yelled Jimmy. 'Leave me alone!'

'Oh, Jimmy doesn't want to play with me,' said the rabbit in a high-pitched, sad voice. 'I'm so, so sad.'

'Please lads, just stop. What do yiz want? Just leave me alone,' pleaded Jimmy.

The rabbit got closer, and soon Jimmy's vision was taken up by a large pink head, two white eyes, a pink nose, and a large smiling mouth with two large teeth. The rabbit slapped Jimmy with its large floppy ears. 'Let's be friends, Jimmy,' it said. 'Don't be afraid. I won't hurt you.'

Jimmy was helpless as the rabbit lay down on top of him. It ran its white gloved paws over his body, and then lay behind him and simulated having anal sex with him. Gunner could no longer keep up his rabbit voice, and shouted: 'Whaddya think of that, Jimmy? Aha! Ever had sex with a rabbit before?'

'Fuck oooooooffff!' shouted Jimmy. 'Leave me alone!'

Gunner was having fun. He reached over to his basket and grabbed a large carrot. He trailed it across Jimmy's body, and shoved it between his buttocks.

Jimmy yelled in pain and shock. Gunner roared laughing again. 'Are ye gonna tell all yer posh friends about this? Wha'?' he shouted.

Hank declared that enough was enough, and sent Gunner out to get changed.

Davey could see that Jimmy was trembling. He found a blanket on a shelf and placed it on the floor, so that Jimmy would have a warm surface to lie on. Then he threw the anorak onto him again, and then a second blanket he found somewhere else. Underneath the pile he could hear Jimmy whimpering.

The three men convened outside the garage. 'All right,' said Hank, 'here's what we're going to do. Gunner, you've got to go home. Shower. Put your clothes in the wash. Even your shoes. Then get down to The Marbler and have a couple of pints. Only a couple, all right! And make sure you buy a pint for at least one other person. Talk to the barman about the football or the horse-racing. I want people to remember that you were there. And I want them to remember that you were relaxed, not all sweaty and anxious.

'Then you're to go into the off-licence next door and buy a crate of beer. Tell them you're off home to drink a few cans and watch a couple of movies. When you get home, pour at least three cans down the sink. Get your ma to join you, or a couple of mates. You need an alibi for tonight.

'Davey, the same. Don't go with Gunner. But get out and about, and make sure people see ye, and remember seeing ye. Don't get drunk. You need to have your mind clear, in case you get lifted. Yiz both slept late this morning, then went out for a couple of early scoops, then home again to watch the telly and drink a few cans. All right?'

The two younger men agreed.

Hank continued: 'In a couple of hours, the Levins will be here. They'll clean up this whole mess. You can watch the news tonight for developments.'

'What are you going to do?' asked Gunner.

'I'll stay here for a while with Tyson, and make sure nobody comes or goes. I'm going to burn this rabbit costume in the stove. Jimmy's DNA is on it, and so is yours, so we can't take any chances.'

*

That evening, the Levins – Jo and Anto – arrived. They were a husband-and-wife team who had their own office-cleaning company. On the side, they removed evidence of crimes on behalf of criminal gangs.

Hank explained the brief to the Levins, and left. He too needed to show himself to be out and about on a day when the Gardaí might be linking him to an abduction.

A live victim meant that they had to hide their identities, so the Levins donned 'alien' Halloween masks. Jimmy had fallen asleep, so didn't see them approach, but when he awoke and saw two aliens looking at him, he screamed in fear.

'Shut up!' shouted Jo Levins, but Jimmy kept screaming.

'Be quiet, or I'll have to knock you out!' shouted Anto.

'Get away from me! Get away from me! Help!' shouted Jimmy.

Anto went to his bag, and returned with a syringe – which he plunged into Jimmy's buttock. Jimmy stopped moving. 'We need to check his pulse every ten minutes,' said Anto to Jo.

The Levins laid a plastic sheet on the ground near the drain, and doused Jimmy's body with bleach. Jimmy screamed as the chemical stung his torn flesh. Then Jo Levins sprayed him down with a garden hose. She produced a shampoo bottle and cleaned Jimmy's hair. Then she sat him up, put gel into his hair, and blow-dried it.

Anto unzipped a small pouch that contained a nail-kit. While Joe cleaned under Jimmy's fingernails, Anto cleaned under Jimmy's toenails. Finally, Jimmy was sprayed with deodorant.

From their van, they brought a bag of men's clothes. They dressed Jimmy in a shirt, jacket, pants, underwear, socks and shoes.

When Jimmy woke, he was on the floor of the Levins' van, surrounded by cleaning products, mops and vacuum cleaners. He was still tied, and was being guarded by Jo Levins, who was wearing an alien mask.

'Where am I?' he asked.

'How are you feeling?' she asked.

Jimmy couldn't put his feelings into words. Although he felt much better than he had at any other time that day, he was still a prisoner – being held by someone wearing a Halloween mask. 'Where am I?' he asked again.

'You wanna go home?' Jo asked.

'Yes. Please.'

'OK, here's the deal,' said Jo, producing a half-bottle of whiskey. 'You're going to drink this – '

'No!' shouted Jimmy. 'Not again! Let me go!'

Jo slapped Jimmy in the face, 'Don't interrupt me again, you stupid posh arsehole. The last time you started crying like a little girl, and we had to knock you out. I'm not going to waste another dose on you. I'll fuck you out of this van while it's moving if I have to, so *shut up!*'

Jimmy was stunned into silence.

'This,' said Jo – pointing at the whiskey – is your ticket home. 'It's only whiskey. Nothing else. You drink it; you go home.'

'But why?' asked a confused Jimmy.

'Fuck knows why!' shouted Jo. 'Just do it, if you wanna go home. You either want to do this or you don't. I couldn't be bothered forcing you.'

'I don't want it,' said Jimmy.

'Fucking take it, or you're not going home,' shouted Jo.

'I told you, I don't want it,' said Jimmy.

'I don't give a fuck what you want, ye miserable fuckin' ejit!' roared Jo. 'I'm too busy for this. Just take it, or I will beat the fucking shite out of you.'

Jo's rage left Jimmy in little doubt that she would carry out her threat. She was so rough that she would probably beat Jimmy in a fair fight; he had no hope while he was tied up.

Jo handed the bottle to Jimmy, who took it reluctantly with his tethered hands. He removed the cap and smelled it. 'Is it really just whiskey?'

'What did I fucking say?' shouted Jo. 'It's just whiskey. If you want to go home, drink it. If not, give it back, and we'll dump your body somewhere.'

Jimmy was disoriented: from the drugs, from the alcohol, from the mental and physical trauma, from being in the back of a van with darkened windows, being chastised by an alien. He could see street-lights whizzing by outside, so he knew it was night,-time but he had no way of knowing what time it was, or where he was. He felt he had no choice, and took his first few sips tentatively.

'So who are you, then?' asked Jimmy.

'You don't need to know. Just drink. Quicker.'

The two sat in silence while Jimmy forced down the whiskey. 'Three minutes!' shouted Anto, from the driver's seat.

Jimmy got drunk quickly. The combination of substances already in his system, and the onslaught of the spirits on an empty stomach, meant that he started slurring his words while he was still halfway through the bottle.

The van stopped, and then reversed. Jo produced a gun, and shoved it into Jimmy's face. 'Now listen to me very carefully,' she said, taking back the remains of the whiskey. 'In a moment I'm going to open this door. I'm going to untie you, and you're going to get out and walk. And you're going to keep walking. And if you turn around, I'm going to blow your head off. All right?

'All right,' said Jimmy, fearfully.

The van stopped. Using a knife, Jo cut Jimmy loose. She opened the sliding door and forced Jimmy out. Just before he took his first step, she put a straw hat on his head, tilted it, to cover his eyes, and squirted him with aftershave.

Jimmy started walking. He didn't dare move the hat, so he didn't know where he was walking. He could see gravel at his feet, and grass. He shouted back: 'How far do I walk?' There was no reply.

He kept walking, slowly and unsteadily. 'Do I keep going?' he shouted. Again, there was no reply.

He bumped gently into a wall. 'What do I do now?' he shouted. But there was still no reply.

Eventually, he dared to look around. He removed the straw hat and saw that the van was gone. He was down a dark lane. He turned back, and after around 30 metres found himself under street-lights. The area was familiar. He was close to his home.

He straightened the hat on his head and made towards his street. It was difficult to walk in a straight line, but he was elated at being alive and heading home. He was hungry, thirsty, sore, disorientated, traumatised and drunk. But he was alive. It wasn't a bad result, considering the day he'd had.

Jimmy turned the corner of his street and walked towards his house. As he got closer, he could see three Garda cars, and two TV news-vans, at the spot where he had been abducted that morning. TV lights illuminated the area, and a reporter was beginning to give a piece to camera.

He could hear her say something about a kidnapping, and a Garda investigation. At first, the other bystanders didn't recognise Jimmy, but then one photographer, and then another, put cameras to their eyes, and there was a succession of flashes and clicks. This alerted some news reporters who were sitting in their cars, and they started running across the street, shouting: 'Jimmy! Jimmy!'

In order to go through his garden gate, Jimmy had to walk behind the reporter who was now live on TV. As he brushed by her, he looked into the camera, tipped his straw hat, and said the only words that came to his drunken mind: 'How're ya, Horse?

14

⊰⊱⊰

Home

Inspector McClean opened the front door. 'Well fancy seeing you here, boy,' he said, in an excessively Cork-inflected accent.

'Ah, g'man Squeezy,' said Jimmy, still looking for keys in his pockets. 'I . . . I . . . dink this is my . . . my house. D'ye mind if I come in?'

As he came through the door, Milfoth – who had just seen her husband live on TV – came running out of the sitting room.

'Jimmy!' she shouted, with a mixture of joy and confusion.

Jimmy stretched out his arms to embrace her. 'Sweetheart! It's good to be home. I had a dreadful day. I must tell you all about it.'

Milfoth took a step forward to hug her husband, but then smelled the aftershave, and recoiled. 'What? What? Where have you been?' she asked in disbelief.

''Tis a long story.'

'Are you drunk?'

'Possibly . . . actually, it's a . . . it's a very strong probability . . . but that's not important now,' said Jimmy.

'It's *very* important,' declared Milfoth. 'We're here thinking you were kidnapped, but you were out getting drunk!'

'Technically, yes,' said Jimmy, 'but not really. I can explain.'

'You fucking better explain!' yelled Milfoth, and she lunged forward and hit Jimmy repeatedly. 'You fucking better. I thought you were dead! What were you doing? Fucking some whore?'

Detective McClean closed the door, to shut out the prying eyes of the media. Jimmy backed into the corner behind the front door, raising his hands to protect himself from his wife. 'My day's been bad enough already,' he pleaded. 'Can you just calm down, please.'

'This *is* calm!' shouted Milfoth. She knocked the hat off Jimmy's head, and kicked him in the leg. Two other detectives, O'Toole and Kearney, pulled Milfoth away. 'Please, mam,' one of them said. 'We need to ask your husband a few questions.'

'No, *I* have questions!' shouted Milfoth, and lunged at Jimmy again. *'Where the fuck were you?'*

The two detectives restrained Milfoth and ushered her into the sitting room, where other uniformed Gardaí were seated.

'Dank you, ossifers,' said Jimmy. 'I dink sometimes she can be very . . . insensitive.'

Jimmy was led into the kitchen by McClean, where he was sat down and offered tea.

'Tea?' said Jimmy in an exhausted tone. 'Dat's the nicest-nicest t'ing enyone did for me all day.' Jimmy shook his head in disappointment, and pointed in the direction of his wife. 'Y'know, sometimes I find her attitude most unhelpful. She let the side down there, in my view. I would like to apologise on her behalf. Whaddyyou . . . whaddayou . . . whaddyou think, Squeezy?'

McClean ignored the question. He pulled up a chair and sat opposite Jimmy. 'Now,' he said, 'we have some serious matters to discuss, and I need to ask you some questions.'

'Right,' said Jimmy, suddenly assuming the same serious tone as the Garda. 'Let's get down to business.'

'We received a call this morning about a suspected abduction.'

'It was more than suspected, Squeezy,' said Jimmy, trying – in vain – to appear serious and coherent. 'I can cato-gor-iclly say it was an abjuction . . . of me.'

'Can you account for your movements today?' asked McClean.

'Account for my movements?' said Jimmy, supressing a burp or a hiccup, or both. 'I was obstructed . . . I mean, objected . . . I mean . . . . let's just say "kidnapped" . . . . Is that ok? Right.' Jimmy moved his hands, as if trying to steady the room around him. 'They took me away at about eight o'clock . . . no, actually, at about seven o'clock. I was going to the gym, a bit earlier than I usually do. And next thing I was ob . . . junted.'

'Who abducted you?'

In his drunken haze, Jimmy still had the awareness that answering this question could have serious implications. 'I dunno,' he said.

'Were they wearing masks?'

'Yes, I think so.'

'You *think* so?'

'Well, it all happened so fast.'

The Garda gave a look that showed he didn't believe Jimmy. 'Your wife said you were getting a little bit of hassle from some thugs recently.'

'She did? What did she say?'

Now it was the Garda's turn to be circumspect. 'Oh, just that you had had some hassle, and that's why she suspected the worst.'

'And what would be the worst, in her view?' asked Jimmy. 'That . . . that's a question that needs a serious answer, Squeezy. D'ya think? Like, in her mind, what would be the worst?'

The Garda took note of Jimmy's question, but didn't answer. For Jimmy, this bought a little time. He didn't know what Milfoth may have said. Perhaps she had mentioned his drug-dealing, but if she hadn't, it would be best if he avoided any discussion of the gang that had grabbed him. He wished he wasn't so drunk.

'You and your wife getting along OK?' the Garda asked.

'I think you can answer that one for yourself, sir.'

'You know, Jimmy, we in An Garda Síochána have invested a lot of time and resources to ensure your safe return here this evening. We would be very . . . disappointed . . . if we felt this was all a hoax.'

'A *hoax*,' said Jimmy in disgust. 'You think I went through all I went through for a hoax?'

'Or if we felt you were withholding information.'

'I know that, Squeezy, sir . . . ah, Guard. And I would like to extend my grantitude . . . grati . . . grati . . . chewed . . . to all the brave women and men in the force. For their professionalism, and fortitude. Thank you very much.'

'Why were you abducted?'

'I don't know. Maybe it was mistaken indemnity . . . I mean inden-nity. I-dentity. Identity, sorry.' Jimmy was clearly physically uncomfortable, and twisting in his chair. 'You know, my underpants are too tight,' he blurted.

'I'm sorry to hear that, but I would like to know where you've been for the last fourteen hours,' said McClean.

'Fourteen hours? Is that how long I was amducted? It felt much longer, believe me. You know . . . ye know . . . my underpants are just . . . too . . . tight.'

'Yes, you've said that.'

'They're not my clothes, you know. I wouldn't normally dress like this.'

'Whose clothes are they?' asked McClean, impatiently.

'How would I know?' said Jimmy, as if the answer was obvious. 'They were on me when I woke up.'

'Woke up where?'

'In the back of the van. With the aliens.'

'Aliens?'

'Yes.'

'So you were abducted by aliens?'

'No,' said Jimmy, slightly irritated. 'I was abducted by the men. But the aliens left me back. In a van.'

'In a van? Not in a spaceship?'

'Yeah. Not in a spaceship! Are you taking the piss?' Jimmy was irritated, and started to stand up and undo his trousers. 'Look, my underpants are too tight. I need to take them off.'

McClean rose too, and ushered Jimmy back to his seat: 'Please, Jimmy, let's just leave your pants alone for a few more minutes. Just a few more questions.'

'Anyway,' said Jimmy, returning to his seat, 'they weren't in a spaceship, because they weren't real aliens. They were just dressed as aliens.'

'So they weren't real aliens, just pretend ones?'

'Well, they had Dublin accents, not . . . like . . . alien accents. They weren't going' – Jimmy moved his hands like a robot – "I. Am. An. Alien." But then I don't know. Like what kind of accents do real aliens have? Y-you'll have to answer that one for me, Guard.'

McClean didn't answer, but wrote another note. 'And they gave you your clothes?' he asked, without raising his eyes.

'How would I know? I was asleep.'

'And where are your own clothes?'

Jimmy was getting more irritated. 'How would I know? They took them off me!'

'Who? The aliens?'

'No,' said Jimmy, getting agitated by what seemed like unnecessary questions. 'The aliens *gave* me clothes. It was the men who *took away* my clothes.'

'OK,' said McClean, also getting tired. 'These men abducted you, took your clothes, and then what?'

'They gave me a magic potion.'

'Right.' The Garda was momentarily stuck for another question. 'And what was so magic about the potion?'

'It was very scary.' Jimmy suddenly remembered the fear he'd felt. 'Like, it was really cool in the beginning, like, trippy and stuff. And actually at the end, it was fine as well. But in the middle . . . I'm not sure I want to talk about it right now. It was very personal.'

'Please, Jimmy. What happened then?'

'Well, first there was a big dog on me.'

'A dog attacked you? Do you have bite-marks?'

'No, he didn't bite me. But I probably have scrape-marks on my back,' said Jimmy, starting to lift his shirt.

'That's OK, continue with the story,' said the Garda, showing no interest in examining Jimmy's back.

'I think they were trying to get the dog to . . . y'know . . . ' he lowered his voice, so the other Gardaí couldn't hear him – 'have rumpy-pumpy with me,' said Jimmy.

'Right. So the dog on top of you . . . . Was this real, or was it the magic potion?'

Jimmy was suddenly cross, remembering the hurt. He waved a finger at McClean for emphasis. 'It was real, Squeezy, I'm telling ye. This was nasty stuff, it was.'

'Right. How nasty?'

'Pretty bad. Pretty scary . . . . And then there was the pink rabbit.'

'The pink rabbit?'

'Yeah, and he . . . ' – Jimmy made a gesture with his hand in the vague direction of his backside – 'he . . . interfered with me . . . with his carrot . . . .' Jimmy lowered his voice. 'He protruded my bung-holio.'

'All right,' McClean announced to his colleagues, and closed his notebook with a loud crack. 'I'm finished here.' He rose, left the kitchen and shouted over his shoulder: 'This is domestic bullshit. A waste of our bloody time.'

'Where's he gone?' asked Jimmy, confused. 'It was just getting to the interesting part.'

Milfoth burst in the door. 'Now, can I talk with him?'

Garda O'Toole turned to her. 'Yes, ma'am, talk to him. And whatever difficulties exist between the two of you, please sort them out before calling us again.'

Jimmy suddenly felt fear again. 'Here, Guard, don't leave me here with her. I . . . I feel I'm in danger.'

'That's music to my ears,' said O'Toole, and strode towards the front door.

'Hey, come back here. I'm not finished,' said Jimmy.

'Sorry,' said Garda Kearney. 'This is a domestic issue.'

'Domestic? That doesn't make it right!'

'I want to talk to you,' said Milfoth.

'Lads, please, she wants to talk to me. That's a bad sign. I need your support,' said Jimmy, with growing hysteria. 'Hey, come back here, and make yourselves useful for a change. Fucking cops!'

The Gardaí continued towards the door.

'Here,' said Jimmy. 'Yer always giving out, saying "Our morale is very low" and "We need more resources". Well, now's your time to actually do something.'

'Like what?' asked Kearney.

'Like . . . I'm about to be a victim of a crime. Don't you care?'

'Not really,' said Kearney, and smiled.

'I was kidnapped, and molested by a rabbit: a pink one, for your information!' yelled Jimmy theatrically. 'My body is a crime scene! I demand to be checked – for DNA evidence. Or at least for traces of fur and carotene!'

Garda O'Toole returned to the kitchen. 'It's only a crime if the rabbit did it against your will.'

'Oh, very funny, little Garda-man. That's really witty! Ha-ha,' said Jimmy sarcastically.

The last Garda left, leaving Jimmy and Milfoth alone in the house. The sound of the front door closing marked the moment she could get answers from Jimmy. 'You have one minute to tell me what the fuck happened today, or I'm leaving,' she said, with her index finger raised.

'As I said to the Garda – '

'I don't want to hear the shit you said to the Garda. I'm your wife. I want to hear the truth.'

Jimmy was about to answer, when the doorbell rang. Milfoth strode down the hallway and opened the door. Several journalists and a photographer stood outside. One of them asked: 'Can you comment, please, on what happened today. Was there – ?'

'No!' shouted Milfoth, and slammed the door.

Moments later, the door opened again. It was Jimmy. 'I would just like to say that, contrary to what you may have heard from An Garda Síochána, I was indeed – '

He was yanked powerfully by the collar from behind, causing him to end up sprawled on the hallway floor. Milfoth slammed the door for the second time in seconds. Jimmy raised his head a few times, in a vain attempt to get up from the floor, but he was unable to do so.

He was aware of Milfoth berating him from above, and the last word he heard before she stomped up the stairs: 'Asshole!'

*

Jimmy woke in the middle of the night, on the cold hallway floor. He rose unsteadily to his feet and stumbled as far as the downstairs toilet, where he dry-heaved. He downed a glass of water, in the hope of weakening his emerging hangover, but it came back up. He clawed his way up the stairs, and managed to remove the underwear that was threatening to cut off circulation in his nether regions, before collapsing into bed.

It was midday before he woke. He was depressed. Without even checking her room, he knew that Milfoth had left. Where? He didn't know – but probably her mother's.

He felt deep anxiety, which needed deciphering. Was it because his body had been filled with toxins the day before? Quite likely. Was it because he had been through a near-death experience, and had endured a series of traumatic events? That would certainly make sense.

Was it because his brief moment in the national spotlight might contribute to the instant demise of his fledgling career in cocaine sales? Yes: his clients would view any publicity as potentially contagious. Would it damage his already damaged career in television? Probably.

There was also the embarrassment of what had happened. Not just for him, but for his wife and daughter too. He didn't want to face the world, and resolved to spend a large part of the remainder of his day in bed. The future looked bleak, he thought to himself. Actually, the present looked bleak too.

He nodded off again, but was awoken by a loud banging on the front door. He tried to ignore it, but it continued, and then he heard his name being called. He looked out through the blinds, to see Danny looking up. 'Hold on, I'll come down!' he shouted.

'Are you OK?' Danny asked, as he sat down in Jimmy's kitchen. 'I'll make the tea myself. Just point to where I'd find tea-bags.'

Jimmy rested his head in his hands – which in turn were supported by his elbows and the kitchen table. Something inhibited his ability to converse: he wasn't clear if it was the hangover, or a kind of wider despair. He pointed in the general direction of a press, and was pleased to see a cup of hot liquid placed under his face.

'Is your wife around?' asked Danny.

'No, she's gone,' said Jimmy, in a coarse voice.

'Gone, as in gone to the shops? Or gone, as in – '

'Gone, as in I think she's left me,' said Jimmy.

'You think?' asked Danny. 'Did she say anything?'

'Oh, she said a lot, but I was just too drunk to remember.' Jimmy suddenly saw the funny side of his night, and both men laughed.

'Well, you're currently the nation's favourite drunk,' said Danny. 'Have you seen the papers?'

'Don't tell me,' said Jimmy. 'I have enough on my plate.'

'Put it this way: you're going to have to get used to people calling out to you in the street "How're ye, Horse?"'

'Maybe I should try a career in comedy.'

'How have you been? Have you been drinking a lot?' asked Danny.

'No, on the contrary,' said Jimmy. 'I've hardly had a drink in months. I think my body has lost its tolerance of alcohol.'

'You do know that tomorrow's the big day?' said Danny.

'What big day?'

'You're pitching your programme idea. Didn't you get the call?'

'What call?' Jimmy instinctively tapped his sides, looking for his phone. 'I don't know if I have a phone any more. I think the cops took it.'

'We're invited to pitch *I'm Offended* to TV Ireland tomorrow. You should have got an email a few days ago too.'

'An email...,' said Jimmy. 'I've been a bit distracted of late.'

'Yeah, no kidding,' said Danny with a laugh.

'Look, Danny, I don't think I can pitch anything tomorrow. You'd better do it yourself.'

'No way, Jimmy. This is your idea. You're pitching it. I'll help, but this is your baby.'

'I can't, Danny. Look at me. I'm just not able.'

'It's just a hangover. Get some sleep. You'll be fine tomorrow.'

'It's more than that. I'm just not up for it,' said Jimmy forlornly.

'It's a big day tomorrow,' said Danny. 'New American owners in town. They want to see what the pipeline looks like: what they're spending their money on. It's a chance for you to shine in front of them.'

As the tea settled in Jimmy's stomach, a wave of nausea overcame him. 'Thanks, Danny, but I've got to go back to bed. I'm sorry,' he said, as he headed for the door. He stopped momentarily. 'How will Monica view my . . . public appearance?'

'You know, she takes a particular view of the kind of men who go off on the razz all day, and leave their wives thinking they've been kidnapped.'

'All the more reason to cancel tomorrow,' said Jimmy, and asked Danny to let himself out.

*

It seemed pointless to apply testosterone gel to his body that day, but he did it anyway. He couldn't help thinking that the magical molecule that was supposed to renew his life had only landed him in trouble. He spread double his usual daily amount on his chest and shoulders. 'I need all the help I can get,' he said to himself.

Jimmy took to the bed for the rest of the day. He was physically and mentally exhausted. He thought he might have the symptoms of Post-Traumatic Stress Disorder, but was too fragile to go to his computer to find out what the symptoms actually were.

He had repeated memories of being mauled by the Rottweiler, and the sensation of the dog's saliva dripping into his ear and along his neck. His skin crawled at the memory of the dog straddling his cowering body; its genitals rubbing on his side; its claws dragging along his bare skin. 'What was the purpose of that?' he wondered aloud.

He remembered how close he'd come to getting shot. Joey Watt's fate had awaited him. He was due to be in a ditch near Finglas by now – soon to be discovered by a farmer, or someone walking their dog. He was due to have been tortured before his death.

The doorbell rang. He looked out, to see a police car, so he felt obliged to open the door.

'Your phone and your keys, sir,' said a stern Garda. 'We are also returning your car,' he said, pointing at his car being lifted off a Garda truck. 'I hope you're feeling better today.'

Jimmy's phone was inundated with texts and voicemails. They started with the concerned calls from Milfoth early in the morning, and then became a flurry of texts and voicemails after the evening news. Typical of the messages was one from a former college friend: 'Jaysus, Jimmy, you're a dark horse. You gave us all a good laugh, but I'd say your missus might have a different view. Glad you weren't kidnapped, by the way!'

Uncomfortable as it was that the nation saw him as a selfish, and perhaps unfaithful, husband, Jimmy felt it was better that that impression was given. The alternative was that he had been kidnapped by a drugs gang – and Jimmy wasn't ready to explain that to anyone, especially to the police.

He rang Milfoth. 'What?' she answered.

'How are you?' Jimmy asked softly.

'How the fuck do you think I am?' she shouted back. 'You've embarrassed and insulted me very, very publicly.'

'Well, I'm sorry about that. It was out of my control.'

'So, what happened?'

'I don't feel comfortable talking about it on the phone.'

'Well, get used to it, because it's the only way you'll be talking to me for a long time.'

Jimmy knew what this meant. 'OK,' he said. 'I understand.'

'So, where were you?'

'I told you, I can't discuss that on the phone.'

'I don't give a shit,' she wailed. 'Where the fuck were you?'

'What part of "I can't tell you on the phone" do you not understand?' he said loudly. 'You'll just have to come to me.'

'No! Goodbye!'

'Wait, wait,' said Jimmy. 'It's only appropriate that I say "Thank you".'

'For what?'

'For saving my life.'

'Oh, here we go,' said Milfoth dismissively. 'How did I do that?'

'With the crucifix. You told the cops. And someone there told someone else. It disrupted their plans – which was . . . erm . . . fortunate.'

Milfoth was silent as she considered the possibility that Jimmy might be telling the truth.

'So, thank you,' said Jimmy.

She hung up.

15

ঙঔ ঙঔ ঙঔ

I'm Offended

It was early morning when the phone rang. 'Just checking you're good to pitch today?' said Danny.

'I don't think I'm up for it,' said Jimmy. 'Really, I just want to be alone.'

Danny softened his tone. 'Are you OK? I thought you were, y'know, better of late?'

'I'm just not feeling up to it right now. Thanks, all the same.'

'I don't want to add to your stress,' said Danny, 'but if you don't do this, you're going to feel a lot worse about your life tomorrow, and worse again the next day, and the next. And you'll be right to feel bad, because this is the best chance you've had in months of getting out of your situation. There's nothing else on the horizon.'

Danny could hear Jimmy breathing at the other end of the line, but no words.

'You still have another couple of hours to decide. Think about it. I can pick you up at 9.30.'

Jimmy snoozed for a little while longer, but because he had spent most of the previous day in bed, he ran out of tiredness. He had also run out of melancholy. His blood felt clean again, and his body ached far less than it had. The morning sun was splitting the curtains.

'Fuck it anyway,' he said as he pulled back the duvet and sent two feet towards the floor. 'If I'm not dead, I might as well live.'

*

'Nigger,' said Jimmy. 'Nigger.'

The room went silent. Monica looked at Jimmy, and mouthed 'What the . . . ?' silently.

Brad Kerzhakov, the representative of the American owners, looked shocked. Even Danny wasn't expecting this. He looked at Jimmy, unsteady on his feet, unshaven, in a crumpled suit, no notes in his hand, and watched as the word came out of his mouth again: 'Niiii-gger!'

Monica looked at Brad in embarrassment, and turned to Jimmy, before hissing: 'This is not acceptable language in this office.'

'Why not?' asked Jimmy, calmly.

'Sir, that kind of language would not be permitted on one of our stations,' said Brad.

'Why not?' asked Jimmy again.

'Because it's offensive,' said Monica harshly.

'Offensive to who?' asked Jimmy.

'I'm offended,' she said.

'Why? Are you a nigger?' asked Jimmy.

'You are being offensive to black people,' responded Monica.

'Er, we would say "African Americans",' added Brad helpfully.

'And are you African American?' asked Jimmy.

Both Monica and Brad looked at themselves as if checking, before denying the suggestion.

'OK,' said Jimmy. 'So although you're not a black person, or – Brad – an African American, you are adopting the persona of such a person, to claim that you are offended.'

'That's an over-simplification,' said Monica sternly. 'Now what's this about?'

Jimmy waved away the question, and looked around the room, before uttering his next word: 'Knacker!'

'Oh for heaven's sake!' yelled Monica.

'Is that an offensive word?' asked Brad.

'Yes it is,' said Monica emphatically. 'It refers to the Travelling people: traditional nomadic people in Ireland.'

'Are you offended, Monica?' asked Jimmy directly.

'Yes I am,' she responded loudly.

'Why? Are you a knacker?'

'No I am no – ' she replied loudly, and then quietened, to say: 'No I am not, but that doesn't mean you are not being offensive.'

'So you are stepping into the persona of a Traveller to let us know that you're offended. Effectively, you're saying: "I'm offended, as a Traveller".'

'I'm not stepping anywhere, Jimmy. But I *am* losing my patience.'

'OK, OK, OK,' said Jimmy, and took a deep breath. Then on the exhale he said: 'Kike!'

Brad stood up. 'Sir, I think this meeting is at an end.'

'Why?' asked Jimmy. 'Are you a Jew-boy?'

Danny didn't want to show disloyalty to Jimmy, but couldn't support him either. He stared at the floor, wanting the pitch to end immediately.

'It doesn't matter if I'm Jewish or not; I'm offended,' said Brad.

'Good,' said Jimmy, smiling. 'That's what I want to hear. You can sit down again, Brad.' He gestured towards the American's chair. 'Please.'

Brad returned to his seat slowly. Jimmy smiled again. 'So, well done everybody, and thank you. You've got the basic premise. Someone says something offensive, and you have responded by announcing that you're offended, and then you have explained on whose behalf you are offended.'

The others in the room looked at Jimmy in silence.

'Now, I've given you the easy ones; everyone knows the word "Nigger" is offensive, and to whom it is offensive. And it wouldn't work on a TV show, as you pointed out Brad, so you get no points for that one.

'But what if I made it a little more difficult? What if I had said "Kano"? What if I had addressed you as a kano? Anybody offended?'

The others were reluctant to answer either way.

'OK, well let me help you. Kano is Filipino slang for Americans. Shortened from the Tagalog word "Amerikano". So before you announced that you were offended, you would have to know a little about Filipino-American relations in the twentieth century. You get a point for that. And for a bonus point, you would have to know that Tagalog is a language spoken by the majority of people in the Philippines; it's the basis of the Filipino language.'

There was still no response from the others in the room. Jimmy continued: 'So, now, I want you to imagine that you have a buzzer at your fingertips. I'm going to say something. It will be offensive. To play the game, you must press the imaginary buzzer and make an *Eeeeh* sound. Then you announce "I'm offended", and say who you represent, and why you are entitled to be offended.'

The others nodded in agreement. Jimmy continued: 'I was walking across the desert and I came across two locust-eaters.'

Danny raised his hand to reply. Jimmy corrected him: 'Use the buzzer, please.'

'*Eeeeh*,' said Danny weakly. 'I'm offended as an Arab person.'

'Good,' said Jimmy. 'That's one point. Now for a second point, who is it that is likely to have offended you?'

Danny shrugged his shoulders. 'Non-Arabs?'

'Specifically, please?' said Jimmy.

'A Persian?' said Brad.

'Yes,' said Jimmy, 'a point to Brad. And where does the phrase come from?'

Nobody offered an answer. 'OK,' said Jimmy, 'nobody wins a third point. The phrase refers to the use of locusts in Arab cuisine.'

There was only silence from the others in the room. 'Let's try another one,' said Jimmy. 'Remember, the rule is that you must buzz, and then you must start your answer with "I'm offended as a . . . ".'

Jimmy cleared his throat and adopted the voice of a TV quizmaster: 'I was enjoying my meal, but was disturbed by a noisy roto.'

Monica smiled: 'I know this one. I travelled in South America when I was a student.'

'Use the buzzer please,' said Jimmy.

'*Eeeeh*,' said Monica, trying to sound like a buzzer. 'I am offended as a Chilean.'

'That gets you a point. Who is likely to have offended you?' asked Jimmy.

'Probably someone from Peru, or maybe Bolivia,' answered Monica, seemingly pleased with herself.

'That gets you another point,' said Jimmy. 'And for a bonus point, what is the root of the word "roto"?'

Monica shook her head. The others shrugged their shoulders.

Jimmy answered his own question: 'The word goes back to the period of the Spanish conquerors in Chile. It means "tattered", and was applied to the Spaniards because they were badly dressed. In time, the term was applied to the Chileans, which has kind of upset them.'

'OK,' said Brad, 'so you're pitching some kind of quiz show?'

'More than that,' said Jimmy. 'It's a quiz show that tests viewers' knowledge of international history and sensibilities. And it would be the only such show that tests a person's knowledge of etymology – which is the study of the origin of words, and the way in which their meanings change throughout history.

'After every few questions, we would deliver a short report explaining, for example, the background of the word "roto", or indeed, the use of locusts in food.'

'So it's a history lesson?' asked Brad.

'Yes, but even more than that,' said Jimmy. 'It's educational, in a wider sense.'

Jimmy watched while Brad added the word 'Educational' to his notes, and circled it.

'That's the first round,' said Jimmy. 'After that, we move to plotlines in books and movies that can be interpreted as offensive, and similarly for popular songs.'

'Oh, like "You scumbag, you maggot, you cheap lousy faggot"?' said Brad.

'I think you're getting the picture,' said Jimmy with a smile.

Brad was pleased with himself too. 'I just heard it for the first time last week.'

'Now every quiz show must have a catchphrase,' said Jimmy, 'something that will be used in everyday conversation. That's why each answer starts with "*Eeeh*, I'm offended".

'We want people in offices and homes, every time they hear a word or phrase that might be a little politically incorrect, they hit an imaginary buzzer and say "*Eeeh*, I'm offended".

Jimmy clearly had Brad's attention. Monica didn't know whether she liked the idea or not, and kept looking at Brad for guidance.

Jimmy continued: 'You see, Brad, you and I both live in societies that have become cesspits of fake outrage and competitive indignation: people jumping to the defence of what are noble causes, but for selfish and deceitful reasons. Every day we hear people announce that they are offended, when really, they have little to be offended about.

'It's the political-correctness culture gone too far. It enables people to police our conversations; to control us; to suppress our work on the airwaves. Someday this culture of censorship will be overthrown, and our show, *I'm Offended*, will be at the vanguard of that movement.'

'But Jimmy, don't you think it's a dangerous strategy? Like, you can be accused of trivialising racism,' said Brad.

'No,' said Jimmy. 'The people who feign and exaggerate offence in the name of attacking racism are the ones who trivialise racism. We will trivialise *them*.'

Monica found an opportunity to take control of this conversation: 'Jimmy, it's an interesting idea, but I'm not sure that the Irish market needs a new quiz show.'

'Good!' said Jimmy. 'I'm glad you said that.' Monica smiled. 'Because what you've said is absolutely irrelevant.' Monica stopped smiling.

'We need to stop thinking of Ireland as a market. There is no Irish market. Having a minority share of a viewership of four million people is not a market in TV terms. Tell her, Brad: would you develop a new show to serve just the people of Austin? Or just the people of Miami? Or just a suburb of LA?'

Brad shook his head.

Jimmy continued: 'It's too small. Too fragile. You incur all the costs of developing a new concept, but can never draw down sufficient revenue to make it worthwhile.'

Monica felt the need to adjust the record for Brad. 'We always try to sell our formats to international markets.'

Jimmy re-corrected: 'We *try* to sell Irish formats to international markets, but with very little success. I'm saying, we need to stop developing Irish shows. Instead, we will develop shows that are born international; it's just that they are tested in Ireland first.'

'And what difference would that make?' asked Monica.

'First of all,' said Jimmy, 'we won't care what people say on social media, or what they say in the press, or what they say when we meet them at dinner parties, or in a pub. We might find it useful feedback, and their observations might inform our development decisions, but we won't actually care because what we are doing is only a test. We won't even care if people watch it or not, as long as we know why.'

'How can I run a TV show without caring if people watch it?' asked Monica loudly.

'Because, Monica, it's not your money. It's Brad's.'

'Hey, we're already investing enough in our Irish network,' said Brad emphatically.

'No, you're not,' said Jimmy. 'Not nearly enough, Brad. You invested $30 million in audience research and programme development last year.'

'What makes you think that?' asked Brad defensively.

'It's in your annual report,' said Jimmy, as if it was obvious. 'You need to switch some of that expenditure to your subsidiary, TV Ireland. It will, of course, make a loss, but you can write that off against profits in the US.

'In addition, the Irish government will grant-aid the development of this and other shows, because it is an R&D project. You avail of a tax credit of 25 percent on all R&D expenditure. So, you get to develop *I'm Offended*, and give it a full-season test run, at a fraction of your normal costs.'

Monica and Brad were riveted. Danny felt like applauding, but tried to look like none of this was new to him.

'And there's more,' said Jimmy. '*I'm Offended* becomes a piece of intellectual property that you sell to your own stations in the US, at a tax-efficient price. And you sell it in other jurisdictions around the world.

'You hold the intellectual property in a separate subsidiary here in Ireland, where the profits accrue subject to a low corporation tax of 12.5 percent. However, the effective tax rate will be even lower, because you're trading intellectual property.'

There was a long silence as Brad formulated his next question: 'And what are you looking for?'

Jimmy seemed nonchalant. 'We can work out the details over the coming weeks, but something along the following lines: Danny and I will create and control *I'm Offended* – subject to terms and conditions, of course. We enter a partnership with you on the ownership of the intellectual property itself, and the intellectual property company. And also, you put me in charge of programme development in Ireland – answering directly to your head of development in the US.'

Monica gulped.

*

'What happened in there?' Danny asked as Jimmy strode across the car park. 'I didn't recognise you. Where did that come from?'

Jimmy stopped as they reached Danny's car. 'I dunno. I was just thinking about stuff the last while. It just made sense. Do you think they liked it?'

'Liked it? I think you've started something very big,' said Danny. 'And by the way, thanks for including me in the plans. I appreciate it.'

Jimmy stretched out his hand. 'You've been a good pal, Danny. In my hour of need, and all that. So thank *you*.'

The two men shook hands, and then Danny burst out laughing. 'And I like the way you cut Monica out of the more lucrative end of the deal.'

'Nothing she wouldn't do for us,' said Jimmy, and winked.

16

❧❧❧

Hank's

Several days later, Milfoth returned to Dublin while Byron remained with her grandmother in Kerry. She leaned against the dishwasher with her arms folded, and said calmly: 'Now, explain.'

Jimmy relayed everything that had taken place on the day of his disappearance. Milfoth didn't interrupt, but at the end said: 'Do you expect me to believe that shit?'

Jimmy replied: 'If I was going to make stuff up, do you think I would come up with this particular flavour of shit?'

Milfoth felt caught between a duty to support her husband, who may have been through traumatic events, and the urge to smack him hard for being a liar. She chose to remind him that he had brought whatever had happened upon himself.

'Well, I didn't expect much in the line of sympathy from you,' said Jimmy, 'but if it wasn't for the crucifix, I would be dead now. So once again, thank you.'

Milfoth seemed to weigh up the pros and cons of that scenario, and eventually said: 'I won't be buying you another one.'

The couple stood silently in their kitchen while each assessed their situation. Eventually Milfoth raised her head and asked: 'So what now? Are you finished dealing?'

'Yes.'

'Are you sure?'

'Yes, I am.'

'Are you still in danger?'

'I don't think so.'

'You don't *think* so?'

'I think both gangs have stated their positions clearly,' said Jimmy, trying to sound reassuring.

'Should we move?' she asked.

'Where to? We both have to be near Dublin for work. And I don't think we could afford to move to another country.'

'So we just sit here helpless, waiting for another attack? Maybe it's time to get a guard-dog, and an alarm, and new windows?'

'Maybe,' said Jimmy. 'These are expensive items, and anyway they mightn't work.'

'Well, what then?' asked Milfoth, throwing her arms aloft. 'Let's go to the Gardaí.'

'And tell them what? That I've been selling cocaine? That I met some nasty people and now I'd like their protection?'

Milfoth could see the difficulty.

'Anyway, word would get back to Hank, and then he'd definitely have to kill me,' said Jimmy. 'Maybe I should have a word with Hank?'

'No,' said Milfoth firmly. 'Don't even think of going near him again.'

'OK,' said Jimmy.

'Are you still spreading that shit on your body?'

'What? The testosterone?'

'Yes.'

'Yes.'

'Has it occurred to you to stop using it?' said Milfoth. 'Has it occurred to you that it might be more trouble than it's worth?'

'Yes, it has,' said Jimmy. 'Yes, it has.'

*

Days went by, and Jimmy didn't leave the house. Vans passing on the road outside made him nervous. Anyone calling to the door had to explain who they were, and what they wanted, before he would open it. Even then, he stood close to the wall when shouting at the visitor, in case a bullet came through the door.

Jimmy was glad that Byron wasn't around, but Milfoth had to keep a regular work schedule. That concerned him. He comforted himself by assuming that any attacker would target him, not her. If he got shot, at least it would be over quickly. If she were shot . . . well, he couldn't be sure how he would feel.

Eventually he came to the realisation that if they wanted to harm him, they would find a way, and there was no point in living his life indoors. He went to the gym.

It felt good to work his muscles again. He tried to avoid eye-contact with other gym-users, so as not to attract conversation about his appearance on the TV news. He went into the sauna, where he had the sensation of sweating out the nastiness of his abduction. His skin, so troubled by man and beast, felt better. He took a cold shower, and returned to a higher bench in the sauna. Sweat dripped from his brow, and he could barely tolerate the heat, but it felt good.

He plunged into the pool, and swam slowly up and down. It was early afternoon, and he had the pool to himself – just the way he liked it. The water was flat and undisturbed, except for the ripples he made.

He held his breath, and tried to swim two lengths underwater. He didn't succeed, but it felt refreshing as he depleted his body of oxygen, and then surfaced for frantic gasps of air.

Underwater, he felt distant from his problems and worries. He wanted to stay there. He wondered if it was possible to just forget to surface. 'It mightn't be a bad way to go,' he thought to himself.

He went to the jacuzzi. The heated water seemed to burn his skin, but that was OK. He could only put his legs in at first, and slowly brought the rest of his body under the bubbles. 'Aaah,' he said. 'Oooh, that's lovely,' and he shut his eyes. He positioned himself over one of the vents, and let it massage parts of his back.

'Did I see you in Arnotts?' asked a voice. Jimmy opened his eyes, to see a man sharing the jacuzzi with him.

'What?' asked Jimmy in horror.

It was Gunner. 'Ye took yer while comin' back here, huh?'

'What the fuck!' shouted Jimmy, rising to his feet. He grabbed Gunner by the throat with his left hand, and drew back with his right, ready to strike him in the face. 'What are you doing here?'

'Relax, pal,' said Gunner raising his hands out of the water. 'No weapons, look. I come in peace.'

'What the fuck are you doing here?' shouted Jimmy, looking around to see if Gunner had any support. 'Don't fucking come near me!'

'Take a fucking chill-pill, all righ',' said Gunner. 'I've only come here to talk.'

'I don't wanna talk!' said Jimmy.

'You don't know that until you've listened, OK,' said Gunner. 'Hear what I have to say, and then decide.'

Jimmy slowly released his grip and lowered his clenched fist. He looked around again, to see if Gunner had anyone with him.

'I tried to call you, but you don't answer your phone any more,' said Gunner.

'It's my business phone, and I'm no longer in business,' said Jimmy.

'I came here so we could have a quiet chat,' said Gunner.

'What the fuck do you want?' said Jimmy in a lowered voice, as he returned to a sitting position.

'It's not me, it's Hank,' said Gunner. 'He feels bad about what happened, and wants to apologise to you.'

'Tell him to fuck himself.'

'Ah, now,' said Gunner. 'These things happen in business sometimes. Luckily, there's no permanent harm done.'

'Tell him to go fuck himself. I don't want to hear from him, or you, ever again. Hank and I had a deal. We agreed that if there was ever a disagreement, we would sort it out ourselves, like gentlemen. He broke the deal.'

'He knows that, he knows that,' said Gunner. 'And this is him now trying to sort things out as a gentleman. He feels bad about what happened. He's been in touch with the Deveneys, and he knows you were telling the truth.'

'I know I was telling the truth,' shouted Jimmy. 'I don't need you sneaking up on me in a hot-tub to confirm that. Now get the fuck out of here, and stay out of my life.'

'Anyways,' said Gunner, raising the palms of his hands in a bid to calm the atmosphere, 'he wants to apologise to you – '

'Tell him I didn't ask for an apology, but I have asked you and him to stay the fuck away from me!'

'And he wants to pay you a little compensation for any . . . y'know . . . inconveniences you may have suffered in the course of his work.'

Jimmy pondered the word 'compensation'. 'How much?' he asked.

'I don't know. He didn't tell me that.'

'Well, then don't waste my time.'

'Last time something like this happened, he gave the lad fifteen grand,' said Gunner. 'And that was for less of a beatin' than you got. But y'know, fifteen grand. The lad was happy. Hank was happy. A handshake. No hard feelings.'

'You know where I live. Put it in an envelope and leave it on my doorstep.'

'That's not the way Hank works,' said Gunner. 'Look, between yourself and myself, my guess is that Hank needs to know that you're not going to talk with the cops. He needs to see the whites of your eyes when he apologises to you, and then he gives you a few bob to help you forget about it. And we all move on.

'And you can call him whatever names you want to call him. Say what you think of him, just say it all to his face. He's fine with that, as long as the two of you shake hands, and you forget all about it as soon as you walk out his door. That's the way he likes to do things.'

Jimmy softened, but still needed convincing: 'I fell for your trap before. Why would I walk straight into another one?'

'If Hank wanted you dead, what would you be now?'

'What?'

'I said,' said Gunner slowly, 'if Hank wanted you dead, what would you be now?'

Jimmy didn't have an answer.

'You'd be dead,' said Gunner. 'I wouldn't be wasting my time sitting here talking to ye.'

Jimmy couldn't argue with Gunner's logic.

'Look, I'll tell ye what,' said Gunner. 'Tell yer missus where you're going. No secrets. Email yer friends that you're going over to Hank's house. So if ye were to disappear, everyone would know where you'd been. Sure, tell the cops if ye really want to. And park yer car outside his house. I'm going to make sure there's a parking spot left for you. Full transparency, wha'?'

Jimmy didn't answer.

Gunner persisted: 'Promise me you'll be there: Hank's house, 6.30 tomorrow evening. I'm going to save a parking spot for ye, so make sure to drive over.'

He still wouldn't answer.

*

Jimmy spent the evening wondering if he should go to Hank's house or not. Something told him he shouldn't go, but he needed the money. If Hank offered him fifteen thousand, Jimmy decided he would demand twenty. He had his arguments ready. Of course, if only ten grand was made available, Jimmy would be grateful for it.

He needed to be business-like and not emotional with Hank. He wanted him to know that Hank could trust him to keep his mouth shut about what he knew. In return, Jimmy would have the assurance that there would be no further abductions. Their business relationship would end honourably and, as Gunner had suggested, they would shake hands as gentlemen.

Milfoth noticed he was pensive, and asked what was on his mind. The two were sitting at dinner, sharing a bottle of wine. They seemed to communicate more with each other when Byron was away. This was the closest they'd had to a date in years.

'I still feel a bit tense after all that happened,' he said. She seemed to accept that. He thought about telling her about the invitation to Hank's, but he knew that she would forbid it.

She looked pretty in the candlelight. That, and the wine, and the relatively pleasant conversation, and his rising testosterone levels caused his mind to wander down from her lips to her neck, and the top of her cleavage.

It was so long since they had done *it* that he didn't know how to initiate it any more. She was talking about something, but he was only half-listening. His focus grew on her body. This was the moment to rekindle their relationship; their sex lives.

With Byron away, they could do it in any room they wanted, just like the old days. Or in several rooms; again, just like the old days.

A bulge grew in his pants, and his eyes dropped to her breasts, which heaved inside a light summer shirt. He smiled as she made a witty remark, but really he was smiling at the thought of seeing her naked again. It used to be so good, and it could be again.

She poured him a glass of wine, and she poured herself one. The signs were good. He remembered how she used to like being surprised by his advances; how she liked him to take control, and how she liked to succumb to his desires. It had been all win-win in those days.

She collected the dinner plates and rose to place them in the sink. Her ass looked good, wrapped in a short denim skirt. Her bare legs, all tanned and slender, seemed to call out for his attention. It was time.

Jimmy rose too, and approached her from behind. With his index finger, he moved a lock of her hair behind her ear. He leaned forward and began to kiss her neck. He caught her scent, and it brought back memories. He placed his hands on her hips and moved them north along her curvy waist to their favoured destination, her breasts. Everything was familiar, yet new. He closed his eyes, exhaled slowly through his nose, and savoured the moment.

'What are you doing?' she asked.

'Just hoping to make love to my beautiful wife,' he said softly. 'Sound like a good idea?'

'No, it certainly doesn't.'

'Oh, come on,' he said, trying to disguise his desperation. 'Help me out here.'

Milfoth moved her hands to his. She held his fingers for a moment, and then raised both his hands high in the air. With the swift twirl of a ballerina, she spun herself out of his reach, and moved towards the door. 'Nobody gave me medication for my libido,' she said, dismissively, and left the room.

Jimmy didn't even turn to watch her leave. He was left facing the kitchen sink and a collection of dirty plates and utensils that were partially submerged in grey water. This too was a familiar feeling.

'Fucking bitch!' he said to himself. 'I fucking hate her!'

*

Hank lived in one of the houses in Rialto that backed onto the Grand Canal. He moved there after the Criminal Assets Bureau took his country estate, with its high walls and CCTV cameras. In Rialto, he felt less safe, but liked being in a terrace, where he felt protected on both flanks; as well as having the canal at his back, which he referred to as his moat.

It was a long walk, or a short drive, to Hank's house, so Jimmy took the car, as instructed. He drove along the South Circular Road until he reached The Bird Flanagan, and then swung a left.

He drove down Hank's road until he found his house. He was nervous, and it wasn't yet 6.30 PM, so he drove around the block again. It gave him the opportunity to see if any police were waiting in cars nearby.

He had second thoughts about parking at Hank's. What if the Gardaí were watching the house? He would prefer it if his car wasn't parked outside. He decided to leave the car on another street, and walked the five or so minutes to his meeting.

He rang the doorbell, looking anxiously around in case a cop or a journalist might be watching. All the cars parked on the street appeared empty, and there didn't seem to be anyone peering out of the windows of the houses across the street. Still, he felt uncomfortable.

Gunner opened the door: 'Yer late. I thought you weren't coming.'

'Sorry about that,' said Jimmy with false cheerfulness.

Gunner looked over Jimmy's shoulder. 'Where's yer car?'

'I decided to walk,' said Jimmy.

'For fuck's sake, ye sap,' said Gunner. He was clearly more tense than he had been the day before. 'Can ye not do what yer bleedin' told?'

'Sorry,' said Jimmy, but he was unsure if he had done anything to apologise for.

As Jimmy crossed the threshold, he was met with the stale smell of a house where a man lived alone; or alone with a dog. Inside the main door was a metal door that served as an extra layer of security. As Gunner closed it, Jimmy observed the short hallway, which was adorned with photos of Hank in his prime, showing off a body that was enhanced beyond its genetic limitations. A large black and white image showed Hank dressed in tiny trunks, snarling at the camera. His fists were pressed together, and his trapezius muscles stood like mounds on his shoulders, either side of his bulging neck.

In another photograph, Hank posed alongside Arnold Schwarzenegger, apparently at some competition. 'Hank knew Arnie?' said Jimmy, trying to sound light-hearted.

'Come on,' said Gunner with a grunt.

Jimmy passed into the kitchen-cum-dining-area at the back of the house. Through a glass door, he caught sight of a Rottweiler patrolling the back garden. It was Tyson. Fear shot through Jimmy's heart as he remembered the dog straddling his naked torso.

Hank was leaning against his kitchen table, which was pushed against what looked like a disused fireplace. 'Well?' he said. 'What can I do for you?'

Jimmy shrugged. 'You tell me.'

The two men looked at each other, waiting for the other to speak.

'Gunner said you wanted to see me,' said Hank.

'No,' said Jimmy, looking around at Gunner, who was busy opening a package. 'He said *you* wanted to see *me*.'

'I wanted to see you? About what?' said Hank.

'To apologise,' said Jimmy, as if it was obvious.

'*Me*, apologise?' said Hank, standing erect, chest out. 'Are you having a laugh?'

Jimmy turned to Gunner. 'You said he wanted to apologise.'

'I'll be with ya in a minute,' said Gunner, still busy with his package.

Jimmy turned to Hank again, and spoke sternly. 'He said you wanted to apologise, and maybe offer some compensation.'

Hank smiled. 'Compensation? You're joking me.'

'Do I look like I'm joking?' said Jimmy, annoyed by Hank's attitude.

Hank looked over at Gunner, and pointed at Jimmy. 'What did you bring this clown over here for?'

As he spoke, Gunner appeared at Jimmy's shoulder. Both Jimmy and Hank looked down, to see blue latex gloves on Gunner's hands. He held a revolver. Jimmy froze.

'What the hell are you doing?' said Hank.

'Sorry Hank, it just has to be this way,' said Gunner. He raised the gun and fired.

Bang! Bang!

'What the fu – ? Aah!' shouted Hank.

Two holes opened in Hank's chest. Blood spurted in the direction of the gun, on the wall behind Hank, and onto Jimmy.

'What the fuck?' Hank yelled as he stumbled backwards onto the kitchen table. He looked at Gunner in horror and disbelief. He turned his head towards Jimmy. 'You set me up,' he said.

Gunner fired two more shots. One entered Hank's sizeable abdomen, and the other missed him, despite the close range.

Hank's body writhed, and his hands touched his wounds, making a vain effort to stem the flow of blood. He grimaced in pain, and stumbled forward, as if trying to grab the gun, but Gunner shot him again, this time in the shoulder. Hank let out a loud 'Aaahhh' and fell to the floor. Gunner shot him once again, this time in the area of his heart.

Hank lay on his back while a pool of blood formed a circle on the floor around him. One hand grabbed his chest while the other lay limp on the ground, a little under his table. Sounds came from his mouth, but it was unclear if he was trying to speak, or gasping for breath.

Jimmy stood, motionless. Gunner, too, was motionless, as if waiting for the sound of the shots to stop echoing around the room, and his ears.

Gunner slammed the gun sideways into Jimmy's chest. Jimmy instinctively raised his hands and grabbed it. Gunner turned away, leaving Jimmy with the gun. He reached into his pocket and pulled out a phone. He dialled a number, and the call was answered immediately. 'You can call that in,' said Gunner. 'It's done.'

He waited a moment while the other person asked a question. Gunner turned towards Jimmy. 'No, the fucking pox-bottle left his car at home,' he said.

Jimmy suddenly gathered his wits. He pointed the gun at Gunner and pulled the trigger three times. *Click. Click. Click.* But there were no more bullets. Gunner pushed the gun away gently, as if Jimmy's attempt to kill him was too naive to bother with. He ended the call and put the phone back in his pocket.

Jimmy struggled to think of something to say. Eventually he blurted out: 'Who was that?'

'That's my alibi,' said Gunner, smiling. 'And you don't have one, do you, bitch?'

Jimmy was unable to react fast enough to the unfolding events. He stood with his mouth open, still holding the gun, looking at Gunner.

Gunner turned and walked towards the back door. 'So long, sucker,' he said as he left. The Rottweiler trotted towards Gunner, wagging his tiny tail loyally. Gunner patted his massive head, and said soothingly: 'All right, Tyson.'

Jimmy came to the door and called: 'Where are you going?'

Tyson looked at Jimmy and lunged in his direction, with a bloodcurdling bark. Jimmy barely managed to get the door closed, and the dog's heavy frame rebounded off the glass with a loud thud.

Tyson sent a series of deep and powerful barks through the glass. He rose on his hind legs and looked at Jimmy, almost eyeball to eyeball. Jimmy retreated to a kitchen chair, but kept looking at the snarling dog, in case it somehow found a way to open the door. Behind the dog, he saw Gunner disappear between the trees at the bottom of the garden.

Jimmy struggled to slow his breath, to help him think clearly. The gravity of his circumstances was clear to him: he was alone in a house with a bloody corpse, and his fingerprints on the murder weapon. He had no alibi. He had a credible motive for killing Hank, if a diligent prosecution team were to examine his recent abduction, his drug-dealing and the murder of Joey Watt. Calling the police was out of the question. They wouldn't believe him. He could spend the next twenty-five years protesting his innocence.

He couldn't leave through the back door because of the dog. There were no side exits. So he would have to leave through the front door – and quickly, because it seemed that Gunner's accomplice may have already phoned the Gardaí.

He wiped the gun with a J-cloth he found at the kitchen sink. He looked around to see if there was anything else he had touched. The handle of the back door: he wiped that.

He wasn't sure what to do with the cloth. He washed it out, in case some of his DNA was on it. Then he cleaned the tap in case he had left fingerprints on it.

He left the room quickly, but resolved to walk down the road calmly. When he got into the hall, he found that the internal security door was closed. Jimmy pulled on the handle but it wouldn't open. He pushed: no luck. He shook the door violently. 'Oh, please!' he shouted in despair.

He looked around for a door-release button, but he couldn't see one. The hallway was dimly lit because of the metal door, so he turned on a light and searched the edges of the door for a button release. Still no luck. He was trapped.

Jimmy crept into the front room of the house, and looked through the net curtains at the street outside. Two elderly neighbours – a woman and a man – were talking at the end of Hank's driveway. They looked concerned. Jimmy surmised that they had heard the gunshots. With them there, he couldn't leave via the front of the house, even if he could open the door.

The woman approached the house, while the man remained at a safer distance. The doorbell sounded with a loud buzz. Jimmy looked around, and saw that the buzzer was in the front room, right next to him. A small screen showed who was standing at the front door; beside it was a button which, he assumed, provided the release mechanism for the metal door.

Did this mean that there was a video recording of Jimmy coming to the house? He couldn't tell.

The lady who rang the doorbell started to shout through the door: 'Hank, Hank, it's Margaret. Is everything all right in there?'

She moved into the garden and put her hands to the window, to see if she could see through the net curtains. 'Hank, Hank,' she said again. 'Are you in there?'

Jimmy darted from the front room back into the room where Hank's body lay. Tyson saw him and became excited again, barking loudly and snarling through the glass. The noise of the dog at the back of the house, and the lady at the front, sapped Jimmy's mind of its ability to concentrate. He flopped in a kitchen chair, put his head in his hands, and said: 'It's impossible. I give up.'

At the front of the house, the sound of a siren announced the arrival of the first Garda car. A second arrived soon after, or perhaps it was an ambulance – Jimmy couldn't tell the difference by sound. He crept into the hallway, and peeped around the door of the front room. He saw the flashing lights of a fire engine, and a small crowd gathering on the street outside.

The doorbell buzzed many times. Jimmy could see on the monitor several uniformed Gardaí standing on the doorstep. As he returned to the back room, he could see the Rottweiler angrily patrolling the side walls of the garden. The emergency crews were trying to access the back of the house via the garden, but Tyson was preventing them from doing so.

Jimmy sat on the lower steps of the stairs and waited for the inevitable. He took out his phone, and thought about calling Milfoth. But what could he say? 'Sweetheart, I am about to be accused of murder, but it's not something you should be worried about?' Or: 'I know you said I shouldn't go to talk with Hank, but . . . .' Maybe he would just thank her for the years they had together, which would now come to an end. He decided against calling her, and put the phone back into his pocket.

He thought about the gun in the other room. If he could find some bullets in the house, he could just end it all there and then. It would be a solution, but perhaps not the best one. Maybe he would leave a message first, explaining exactly what had happened, and then do it. His mind wasn't helping. His stomach was in a knot. He felt sick.

The emergency services pounded on the front door, not just with their fists, but with something much heavier. Jimmy could hear the splitting of wood coming from the door and its frame. *Boom. Boom. Boom.* Jimmy could hear splinters of wood landing on the tiles between the front door and the metal one.

He thought about saving everyone's time by just opening the door to let the emergency crews in. He looked at them on the monitor, bashing away at the door – and his liberty. A wave of apathy overcame him. He sat on the floor and joined in the noise: '*Boom. Boom. Boom. Woof! Woof! Woof!*'

The front door gave way. Jimmy could hear the swearing of the emergency crews as they discovered the metal door inside the house. 'For Jaysus sake!' shouted one, and kicked the door. Jimmy found this funny, and laughed to himself.

A short while later, he could hear a fire crew assemble a cutting machine. The noise it made as it cut into the reinforced metal door was so deafening that he returned to the back room. Tyson hurled himself at the glass door again, and snarled at him.

Jimmy looked down at Hank. The crimson pool was drying. He sat on a chair beside the dead man and spoke to him: 'Well Hank, looks like this is the end of the line for both of us. Maybe we both deserve it. Pity, huh? In another time and place, we could have been . . . friends.'

Jimmy looked out into the hallway. Sparks flew from the metal door as a small slit began to open in it. The noise was uncomfortably loud, so he returned to the back room and shut the door. He felt the presence of his father in the room. He turned to see Jacko sitting in the corner, looking ashamedly at his soon saying: 'Not good enough, James. You've only yourself to blame.'

'Leave me alone, Dad,' Jimmy shouted. 'Or at least try to help me.'

Jimmy looked at the pictures on the wall. A large framed poster of Mohammed Ali dominated the room. It was the iconic one: part-beauty, part-beast; his lithe, ebony body standing in triumph like a crazed Adonis above the unseen Sonny Liston.

Under the photo, a quote from Ali read: 'Impossible is nothing.' Beside it, a clarification by Ali: 'Impossible is not a fact. It's an opinion.'

Jimmy meditated on that for a moment: 'Impossible is not a fact, it's just an opinion. Just a silly ol' opinion. Just a view someone has at a certain point in a certain place, in certain circumstances.' He thought of some of the times in his life when it had seemed there was no option but to act in a particular way, yet later, in a calmer state, he realised there had been other options. Could this be one of those moments?

In the hallway, the noise of the angle-grinder reached a crescendo and then stopped. The sound of the metal door clashing against an inside wall indicated that the door was open. Then there were voices: 'Anybody in there? This is An Garda Síochána. We are armed, and we are coming in.'

Armed detectives entered the room. Their guns came first, then their faces, and, tentatively, their bodies.

17

⋘⋘⋘

Impossible?

The room filled quickly, led by Inspector McClean. He pointed his gun at Hank, on the off-chance that he was only pretending to be dead. Another poked his gun into the corners of the room and some presses in the kitchen. Some uniformed Gardaí entered, followed by paramedics.

McClean halted the procession: 'OK folks, this is a crime scene: a murder scene, we believe. We must preserve it, so I need everybody out. Everybody out, please. Don't touch anything. Be careful what you stand on. Don't venture into any other rooms unnecessarily. Lads,' he said, pointing at two detectives, 'I need you to check all the other rooms.'

Tyson was in a frenzy of barking and growling at the sight of so many strangers in his master's house.

'And can someone do something about that dog, please,' said McClean.

'We've called the canine unit, sir,' came the reply.

As quickly as the room had filled, it emptied again. The house went quiet, except for the noise of the dog – and perhaps the pounding of Jimmy's heart. He was on all fours, hidden in the tiny space between the table and the disused fireplace; obscured by the legs of the table and three chairs.

He had watched the others enter the room. Seeing only their footwear and the lower parts of their trousers. It seemed silly to hide, particularly in such an easily revealed place. When McClean cased the room, Jimmy was sure he would be found – perhaps even shot. Evading the law seemed . . . impossible. But, perhaps, impossible was nothing.

The two detectives returned to the room wearing plastic covers on their footwear. Jimmy could see the flash of a camera documenting the scene.

'Who do you think did it?' said the first. Jimmy recognised the voice of Detective Kearney. He was in his house on the night of the abduction, and he had met him previously at a recording of *The Redeemables*. Jimmy didn't like him, or trust him.

'I'd say an inside job, what about you?' said Detective O'Toole, who was also there on the night of the abduction, and who was also a regular in the TV studio. Jimmy didn't care much for him either, but had no reason to dislike him.

'Yeah, probably one of his own. An outsider couldn't have got through that metal door,' said Kearney.

'What about an attack from the rear?' said O'Toole, checking to see if the back door was unlocked.

'And negotiate that dog?'

Jimmy's heart pounded so loudly he was convinced the Gardaí could hear it. His stomach was in knots and he wanted to visit the toilet. Sweat oozed from his brow. He didn't want to move an arm to clear it, so a succession of drops left his forehead and crashed onto the wooden floor below. The noise was deafening – at least to Jimmy. Surely the cops could hear it? He wondered if the cops knew he was in the room, and were just having fun with him.

Kearney put his foot on Hank's shoulder and shook his stiff body. 'Well Hank, you finally got what was coming to you,' he said.

'Be careful,' said O'Toole, 'you could contaminate the scene.'

Kearney didn't seem to care. 'Do you think whoever did this left any evidence to contaminate? This was a professional job. The place will be clean.'

He shook Hank's body again. 'Who killed you, Hank? Give up yer ol' secrets.'

Hank's eyes, partially open, stared at Jimmy. His mouth, encrusted with blood and sputum, moved. '*He* did,' said Hank, pointing his outstretched hand at Jimmy. 'It was himmmmm,' he said, almost touching Jimmy.

That's what Jimmy thought he saw. He shut his eyes to remind himself that it was a trick of the mind. He wanted to get away from the body so badly that he was ready to stand up and turn himself in. Hank's outstretched hand was less than a metre from his own. He had rarely been so close to a corpse, and had never been close to a body that hadn't already been made up and placed neatly in a box.

'That bloody dog,' said O'Toole. 'What are we going to do about it?'

'Shoot it?' offered Kearney.

'Maybe we can tranquilise it,' said O'Toole. 'I don't think it would look good in the papers if we just came in and killed Hank's dog.'

The two men left the room, but as they did, Jimmy received a text, and his phone buzzed. The two detectives stopped and returned to the room.

'Did you hear that?' asked Kearney.

'It could have been a phone upstairs,' said O'Toole.

'No, it sounded like this room. I wonder if Hank has a phone on him.' He bent down to check Hank's pockets; his hands were within touching distance of Jimmy.

'I don't think that's a good idea,' said O'Toole.

'I'm just looking for evidence. There could be clues to the murder in his pocket,' said Kearney. 'Anyway, Hank owes us money. Don't you, Hank? You didn't pay up in life, so you might as well pay up in death.'

Jimmy could hear the sound of drawers being opened by O'Toole. 'I don't think he'd leave much lying around here, do you?' he asked.

Kearney didn't find a phone, but pulled a bundle of €50 notes from Hank's pockets. 'Well done, Hank,' he said. 'But you owe us much more than that.'

A moment later he returned a fifty-euro note to Hank's pocket. 'Always leave something behind,' he added, 'to avoid suspicion.'

'I'm dying for a cigarette,' said O'Toole. 'But I don't want to smoke at the front of the house with all the cameras around.'

Kearney agreed. 'We need to get that stupid dog away from here, so we can relax out the back. It's going to be a long night.'

Kearney and O'Toole left the room, and Jimmy almost collapsed as the tension gave way to relief. He rested his forehead on the floor and cradled it with his hands. He rubbed away his sweat from the floor with his sleeve, and then tried to rub his fingerprints off the floorboards. It seemed like a pointless exercise.

He reached into his pocket, grabbed his phone, and put it on silent. A news-feed on his phone had already reported Hank's murder. It was described as 'Dublin's latest gangland shooting'. It didn't name the victim but said that he was 'known to Gardaí'. It carried a photo from outside the house, which was sealed off, with uniformed personnel present.

Jimmy noticed that the grate had been removed from the fireplace: it made a suitable place for hiding. He moved his body inside, while his legs remained outside. He felt a little safer. Above, he could feel the cool evening air coming down the chimney. He looked at his phone again.

The report said that the man's body was still at the scene, which was sealed off pending the arrival of the State Pathologist in the morning. 'In the morning!' Jimmy whispered in disappointment. He wanted the ordeal to end immediately.

O'Toole and Kearney re-entered the room and took more photos. The flashes were more intense this time, and Jimmy assumed that a professional camera was being used, rather than a phone. They had a conversation about the dog. Jimmy learned that they were trying to feed it meat that was laced with a sedative, thrown from a neighbour's garden.

Later again, an excited group of people passed through the room, all wearing white protective gear. Minutes later, they returned from the back garden with the dog in a crate, sedated.

With the dog removed, Jimmy had an opening. Tentatively, he left his hiding place, only to dart back inside when he thought he heard a noise in the hallway.

It was now almost dark outside, and the room was full of shadows. He crept out of his hiding place again, and tiptoed across the room towards the back door. His foot slipped a little, and he realised he had stepped in blood, and had put bloody footprints on the otherwise clean part of the floor. He took a tissue from his pocket and wiped away the footprint. But as he did that, he created another footprint, and then another. He put the contaminated tissue back in his pocket. He didn't know what else to do with it.

He was just outside the back door when he had a realisation that caused him to freeze: earlier, when he was trying to get out of the metal door, he had left fingerprints all around its edge as he looked for the release button. But what should he do? Freedom was at the bottom of the garden: he was nearly there. But what kind of freedom, if he left fingerprints behind him? 'What'll I do? What'll I do?' he asked himself.

He crept back inside, and crawled under the table to think. He could sneak into the hallway and start to erase his fingerprints, but he wouldn't know until he entered the hall if there was a Garda sitting there or not.

If he was caught, he could claim that he had only just arrived, having come through the back door, which had been left unlocked. But what was his reason for entering the crime scene? He couldn't think of one. Anyway, he had probably left prints and sweat under the table and in the fireplace, despite his efforts to clean them away. He had a bloody hankie in his pocket, and prints on the metal door.

Suddenly he remembered a Jason Bourne movie – the one in which he exploded a house by filling the kitchen with gas, and putting a newspaper in a toaster to ignite it. If he could cause an explosion and a fire in Hank's house, it would destroy most of the evidence. And anything that was not destroyed could be ruined by water damage as the fire brigade put out the flames. Jimmy could think of no better plan.

He fumbled in the dark to see if Hank's cooker was gas-operated. It was. And he fumbled some more to see if Hank had a toaster. He had. At this point, his fingerprints were all over the kitchen, but he was beyond caring. It made little difference if they found lots of prints, or just a few.

He found a newspaper, folded it and put it in the toaster. He turned a knob on the cooker and one of the rings lit automatically. He blew hard, and managed to eliminate the flames. The gas continued to hiss. 'Perfect,' he whispered.

He got all four rings to hiss this way, and an odour of rotten eggs started to fill the room. He had to move quickly, to avoid inhaling the gas. He turned on the oven, then opened the oven door, and blew hard again. The flames disappeared, but the hissing remained. This was good. He backed away from the cooker, turned on the toaster, and left quickly through the back door.

The trees at the bottom of the garden appeared like a black wall in front of him. Jimmy tried to remember where exactly Gunner had found a path through. He squinted, to avoid branch-injuries to his eyes, and in the darkness he walked into a fence. He scaled it quickly and found himself on the bank of the canal. There was no option but to cross it.

He passed through thick vegetation until his feet felt the water. It was cold, but he had to proceed. The water crept up his legs. He hated cold water, but he had to keep going. The water rose to his groin and he nearly yelped. Onwards, onwards, and he was submerged up to his chest.

Inside Hank's house, the cooker hissed. The toaster spat upwards a relatively undamaged newspaper. There was no flame; barely a spark. Nothing happened.

Jimmy waded across the canal. The edges were shallow, but the middle part was deep enough to drown in. It wouldn't have been a difficult swim, but he was weighed down by his shoes and clothes. He'd felt he had to keep them with him, rather than leaving them around, as evidence.

Reaching the reeds on the far side of the canal, he disturbed a couple of moorhens, which chirped their disapproval before swimming away. This disturbed some ducks, who also had something to say. Suddenly, the canal seemed come alive in the darkness.

He looked back at Hank's house, hoping to see flames erupting through the roof, but there were none. He knew that he had been out of the house for longer than it took a toaster to pop, so his plan hadn't worked. His escape seemed pointless now, but he staggered on.

Jimmy found a grip on the steep bank and raised himself out of the water. He could now see the canal path that he had sometimes jogged along; dimly lit because the trees were in full leaf and obscured the street lights. Nobody was out walking, which was a relief.

He reached the path and put one soggy foot in front of another. He wanted to run, but was weighed down by his sodden clothes. He walked as quickly as he could, and tried to stay in the shadows of the trees. He felt dirty and cold, and was still a long way from home.

In the house, Kearney and O'Toole returned to the room where Hank had been murdered. As they crossed the room towards the back door, O'Toole took a cigarette from a pack and held it in his lips.

'Jaysus, I need a smoke,' he said.

'What's that smell?' said Kearney.

'I don't know,' said O'Toole, as he sparked his lighter.

'I don't think you should light that in here . . . .'

There was a loud *whoof* as the gas ignited. The force of the explosion blew out the windows of the kitchen and living room. It shattered the ceiling above, sending plasterboard up into the bedroom and bathroom above, and creating a large hole. Then everything that had been blown up came crashing down again, followed by the contents of the bedroom and bathroom, in a crescendo. The fireball torched the walls and the rafters, as well as anything flammable in the living room and bedroom.

A hole was created in the ceiling of the bedroom too. Many of the tiles on the roof were dislodged, and came crashing down on the garden patio. Within seconds, the back half of the house was on fire and the whole house was filled with smoke.

The noise made Jimmy jump in fright. From the bank of the canal, he looked around, to see a fireball rise into the air. It almost took his breath away. 'It worked!' he said. 'It worked!'

He clenched his fists and raised them in the air. 'Yes!' he shouted, and then realised it would be unwise to make any more noise. There was no time to celebrate. He had to keep moving.

The path dipped below the Herberton Bridge, which allowed Jimmy to cross Herberton Road, the busy entrance to Rialto, without being seen. His presence under the bridge seemed to rouse two homeless people who were sleeping there, but it was too dark for them to see him clearly.

The next stretch of path was directly beside the canal, and out of view of the road, so Jimmy made swift progress. This led to Dolphin's Barn Bridge, where the path crossed under the road again, allowing Jimmy to remain unseen.

As he passed Dolphin's Barn Fire Station, three fire engines and two ambulances emerged amid a cacophony of sirens and flashing lights, and hurried in the direction of Hank's house. Jimmy continued in the opposite direction, half running and half walking, until he got to Sally's Bridge. He crossed the canal at street-level, and re-entered Dublin 8.

From now on, his journey was along populated streets. He was very cold, and desperately wanted to get home, but he knew that running would only attract attention. So he walked in as casual a manner as possible.

When he reached his house, the lights were off – indicating that Milfoth was already in bed. 'Excellent,' he said to himself, 'it's the wrong time for questions.'

He let himself quietly into the house, and went straight to the washing machine. He stripped, and put everything he had been wearing, including his shoes, into it. As he fumbled with the buttons, Milfoth appeared at the door in her dressing gown.

'What'cha doing?' she asked.

'Oh,' said Jimmy, grabbing a towel from a shelf and wrapping himself in it, 'just putting on a wash.'

'At this hour?' she asked.

'I thought "Why not?",' he said. 'I got a bit wet on the way home. Sorry if I woke you.'

'Why are you washing your shoes?' she asked.

Jimmy fumbled for an answer. 'Y'know, I heard recently that it's OK to put runners into the wash. I just want to try it out.'

Milfoth didn't seem convinced. 'They said on the news tonight that there had been a gangland shooting over in Rialto.'

'Oh, really?'

'But you probably knew that already,' she said.

Jimmy couldn't decide if he should or shouldn't have known, so chose only to nod. Milfoth returned to her bedroom, and Jimmy headed for the shower. He ran shampoo through his hair twice. Using his teeth, he cleaned under his fingernails and spat down the plughole.

He dressed in fresh clothes and left the house again, this time to collect his car. He cycled back to Rialto, and found that the police cordon was close to where he had parked. Jimmy could see that a large crowd of onlookers had gathered.

He put down the back seats of his old Mercedes, and put his bicycle into the boot. As he steered slowly towards home, the radio delivered a news update: 'It is believed that a bomb left in the house of a murdered gang-leader is responsible for the killing of two Gardaí last evening.'

Jimmy felt sick in his stomach. 'Two Gardaí dead!' he said, in horror. 'Noooo!' He assumed it was Kearney and O'Toole who had been killed. They were crooked cops, but he didn't want to see them killed. He thumped the steering wheel several times. 'Damnit!' he said. 'Damnit'.

He cried for a moment – not for the dead cops, but out of frustration. Each time he tried to leave his criminal life behind him, it seemed to pull him back in. He was now a central player in the deaths of three men.

'Please just let this be over,' he pleaded, to a god or some other force; he didn't know which.

He reached home just as the clothes finished their wash-cycle. He stuffed them in the dryer and planned his next action.

Washing his clothes wouldn't be enough. In his shed, there was a fire-pit that they had bought on a whim and used only once. He retrieved it from under some old paint cans, and brought it outside. Also in the shed, he found barbecue lighter fluid.

When his clothes were dry, he sprinkled them with lighter fluid and burned them in the pit. As the ashes cooled, he put them in a saucepan and drove to the Phoenix Park. There, in the dark quiet road near the Magazine Fort, he opened the door of his car and slowly poured the remnants of his clothing onto the road.

When he got home, it was close to 6 AM. He flopped into bed. Although he was very tired, he had trouble sleeping. His mind was racing, and the vision of Hank's face – dead, but bloodied and angry – returned him mind again and again. He entered into a shallow, fitful sleep. He had dreams, but Hank was in them, and so was Gunner.

18

❧❧❧

Bastion

When Jimmy emerged from his difficult sleep, it was almost noon. He spread two sachets of testosterone solution on his upper arms and chest, but it all seemed so pointless. His life was too painful. He felt shaken. He felt ill at ease. He felt tense and sad. He felt, upon waking, shocked that what he had witnessed and experienced the day before was not a dream, but a horrendous reality. He felt exhausted.

He wanted to tell someone about the murder, but he knew he couldn't – perhaps ever. Images from the killing came back into his mind every few minutes. Several times he swore: 'Jaysus Hank, don't start haunting me.'

In the mirror, his face had an ashen hue – the pallor of a man who was tired and sad. His eyes seemed to have developed a distant stare. He whispered a line from his favourite Johnny Cash recording: 'What have I become?'

He felt guilty. Two Gardaí were dead. He assumed he was responsible for their deaths, but couldn't be sure. How had his life got to this point? Two men were dead, and he could only *assume* that he had killed them. 'What have I become?' he asked himself again.

In the kitchen, Milfoth was chopping vegetables when Jimmy lumbered in wearing pyjamas and slippers.

'So they named the man who was shot in Rialto yesterday,' she said, without turning towards Jimmy.

'Oh?' said Jimmy.

'His name was "Hank Savage".'

'Right,' said Jimmy.

'Same name as one of your business associates, I seem to remember.'

'I suppose,' said Jimmy.

'Two Gardaí dead as well.'

'Yeah,' he confirmed.

'Did you kill these men?' she asked as she turned towards Jimmy, pointing the knife in his direction.

'No.'

'Honestly!'

'No, I said.'

'Don't tell me a lie!' she shouted.

'I'm not lying,' he retorted.

'Did you have anything to do with their killings?'

Jimmy wanted to answer, but any of the words he considered using would not be helpful to his position. He didn't answer.

'Oh God,' said Milfoth quietly, looking at the ceiling as if for answers. 'Oh Jesus,' she said breathlessly. 'What am I going to do?'

Jimmy sat down, almost deferentially, and spoke slowly: 'First of all, I would be grateful if . . . if anyone asks where I was last evening, please say that I was here with you.'

'You want me to lie for you?' she hissed.

'I want you to . . . say this . . . for our daughter's sake, and for your sake. It will be in your best interests. We watched our *Pulp Fiction* DVD. If you can't remember the details, it's because we were drinking wine and you fell asleep towards the end of the film.'

'Tell me what happened yesterday,' demanded Milfoth.

'No.'

'Tell me. I need to know,' she said.

'No you don't. The less you know, the better it will be for you if anything goes wrong,' he said coldly.

'Goes wrong? Goes wrong? As opposed to what – things going right, as they are now?'

Jimmy spoke slowly. 'You're right, things aren't good now, and haven't been for a while. But things could get much worse, so we have to be calm and careful.'

Milfoth tried a different approach: 'The people who carried out the killings, are they your friends, or are they your enemies?'

'Enemies.'

'So, now they'll come after you?' she asked.

He couldn't maintain eye-contact. He looked away and shrugged.

'Am I safe?' she asked.

'I don't know. They don't usually go after the women.'

'Usually?'

'I think you're safer than me,' said Jimmy.

'What about Byron? She's due back from my mother's today.'

'Today?' This presented Jimmy with a new concern. 'Really? Could she not stay another week where she is?'

'What difference would a week make?'

Jimmy didn't have an answer.

'She has been away a long time. She misses her home and her friends,' said Milfoth.

Jimmy exhaled: 'Shit!'

'Why don't we just go to the Gardaí?' she asked.

'No,' said Jimmy, quickly and firmly. 'I think we've missed that particular boat.'

There was a long pause while both of them searched for a solution to their difficulty.

'Would we be safer without you?' she asked.

'If you're asking me to move out, then the answer is no,' he spat back.

'Perhaps you're being just a little selfish, considering the circumstances?'

'First of all, I have nowhere to go. Secondly, I think it's better that I'm here to protect you – '

'*You*, protect *us!*' she scoffed.

'To protect you, and my daughter. I think it's better than leaving you here on your own while I hide out somewhere far away.'

'You've brought danger right into this house. Ruined this family. And now you think you can protect us?' she shouted.

Jimmy matched her anger: 'Everything I have worked for has gone into creating a better life for us. For all of us. Everything. Every euro I've made. Everything. And if this family has been ruined, it was done several years ago, not by me, but by you!'

'Oh, here we go again,' she said, throwing her arms in the air.

'Yes, here we go again. I have made mistakes. I admit that. But the mistakes I've made have been while trying to provide for my family. Nothing else. There was no joy in it for me. Just duty.'

He held up his thumb and index finger, with a small gap in between: 'I was this close to hanging myself a few months ago, but I chose instead to provide for my family. So at least I tried. I tried! And if I get a bullet for that, or get twenty years for it . . . well, they're the risks I have accepted – *for my family.*'

'Nobody asked you to do those things,' she said defiantly. 'You could have got a job in a pub, or a café, or somewhere that didn't involve *murder.*'

Jimmy took a moment to compose his response. 'I accept that this is a very stressful time for you. But it's not unreasonable to ask you to be supportive.'

'Supportive! Supportive? I have been more than supportive,' she said, through gritted teeth. 'I have been sexually assaulted in my own home. I have been terrorised. I have been humiliated in front of the nation. You have brought the murder of three men to my doorstep, and you ask me to provide an alibi. You treat me as if none of this is any of my business. And if I question you on all of this, you ask me to be supportive!'

Both of them seemed to want the heated discussion to end, so a silence followed, punctuated only by Jimmy's heavy breathing. 'Sorry,' he said, 'just trying hard to think of solutions at this point.'

'Do we need to get a guard-dog?' she said, supportively.

Jimmy nodded. 'Yeah. Today, if possible.'

'What about reinforced windows?'

'I'll make some calls about that.'

'We're vulnerable in two areas,' said Milfoth. 'The house over our back wall is vacant, so anyone who knows the area could come through that garden to get into ours.'

'What can I do about that?' asked Jimmy.

Milfoth ignored the question. 'The other weakness is our front door. It's a cheap composite thing that I could probably kick in myself. We need something that's reinforced, with multiple dead-bolt locks.'

Jimmy shook his head. 'I don't think we can afford that.'

'I don't think we can afford *not* to,' she said, handing him her credit card. 'Get something that makes us safer. We can worry about paying for it some other time.'

*

Milfoth met Byron as she arrived off the train in the early afternoon. They headed straight to the animal-rescue centre in the Dublin mountains to procure a guard-dog.

Jimmy spent the afternoon calling window companies to price bulletproof glass for the house. The prices were far beyond what he could afford without taking out a loan. And taking out a loan while he was still unemployed would be difficult.

He checked with one supplier: 'Are you sure double-glazed windows wouldn't stop a bullet?'

'Yes, mate,' came the reply. 'Glass is very brittle. It offers a little bit of resistance and then shatters. Best it can do is maybe knock the bullet off its trajectory a bit.'

Another difficulty for Jimmy was the six-week waiting period for ballistic glazing. 'It's a bespoke solution,' said another sales agent. 'You can't just buy it off the shelf.'

Jimmy felt that if he was attacked, it would happen within days, not months, so it seemed pointless to begin a six-week waiting period.

'I do have a security door in the showroom,' said one sales agent. 'If you have a standard-size doorway, we could install it tomorrow.'

'How much?' asked Jimmy.

'Seven grand, plus VAT – but that includes installation.'

Jimmy baulked at the price; it seemed far too much to pay for a front door.

'It comes with a multi-point locking system, and reinforced steel,' said the sales agent. 'What price do you put on peace of mind?'

Jimmy had little negotiating power. He felt grateful to Milfoth as he put the charge on her card.

He called several house-alarm companies. Despite his pleas for urgent service, they all lacked a suitable sense of urgency. He provisionally booked an alarm – fully monitored, and with a panic button. But it would be a minimum of ten days before it could be installed.

His only other purchase was made online, where he found an integrated doorbell-and-video-camera device. This would enable him to see on his phone who was calling at his door.

He listened to every news bulletin on both radio and TV, and read every online article he could find about the previous day's events. The headlines were dramatic and simple: 'TRIPLE MURDER IN HOUSE OF HORRORS', 'GARDAÍ KILLED BY BOOBY-TRAP BOMB', and 'SAVAGE WHACKED IN DUBLIN 8 BLOODBATH'. Each was followed by speculation that someone close to the gang-leader may have been responsible for his murder.

There were many photographs of Hank in his prime as a bodybuilder and ladies' man. His position at the nexus where gangster meets celebrity meant that there were scores of photos of him with famous actors, musicians and sports stars.

The killing of the Gardaí was the top story throughout the day. It started with speculation about a bomb, but by late afternoon Jimmy noticed that it was referred to merely as an explosion. On the 6 PM news, the suggestion was made – for the first time – that the explosion may have been caused by gas igniting. An 'informed source' speculated that the killing may have been accidental, 'possibly a result of the earlier shooting having ruptured a gas appliance'.

Garda representatives, journalists and politicians all agreed that the killings highlighted the dangers that 'rank-and-file Gardaí face every day'. They saluted the men's bravery and selflessness, and called for increased resources to be made available to 'tackle the scourge of organised crime'.

Reports said that Kearney had left behind a widow and three children; O'Toole was also married, with two children. Jimmy struggled with this so much that he returned to his bed. He reminded himself that their deaths were accidental, and that they were corrupt, but he knew this would not diminish the suffering of those children.

Late in the day, reports emerged that Gardaí had raided buildings that were associated with Hank. These included a disused garage, a city-centre stable, and a country residence near Rathfarnham. One reporter, quoting an unnamed Garda source, said that Gardaí believed that members of the Savage gang may have moved money and drugs from the buildings shortly before they were searched.

Jimmy assessed each news report. Gang-members clearing out Hank's premises before the cops arrived should mean that they had been cleansed of fingerprints and DNA evidence. That would make it difficult to link Jimmy to those buildings.

Hank killed by his own people: that would leave Jimmy out of the frame in the eyes of the Gardaí.

An explosion that wasn't a bomb: this meant that the Gardaí would be less vigorous in their investigations, which would also lessen the change of Jimmy being linked to the scene.

But where did it leave him in the eyes of Hank's gang? They would have hoped by now that Jimmy had been arrested for the murder. Now that he hadn't been, what would come next? It seemed to Jimmy to be a classic case of prisoner's dilemma: if he and Gunner remained silent, it would be unlikely that either of them could be prosecuted for Hank's murder. In that scenario, both had an incentive to stay silent.

If they ratted on each other, they could both be convicted. If one ratted while the other stayed silent, the silent party could be convicted. In that scenario, each was incentivised to rat out the other before they could talk to the cops.

Jimmy asked himself what he would do if he were Gunner. The answer was clear: don't wait to find out if Jimmy would rat or not. Just kill him.

Jimmy was desperately anxious. The strain of the previous day, coupled with a night of poor sleep, had left him listless. His concentration was poor. The thought that there were people living nearby who may want to kill him, meant that he couldn't relax. He kept the curtains closed, and peeped out the windows every time he heard noise outside – which was every couple of minutes.

In the absence of an *immediate* threat, Milfoth provided. He went back over their most recent arguments and, of course, her rejection of him. He called to mind her many and frequent callous remarks, and it made him angrier. In his mind, he rehearsed his lines in preparation for their next dispute.

*

Shortly before 7 PM, Byron burst through the door. 'Dad! Dad! We got a dog!'

'Welcome home,' said Jimmy sarcastically. 'Nice to see you after so long . . . .'

'He is just gorgeous – wait 'til you see.'

Milfoth came in the door with a dog-basket, some dog-toys and a large bag of dog-food. 'He's in the car,' she said.

Byron ran back out to the car excitedly. Milfoth explained her afternoon to Jimmy: 'First we went to the dog-pound. We found a really suitable dog, but they wouldn't give her to us until they came to inspect our house. Then we would all have to go together to visit the dog in the rescue-centre. And then we would have to go to an adoption-seminar to learn how to take care of a dog. I thought none of this would work, because you said you wanted a dog today.'

'OK,' said Jimmy. 'It didn't have to be today . . . .'

'So we went online and looked for dogs for sale, and we met a guy in Lucan, who sold us Bonnie. He says he would make an excellent guard-dog.'

At that, Byron walked proudly through the door with a small white dog. Jimmy was confused. He was unsure if it was a puppy form of a big dog, a fully grown small dog – or a lamb. Or a cuddly toy.

'What's that?' asked Jimmy.

'This is my new baby brother,' said Byron. 'Isn't he gorgeous?'

'What's that?' asked Jimmy again. 'Seriously . . . what is that?'

'Bonnie is a bichon frise,' said Milfoth helpfully. 'They bark if they hear the slightest sound, and they are excellent with children.'

'We don't have any children,' said Jimmy.

'Ahem, excuse me,' said Byron. 'I'm a child.'

'This is not a guard-dog,' said Jimmy.

'Yes, it is,' countered Milfoth. 'The man said they make excellent – '

'Guard-dogs aren't white!' shouted Jimmy.

'Dad, that's a kind of racism,' said Byron. 'If the colour of his hair was different, would you be less prejudiced against him?'

'What difference would that make?' shouted Jimmy. 'I asked ye to get a guard-dog, and you come back with *this*.'

'What's wrong with him?' asked Byron.

Jimmy was agitated. 'It's not a guard-dog! It's barely one grade above a cat!'

'Now you're being offensive to cats,' said Byron.

'I'm not being offensive to anything,' said Jimmy. 'I'm just concerned that if some guy comes through that door tonight to do us harm, what's going to happen? Is Bonnie going to hurl himself at the guy and rip through his carotid arteries with the power of his tiny little jaws? Or throw his teddy-bear body in front of a bullet to save his new family? Maybe he could lick the intruder to death!'

'The man said that 90 percent of being a guard-dog is about alerting your owners when there's an intruder,' said Byron.

'Oh, and how would this fella know? Was he a guard-dog in his early life? Or perhaps he went to college and studied guard-doggery?'

'I think you need to stop shouting, Jimmy,' said Milfoth. 'You'll frighten Bonnie.'

'Oh dear,' said Jimmy, sarcastically. 'Stop shouting or you'll frighten the guard-dog! What if someone gives the guard-dog a fright? Will we have to take him to a doggy therapist? I hope whoever breaks into our house has good enough manners to keep their voice down. We don't want the guard-dog getting a fright. Maybe I should put up a sign saying "QUIET PLEASE, GUARD DOG SLEEPING". And I hope that whoever comes to kill me will refrain from making remarks that could be interpreted as offensive by certain colours of dogs, or cats.'

'You're being silly, dad,' said Byron. 'I think we should discontinue this conversation until you've learned to discuss matters civilly.'

Byron picked up the dog and left the room. Milfoth followed. Jimmy was left alone, standing in his kitchen.

*

The evening was spent trying to accommodate the new member of the family. Jimmy watched Milfoth and Byron hug the dog, play with it, and screech with joy when he seemed to obey a command or do something they found funny. They put Bonnie on Jimmy's lap, but Jimmy's body stiffened. Intellectually, he could tell that the animal was cute, but as a matter of principle, he would not show it affection.

Several times Jimmy patrolled the house to make sure the doors and windows were locked. He kept a hurling stick nearby at all times. He poured himself a whiskey to help him sleep, and went to bed early.

It was several hours before Milfoth and Byron went to bed. Jimmy knew this from the murmur of conversation that rose through the floorboards from the rooms below, punctuated by shrieks of laughter. He must have dozed off sometime after midnight, and fell into a deep sleep. Some hours later, Bonnie, in the kitchen below, went crazy.

'Woof, woof, woof! Woof, woof, woof!' The barks were loud and continuous, and so fast that they sounded almost mechanical. Jimmy sat bolt upright, wide awake as adrenaline raced through his system. He grabbed his stick, and peeped out of his bedroom window. There was nothing unusual happening on the street.

As he left his room, Milfoth came out of hers with her phone in her hand. 'Where are you going?' she said. 'Don't go downstairs.'

'I have to go downstairs,' he said. 'I'll be careful.'

'I'm ringing the police,' she said. Jimmy didn't object.

He crept down the stairs, listening in case someone had already entered the house. He left the lights off, hoping to surprise whoever had come in. He figured he knew the house better than they did, so he would have an advantage in the dark.

Upstairs, he could hear Milfoth repeat the address of their house on the phone. 'Please hurry,' she said. 'Please!'

In the kitchen, Bonnie maintained his barrage of barking. 'Woof, woof, woof! Woof, woof, woof!'

Jimmy opened the door slowly and carefully in case someone was hiding behind it. He could see Bonnie, on his hind legs, jumping up and down, and scratching at the patio-door. That his attention was turned towards the garden, suggested that the intruder was still outside, not inside.

Jimmy crawled across the floor to the kitchen island, his eyes fixed on the kitchen window and the patio doors, in case someone was pointing a gun inside. His heart was pounding, and sweat oozed from his forehead. On crossing the floor, he placed his back against the island, and considered his options.

If someone came through the patio-door, he would hit them hard across the head before they had a chance to assess the geography of the room. He would then grab their gun, and hopefully end the confrontation quickly. The same if they came through the kitchen window. He would wait.

Bonnie wouldn't stop: 'Woof, woof, woof! Woof, woof, woof!' There was no change in the volume of the dog's barking, or where its attention was directed, so Jimmy couldn't tell if the intruder was getting closer or backing away.

He decided to put the patio-lights on. That might give him a clear view of the intruder in the garden, make it more difficult for them to see inside, and hopefully discourage an attack. But it meant crossing the dining area of the room to get to the lightswitch. He crawled again, this time very close to the patio-doors, just behind the barking dog.

Jimmy stood carefully to reach the switch. He was now exposed, should someone point a gun through the window. He decided to flick the switch, then dive across the floor to the safety of the kitchen island again.

'One, two, three,' he said to himself. He pushed on the switch, then tumbled across the floor with all the grace of an elephant on ice-skates. Bonnie maintained his barking. 'Woof, woof, woof! Woof, woof, woof!' Jimmy waited for a bullet or some other development; there was none.

Moments later, Jimmy peeped out from the safety of his hiding-place. The patio and part of the garden was illuminated, and Bonnie – still on his hind legs – was in silhouette. 'Woof, woof, woof! Woof, woof, woof!'

Jimmy crept across the floor – and for the first time could see what Bonnie was barking at. Lazily resting on Jimmy's lawn, and indifferent to Bonnie's protest, a fox scratched itself.

'Jimmy, are you OK?' shouted Milfoth.

'False alarm,' shouted Jimmy. 'It's just a fox in the garden. Shut up, Bonnie!'

'Are you sure? Is it safe to come down?'

'I think so,' said Jimmy wearily. 'Can you shut this stupid dog up, please!'

Byron rushed by Jimmy, still tying her bathrobe. 'Oh, you're such a brave boy,' she said to Bonnie in a high-pitched voice. 'You're a good guard-dog. Aren't you? Aren't you? See, Dad, I told you he would be good.'

Jimmy was too tired to argue. He couldn't deny that the dog was good at raising an alarm, but wished he had the judgement to go with it.

He instructed his daughter to place Bonnie's basket in the front room, where he mightn't be disturbed by a fox. He slowly ascended the stairs and returned, wearily, to his bed.

Jimmy wanted desperately to sleep, but he couldn't. He checked the time: 2.30 AM. His heart was still pounding fast, and his body, especially his shoulder areas, was tense. He checked the time again: 2.45 AM. Several times he was startled by noise on the street, but it was only taxis, or people coming home drunk and chatting loudly. This kind of noise had never disturbed him before. He checked the time: 3.11 AM.

Sometime after 3.30 AM, he went into the bathroom and found some sleeping-pills in the cabinet behind the mirror. He popped two, had another nip of whiskey, and returned to bed. He was soon fast asleep. It seemed like only minutes later that Jimmy was woken again, this time by the doorbell: *Ding-dong.*

Jimmy sat bolt-upright again, but this time very disoriented. He didn't know why he was awake, and lay down immediately and went back to sleep.

Ding-dong.

The dog started to bark, but not with the same intensity as before.

'Jimmy, are you awake?' It was Milfoth's voice from the next room.

He jumped out of bed and fumbled in the dark, not knowing what he should do. 'What?' he shouted to Milfoth.

'Someone's at the door,' she shouted.

Jimmy looked out the window and saw a Garda car outside. 'No!' he shouted. 'No!'

Milfoth ran into his room and found Jimmy sitting on the floor with his head in his hands. 'They've come for me,' he whimpered. 'I'm sorry. I knew it would happen. I knew it would happen.' He was hysterical. 'I'll need to pack a bag. Can you find a good solicitor? I can try, but it might be easier for you to make a few calls.'

Milfoth looked out through the curtains, then opened the window and called down. 'Hello?'

A uniformed Garda stepped back from the doorstep, and looked up. 'Sorry to disturb you, ma'am, but we received a call about an intruder at this address.'

'Oh, I already called to say that there was no intruder,' said Milfoth. 'That was a couple of hours ago.'

'Well, just checking, in case there was a hostage situation,' said the Garda.

'No, everything is fine. Thank you,' said Milfoth, and closed the window.

'Fuck's sake!' shouted Jimmy. and pounded down the stairs. He threw open the front door and shouted at the Garda: 'What the fuck are you at?'

'Excuse me?' said the Garda.

'We thought we had an intruder two hours ago, and you're only showing up now?'

'You cancelled the emergency call. I'm just following up to make sure that you're OK.'

'Well, how do you know if we *are* OK?' bellowed Jimmy.

'The lady said you were OK,' said the Garda, pointing to the upstairs window.

'How do you know that there isn't an intruder with a gun at her back?'

'Is there?' asked the Garda.

'You tell me!' roared Jimmy. 'You're the fucking Garda.'

'Jimmy!' shouted Milfoth, appearing at the door. 'I'm sorry, Guard, my husband isn't usually like this.'

'That's because I'm not usually woken at five in the morning by a cop who's just going through the motions.'

'Sir, I am very sorry for waking you. I just wanted to make sure that you're safe.'

'You didn't make sure!' shouted Jimmy. 'You're walking away, and you don't know if we're safe or not.'

'We're safe, Guard. Thank you,' said Milfoth.

'No we're not!' shouted Jimmy. 'I think I saw a fella with a knife in my kitchen a moment ago. Come on, Guard, you better check it out! Come on, Guard. Let's see how brave you are!'

Standing on his garden path wearing only a vest and boxer shorts, Jimmy made the gestures of a traffic cop at a busy intersection. 'Come on, Guard! I want you to check the house to see if there's a hostage situation.'

The Garda didn't move, but looked at Jimmy with pity. 'Sir, you know it's an offence to make a false report?'

'Oh, you want to charge me now, do you?' shouted Jimmy. 'You show up late for a possible break-in, and now you're going to arrest the victim?'

Milfoth manhandled Jimmy back into the house. 'Good night, Guard, and thank you for dropping by,' she said, and slammed the door.

*

Jimmy went through the next day bleary-eyed and drowsy. Several cups of coffee didn't seem to wake him fully, and he didn't eat much. He tried to avoid Milfoth, who had scolded him for 'Behaving like an idiot – yet again' the night before.

He watched TV for a while, mostly flicking from channel to channel. Nothing held his interest for more than a couple of minutes. Even when there was TV coverage of deceased Gardaí, he couldn't concentrate. When footage appeared of Hank's funeral, he couldn't believe that his death had only happened two days earlier. It seemed like weeks had passed.

He drank a beer to help him sleep in the afternoon, but the bright sun outside had told his body that this was a time to be awake, so he enjoyed little more than a short nap.

He wanted to go out for a walk, to tire his body and breathe fresh air, but thought that this would be too dangerous. So he stayed inside, with the curtains drawn, and all the external doors, and downstairs windows, locked.

Milfoth and Byron went to the War Memorial Gardens in the afternoon to walk Bonnie. As his wife went out the door, Jimmy raised his middle finger in her direction, as he had done many times before. He was angry at her. Why exactly? He didn't know. Perhaps because she had been nagging him about the night before. 'She's always giving out about something,' he mumbled to himself.

Early in the evening, he drank a glass of whiskey and took a couple of sleeping-pills. He fell into a deep unconsciousness.

Sometime after 3 AM, Bonnie went crazy. 'Woof, woof, woof! Woof, woof, woof, woof!' sounded through the house again, like a machine-gun.

Jimmy sat bolt upright. He grabbed his hurl and went through exactly the same procedure as the night before, except this time in a half-hearted manner. Milfoth didn't ring the police this time, but kept her phone in her hand while Jimmy crept into the kitchen again, to find Bonnie transfixed by something in the back garden. It was the fox again.

'We can't live like this,' announced Jimmy, over a late breakfast. 'The dog either has to learn the difference between humans and foxes, or he'll have to go.'

'No,' said Byron. 'You can't get rid of our dog just because he was doing his job too well.'

'Doing his job? His job isn't to bark at foxes,' said Jimmy, trying to raise his voice, but only sounding hoarse.

'Well, how is he supposed to know? You haven't trained him yet. You haven't given him any attention. How is he supposed to know what you want?'

'Or we can get rid of the fox,' said Milfoth.

'How?' said Jimmy and Byron in unison.

'I read on the internet that foxes are very sensitive to smells. And they can tell from the smell of urine if it's from a larger animal or not.'

Jimmy and Byron looked at her blankly, as if to ask: 'Where is this going?'

'So, if the larger animal sprays its urine around the perimeter of the garden, it will stop the fox coming in,' said Milfoth, looking at Jimmy.

Jimmy looked confused: 'What larger animal? You want me to get a horse now?'

'*You're* the larger animal,' said Milfoth, as if Jimmy was slow on the uptake.

'You want me to piss in the garden?'

'Yes,' said Milfoth.

'*You* piss in the garden,' said Jimmy, angrily.

'No, it has to be you,' she replied sternly. 'Foxes know the difference between male and female pee, and they're more afraid of males.'

Jimmy was irritated at the suggestion. 'So, you want me to go out now and piss in the garden?'

'Not now,' said Milfoth. 'Tonight, just before you go to bed. So that it's fresh when the fox comes around.'

'Oh, sorry,' said Jimmy sarcastically, 'only the freshest of urine will do for our fox.'

'Yes, it must be male, and it must be fresh. And perhaps sprinkle it high, so that the fox is sure that it's coming from a much larger mammal.' Milfoth had clearly done her research. 'And you need to put it in the areas where the fox is most likely to enter the garden.'

Jimmy remained dismissive. 'You want me to walk around the garden with my todger out, giving a little squirt here and there at the places where I think a fox is most likely to appear?'

'It's about quantity and consistency,' said Milfoth confidently. 'It's about delivering the right volume at the right places. I think if you walk around with your . . . thing . . . in your hand, your bladder might empty before you've got to the right places. Therefore it's better if you urinate into a container over a period of hours, and then choose the best spots to sprinkle.'

'A container? Like a bucket?' said Jimmy.

'I'm thinking of the watering-can in the shed,' said Milfoth. 'It already has a handle, and a sprinkle.' She smiled to herself. 'For your tinkle.'

Byron laughed, and Jimmy slapped the table with both hands. 'I'm not sticking my todger into the watering-can,' he shouted.

'If it helps you get a good night's sleep, isn't it worth it?' said Milfoth.

'No, it's not worth it,' said Jimmy loudly and defiantly. 'So I'm not doing it.'

But they both knew that he would.

*

After three hours of sleep in the afternoon, Jimmy felt more alert and in better form. His appetite returned too. Following dinner, Milfoth interrupted his plan to watch TV. She presented him with the watering-can and said: 'It's time.'

'Oh, for Jaysus sake, you really want me to stick my dick in there?' said Jimmy.

'Shut up and just do it,' she said. 'Since when are you so particular about where you stick your dick? At least you don't have to pay the watering-can!'

Jimmy closed the patio-door behind him, and sneaked into the darkness of the garden. The part of the garden closest to the house was illuminated by light coming from the kitchen and dining areas, so he went to the back of the garden, to the shadows cast by the garden-shed, the walls and the tall bushes.

It wasn't beyond Milfoth to call the neighbours, and invite them to shout words of support out their windows to Jimmy as he went about his task. So he opened the door of the shed and stood in the doorway. It was a good place to survey the neighbours' upstairs windows. There was no indication of an audience.

In his own house, Milfoth washed dishes at the sink just inside the kitchen-window. Upstairs, there was a light on in Byron's room. Her curtains were open and he could see her busily putting clothes into her wardrobe. Downstairs, Bonnie was on his hind-legs, looking out the patio-door, presumably wondering what Jimmy was doing.

From Jimmy's vantage-point, everything looked so peaceful. The warm glow of his home in the dark night showed the sum-total of his life. If he were to die now, there would be no need to write an obituary; just a photograph of that scene would suffice. Most of his assets were on view: the house he had nearly paid for; the garden he had managed. The key relationships of his life were there: his wife and his daughter; not the dog. Sadly, he noted that if such a picture were made, there would be no friends on view. He wondered how he had arrived at this point in his life where he had no close friends.

As he unbuttoned his fly, he heard a noise from somewhere behind the shed, but thought nothing of it. He held the watering-can with one hand, and his male appendage in the other. Nothing came out; his body seemed to recoil at the idea of peeing into a plastic container.

'Come on,' said Jimmy to himself. His bladder was full following dinner, so there should be little difficulty.

'Come on,' he said again, but his 'todger' refused to obey. As he spoke, he heard another noise from outside the shed – this time like something brushing off the trees.

Jimmy focused on his bladder. He closed his eyes momentarily, took a deep breath, and told himself to relax. He thought about peeing. He thought about a waterfall. And then his blood ran cold.

A dark figure passed in front of the garden-shed door, barely more than an arm's length from Jimmy. He froze. What felt like fire passed from his heels up to his scalp. His body knew before his mind could comprehend: he was in danger. Instinctively, he held his breath. He didn't – couldn't – move.

The figure walked away from the shed towards the house. It stepped on the gravel patch, which made a crunching sound, so the figure skipped to the grass, which was silent underfoot.

Jimmy watched. His only possible weapon of defence – the hurl – was inside.

The figure crept behind the apple-tree and peeped in the direction of the house. With the light coming from the kitchen and living-room, the figure was in silhouette, and Jimmy could see the person's outline clearly. The person was male, and familiar. He was of short stature, with broad shoulders. A small head sat on a thick neck. His gurrier gait was still evident as he crept by. It was Gunner.

As Jimmy drew breath, he saw Gunner take something from his pocket, adjust it, and hold it by his side. It was a gun.

In seconds, Jimmy's options flashed through his mind. He could stay silent, and hope that Gunner wouldn't find him, then escape over the back wall and raise the alarm. Jimmy would be safe, but Gunner might still shoot Byron and Milfoth.

But maybe Gunner was only there to scare Jimmy? It might be just show. And maybe he could talk with Gunner, man to man. After all, he had no incentive to finger him for Hank's murder. That plan could deliver the best outcome, but Jimmy would be reliant on Gunner showing appropriate judgement.

The only other option was the one he followed. Deep inside, something stirred; something he had never felt before – an atavistic reaction to extreme danger. An intruder was about to enter his cave and attack his kin. Adrenaline coursed through his veins. Fight or flight? He would fight. Kill or be killed; there was no other option. He felt calm and determined.

Jimmy placed the watering-can gently on the floor of the shed. In the darkness, his hand roved the surface of his workbench until it found something hard and heavy: a large pipe-wrench.

He moved quietly but swiftly in Gunner's direction. He avoided the noise of the gravel path and tiptoed along the grass, past the apple-tree, towards his prey. Gunner had now left the shadows and was in the illuminated part of the garden. Milfoth was still busy in the kitchen, and easily within range of a handgun. Gunner moved towards the patio-door. Inside, Bonnie kept watch – silently.

Jimmy rushed at Gunner. Like a fast-bowler, he raised the hand that held the wrench high above his head, and his other hand reached forward. As he closed in on his target, he swung his leading arm behind himself, propelling the raised arm forwards and downwards with force. The wrench crashed into the side of Gunner's head. There was a loud crack. There was such power in the blow that it knocked the wrench out of Jimmy's hand. The gun flew from Gunner's hand, and both men went head-first into the ground.

Jimmy lay on the grass for a moment, wondering what should happen next. He had never before performed such an act of violence. He was sure the intruder would not rise again, but he was wrong.

Gunner seemed dazed as he staggered to his feet. Instead of attacking Jimmy, he stumbled around looking for his gun. As he reached down to pick it up, Jimmy slid over and kicked it away. This put his body under Gunner's, and left his head exposed.

Gunner saw the opportunity, and hit Jimmy hard across the temple. What looked like an electrical current passed through Jimmy's vision, and his head shot back onto the ground. Gunner sat on his chest, and delivered three fast, powerful punches into Jimmy's face.

Pain radiated from the centre of his face, and blood spurted from his eyebrow and his nose. Somewhere in Jimmy, perhaps owing to months of abdominal training in the gym, he found the strength to raise his hips – with such force that Gunner was propelled forward, into the grass.

Jimmy got to his feet quickly. As Gunner tried to raise himself, Jimmy came from behind, to deliver a hard kick into his groin, a second one into his ribs, and a third that glanced off his head. Yet, Gunner still raised himself.

Jimmy had learned how to punch hard, and delivered two strong blows to Gunner's head, but they didn't seem to faze him. Gunner grasped at Jimmy's fingers, but Jimmy had learned how to evade such manoeuvres. He put Gunner in a headlock, and delivered some punches to his head, but they seemed to be more painful for the giver than they were for the receiver.

Gunner turned his head and bit Jimmy's waist. Jimmy let out a roar of pain, and loosened his grip. Gunner put an arm between Jimmy's legs, and lifted. This unbalanced Jimmy, and Gunner slammed him backwards onto the ground. Jimmy was winded.

Gunner sat on Jimmy's chest again, and this time, Jimmy hadn't the strength to knock him off. Gunner used his left arm to push away Jimmy's efforts to defend himself, and his right to pound Jimmy's face and head. With each blow, Jimmy's ability to fight back waned.

Jimmy summoned up enough energy for another move. He tried to headbutt his oppressor from below. Gunner saw it coming, and stayed clear. He grabbed Jimmy's wrists, and held them down. Jimmy was now defenceless, and Gunner delivered a powerful headbutt to Jimmy's mouth. Jimmy felt sharp pain as four of his front teeth were knocked out.

Jimmy's head area was opened in several places. Blood poured from above both eyes, obstructing his vision in one. His nose was broken, making breathing difficult. His energy was sapped; there was little fight left in him.

He received a punch to the side of his mouth, and felt his jaw dislocate. His head turned in the direction of his home, just a few metres away. He could see Bonnie, still on two legs, amused by the sight of two humans fighting.

'Bark, you little shit, bark!' Jimmy tried to say the words, but nothing would come out. The dog remained quiet, standing on his back legs and looking pensive. 'Milfoth won't be happy, you naughty boy,' said Jimmy, under his breath. 'Smearing the glass with the tip of your fun-size Mars bar.'

The blows continued. *So this is how it ends*, Jimmy thought to himself. *Beaten to death in my own garden by a scumbag who I brought into my life because I decided to be a criminal. And my last thoughts as I leave this world are of the back door, and Bonnie's dinky dong. Funny, really.*

The pain was no longer severe; he was too dazed. He could feel injuries all over his head and body, but it was no longer his pain. He felt detached. His spirit and his battered body were separating.

Somewhere above him, Gunner continued his work, his punches weaker now. He too was leaking blood, particularly from the ear where Jimmy had landed the wrench. Blood from Gunner dripped onto Jimmy's face. For a moment the two men looked each other in the eyes. It seemed oddly intimate. The two had played significant roles in each other's lives of late, but Jimmy didn't even know his real name.

Gunner hit Jimmy again, but it was a weak strike. He tried again, but he was off balance, and he failed to connect. He threw another punch, but either he had no strength left, or Jimmy was beyond feeling anything. Gunner tried again, but his coordination failed him. He missed Jimmy, and grazed the ground.

Gunner stared at Jimmy. His face was troubled. He whimpered; he seemed to be in distress. He was crying. He swore at Jimmy, and tried to say something. Then, slowly, Gunner put his hands on the grass. His breathing was heavy, and soon his forehead lowered and rested on the back of his hands. He cried a little more, then stopped moving. All went quiet in the garden.

Jimmy tried to call out for help, but his broken jaw prevented him from forming the words, while the weight of Gunner on his chest made it difficult for him to breathe. 'Hewwww,' he said, as loud as he could – but it was little more than a whisper.

'Heaaaaww,' he said, but Milfoth didn't hear him. She just worked away inside the kitchen window, while Bonnie observed quietly. He tried again: 'He-llph.' But it was barely audible.

He heaved Gunner off his chest, who fell lifelessly onto the grass beside him. Jimmy couldn't be sure if Gunner was dead, or just resting, so he delivered a blow with his elbow into the side of his head. There was no reaction. He did it again. Still nothing. His hands were too bruised, and he hadn't the energy to swing them, so he delivered several more elbow-blows, this time into Gunner's body. There was still no reaction. 'Fucker,' said Jimmy. It seemed to be the only word he could enunciate.

He cleared blood from his eyes, and began to regulate his breathing. Suddenly, a wave of elation washed over him. 'I've killed him,' he thought to himself. 'I've done it! I've done it.'

The finality of a kill touched that atavistic core again. He had been challenged. He had risen to the challenge, and he had killed his attacker. A man's job was to protect his family, and he had done that – excellently. He had killed for his family. It was an achievement that couldn't be taken away from him. Death was final. It was the ultimate victory. Victory was Jimmy's. His spirit soared.

For a moment, he forgot his pain. He forgot the rage inside him; the insult of a person entering his territory uninvited. His body was still on high alert. Adrenaline still pumped through his system, but it had no outlet.

He looked around to share his moment of triumph but there was nobody, except her – the woman in the window. Milfoth. 'Fucking Milfoth,' he mumbled.

Somewhere in his body, he was still raging. Seeing her, reminded him of pain. It reminded him of humiliation. She was taking from his moment of triumph by just being there. He had just slain one oppressor, but there was another one – one who had damaged him over a much longer period. So much of his pain was her fault.

In an instant, his rage found an outlet. And his mind was quick to locate a means to satisfy his sudden and overwhelming desire. Gunner's weapon was beside him, and so were Gunner's fingers. It was the perfect moment to remove Milfoth from his life.

Jimmy reached across the lawn for the gun. He clutched it, manoeuvred himself towards Gunner, and put it in the dead man's hand. Gunner's fingers had already stiffened, but he managed to put Gunner's index-finger on the trigger. He held Gunner's hand in his hands, and took aim at Milfoth's head. She kept moving, and his vision was blurred, so aiming the weapon was difficult.

'Stay still, for fuck's sake,' he said. He closed one eye, in the hope of clearing his vision, but it remained blurred. It would have helped if he could move closer to the window, but that was difficult, and he had no way of moving Gunner.

He needed Gunner to twist his wrist slightly. 'Help me out, Gunner, for fuck's sake,' he whispered to the corpse. 'Move, ya prick!'

Milfoth stopped moving. She was perfectly positioned. Jimmy's open eye seemed to focus. He aimed again. Then his mind cleared a little. *What am I doing?*' he asked himself, looking at the gun instead of his wife. *Why am I doing this?* He lowered the gun slightly.

Bang!

The gun sounded, its noise ripping through the cool summer air. The bullet sped from the chamber, but instead of penetrating the kitchen-window, it collided with the masonry beneath it. There was a 'ping' as the bullet ricocheted, and returned in the direction from whence it came. A split-second after leaving the gun, the bullet hit Jimmy in his lower abdomen.

Pain shot through the lower half of his body. It travelled along the nerves and blood vessels until his brain was ambushed with news of a catastrophic injury. His mouth and vocal-cords, so unable to produce sounds just a few minutes earlier, let out screams which were so high-pitched and mournful, they could only have been made by a man who had shot off his own testicle.

19

❧❧❧

Hospital

Jimmy had emergency surgery on his groin and other surgeries on his broken jaw, his gums and palate, and the lacerations to his face and head. Several of his ribs were fractured, as were bones in his hands and wrist. His nose was broken, he had puncture-wounds to his waist, and he had concussion. With so much going on, the doctors heavily sedated him for several days to allow the initial healing to begin while he slept.

When he regained consciousness, Jimmy was in extreme discomfort. Breathing through his nose was impossible, and breathing through his mouth was difficult because his jaws were wired shut. His doctors were concerned that a build-up of fluids in his stomach could trigger vomiting, and lead to drowning, so a pipe was inserted through his crushed nose to remove the contents of his stomach.

He was fed through a tube, and a separate line delivered antibiotics to prevent infections. A catheter removed his urine. Its presence caused pain in an area that was already in distress. Actually, most of Jimmy was in distress. The only counterbalance came via a line that gently delivered into his arm a powerful cocktail of Class A drugs.

When he awoke from surgery, Milfoth was there. And in the days that followed, as he passed in and out of consciousness, she was there too.

He wasn't permitted to drink fluids, so his mouth went dry frequently, causing him discomfort. Over the next few days, Milfoth dipped a spongy material in water and held it to his dehydrated lips, with what looked like a short wooden stick from an ice-pop. She spread balm gently on his lips to prevent them from splitting, and moisturiser on his swollen face. She rubbed hand-cream on the parts of his hands that were not covered by bandages. Jimmy couldn't smell the cream, but he appreciated the gentle, sensuous, feminine touch.

'I brought your toiletries bag. It's there in your locker,' she said. 'I'll ask the doctor when it might be OK to brush your teeth.'

Jimmy raised a thumb in a sign of appreciation.

Propped up in his bed, he looked down at Milfoth, busily making his hands feel better. This wasn't the stern, argumentative, perma-scowl person he had lived with for several years. This was more like the person he had married: pretty, kind and attentive.

He wanted her to know how much he appreciated her tenderness. He closed his fingers on hers, and held them until she stopped what she was doing. She looked at their joined hands, and then at his face. For a moment their eyes met, and she smiled. Then she looked away, as if embarrassed.

Jimmy thought about Milfoth, out having a good time on *that* night. Maybe she had done nothing wrong. Maybe she was the victim of someone else's inappropriate behaviour – a high-testosterone individual, of course. Maybe she had deserved his support, not his scorn. He resolved that it was time to put that bitter episode behind them.

How could he have tried to kill this beautiful person? He felt overcome by guilt, and tears filled his eyes. She tried to continue applying cream to his hands, but he held her fingers tight. She looked up to see he was crying.

'I'm sorry,' he tried to say – but all she could hear was an indecipherable hiss.

Somehow she understood what he wanted to say. She stood up, rubbed the side of his face with the back of her fingers, and kissed him on the cheek. 'The consultant wants to speak with you,' she said. 'I'll let her know you're ready.'

Alone in the room, Jimmy had time to contemplate the events that had led him to St James's Hospital. *What have I become? That* question seemed to follow him from crisis to crisis.

He pondered the double-edged sword of testosterone. The surge of the hormone had given him the strength and aggression to kill his attacker, and protect his family. But it also fuelled a very destructive and violent impulse. For the first time, he understood *roid-rage*.

There was a knock on the door. A sombre-looking consultant entered, sat beside Jimmy's bed, and explained the full extent of his injuries. She took extra time to discuss the loss of a testicle. She spoke softly, and seemed to assume that this would be a greater loss to Jimmy than he seemed to feel it was.

'We believe it will not overly impact on your ability to have children,' she said.

That wasn't a concern for Jimmy.

'When your injuries have healed in the coming months, we propose bringing you back in for a testicular prosthesis.' She delivered the options as casually as a salesperson discussing running shoes. 'We can offer you a selection of sizes. Some are made of a kind of rubber called reinforced silicone elastomer. Some feel solid. Others are filled with a gel, which makes them feel slightly soft.'

Jimmy could only feel disappointment that he was unable to crack a joke about it all.

She continued: 'Because of your injury, you will be naturally low in testosterone. This could hamper the healing of your wounds. Basically, your body needs to form new tissues, and that is done through an interrelationship between hormones and nutrition. So I will recommend that we supplement your testosterone levels, artificially.'

Jimmy raised a thumb of approval.

As the consultant rose to leave, Jimmy clicked his fingers to get her attention.

'Yes, Jimmy,' she asked. 'You have a question?'

Jimmy pointed towards his bedside locker, and the consultant opened it to see what he wanted. 'Is it your toiletries bag?' she asked, and Jimmy raised his thumb to indicate 'Yes'.

'Would you like me to get something from it for you?' she asked.

Jimmy turned his thumb down to indicate no, and reached out his hand for the bag. She placed it on his chest gently, and left.

With the limited range of finger movements that was available to him, Jimmy pried open the zip of his toiletries bag. His better hand rummaged inside, and emerged with a pre-filled syringe covered in some eastern European language. It was from the Serbian website, and he hoped that they had had the decency to fill the syringe with the volume of testosterone that he had paid for.

He fumbled with the cellophane, and then the protective cover. With his right thumb on the plunger, he pointed the needle to his left shoulder, and injected his deltoid muscle.

On his bedside locker stood a yellow plastic container marked 'Sharps'. Jimmy dropped the expended syringe through a hole in the blue lid.

*

Several days later, the consultant gave permission to the Gardaí to interview Jimmy. Inspector McClean entered the room with a uniformed Garda and a suited man. McClean asked Milfoth to leave the room – which she did, reluctantly.

'How are you today, Jimmy boy?' asked McClean, loudly – as if Jimmy's hearing had also been damaged.

Jimmy could do little more than raise a thumb.

'Good,' shouted McClean. 'I hear you'll make a full re-co-ve-ry.' McClean seemed to think his words needed extra enunciation.

McClean introduced Garda Helen Sweeney from the Press Office, and Dan Sleator, his head of communications, in the suit.

'Jimmy, we would like to commend you for your bravery. What you did that night in your garden was quite a feat,' said McClean.

Jimmy indicated his acceptance of the praise by raising his thumb again.

'You don't have to try to speak,' said McClean. 'I know that's very difficult for you at the moment. But we would like to ask you a few questions. Your doctors said you should be strong enough by now.'

Jimmy raised a thumb.

'Here,' said Garda Sweeney. She handed him a notebook with the words 'Yes' and 'No' written in large letters. 'Just point to the appropriate word if we ask you a question.'

McClean continued: 'Jimmy, we would like to portray this event in a certain way in the media. William "Gunner" McNamara was a thug who intimidated a lot of people. We think your . . . victory . . . over him . . . you being – and I hope you don't mind me saying it – an older man, unarmed . . . we think it will inspire younger men in the community to stand up to people like Gunner. We think it will help them fight back against the drug-pushers and the thugs. So we would like to have a piece run about you. Y'know: "Brave dad who stood up to the bullies".'

Jimmy held up the notebook and pointed to the 'No'.

Dan Sleator stepped forward, and also spoke in a raised voice. 'Hello, Jimmy. We're thinking of using a photo of you, like you are now: all bandaged up, but looking heroic. It would appear like a leak to one of the papers: we have a journalist in mind who does us the odd favour. We'd have a quote from a "source close to the hero dad" saying you're glad to have stood up to the scum.'

Jimmy held up the notebook again, and pointed to the 'No'.

Garda Sweeney stood forward and took her turn to convince Jimmy. 'I suppose, Jimmy, we have a special interest in Gunner. We believe he and his gang may have caused the death of two of our members recently. We want them to know that even the toughest of them can be beaten by, y'know, an average man like yourself.'

'No', again.

McClean took a deep breath, then let it out slowly. 'We would really like it if you agreed to this, Jimmy,' he said. 'It would provide a nice bookend to this sorry story. If not, we have to keep the file open and keep asking awkward questions. So help us out, huh?'

Jimmy exhaled loudly. Instead of pointing to the notebook again, he took a pen from Garda Sweeney, and drew something on the page. When he'd finished, he held up the notebook to show the others. It was a drawing of the back of a hand with the middle finger raised.

McClean shook his head sadly. 'OK, Dan, you'd better go,' he said, and the younger man left the room. McClean continued: 'Jimmy, we do have a few other questions to ask you. We're trying to understand why Gunner would have attacked you. Any idea?'

Jimmy shrugged his shoulders.

'Had you met him before?' asked McClean.

Jimmy pointed to 'No'.

McClean asked again: 'Did you meet him before the night in the garden, either socially, or in some other way?'

Jimmy pointed to 'No' again.

McClean looked to Garda Sweeney with disappointment, and then turned to Jimmy again. 'Y'see our information suggests that you and he sat in the hot-tub together several times in the local gym.'

Jimmy didn't like the sound of the question, but was able to hide his concern beneath his bandages. He shrugged his shoulders.

'What about Hank Savage? Did you know him?' asked McClean.

Jimmy shrugged.

'Ever meet him before?' asked Sweeney.

Jimmy pointed to 'No'.

Sweeney stepped towards Jimmy. 'Y'see, we're trying to find out what happened to Hank Savage. We think he may have been killed by Gunner, but we're not sure. We would ask him, but he died at your house. Now, that wouldn't necessarily be significant, if you had no connection with Hank. And you said you never met Hank, right?'

Jimmy nodded in the affirmative.

'But our information suggests that you and Hank met more than once in The Bird Flanagan,' said McClean.

There was a silence in the room as both cops looked to Jimmy for a response. But he offered little more than a shrug.

McClean turned to Garda Sweeney. 'Helen, did you have a ballistics question for Jimmy?'

'Yes,' she replied. 'Jimmy, what puzzles us is how the shot that injured you was fired. We had assumed that Gunner fired it, but the shot was fired at the end of the struggle, and Gunner was more or less deceased at that point. So it's unlikely to have been him.' She looked at Jimmy, but he remained motionless. A feeling of dread rose in his stomach.

'And then we wondered if a third party might have been involved,' she continued. 'But the only other fingerprints we found on the gun – on the trigger and the grip – were yours.' The two Gardaí stared at Jimmy, waiting for a reaction, but there was none.

McClean took over the theorising. 'So, Jimmy, it seems that you may have fired the shot, but how? You didn't shoot yourself from close range. It was a ricochet. And we found the ricochet-mark just below the kitchen-window, where your wife says she was working at the time.'

Jimmy stared at the two cops, who in turn stared back at him from the end of his bed. They waited patiently for a response. Jimmy took the notebook, and scribbled a note on it: 'PR guy.'

'Ah, of course,' said McClean.

He opened the door and beckoned to Sleator, who returned to the room and spoke as if he had never left. 'So, we'll go with the story then. Probably in tomorrow's paper, but maybe the next day. OK with everyone?'

Sleator smiled and turned to leave, followed by his two colleagues. They were interrupted when Jimmy rapped his pen on the notebook. 'Yes, Jimmy?' asked Sleator.

Jimmy scribbled a note: 'Photo?'

'Don't worry about that,' said Sleator. 'We got that earlier when you were asleep.'

20

⋘⋘⋘

Convalescence

The recovery period was slow, but Jimmy didn't mind. After the dramatic events of the months before, he appreciated the period of quiet at home. With Gunner dead, he no longer feared for his life. He couldn't think of anyone else who might want to attack him.

The quiet life also suited his recovery from concussion. He had frequent headaches, and the doctors encouraged him to rest as much as possible. He was encouraged to limit screen-time, bright lights, and vigorous exercise.

Initially, his energy levels were low. The pureed food he consumed every day through a straw placed inside his wired jaw contained insufficient calories for him to maintain his weight.

He felt as though he was wasting away. Losing fat was a welcome development, but not muscle mass. He set himself a goal of five hundred press-ups, five hundred sit-ups, and five hundred squats per day. It was against medical advice, and more than he had ever attempted before, but he figured that a hundred of each, every third waking hour, would be achievable.

It was a struggle, but after several weeks he achieved his goal, and upped his target to eight hundred of each exercise per day; a hundred every second hour, on average. Weeks later, he increased the goal to a thousand of each exercise per day. He bought some dumbbells second hand, and used them to strengthen his biceps and improve his squats.

He found a punchbag on a free-trade website, and hung it from the apple tree in the back garden. There, he practised the punches and kicks he had learned months before in the gym.

The testosterone supplements helped. His strength had markedly increased over the months, and his physique had also improved. This motivated him to work harder. He was now injecting himself with around 400mg of testosterone per week, and smearing another 350mg each week on his torso. The injected material continued to arrive from the Serbian website, but the testosterone sachets were 'legitimate', having been prescribed by his consultant following his shooting injury. Jimmy had learned to stop taking any steroids ten days before each 'legitimate' blood-test, so that his testosterone levels appeared lower than they actually were. That way, he was found to have 'a medical need' for the drug, and he secured a long-term prescription for it.

Although his consumption of the steroid was still less than what some body-builders might take, it was more than four times the dosage he had started out on. The results of his mail-order blood-tests reflected this. His testosterone levels had reached 30 nanomoles per litre: five times higher than his first reading, and around 50 percent higher than what some 'experts' considered optimal.

He worried that he could be overdosing, particularly because he wasn't confident in the product he received from Serbia. This supplement could be stronger than it should be, or weaker; he couldn't tell, because the instructions were written in the Cyrillic alphabet. Despite his doubts, he found it difficult to cut back on the steroid while the benefits seemed so obvious. His confidence was strong now. He had regained his self-belief.

Also, he appeared to be experiencing few of the side-effects associated with juicing. His hair remained intact, and he hadn't suffered an outburst of acne. However, his sleep was still affected. He found himself awake most nights at around 4 AM, largely because – according to his consultant - his central nervous system was struggling to cope with the onslaught of testosterone on his biological systems.

In addition, he needed to pee small amounts frequently each night – which, worryingly, was consistent with an enlarged prostate gland. Most days he napped in the afternoon, to compensate for the nocturnal disturbances.

He introduced long periods of fasting most days, to further reduce his body fat. He started to use a nicotine nasal spray to suppress his appetite during the periods that he deprived himself of food. Then he upped his consumption of protein shakes and carb shakes to build muscle mass during his feeding-windows. Because of the fasting and the nicotine supplement, he felt his short- and long-term memory improving.

He found yoga classes on YouTube, and worked on his flexibility each day. He did his tap therapy every morning and evening, telling himself: 'I may be lucky to be alive, but I make my own luck.'

His measured his body fat at eight percent, which was unhealthily low, but he enjoyed the look of his new sinewy physique – which was reminiscent of how he had looked as a teenager. One afternoon while watching *The Simpsons*, he realised he was progressing towards 'a Ned Flanders body': a physique that was hardly noticeable when he wore a shirt, but when the shirt came off, he looked ripped.

Nevertheless, he continued to avoid social situations, principally because he didn't enjoy the sudden fame, or infamy, associated with having beaten a man to death. Also, he found non-verbal communication frustrating. Mostly he remained in his house, drinking smoothies, exercising, stretching and sleeping. He had no visitors; this didn't bother him, although he worried about what social isolation might do to his mental health.

Most days, the only company he had was Bonnie. The little dog was affectionate and non-judgemental. They slept alongside each other on the sofa every day, and on his bed whenever Byron was away. They played together in the garden and in the park, and went on long walks together. He had grown to love Bonnie.

Financially, however, Jimmy was in a bind. The three-month suspension that had been granted on his mortgage payments had expired, and he didn't know where he was going to get his next payment. When the wires came off his jaws, one of the first people he called was Monica – to see how his TV proposal had been received.

'No decision has been made, Jimmy, but I wouldn't get your hopes up,' she said. She sounded bothered that he had called her, and only made passing reference to his injuries. 'I've got to be honest with you, Jimmy: I'm not sure if your lifestyle is compatible with the image we like to project of our station.'

'My lifestyle?' asked Jimmy, through a sudden flush of anger. 'What do you mean?'

'I don't know what you're up to, Jimmy,' she said. 'But first, you're involved in a so-called abduction. Next, you're in an altercation with one of Dublin's most dangerous criminals.'

'Yes, all stemming from a show that I made for your station,' Jimmy shot back. 'My work for you put my life in danger. You should show a lot more concern.'

'Yeah, whatever,' she replied. 'If you'd like to show us how your work for us led to you being "abducted", I'm sure our HR department will be happy to consider a compensation package.'

Jimmy was silent. Monica excused herself, and ended the call. Jimmy exhaled loudly, and swore. *I'm Offended* was his best hope of earning a living. There was nothing else in the pipeline.

21

✺✺✺

Spoils of War

Although his finances concerned him, Jimmy found that having killed a man gave him confidence. If he was able to overcome an armed thug in his garden, he should be able to find a solution to his money challenges.

One day, he recalled an important detail from media coverage in the wake of Hank's death: Gardaí believed his gang had removed money and drugs shortly before they raided several of Hank's premises. Further coverage after Gunner's death said he had a gun, cash and drugs from his flat, but not in sizeable quantities. So where was Hank's cash?

He needed to find Davey and Midget, but he didn't even know their full names. He didn't know where they lived, and he didn't have the necessary contacts in the Gardaí or the underworld to help him find them.

He started to take slow drives through Crumlin, Dolphin's Barn, Rialto, Inchicore and Drimnagh, looking for the two men. For hours on end, he drove through housing estates, and parked outside supermarkets, chippers, off-licences, pubs and bookies. He took Bonnie on long walks in those areas, looking for them.

Inadvertently, his walks became a tour of notable deaths that had happened in the area since he had moved in. He passed by the Herberton apartments, where a German student had died from stab-wounds on the night of a party. He passed the chipper in Drimnagh where two

Polish men had died after receiving screwdriver injuries to their temples. Near the Luas line, he saw a cross marking the spot where a young man had been shot in a gangland dispute. Nearby, under a bridge over the canal, another cross remembered two homeless people who had drowned there one cold night.

His mood was lightened at the flats in Pimlico, when he saw something looking out from a top-floor balcony. It was a horse.

His mood was also lightened by the recognition that seemed to greet him wherever he went in the area. He was now a sinister-looking figure, all dressed in black, and in shades, with a small white dog on a lead. Some men needed a big dog to feel threatening; others didn't have to try. Locals seemed to understand that he was a tough guy who should not be crossed. People stayed out of his way. Even the hard boys – the sort who walk around with their hands down the front of their tracksuit pants, as if they are hiding a pistol – grunted a deferential 'Hello'. For the first time, he felt respected in his own community – and he liked it.

The long walks were good for Jimmy's aerobic fitness, but they were tiring, and even Bonnie started to hide when Jimmy produced the leash. Still, there was no sign of Davey or Midget.

Then Jimmy remembered something Davey had said in the back of the van on the day of the abduction. Davey said he had visited Joey Watt's girlfriend Samantha, and their daughter Coleen, every week.

Jimmy had interviewed Samantha for the last edition of *The Redeemeables*, and remembered where she lived. He decided against approaching her directly, in case this spooked Davey; instead, he would stake out the house. If Davey visited once a week, he would make sure to be there when it happened.

Samantha lived in a red-brick terraced cottage on one of the side streets near the St Teresa's Gardens flats. Jimmy parked his car across the street, giving himself a good view of the front door, and waited.

He saw that Samantha took Coleen to the crèche at the nearby Mercy Family Centre on weekday mornings. He followed her the first and second mornings, and again when she left the house to collect Coleen at lunchtime. He followed her to the nearby Lidl, and back again to her house, but there was no sign of Davey.

He found Samantha's life somewhat sad. She seemed so burdened for someone who was barely out of her teens. She always wore patterned leggings that stretched over her plump thighs, and each morning pushed

Coleen's buggy in a hurried fashion. There was no sign of joy on her face, except when she lit a cigarette outside the crèche with other young mothers. Coleen always seemed to be reaching into a bag of Tayto.

He found the stakeout of Samantha's home boring and time-consuming. From one of the houses, the pleasant sound of piano-music wafted into the air. He recognised one of the pieces as Beethoven's *Fur Elise*, a gateway composition for any moderately serious piano player. It raised his mood somewhat, but overall he disliked being confined to his car for hours on end.

On the third day, Jimmy saw Davey. He left the house in the afternoon with Samantha and Coleen, and the three went to the nearby playground at Weaver Square. Davey showed endless patience as Coleen went up a short ladder and came down a slide into his open arms. Again and again they did it. Davey shared a kiss with Samantha, and they both kissed the toddler. They looked like a regular family.

Jimmy concluded that Davey was no longer just a weekly visitor at Samantha's: they were a couple, and he had moved in. *That's good,* he said to himself. *A man is more vulnerable when he has a family.*

The next day, Davey left the house in the late morning. Carrying a bag, he walked swiftly to the bus-stop and got the 150 into town. Jimmy followed on his bike. He watched as Davey alighted at Hawkins Street, and followed as he walked across O'Connell Bridge to the boardwalk along the Bachelor's Walk side of the Liffey.

Standing on the bridge, Jimmy watched for the next two hours as Davey was approached by strangers, engaged in conversations, and transacted deals.

*

The next morning, Jimmy waited until Samantha left the house with Coleen for the crèche. Once they were out of sight, he got out of his car, donned a backpack, put on a baseball cap, and pulled on black leather gloves.

He crossed the road, and banged on the door loudly. 'Davey, open the door, I'm after forgetting me keys!' he shouted in his best "Samantha" accent. There was no sign of life inside the house, so Jimmy banged again, louder, and screeched through the letterbox: 'Davey, open the bleedin' door, would ye! I forgot me keys!'

Through the frosted glass of the front door, Jimmy saw movement. He banged on the door again. 'Hurry up, wud ye!'

A voice from inside shouted: 'All right, all right, I'm coming! Hold yer bleedin' horses!'

The door opened. Inside stood a sleepy-looking Davey, in a T-shirt and boxer shorts. It took him a moment to realise that it wasn't Samantha, and he tried to close the door, but Jimmy was too quick for him. In one movement, he blocked the door with the outside of his right foot, and took a step into the house with his left. He grabbed Davey by the throat and slammed him against the wall. Davey stiffened, and looked scared.

'If I wanted to kill you, what would you be now?' growled Jimmy into Davey's face.

'Wha'? What?' said Davey, trembling.

'If I wanted to kill you, what would you be right now?' Jimmy asked again, in a menacing tone.

'Wha'? I dunno.'

'What would you be?' said Jimmy, raising his voice suddenly. 'If I wanted to kill you, what would you be?'

'I . . . I dunno,' shouted Davey. 'D . . . dead?'

'Yes, dead!' said Jimmy, applying extra pressure to Davey's throat. 'Very dead. And are you?'

'What?' said Davey, both confused and frightened. 'Am I what?'

'Are you dead?'

'N . . . no, I'm not. I'm not dead.'

'That's right,' said Jimmy. 'You're not dead. So what does that mean?'

'I dunno.'

'It means I didn't come here to kill you,' said Jimmy. 'As long as you don't piss me off. Coz I might change my mind.'

'Right,' said Davey.

'You fuck with me,' said Jimmy, 'and I'll make sure that Coleen loses a second daddy in the space of a year. Y'hear me?'

'Y . . . yeah,' said Davey.

'I might even do a job on Samantha. Do you understand?'

'Yes.'

'Good,' said Jimmy, relaxing his grip on Davey's throat. 'Now move it,' he said, and pointed Davey in the direction of the sitting room.

A worn faux-leather couch lay just inside the door. Davey sat on it, but was pulled to his feet again by Jimmy. 'Sit over there,' he said, pointing at another couch further into the room. Jimmy sat on the seat closest to the door. He kept one hand in his jacket pocket, as if he was holding a weapon. 'Anyone else in the house?' Jimmy asked.

'No,' said Davey.

Jimmy looked around the room. From his previous visit to the house, he remembered how the large TV dominated the corner nearest the window. A play-pen and some toys occupied another corner. The walls were bare, as before, except for a child's handprints, which were sellotaped to the plaster. A photograph of Joey now rested on the mantelpiece, in a frame that was labelled 'Dad'.

An electric piano had been added to the room, adorned by handwritten music notes, and a printed copy of *Fur Elise*. 'Who's the musician?' asked Jimmy.

'I am,' said Davey. 'I write my own songs, and stuff.'

'Where did you learn to play the piano?' asked Jimmy.

'I learned myself,' said Davey. 'Learned off the internet and YouTube.'

'Very impressive,' said Jimmy.

'It's just logic,' said Davey. 'It's just the major keys, and the basic chords, and a bit of a beat. Then practice.'

Jimmy nodded in agreement. 'You know why I'm here?' he asked.

'No,' said Davey.

'Fucking think!' said Jimmy, in a raised voice.

'I don't know,' said Davey quietly.

Jimmy leaned forward, as if getting a better look at Davey. 'Davey, I've told you I will do you no harm, and I will do no harm to Samantha or Coleen. But that's if you don't waste a minute of my time. So don't fuck with me, coz if I change my mind I will hurt you all.'

'I don't know what you want,' said Davey, looking deeply uncomfortable.

'Where's the money?' asked Jimmy.

'I don't know.'

Jimmy looked at Davey with disgust. 'Jesus Christ, Davey, I'm trying to be fair here. I'm going to count to three, and you'd better tell me. One, two, th – '

'Why do you want to know?' shouted Davey.

'Because it's mine,' retorted Jimmy.

'How's it yours?'

'Because I'm the boss here. I'm the gaffer,' said Jimmy. 'It belongs to me.'

'What makes you the boss?'

'Because I killed Hank. And I killed Gunner. That leaves me in charge. Unless you want to challenge me – and if so, I will kill you too. Understand?

Davey didn't answer.

'So the gang's money is my property,' said Jimmy.

'Yeah, but me and Midget rescued it, otherwise the cops would have it,' said Davey defiantly.

'I admire that, and I will look kindly on that,' said Jimmy, calmly. 'You will be rewarded – *when* I have it.'

'Me and Midget took the risk and got it. What did you do?'

'What did *I* do? What did I do? You fuckers kidnapped me. You beat me, and you tortured me, and if it wasn't for a stroke of luck, I would have been found dead in a ditch with my balls in my mouth. So you little fucks owe me compensation.'

'I tried to be nice to you that day, I did,' said Davey.

'I know that. But you weren't willing to save my life, so don't expect my gratitude. Fuckin' chicken-shit. Gunner wasted your best mate, and you wouldn't waste Gunner. You owed it to Joey, and you didn't do it.'

Davey went quiet.

'You wouldn't even let me do it. All you had to do was give me the gun,' said Jimmy.

Davey looked ashamed, and stared at the ground.

'Where's Midget?' asked Jimmy.

'He done a runner to England, he did,' said Davey. 'He has a brother over there.'

'When you speak with him again, tell him I want to see him,' said Jimmy.

Davey didn't answer.

'So,' said Jimmy, 'where's the money?'

'It's all gone. I went on the lash, I did.'

'Don't waste my fucking time,' said Jimmy. He lifted up a cushion that was beside him on the couch and looked around the room. 'Where's the money?'

'Not here.'

'Davey, I don't believe you,' said Jimmy. 'I don't believe you – which means I'm going to search everywhere in this house before I leave. That means every inch of the attic, under the beds, in the wardrobes, in the child's toy-box. I will rip open the sofas, and the mattresses, and I will rip up the floorboards: whatever I have to do. And that's gonna take longer than it takes Samantha to get back from the Mercy Centre.'

Jimmy paused to let that scenario play out in Davey's mind.

'And I don't think that she will be as calm as you are,' continued Jimmy slowly, 'which means I'll have to pacify her. And I was hoping to avoid that. Davey, if you love her, you're going – '

'It's in the coal bunker out the back,' blurted Davey.

Jimmy nodded his approval. 'Good. OK, let's have a look.'

Jimmy followed Davey through the kitchen into a tiny yard at the back. A tricycle and a bike with stabilisers stood beneath a short clothes-line. There were some flower-pots, an outdoor sweeping-brush, and a coal-bunker.

'It's in there,' said Davey, pointing.

'Get it out,' said Jimmy, making it clear that he was not going to get his hands dirty.

Davey lifted the lid of the bunker, and moved much of its contents with a garden trowel. He reached inside, and pulled out a football bag, covered in soot. Jimmy beckoned to Davey to put it on the kitchen table. He cleared a space between dirty dishes for the bag, and opened it.

Inside were bundles of fifty-euro notes, all shrinkwrapped. Jimmy had never seen so much cash before. He tried to remain calm, but inside, a flush of excitement warmed his body. He took off his backpack and laid it on the table. 'Fill it up,' he said to Davey.

'Fuck off,' said Davey, and walked into the corner of the room. He couldn't watch his money being stolen.

Jimmy helped himself to the stash. He fired the bundles into his backpack until it was bursting at the seams.

Davey turned around and said quietly: 'It's bad form, crims stealing off other crims.'

'If you had done the right thing by Joey, this wouldn't be happening.'

Davey seemed to physically weaken each time that charge was levelled against him.

Every cell in Jimmy's body was alive. If Davey wanted a fight, he would take him on. If he opted for an argument, Jimmy had point after point lined up on his tongue. If all Davey could do was whimper from the corner, Jimmy would treat him with the requisite contempt. 'You scumbags put my life in danger. I should hack your fuckin' head off!'

Davey had little opposition to offer. 'What's my commission?' he asked.

'I left you a bundle,' said Jimmy, trying unsuccessfully to close his bag. The uppermost bundle was preventing the zip from joining. He took it from his bag, and threw it back into Davey's. 'There, I'm leaving you two bundles.'

Davey didn't react.

'Say thank you, you little shit,' said Jimmy. 'I could still leave you with nothing.'

Davey still didn't react.

'With all this money, how come you're selling bags down on the boardwalk?' asked Jimmy.

Davey shrugged. 'Have to do sumptin'. That's all I know what to do.'

'Do the Deveneys know you're selling there?'

Davey shrugged. 'Yeah, I told them. I have to throw them a few bob every week.'

As Jimmy slung the backpack over his shoulder, he thought of another question: 'Tell me something before I go. When you fuckheads kidnapped me that day, what was that liquid you made me drink?'

Davey smiled weakly at the thought. 'They call it *ayahuasca*. It's some drink made by the Indians in South America. A few gallons of it arrived in a shipment of coke. Hank thought he could make some money from it, but there doesn't seem to be much of a market; just a few hippies in Wicklow were interested.'

'What did they want to do with it?' asked Jimmy.

'They go to secret locations and do ceremonies and stuff. Sounds stupi'. Anyways, Hank wanted to see how it worked, so they decided to try it out on you.'

'So I was a guinea pig?' sighed Jimmy.

'Yeah, but they didn't give you much. It was mostly whiskey. Did ye see any visions on it?'

'Yeah,' said Jimmy. 'It was nasty shit in the beginning, but when ye left me alone and I warmed up, it was kinda nice. Deep thoughts, y'know.'

'I never tried it,' said Davey. 'It looks boring. And I hear it makes ye puke. Yer not going to go out with yer mates for a few scoops of it.'

'Do you have a number for the buyer?'

Davey shrugged.

'Just give me the fucking number,' said Jimmy, impatiently.

'Or wha'?'

'Or I'll take back the two bundles I've left you!' Jimmy seemed annoyed at having to negotiate.

Davey took his phone off the table and searched for the number. 'He calls himself "Brother Amos". It's 086 . . . .' Jimmy scribbled the number on the back of a child's drawing using a crayon, and put it in his pocket.

'Are ye going to start supplying him?' asked Davey.

'It doesn't sound like there's much of a market for it,' said Jimmy. 'But let's see.'

'Are we still a gang, then?' asked Davey.

'Maybe. I'll let you know.'

'I don't think the Deveneys will be happy to hear that,' said Davey.

The thought of being the focus of the Deveneys again caused a pang of concern for Jimmy. 'They don't have to know,' he said, and left the house.

Every atom in Jimmy's body wanted to scream as he crossed the street to his car. How much money did he have? He didn't know. But it was all his.

He threw his bounty onto the passenger-seat, and pulled away slowly, so as not to draw any attention to himself. Once he was a good way down the street, he let out a shout at the top of his lungs: 'Yeeee-haaaah! What the fuck? What the fuuuuuuck! You're a fucking legend, Jimmmmmmmmy! Wah-whooo!'

As he came to a stop at the intersection with Donore Avenue, a woman stepped off the pavement and crossed in front of the car. She waved politely, as if to say thanks for stopping. It was Samantha. She didn't recognise Jimmy in the car, with his baseball-cap pulled down low. He waved back in an equally polite way. Suddenly he felt bad. He had just stolen from her home. He wondered which of them had the greater need for the money.

Scarcely more than half an hour after the raid, Jimmy was tending Mrs Kennedy's front garden. He mowed the lawn, then raked and disposed of the clippings, while his senior neighbour complimented his work to anyone who happened to be passing.

Jimmy had stashed his loot in her shed. A quick count suggested there was €10,000 in each bundle, and he had taken twenty bundles from Davey. He could hardly believe it: €200,000. For the first time in his life, he was ahead. Ahead! He wanted to jump around Mrs Kennedy's garden, but he had to remain calm. He hadn't even decided when, or if, to tell Milfoth.

As he put Mrs Kennedy's cuttings into the composter, he tried to assess €200,000 in the context of his life. It was a relatively small amount of money compared to the Lotto win he had so hoped for in the previous months. But in any single year of work, he had never cleared €50,000 after tax – and often far less. He calculated how long it had taken him to earn his last €200,000: it came to five years – six, if he included time spent unemployed. And this didn't account for the cost of working in terms of food, clothes and transport.

So his morning's work was the equivalent of six years of toil. 'Six years of putting up with arseholes,' he said to himself. 'Six years of amending my work to suit the opinions of gobshites and politically correct fuckers. Six years of worry. Six years of anxiety. Six years of humiliation. Six years of suppressing my own true self, to fit into a world created by small-minded, difficult people. Six years! Six bloody years!' And he had just earned the equivalent in little more than fifteen minutes.

For the first time in his life he had 'fuck-you' money. He thought about all the people in the previous six years who had wounded him, and not suffered the consequences. Now he could shout 'Fuck you!' at them. And he would.

He was on the high of highs. It was as good as sex, but lasted much longer. He wondered why anyone would earn money legitimately, if they could just steal it. He understood career criminals now: the high from pulling off a job must be addictive.

Back in his own house, Jimmy couldn't sit still. He wandered from room to room, unsure of whether he should go out to celebrate, or just relax in his newfound financial security.

When Milfoth arrived home, she found him singing loudly in the front room. 'What's going on?' she asked suspiciously.

'Nothing, just heard a tune on the radio earlier,' said Jimmy, guiltily.

'Well, why don't you leave singing to the professionals?' she said, and left the room.

Jimmy thought about shouting 'Fuck you', but didn't.

He had a sudden urge to check the prices of cars. He had never owned a new car before; never even thought it could happen for him. But now he could have any one he wanted.

He opened his laptop and checked some car websites. A new Mercedes? No, he would feel too self-conscious.

Maybe a used Mercedes for €40,000? It still seemed too much to pay for a car.

Something for €20,000? That would be more in his comfort-zone.

Ten thousand? Why would he stay at that level if he didn't need to? His cash seemed to cry out from Mrs Kennedy's shed, asking to be spent.

He clicked on myhome.ie, as he had often done before, to check what properties were for sale in Rathmines. Around the Palmerston Park area, even now, they were all out of his reach. All except for one house – which was a wreck.

'Clara' was a small old house that had been the subject of a prolonged probate dispute, and had lain empty for years. Now it had come to the market 'as a dream project for a tasteful restorer', according to the blurb. Jimmy laughed that the only house he could afford in his desired area wasn't even fit for human habitation. But he still made an appointment to view it.

22

⊰⊱⊰

Kindred Spirits

Danny phoned. 'The Americans are back in town,' he said. 'D'ye hear anything?'

'No,' said Jimmy. 'I'm not holding out much hope, either.'

'Why don't we go over and show our faces in the studio?' asked Danny. 'Maybe make some excuse about collecting paperwork?'

'A lot of the team sent me cards when I was in hospital,' said Jimmy. 'We could go and meet them for lunch in the canteen?'

'Done,' said Danny, and set about organising the lunch for the following day.

It seemed strange for Jimmy to pass through the gates of TV Ireland again. It had been home to him for so many years, but now he felt very much an outsider.

That changed in the canteen where Jimmy was swarmed by his former colleagues. Each person greeted him with a hearty: 'How're ye, Horse!' Clearly, his recent exploits had attracted a degree of notoriety and mystique.

Nobody knew for certain whether Jimmy was a pure victim of thuggery, or if he had a side to him that they had not realised before. He dodged questions that might have put some of the rumours to rest. The scars around his eyes attracted positive attention from some of the females. He was reminded that women like bad boys.

'You've lost weight,' declared one of his former assistants.

'That was my special diet,' said Jimmy. 'Six weeks with me mouth wired shut.'

'I must try it sometime,' giggled the young lady.

'It was great,' cried Danny. 'Six weeks, and the fecker couldn't talk.' They all laughed.

Even those who chose not to take part in the welcome couldn't help watching what was going on. One of them was Monica. Jimmy made a point of waving over to her. She waved back politely, and looked away.

'There he is!' shouted a man with an American accent. Jimmy turned, to see Brad Kerkhakov arriving with his tray.

'This is the guy I told you about,' said Brad, turning to another American at his side. 'He killed a guy! Man, he killed a home-invader with his bare hands.' Brad put down his tray, and slammed his right fist into the palm of his hand for emphasis. 'No gun: just beat the guy's fucking brains out!'

His companion put down his tray. 'No way! Not even a gun. How did you do it?'

'Like this,' said Brad, raising and lowering his fist as if re-living the fight. 'Pow-pow-pow!'

'You're a hero, man,' said the other. 'I'd love to kill an intruder. Can I get a selfie?'

'Sure,' said Jimmy, and the three men posed, each with their fists raised.

'So, when are you back in action?' asked Brad.

'Oh . . . ' said Jimmy, not expecting the question, 'whenever someone needs me.'

'You gotta let us know,' said Brad. 'We're waiting to hear from you.'

'Hear from me about what?' asked Jimmy.

Brad looked at him with a puzzled expression. 'The project,' he said, as if Jimmy should know. 'Didn't you receive the offer?'

'No,' said Jimmy.

'We have it all ready to go to him,' said Monica, appearing suddenly at Brad's shoulder. 'We didn't want to send it until now, because we didn't want to put pressure on Jimmy during his recovery.'

'What's the offer?' asked Jimmy.

'It's what you asked for,' said Brad. 'We'll sign you up for three years of project development, reporting directly to our Executive VP in Austin.'

The vagueness of the term 'project development' excited Jimmy. It suggested room to roam; an opportunity to create his own niche. And he no longer had to answer to Monica.

'And we'll pilot *I'm Offended*,' said Brad. 'We can't make a full commitment until we see it in action. You understand.'

'Sure,' said Jimmy. Danny also nodded.

'The guys in Texas can't wait to meet you,' said Brad. 'Wait 'til they see the photo! We gotta get you guys over there soon.'

Jimmy and Danny exchanged smiles. Jimmy glanced at Monica, who could barely suppress a scowl. 'I'll send you the letter during the week,' she said, and walked away.

'Life is good,' Jimmy said to himself. 'Life is good.'

*

Jimmy found himself in Rathmines again, this time at a viewing of 'Clara'. It really was in poor condition. Another viewer arrived, then turned and left quickly. Jimmy didn't. He had a plan, and the poor condition of the property was a crucial factor in that plan.

'No,' said Milfoth, that evening. 'We're not moving.'

'Why not?' asked Jimmy with his arms outstretched. 'You always said you wanted to get out of Dublin 8.'

'Yes, but not to move into a condemned property!'

'That's a temporary state,' said Jimmy. 'We're going to fix it up.'

'Who's going to fix it up? You? You can't hammer a nail straight.'

'I will arrange for nails to be hammered straight,' said Jimmy, with confidence and calmness. It was time to tell her about the money.

'I have residual cash from my drug-dealing,' he said.

'What? How much?'

'Six figures,' said Jimmy, instinctively reluctant to reveal his finances to his wife.

'Well, give me half, and do what you want with the rest,' she said.

'I can't. I have to clean it first. If you and I start spending money, or even lodging large amounts in the bank, the cops and Revenue will be down on me. And it will be worse than just losing the money.'

Milfoth knew this made sense, but she explained that his point was defeated by the prospect of buying a house in an expensive area.

'If we sell this house, we can buy the house in Rathmines. They balance each other out,' said Jimmy.

'But it needs a lot of money . . . .'

'Yes,' he said. 'A great way to launder money is through home improvements. I get a builder in to knock a wall, put in new ceilings, put in insulation – all for cash. Who's to say I didn't do it all myself? Get the driveway done. Get the back and front gardens landscaped. Paint the place. All for cash. As far as anyone is concerned, I did it myself.'

Milfoth shook her head in disbelief.

'And then . . . ' said Jimmy. 'And then, after two years living there, we sell. A newly refurbished house close to Palmerston Park. It will make great money. And it's all tax-free, because there's no capital-gains tax on a principal residence. At that point, our money is clean.'

Milfoth shook her head again. 'No, we're not moving.'

'We've got to. We must. If you really want, we can move back here in two years' time. Two years in exile in Dublin 6, and you move back here debt-free. It's like getting a job in the Middle East for a couple of years, except you don't have to cover your head.'

'You move if you want to.'

'The plan requires your co-operation.'

'Just give me half the cash, thank you.'

Jimmy took a deep breath and shook his head. 'No.'

'Let's just stay where we are,' pleaded Milfoth. 'We're happy here.'

'We're not happy here.'

'Yes we are,' asserted Milfoth.

'We moved here by accident. You always wanted somewhere better. I always wanted somewhere better. Now's our chance.'

'I've grown to like the place,' she said.

'You'll grow to like the next place,' said Jimmy. 'And there's more to like.'

'You just want to be hanging out with doctors and lawyers, and sipping your Heineken in McSorley's,' she said, putting on a posh accent. She knew it would irritate him.

'That's not true,' said Jimmy.

'It is true. You're a snob and you've always been disappointed with yourself for moving here.'

'That's not true,' said Jimmy again.

'It is true, and you feel your family looks down on you because of where you ended up.'

'That's not true – and anyway I don't care what they think.'

'You do care. Not one of them came to visit you after you left hospital. Not even one. Your own family. What were they afraid of? That their car would be burned out if they parked outside our house?'

Jimmy brooded for a moment. He held his breath, and then slowly let it out. 'Can we discuss the exciting opportunity that awaits us, please?'

Milfoth had her own idea. 'Let's build a nice extension here. Let's just brighten up this place. Spend the cash here, where money goes much further. And with the money left over, buy a nice car. Go on a few nice holidays. Let's keep the same neighbours and friends, and just improve our quality of life.'

'No,' said Jimmy with conviction. 'I'm putting a bid on Rathmines tomorrow. Are you with me or not?'

'What if I'm not?'

Jimmy didn't want to lay down an ultimatum. He just shrugged, smiled and left the room.

The next day, Jimmy made an offer on 'Clara', and it was accepted. He put down a small cash deposit, and raced over to an estate agent in Dublin 8 to put their house on the market.

Milfoth wanted no part in what she called 'tarting up' her home so that it could be 'inspected by strangers'. 'Do it yourself,' she said, and disappeared with Byron and Bonnie to Kerry, on 'a stay of indefinite duration'.

Jimmy had a long list of cleaning jobs to complete before the house could be photographed for sale. He hoovered upstairs and downstairs, for the first time ever. He cleaned both bathrooms, also for the first time. And he removed many boxes of papers and placed them in the shed. He tidied up the garden and the patio, and hung flowers in a basket beside the front door.

Upstairs, he cleaned mirrors in the bathrooms and the bedrooms for his first time. He couldn't manage to clean them without leaving streaks, and he cursed the whole process.

The wardrobe in Milfoth's room had always been problematic. Because of the uneven floor in the old house, the wardrobe tilted forward and its door never closed properly. Jimmy decided to fix the lean by tilting it back and placing cardboard underneath its front feet. It was a heavy and tricky job, and he wished he had someone to help him.

As he lifted the front part of the wardrobe, he heard something slide from the top and wedge itself between the back of the wardrobe and the wall. Jimmy cursed again. Now he had the difficulty of getting the item out from behind the wardrobe without tilting the whole piece of furniture too far forward, and risking it crashing onto the floor.

He got his hand behind the wardrobe and the wall, and through a series of shunts, managed to get the item up and back onto the top of the unit. He checked what the item was, and saw that it was familiar. For the first time in years, he held Milfoth's worry-box.

Shortly after Byron was born, it became clear that Milfoth suffered from anxiety. One remedy suggested by her therapist was that she would write each of her worries on a piece of paper, and put them in a box. Then days or weeks later, when the worry had passed, she would take out the piece of paper and remind herself how she had felt at the time of writing the note, and ask herself how real or otherwise the worry had been. The idea was to enable her to see just how groundless many of her concerns were. She would then rip up the worry, leaving only current worries in the box. In solidarity, Jimmy had bought her a beautiful wooden box with an inscription on its lid that read: 'Don't worry, be happy'.

Jimmy knew that reading Milfoth's worries was akin to reading her diary or her private letters, but he couldn't resist the urge. The first note read: 'Worried that MIH might leave me. I think he is seeing someone else.'

Jimmy racked his brains. Was Milfoth seeing someone with the initials 'MIH'? His mind raced through the names of men she knew, but none seemed to be a match. The date on the note was four months earlier, when Jimmy's focus had been not on his wife, but on selling cocaine.

Jimmy picked up another note, dated around the same time, that read: 'Worried MIH has someone new. Out again, with no explanation where. Very sad.'

Suddenly Jimmy realised that the person referred to as 'MIH' was himself. The explanation was on another note – which helpfully linked the acronym to the words 'My Idiot Husband'.

So *Jimmy* was MIH. But that would suggest that Milfoth cared about their relationship. He found that difficult to believe.

He picked up another note: 'Very worried about MIH. Very down about no job. Hope he doesn't do anything stupid.'

The date coincided with times that Jimmy had considered suicide.

'Worried about MIH's mental state,' said the next note, dated a week later. 'Wish he would discuss with me or get help. Stupid men can't talk about their problems.'

Jimmy recalled how sad and alone he felt at the time, but he had no recollection of Milfoth trying to help him. But she must have tried, and he hadn't noticed.

The note was also a reminder of how much his mental state had changed in just a few short months. The confidence that had eluded him then, was now present in abundance. He had regained his masculinity.

Jimmy picked up another note. It was undated, and read: 'Paralysed with worry. Matter too serious to commit to paper. OMG MIH!' Jimmy guessed that it related to his criminal activity.

Another note, also undated, read: 'Can't believe what MIH puts me through. 'Worry' doesn't cover it. Too serious! Oh my God! Can't even write what I'm feeling.'

A note from his time in hospital read: 'Worried MIH will die, or won't fully recover. Praying for my love.'

Jimmy was surprised to see the 'l' word in Milfoth's notes, and he felt guilty. He had never appreciated her predicament. 'I wonder why she never said anything,' he said to himself.

*

Jimmy went to Rathmines to acquaint himself with his new environment. He walked the streets, just observing. He was disappointed to have to do it alone, but he viewed Milfoth's reluctance to move as just another process that had to be worked through.

He called on his new neighbours. On one side, the gates were closed, so he buzzed the intercom on the pillar.

'Hello?' came a refined voice.

'Hi, I'm James,' said Jimmy, adopting a more upmarket tone. 'I've just put a deposit on the house next door. I thought I might say hello.'

'Well that's very nice of you,' said the voice. 'I hope you will be very happy there.'

'Thank you,' said Jimmy, and waited for an invitation inside. Perhaps the gates would open, and tea would be served. On the lawn. But there was just an awkward silence.

'Well thank you,' said the voice, and the conversation concluded with a click.

On the other side, the gates were already open, and the man of the house was hosing down his new Jaguar F-Pace. Suddenly Jimmy felt self-conscious about his old Mercedes. It had an air of faded glory in Dublin 8, but in Dublin 6 it appeared a little shabby.

'I'm delighted the old house is getting sold,' said the man, in a broad south Dublin accent. 'I was going to buy it myself but it seemed so much work for such a small place.' The man seemed to be talking at Jimmy's scars.

'Well, nothing like a bit of hard work to make you love a place more,' said Jimmy, not even sure if he believed what he had just said.

'Roight,' said the neighbour. 'Well, lucky for you: you're probably very good with your hands.'

Jimmy wasn't sure if that was a compliment in this neighbourhood. 'Sure, I'll have a go,' he replied.

'Roight,' said the neighbour. 'Hey, you look familiar. What line of work are you in?'

Jimmy felt anxious. To be half-recognised for his recent exploits was a badge of honour in Dublin 8. But he didn't want his new neighbour linking him to a kidnapping and the killing of a drug-dealer. 'I'm in television production,' he said.

'Great. I know lots of people in RTÉ. I play golf with the DG.'

'Well, I'm over in TV Ireland,' said Jimmy sheepishly.

'Oh, I see,' said the neighbour, sharing Jimmy's disappointment.

'And what do you do yourself?' asked Jimmy.

'Oh, I'm over in Vincent's Private. A consultant radiologist.'

23

❧❧❧

North Side Return

Life was good. Financially and physically, Jimmy had recovered from recent setbacks, and now he felt strong. He drew up a new weight-resistance programme and went to the gym to start it. He put in a hard two hours, moving between push, pull and leg exercises, as well as some cardio. It was exhausting, but in a good way.

He downed a post-workout carb-shake and went into the sauna. He stood under the cold shower, and counted to sixty. His muscles felt hard as he moved to the steam room.

Despite this moment of peace, he felt an undercurrent of anger. With less focus on immediate issues, his mind had time to dwell on matters from the previous months. He thought about TV Ireland, and how they lacked loyalty; how Monica cut him off at the first sign of trouble. That still angered him.

The humiliation he had experienced at a succession of job interviews still annoyed him. He resented each of the interviewers: people who sat in judgement of him and denied him work he so badly needed.

And he remembered Colin Deveney and his henchman Igor: how they had entered his home and assaulted him and his wife. Deveney had damaged him in the eyes of his Milfoth and started a chain of events that ruined his business and nearly cost him his life. That burned inside him. It was a score he wanted to settle.

He was also angry at the estate agent about the house in Rathmines. They had called that morning saying that another bidder had made an offer that was €10,000 more than Jimmy's. 'But I've already bought the place,' said Jimmy. 'I've paid my deposit.'

'Sorry,' said the estate agent, and blamed an administrative error. They invited him to add €15,000 to his own bid if he wanted to stay in the race. Otherwise, they would return his deposit.

Jimmy had no way of knowing if there really was another bidder, or if he might be just bidding against himself. If he was still in his old job, he would like to do a sting on estate agents – although he doubted if any of them were redeemable.

The call put him in a predicament. If he didn't come up with another €15,000, he might lose his dream home. He was so near to achieving his goal, and yet so far from it. The cash he had in storage would just about cover the necessary renovation of the house, so couldn't be used for the deposit. He wouldn't qualify for a loan from any financial institution. He couldn't ask Milfoth. He doubted that Davey would be open to another shakedown, or that Midget would wander back into his life with another bag of cash.

He cursed Deveney, remembering how he had stolen €18,000 from him that night in his house. If that hadn't happened, he could make his bid now. He cursed Deveney again. If we were to lose his dream home, it would be because of Deveney.

Then he remembered Davey's comment that suggested that Deveney might be displeased to hear that Jimmy was still active as a dealer. Could he sit and wait for Deveney to come visiting again?

The rage burned inside Jimmy. Deveney! Deveney was the answer. It was time to sort him out. He started to formulate a plan.

*

Jimmy retrieved his old notebook from Mrs Kennedy's shed. In it, there was a code for Deveney's underground car-park. If the code hadn't changed, that would help him get inside the building. If the code had changed, his plan would have to be aborted. He was so nervous, that part of him wished for the latter.

He waited that evening on the Sheriff Street side of Spencer Dock. As darkness fell, he could see clearly – using binoculars – into Deveney's well-lit penthouse. There were six figures inside: far too many for him to control. Maybe it was time to forget about it all.

He took a long walk, down by the Point Square and back up by the convention centre. When he got back to Sherriff Street, he could see only two men in the penthouse. He waited a long time, and there was no sign of the others. He was sure that only Colin and Igor were still present.

Jimmy's stomach was in a knot as he drove down the back lane to the underground car-park. When he came to the gate, he keyed in the code that had granted him entry some months before. There was a long wait as the system seemed to deliberate on the validity of Jimmy's code. Eventually the gate opened and he drove in.

He waited in his car near the elevator until another resident arrived. As that person entered the elevator, so too did Jimmy. 'Top floor, please,' he said confidently, and the other person obliged.

As he arrived at Colin's door, his heart was pounding. Why was he here? Did he really want to do this? What exactly was his plan? It wasn't too late to back out.

He reminded himself that this was an all-or-nothing situation. He couldn't enter Colin's apartment half-heartedly. The risks were too high. He had to deliver the performance of his life; anything else could get him killed. He wondered if he was mad to do what he was doing, yet underneath it all, he felt excited. The adrenaline pumping through his system had an addictive quality. So too did the testosterone: he felt masculine. Men were designed to take risks. 'Who dares wins,' he said to himself as he knocked on the door.

Moments later, he was aware that he was being viewed through a peephole. The door opened, revealing a puzzled-looking Igor.

'Good evening,' said Jimmy with a smile. Before Igor could answer, Jimmy rammed two fingers into Igor's eyes. Then he slammed his elbow into Igor's throat, as he had been taught by his fellow gym member. He kicked hard into the side of Igor's kneecap, and the bigger man went down quickly, making choking noises and whimpering in pain. Jimmy entered the hallway and kicked the door closed behind him. He grabbed Igor's arm and twisted it behind his back. He took Igor's middle finger and bent it until it was at an impossible angle to the rest of his hand. It was the same manoeuvre Igor had performed on him in his own house. Igor let out a shout of pain.

'Move it,' said Jimmy, forcing Igor to his feet and pointing him towards the living room. Colin looked stunned as his door flew open and the two men entered. The large TV in the room had blocked out any sound of the attack, so Colin was unprepared.

Colin rose to his feet, but Jimmy ordered him to sit. 'And turn off that TV!' he shouted. 'You and I need to talk.'

Jimmy dumped Igor on the living-room carpet, at the angle where the two couches met. 'Don't move,' he said to Igor, 'or I'll really hurt you.'

Colin looked angry; his eyes darted around anxiously. 'What the fuck is going on?' he asked. 'Are you fucking crazy, to enter my home?'

'You're fucking right, I'm crazy!' shouted Jimmy. 'So, you better do exactly as I say.'

Colin raised his hands, as if to plea for peace. Then he lowered them, to grasp the TV remote control. 'I'll just turn this off.'

'Is anyone else here?' asked Jimmy, taking a seat on the unoccupied couch.

'No, it's just us,' said Colin calmly. 'Nobody to interrupt our conversation. Now, how can I help you?'

'Did you ever hear of M.A.D.' asked Jimmy.

Colin struggled to find an answer: 'M.A.D.? Mad? Did I ever hear of mad? Of course.'

'It stands for Mutually Assured Destruction,' said Jimmy with assurance. 'Did you ever hear of it?'

Colin looked back blankly. 'No,' he said.

Jimmy continued: 'During the cold war, the Americans and the Russians built up enough nuclear weapons to wipe out the other side many times over. The Americans said they could destroy the world 10 times over, whereas the Russians could only destroy the world seven times over. What did it matter? If war broke out, they would both be annihilated.'

'OK,' said Colin. 'Is that . . . how is that . . . ? What's this to do with us?'

Igor tried to raise himself off the carpet. 'Lie down, Igor,' said Jimmy in a threatening tone. 'Don't make me have to say it again.'

Jimmy returned his attention to Colin. 'You and I are in a Mutually Assured Destruction situation. You think you can kill me, and you're probably right. But I can kill you too. I can wipe you out, and every semblance of this sorry-ass piece-of-shit gang you have.' He pointed at Igor. 'I can wipe you out even from the grave. I have backers now: powerful people who want me alive and well.'

Colin looked unimpressed. 'Is that it?' he asked. 'Is that why you're here?'

Igor made a determined effort to stand. In a swift movement, Jimmy put his hands behind his head and grabbed a baseball bat from the top of his rucksack. *Whack!* He landed the weapon across Igor's back, causing him to cry out in pain and slump back down.

'I told you to lie down! I fucking told you!' shouted Jimmy, as he stood over Igor. 'Did I not tell him . . . ?' he repeated, turning to plead his case with Colin, but he had already darted for the door. Jimmy was even quicker. As Colin opened the door to leave, Jimmy landed his foot on it with force, causing it to slam shut again. He flung Colin against the wall and raised the baseball bat over his shoulder, ready to deploy it with full force across his head. The two men stared into each other's faces.

'Go on,' said Jimmy, 'give me an excuse. Just give me an excuse.' The muscles in his shoulders and arms twitched and he struggled to restrain them. Sweat poured from his brow. His face was red, and veins protruded from his temple. 'Just give me a reason, and I'll splatter your brains across your panoramic windows,' he said.

Colin was sweating too. He wanted to grab the bat, but Jimmy was so volatile and fit-looking, he couldn't be sure he could win that fight. 'It's fine,' he said. 'It's all fine. I'll go back to my seat.'

Jimmy heard a noise behind him, and out of the corner of his eye he saw movement from Igor's direction. He recognised the difficulty of taking on two men with just one weapon. He needed to disable one of them, if not both. He crashed the butt of the bat into Colin's face, drawing blood instantly. 'Fuck you, Colin,' he said, as he grabbed him by his shirt-collar and threw him back onto the couch where he had been sitting moments earlier.

Moving quickly, Jimmy went behind Igor as he rose up on all fours. He swung the bat with force between Igor's legs and up into his groin. Igor slumped on the floor in obvious pain.

Jimmy returned his focus on Colin. 'I'm protected, you understand that?'

'No, I don't,' said Colin, as he examined the blood that was dripping from his nose onto his hands. 'You're just a crazy bastard who's making a big mistake.'

'I killed Hank. I killed the two cops. I killed Gunner. And I'm free,' said Jimmy. 'Coz I'm protected.'

Colin smiled back through his blood. 'You didn't kill Hank. I did.'

'Jimmy realised he had been caught out in a lie, but he doubled down. 'You weren't there. I was. I killed him, and you're reliant on unreliable thugs like Gunner for your information.'

The force of Jimmy's argument defeated Colin. What Jimmy was saying was hard to believe, but quite possibly true. 'So whaddya want?' asked Colin.

'I want you to know that if you ever cross me again – come near my home, or my family – I will wipe you out, and your little gang.'

'What do you care if I come near your family?' said Colin. 'I heard you tried to shoot your wife.'

This caught Jimmy by surprise, but he responded with a smile. 'If that's what I'd do to the woman I love, imagine what I'd do to a prick like you.'

'Look, why are you here?' pleaded Colin.

'I need you to know that if you kill me or harm me in any way, you will be wiped out by my people. That's Mutually Assured Destruction.'

'OK, OK. But we were done. I had no plans to harm you.'

'We weren't done,' said Jimmy. 'You took €18,000 from me. And I want it back, with interest.'

'Why?'

'Because I'm a key player on the south side now. And if you want to sell on my turf, and use my men, like Davey, you'll pay me a little bit of respect-money. I'd say €25,000 will do.'

'For what?'

'It's a peace-offering,' said Jimmy. 'It's a sign of respect.'

'Or what?'

'Or I will consider you as a threat, and I will neutralise you,' said Jimmy.

Colin looked back at Jimmy in disbelief. He was unfamiliar with the feeling of being bullied. Jimmy didn't seem credible as a peer-player, but his sheer volatility and confidence made Colin think he might be telling the truth.

'And supposing I say yes?' said Colin. 'What do you want me to do?'

'You have forty-eight hours to drop a package at my house. You know where I live. I'll be waiting. I don't need to meet you. Just leave a package on the ground, with €25,000 in it, between the green bin and the black bin outside my front-door. Ring the doorbell as you leave. You drop the money off, and I will understand that we are even. You go ahead and expand into the south side, and I won't stand in your way. You could soon be number one in Dublin. *Number one.*'

This seemed to resonate with Colin – which had been Jimmy's intention.

'If the package doesn't arrive, I'll know you're not at peace with me,' said Jimmy. 'I don't want to spend my time wondering if you'll come and visit again, so I'll have to come looking for you – to bring clarity to our situation. So make up your mind, and send me a message about your intentions. Use cash. And do it within forty-eight hours, OK?'

'OK,' said Colin. 'OK.'

'Don't make me come back here,' said Jimmy, as he left the room. 'Don't make me angry again.'

'OK,' said Colin. 'OK.'

As Jimmy drove away, he was elated. He shouted at the top of his lungs, and cheered: 'Waa-hoo!' The look of fear on Colin's face, the whimpers of pain from Igor: revenge was sweet, and it was funny. He laughed loudly at what he had just witnessed.

And 'witnessed' was the word: it was as if he had only been a bystander to the operation. Something inside him had taken over, and the rest of him just went with it.

Despite his outward joy, Jimmy felt dread inside. What was he thinking when he put that plan together? How could he be so reckless? Why did he put himself in such danger for relatively little return? And what return? It would be days before he would know if his operation had been a success – or otherwise. And even then, would Deveney let the matter lie? *What have I become?* he asked himself again.

Jimmy locked his car and crept into his house. He felt defeated. How could he have been so stupid? He felt in danger again.

With no Bonnie in the house, he had no second set of ears to warn him of intruders while he slept. He retrieved a blanket from upstairs and made a bed on the sofa in the living-room. He didn't remove his runners and jeans, in case he needed to fight, or run. He kept his baseball bat nearby, and a phone. He found it difficult to sleep. His mind was racing.

*

All the following day, Jimmy remained in the house, looking out through the blinds as cars and pedestrians passed. He wondered what the Deveneys were thinking; what they were planning. How would he react if he was in Colin's shoes? He was so stressed he could barely eat. Part of him felt like dropping over to Colin to apologise, and ask him to forget about the whole thing.

It was also a time for introspection. He pieced together the events that had led him from the high of getting a new job, and a financial bounty, to the low of being stuck in his own house again, in fear of his life. He thought about his use of steroids, and the strong link between high levels of testosterone and risk-taking. Although the willingness to take risks can pay back handsomely when it is successful, right now he understood how disastrous risk-taking can be when it is unsuccessful. He decided it was time to reduce his usage of the drug.

Jimmy thought about his conversation with Davey about ayahuasca and the ceremonies performed by hippies in Wicklow. He googled the word, and read about potential psychological benefits – 'spiritual awakenings' – experienced by users. He recalled feeling a degree of peace, albeit short-lived, when Hank's gang forced him to take the drug.

Jimmy found the piece of paper where he had scribbled a number in Davey's house. He called it using his 'work' phone, in case his regular one was being monitored by the Gardaí.

'Hello, is that Brother Amos?'

'This is Amos,' came the reply.

'Hi, this is . . . Jonathan,' said Jimmy, aware that what he was proposing might be illegal. 'Do you do a ceremony kind of thing, with this South American, stuff, aya . . . wa . . . .'

'Ayahuasca?' said Amos.

'Yes,' said Jimmy.

'Yes, we do.'

'Good. Do you take beginners?'

'Sure.'

'By the way, maybe I shouldn't ask you about drugs on the phone,' said Jimmy.

'It's not a drug, it's a medicine,' said Amos calmly. 'Why do you want to take it?'

'I dunno,' said Jimmy. 'I took some by accident a while back, and it was an . . . interesting . . . experience.'

'By accident?' said Amos.

'It's a long story, but I'm just interested in trying it properly now.'

'What are you hoping to achieve?'

Jimmy couldn't think of a good answer. 'I dunno. Maybe I'll know it when I feel it.'

'Are you looking for a good time, or are you seeking insights into the very essence of your being?'

Jimmy guessed that looking for a good time was the wrong answer. 'I just want to . . . know myself better.'

Amos took a moment to consider. 'We have an overnight ceremony on Saturday. Meet behind the Glendalough Hotel at 7 PM. Bring a change of clothes, a sleeping-mat, a sleeping-bag, a bottle of water, and some fruit.'

'OK,' said Jimmy. He hadn't expected such a quick response.

Amos continued: 'Don't consume alcohol or other drugs between now and then. Don't drink or eat anything for five hours before the ceremony. Mother Ayahuasca is very jealous of other substances: stimulants, depressants, and so on. Are you on any medication?'

'No,' said Jimmy.

'Any antidepressants or anti-anxiety medication? You must tell me if you are.'

'No,' said Jimmy.

'OK,' said Amos. 'See you then.'

*

Early the next morning, Jimmy heard the sound of the latch on his gate lifting, and the squeak of the hinges as someone entered his garden path. He dropped gently from his couch, crawled across his sitting-room floor, and peeped through a crack in the blinds.

A flush of fear rose inside Jimmy as he saw Igor approaching the house. He squinted to see what was in his hands. There was a long brown item that looked more like a package than a gun. Still, he braced himself for an attack.

For a moment, the big man shuffled around at Jimmy's bins. Then he appeared to bend over: an action consistent with placing an item on the ground. He rang the doorbell, and walked slowly back towards a waiting car, which then drove away.

Jimmy took time to survey the scene. He looked out the front windows, both upstairs and downstairs. The front hedge partially obscured the street, but there seemed to be nothing of note on the far side of it. He checked the back of the house, in case Igor had only been a diversion. He waited a full fifteen minutes before going near his front door, and even then opened it slowly, in case it was wired to a bomb.

He looked up and down the road, before putting a step past the doorframe. There was no sign of anyone who looked threatening. He took a few tentative steps away from the house towards the bins, but there was no sign of a package.

He checked the ground between the bins, but there was no package. 'That's odd,' he thought. He wanted to check inside the bins, but feared they might be booby-trapped.

He crouched down low and used a stick to lever up the lid of the green bin. Would this method have saved his life if there had been a bomb inside? Probably not, but at this stage he was very anxious to retrieve his money. There was no money in his green bin.

He opened the lid of the black bin in the same way, but there was no sign of the money there either. He rummaged in both bins, in case Igor had placed the package under other material, but again, nothing.

He opened the brown bin. It stank, and was crawling with maggots. It was too disgusting to touch, so he moved some of its contents with the stick. There was still no sign of his money. He checked the mailbox, which was attached to the house. He unlocked it gently and stood back, in case it was wired. Again, there was nothing inside.

He checked the grass, and the shrubs, in case it was there. Nothing. Perhaps a dog could have picked it up and dropped in a neighbour's garden? He checked, but no sign. Was this a trick played by Igor? This was not an outcome he had anticipated. Would he have to go back to Colin and ask for a clarification on the matter? Would he dare?

'Looking for this?' The voice came from a man standing at the garden gate with a package in his hand. Jimmy looked up, to see Inspector McClean.

'Squeezy, what are you doing here?' asked Jimmy suspiciously.

'Oh, just passing by. I saw this in your garden, and thought I might hold it for you, in case it fell into the wrong hands,' said the Garda.

'Thank you,' said Jimmy, reaching out to take the package. 'Now, can I have it back?'

'Sure,' said McClean, but he moved the package out of Jimmy's reach. 'Let's have a wee chat first.'

Jimmy tried to remain calm. Had he been set up by the Deveneys? Was it just coincidence that McClean was passing? Hardly. It looked like he had little choice but to talk with the cop. 'Sure. What do you want to talk about?'

'That's quite a stunt you pulled at Colin Deveney's apartment the other night,' said McClean.

'I don't know what you mean,' said Jimmy.

The detective smiled. 'This is an off-the-record conversation, so we can be honest with each other. OK?'

'Who's been talking to you?' asked Jimmy. 'Deveney?'

'You wouldn't expect that, would you?' countered the detective.

'Igor?' asked Jimmy.

McClean laughed at the thought. 'Let's just say, we have our ways of finding out what's going on.'

Jimmy surmised that the cops had Colin's apartment bugged, but he didn't see the need to pursue the point. 'Can I have the package, please?' he said.

The cop ignored Jimmy's request, and continued: 'So, *you* killed Hank?'

'What makes you say that?' asked Jimmy.

'That's what you told Colin.'

'It was a private conversation. Men say things to other men in order to impress them. I think if you investigate the claim, you'll find there's no evidence to support it.'

'Possibly,' confirmed McClean. 'To tell you the truth, I don't care. Crims killing crims is usually a good thing for society. To interfere is, in a way, unpatriotic.' He smiled at the thought. 'But you also said you killed two Gardaí.'

'I expect you would find no evidence to support that either.'

'I know what you mean, boy,' said McClean. 'The problem is that if you make a claim like that, there are people in my division who will take it very seriously. And investigate it. And bring it to a conclusion. These were two good men with families . . . .'

'Crooked men,' interjected Jimmy.

McClean shrugged. 'Maybe, maybe not. But a colleague is a colleague, and if there's someone out there who's claiming to have killed them, that's a matter worth investigating.'

Jimmy looked indifferent. 'Let them try.'

'Oh, the bravado, the bravado,' laughed McClean. 'The arrogance, the belligerence, the swagger. I see so much of it with you Dublin fellas.'

'Can I just have my money?' blurted Jimmy, with his arm extended.

'Jimmy, making money from crime isn't difficult. A lot of lads do it: lads who are unable to make a cent in any other walk of life. But making the money is the easy part. The difficult part is knowing when to stop; knowing how to get back out of the criminal world without losing your money, or your life. And some of the biggest obstacles . . . are the bravado and the arrogance, and the recklessness.'

'Did you just come here to give me a lecture?' shouted Jimmy.

'I came here to save your life, you stupid man,' said McClean, crossly. Jimmy went silent. 'I came here to let you know that what you did the other night was enough to land you in a shallow grave, or a prison-cell.'

Jimmy couldn't make eye-contact. 'OK, thank you,' he said grudgingly.

McClean continued: 'There was a movie back in the eighties, Jimmy, called *Body Heat*. Do you remember that one at all?'

'Was that the one with all the sex in it?'

'Well,' said McClean, pitifully, 'they didn't show very much, so it hardly counts.'

Jimmy nodded in agreement.

'Anyway,' said McClean, 'there's a scene it in when the Mickey Rourke character says to the John Hurt fella: "Any time you try to do a serious crime, there are fifty ways you can mess it up. If you can think of half of those ways, then you're a genius." And Jimmy, you ain't no genius.'

Jimmy looked blankly at the cop. He had an urge to swap insults with him – and a greater urge to take his money and go back inside. 'Thank you for the lecture. Now, can I have my package please?'

'If I give you this package, Jimmy,' said McClean, 'then myself and Garda Sweeney here' – he waved to the Garda sitting in a car nearby – 'will have to report that we witnessed a known criminal leave a package, presumably cash, at a suspect's house. And that package was then retrieved by said suspect. We will then have to get a warrant to search your house, as you can understand.'

'You don't have to do this,' said Jimmy.

'With my limited knowledge of the legal system, I don't think you'd get a prison sentence for receiving a large amount of cash from a dubious source, but it would still be a conviction. It could be something that would, for example, hinder someone's life if, y'know, they ever, let's say, wanted to work in America.'

McClean had done his research, and his threat chastened Jimmy. The fear of losing his new job with the American TV network would pose a bigger problem than the other scenarios McClean had outlined. 'So what are you proposing?' he asked.

'Maybe I'll hold onto the package for a little while?'

'No fucking way!' shouted Jimmy.

'Think about it,' said McClean.

'You want to hold onto it for how long?' demanded Jimmy.

McClean shrugged his shoulders nonchalantly. Jimmy was furious, and snorted heavily. 'I want a receipt,' he said.

'Jimmy,' said McClean in disbelief, 'you want to make it official that you are aware of cash being dropped off at your house by a criminal?'

'Well, what then? You wanna just walk away with my money?'

'It's your choice,' said McClean, his gloved hand placing the package on the pillar of Jimmy's gate. 'You decide.'

'You're corrupt,' said Jimmy, eye-balling the Garda.

'No, *you're* corrupt, ye pup ye,' countered McClean. 'You're corrupt. Most criminals are good for nothing else but stealing and dealing; that's all they can do. But you had other options. You had a choice, and you chose to sell poison to your fellow citizens – knowing it could kill them. That's corruption!

'I'm just a policeman trying to keep the neighbourhood safe from people like you, and it's an awfully hard job. It's very hard for me to stop people like you; very hard to catch you red-handed. It's a lot of work to gather evidence, and then watch the likes of you walk out of the courts with just a tut-tutting from a judge. Sometimes the best a Garda can do is just manage the situation. And this . . . ' – he tapped the package with this finger and exhaled loudly – 'is a management fee.'

Jimmy looked at the package. The money he needed for his new house – his new life – was just an arm's length away. There was also a little extra to help him change his car, and buy new clothes, and go on a nice holiday. He had risked his life for that money. All he had to do now was stretch out his hand and take it.

'The package is yours if you want it,' McClean reiterated.

'And if I don't take it, do I get anything in return?' asked Jimmy weakly.

McClean shrugged. 'I can help you stay out of trouble – *if* you stay out of trouble.'

'How can I trust you?' said Jimmy.

McClean laughed to himself, and looked up and down the street as if to check that their conversation was not being overheard. 'Well, I saved your life before,' he said.

'When?' challenged Jimmy.

'The day you were kidnapped by a certain pink rabbit.'

'What are you talking about?'

'Someone had to tell Hank not to kill you,' said McClean confidently.

Jimmy's face dropped. 'So, you were Hank's mole?'

'Ah, I wouldn't use that kind of language.'

'So I suppose you want me to thank you now?' said Jimmy.

'Well, you can thank me, or you can thank the good Lord who was hanging around your neck,' smiled McClean. 'Or indeed thank your wife – although you've a very odd way of showing your appreciation to her.'

Jimmy wanted to find out more, but they were interrupted by Kenneth, a neighbour, who came out of his driveway, and turned to pass Jimmy's house. 'Lovely morning,' he announced to Jimmy as he passed by.

'Yes,' said Jimmy. 'It's supposed to be dry until the weekend.'

'You're putting the house up for sale,' said Kenneth. 'You're finally leaving us.'

'Not moving far, Kenneth,' said Jimmy. 'You'll see me again.'

'I always knew you'd move on, Jimmy. I think the area was never really good enough for you.'

'Not at all,' said Jimmy. 'Just a matter of being close to a school for Byron.'

'Y'know, Jimmy,' said McClean, as Kenneth passed out of earshot, 'this was the first place I was stationed when I got out of Garda college. They used to send us country boys to Dublin 8 to toughen us up.' He looked up and down the street as he reminisced. 'This was a rough spot then. Fellas drinking and fighting, and beating up their wives; the beginnings of the drugs trade. And as the years went by, your sort of people started to move in. And I thought things would be better. Ye certainly think you're better. But it seems to me that your crowd often do the same things, just with different accents.'

Jimmy was still fuming, and didn't respond.

'So, what have we decided about the package?' asked McClean.

'You can fuck off with it, if you want,' said Jimmy, unable to make eye-contact.

The detective was very calm. 'I'll take it, so, that you don't want this package then.'

'Just fuck off!'

'Ah now, Jimmy boy, there's no need for that language.'

McClean put the package into the pocket of his overcoat. As he returned to the car, he turned to Jimmy, who was still standing resentfully in his garden. 'You know, Jimmy, I wouldn't be so hostile, if I were you. You haven't lost anything today.' He tapped his pocket. 'Consider this as an investment in your future.'

24

❦❦❦

Ayahuasca

Jimmy was still angry when he drove to Wicklow a few days later. He played his music loud and drove aggressively as he followed the M1 towards Glendalough. He stopped for a burger and chips at Enniskerry. He knew he shouldn't, but he felt defiant.

He arrived early at the Glendalough Hotel and went for a pint. It was a warm evening and he walked with his drink over the bridge onto the grass behind, to enjoy the views. He felt tense as he considered what the ceremony ahead would entail.

At the appointed time, he stood beside his car in the car-park. He made eye-contact with other motorists as they came and went, hoping they might be Brother Amos. By 7.15 PM, he wondered if he had misheard the day, or the time. He looked around to see if there were undercover Gardaí lurking. Perhaps it was a set-up? He tried to phone Brother Amos, but he couldn't get a signal.

At 7.45 PM, a dark van entered the car-park. A shabby-looking Englishman wearing a grey pony-tail and tie-die T-shirt came over and asked: 'Are you Jonathan?'

'Yes', said Jimmy. 'Are you Brother Amos?'

'No, Amos is at the house. I'm Rex. Hop in the van, please.'

'Why don't I drive behind you?' suggested Jimmy.

Rex didn't entertain the idea. 'It's a secret location,' he said, as he beckoned Jimmy to follow him to the van. 'You travel in the back of the van.'

The side door slid open. Jimmy had a sudden rush of fear. The previous time he had heard a van door slide, he was a prisoner. He steadied himself and looked inside. Five younger adults sat on the floor of the van, and waved out at him. 'Come on in,' they said in unison.

Jimmy hesitated again. He realised what a strange situation he was putting himself into: heading to an unknown location, in the back of a darkened van with a group of people he didn't know. It was not what a man with his responsibilities should be doing. But that's what made it right for him. He smiled, and said to himself: 'Feel the fear, and do it anyway.'

The back of the van was dimly lit. Through the translucent windows, he could see the tops of the mountains around Glendalough. But which mountains, and in what direction he was travelling, he did not know.

His travelling companions included a couple from Latvia. They had taken ayahuasca before, in their home country and in Poland. There were two were Irish guys, both former drug-addicts, with neck tattoos and nasal inner-city accents to prove it. Both said the ayahuasca had helped them kick heroin. One was now working as a drug counsellor, and said he had travelled to Peru to take it 'at source'. The other had done it before with Brother Amos.

'What's he like?' asked Jimmy.

'I'd say, unconventional, so he is,' was the assessment. 'He has his own style.'

His fifth travelling companion seemed to be travelling on her own. Her fair hair fell lightly over a revealing buckskin halter-top that reminded Jimmy of a 1970s country music album cover. Jimmy's eyes kept venturing towards her pretty face, and he tried to guess where she was from. *Probably Holland, Germany or France*, he said to himself. *Certainly one of Europe's great breast-showing nations.*

The others in the van were impressed when Jimmy explained it would be his first time taking ayahuasca. The Latvian woman said: 'It is amazink . . . you try it for first time, and you are old man.' The others in the van laughed loudly, and Jimmy felt more at ease.

After around twenty minutes, the van pulled onto a gravel roadway. Jimmy heard stones hitting the body of the van, and grass brushing its underside. Butterflies rose in his stomach. He was excited and apprehensive.

The van came to a stop and the side door slid open. They were at a large country house that looked like it had been built in the 1800s. Certainly it had once been grand, but was now in need of work.

Five other people were standing around the portico. They looked similar to the people Jimmy had travelled with: young, mostly foreign, alternative, with lots of tattoos and face jewellery. Jimmy was the odd man out.

'Which one of you is Brother Amos?' he said.

'I'm Amos,' said a man, walking out of the main door of the house. He was dressed in long brown robes, like a monk, or an extra in a biblical film. He raised his arms, and his voice, and said: 'Welcome, everybody.'

Jimmy's face dropped. His heart dropped. His anger rose. There, under the unmistakable head of curls and behind the mid-Atlantic accent, and oozing confidence, was Malcolm – the medical advisor.

'What the fuck!' shouted Jimmy. 'What are you doing here?'

Everyone else went silent. Feeling sudden tension, people stood aside, and a pathway opened between Jimmy and Brother Amos.

'I am your shaman,' said Brother Amos.

'Oh, you're a shaman now?

'And I am Brother Amos,' he said, calmly.

'*You* are Brother fuckin' Amos!' shouted Jimmy. 'You are a fraud, and a charlatan, and a fucking quack!'

Amos seemed unperturbed. 'I am here to guide you on a very important journey tonight.'

'His name is not "Amos"!' shouted Jimmy to the people who stood around. 'His name is "Malcolm".'

'And your name is?' replied Amos calmly.

'My name is Jimm . . . Jonathan . . . ' said Jimmy, hesitantly.

Amos smiled. 'Names are just labels; they are not who we really are. What we call each other is not important. What is important is that we respect each other, and respect Mother Ayahuasca.'

'Respect, my hole!' exclaimed Jimmy.

'Hey, man, why don't you chill out a little, huh?' said one of the other participants, who had an American accent.

'Because,' said Jimmy, 'he's not who he says he is.'

'What does it matter?' said the buckskin lady as she walked by Jimmy. 'What does it matter if we don't know him?' she said breezily. 'He knows us.'

'Knows us? He knows us? He doesn't know shite!' said Jimmy, irritated by the logic of her argument. He pointed at her, and shouted at Amos: 'Are you paying these people to be here?'

'You are free to leave,' said Amos. 'No charge. I'll have Rex return you to your car straight away if you don't want to be here.'

'I didn't say I didn't want to be here,' said Jimmy, unsure of what he wanted.

'Three times,' announced Amos, holding up three fingers. 'Three times, you called out to the universe for help. Three times, you said: "Universe, help me." And three times, the universe brought you to me. What is that telling you?'

'The universe is a fuckin' eejit,' Jimmy muttered to himself.

Brother Amos had the upper hand. Standing in the raised portico, which resembled an altar, he looked to Jimmy like a charismatic religious leader, in his robes, and surrounded by his disciples. Jimmy stood on the driveway, three steps lower, and alone, like a sinner, separated from the flock. 'The Law of Attraction has brought us together,' continued Amos. 'You asked Mother Universe for help, and she manifested me in your life.'

'Bollocks!' said Jimmy.

'You are free to accept or resist what the universe has to offer. I will support you in either decision, but you must make it now,' said Amos, and with a whoosh of his robes he led the others inside. Jimmy stood alone, just outside the portico. He looked around to see Rex leaning against the van, waiting for him to make a decision.

The sun was starting to set over the nearby Wicklow hills, casting long shadows beside the barns and trees. Lights had started to warm the windows of the distant farmhouses. The sound of baa-ing sheep filled the valley, displaced occasionally by the *put-put-putt*ing of a busy tractor completing the last of its tasks for the day. Beside him, an army of bees and hoverflies rummaged through a line of lavender. On the roof of one of the outbuildings, a flock of housemartins gathered, presumably to discuss their impending return to southern Africa.

Jimmy contrasted the peaceful pastoral scene with the prospect of the drive back to Dublin 8. 'Fuck it anyway,' he said to himself, and turned to join the others in the house.

The main hall was a large drab space dominated by a once-elegant marble fireplace. Jimmy crossed the black and white flagstone floor to a large reception room, where each member of the group had taken their positions around the edge. The walls were decorated with mandala shapes printed on thin pieces of cloth, which looked like they came from some far-off place, probably India. Above a makeshift altar at the top of the room hung the colourful image of a decorated elephant painted on linen. Jimmy unfurled his sleeping mat and sleeping bag, and listened as Brother Amos explained how the night would proceed.

'This is not a drugs trip,' he said. 'You're not here to get high. You're here to work. You are here to see, to feel, to learn. You're here to ask questions; to ask Mother Ayahuasca questions. And to understand what insights she provides. It won't be easy.

'When people talk about the great journeys a person can take, they often talk about a safari in Tanzania, or hiking in the Alps, or riding on the Orient Express. But you are about to go on the journey of your lifetime. This is the most important journey a person can take: the journey within. You may experience very strong emotions. You may feel very happy, or very sad. Or both. But don't worry, Rex and I will be here to help you.'

Jimmy found it all of this overly serious, especially when Amos rose with a large pipe in his hands. He circled the room, blowing smoke loudly into every corner of the room and around the door-frames. 'This is to keep evil spirits out,' he said.

Amos came around the room with a thick black liquid in what looked like an ancient tea-pot. 'This is tobacco,' he said. 'Not the stuff you get at your local shop: it's a native-Amazonian tobacco-strain called *mapacho*. I will pour it on your hands, and you snort it.'

Jimmy did as he was told. The liquid shot up his nose and caused an instant stinging at the back of his head. He grimaced.

'That's OK if it hurts,' said Amos. 'It is releasing toxins from your body. It's good for dissolving anxiety and other negative feelings. Here, have some more.'

Amos wandered around the room, barefoot, uttering prayers and blessings in a language that sounded like Spanish. He put on soft trance music, and lit an array of candles around the room. On his altar he burned more candles, and something that smelled like incense.

Jimmy had expected a more social event: a party. Instead, he was in a room with strangers, and they were discouraged from talking to each other. 'Be still, and be silent,' advised Amos. 'Prepare your mind and your spirit for the great journey. When you talk, you look out. Tonight, you look inwards.'

Some of the others sat like yogis. Although this looked a little pretentious to Jimmy, he too sat upright with his legs crossed and rested the backs of his hands on his knees. He closed his eyes and muttered to himself: *When in Rome.*

Before long, Amos announced that the time had come to drink ayahuasca. 'You will soon partake in a ritual that goes back thousands of years,' he said. 'The medicine is from the leaves of the *psychotria viridis* shrub, along with the stalks of the *caapi* vine. It can only come from the rainforest.'

Amos called each participant to kneel beside him at the altar, and drink the sacred brew from his small wooden goblet. When his turn came, Jimmy did as the others had done. Instinctively, he cupped his hands together as if he was about to receive Communion. He knelt, took the goblet, and drank the thick brown liquid. It looked, smelled and tasted vile. He remembered the torment of the previous time he had consumed the liquid, and this added to his discomfort. He shut his eyes, swallowed hard, shook his head and grimaced.

Amos took the goblet, and offered him a glass of water. 'Don't drink it; just wash out your mouth, and spit into this bucket,' he said.

When the final person had drunk the brew and returned to her seat, Amos rang a small bell. 'That's it,' he said. 'There is no going back. Now you must let the medicine do its work. Stay upright as long as you can – at least for half an hour.'

It all seemed harmless pantomime to Jimmy. There was no effect, on himself or anyone else. With no conversation, and a dimly lit room, the experience so far was one of boredom. His view changed when Rex moved around the room, giving everyone a bucket and a roll of toilet paper. There was no need for words, just a knowing and sympathetic look from Rex. 'No going back, huh?' said Jimmy.

After around twenty-five minutes, he felt tired, and lay back on his mat. As he closed his eyes, some colours and shapes flitted into his vision, like two butterflies frolicking in the sunshine. More colours arrived, unifying with the others, and forming a double-helix. They multiplied and divided. They formed chains and twisted and turned across his vision like a rollercoaster that formed its own track as it moved along.

The colours took the form of lilies. Their petals closed, and then opened again to reveal more shapes and colours within. They danced together. They became swirls, and spun into the centre and back out again, forming geometric patterns. Wave-motion passed through them; they seemed to have a pulse.

The colours became a series of rainbow rays that lit up Jimmy's senses for a moment, before diffusing into blacks, whites and greys, like a large undulating checkerboard. The sight reminded him of the old BBC test transmission picture, which used to appear before programmes started. 'So that's where they got the idea,' he said to himself – but there was little room in his brain now for words.

The colours changed to lime greens and yellows, warm oranges and light reds. It looked to Jimmy to be the same palette that had been used in the Book of Kells. Jimmy smiled at the thought of the famous artwork being the product of tripping monks.

The visions took the form of ferns. They started as young fronds, uncurling, and forming large leaves. They moved with the motion of underwater plants. Abruptly, the vision in his mind stopped. His eyes opened, and he could see reality, which was much less interesting. He was in a plain room surrounded by other people lying down. It was quiet. The calmness outside his head contrasted with the riot of colours and action inside it. He preferred the internal picture.

In an instant, it was clear why his visions had stopped. His stomach sent a message to his brain that he should grab his bucket. As he did, his diaphragm locked hard against his stomach, forcing its contents through his oesophagus with speed and power.

Jimmy projectile-vomited into his bucket with such force that it was nearly knocked out of his hands. Again he spewed, and again. His retching was so violent that he followed each burst with a loud 'Aaah'. He wanted to stop the trip, but he couldn't. He flopped back onto his mat, and shut his eyes; the visions started again.

This time he hovered above what looked like a busy automated factory floor. Everything was moving in, out and around, and he glided above it all as if he was being moved slowly by an overhead crane. The factory roof opened, and he was sucked upwards, emerging onto a giant blooming lotus flower.

The petals slowly opened, then closed, and reopened as a beautiful magnolia flower. Then the petals closed again, and when they reopened it was an orchid. All of this was in close-up. Either the flowers were the size of houses, or Jimmy felt he had shrunk to the size of a bee.

The centre became a black hole that swallowed him. Then his vision changed to a mosaic of spinning kaleidoscope patterns. They became wheels within wheels. The outside forms spun in an anticlockwise direction, while the inside ones did the opposite.

Everything in his vision moved like a Fibonacci spiral. It was like a close-up of a Romanesque broccoli, and every part was turning. The dominant centre of his vision spiralled inwards, and he was drawn into a hibiscus flower, into its centre, past its pistil into its reproductive core. It was as though he was returning to something. It wasn't hostile; it was warm and welcoming. It was vaginal.

Jimmy opened his eyes to see Amos circling the room with a didgeridoo, blending its tuneless pipe-sounds with the soft trance music from the altar. Later, Amos came by with bongos, beating out a soft rhythm, and chanting a prayer in some indecipherable language.

Jimmy watched for a moment, then fired more contents of his stomach into his bucket. So much came out that he didn't think there could be more, but it kept coming – and violently. He worried that he might accidentally spill the bucket onto the floor, or that it might overflow.

He lay down again. The tripping got harder. It was like he was on a speeding motorbike. Everything was too fast. It seemed dangerous. His senses were overloaded. He was spinning so fast that it seemed he would be propelled off his sleeping mat. He grabbed it tightly. 'I need to stop. I need to stop,' he heard himself say. 'It's too much!'

'You're OK, Jimmy.' It was Amos. 'You're doing OK, just breathe.'

'I *am* breathing,' gasped Jimmy. 'How do I stop it? It's too much. It's too intense.'

'Just take a deep breath,' said Amos.

'I am taking a deep . . . Oh Jesus!'

Jimmy sat upright, grabbed his bucket and spewed again. His stomach muscles ached from the stiff contractions. 'What did you give me? Why am I so sick?'

Amos spoke softly. 'Remember I told you that *Madre Ayahuasca* is a jealous medicine?'

'Medicine?' shouted Jimmy. 'It's poison!'

'Keep your voice down, please,' said Amos. 'You might upset the others.'

'I can't, for fuck sake,' said Jimmy. 'I'm dying!'

'Your body is cluttered with all kinds of nasty stuff, and *Madre Ayahuasca* is attacking them. She is helping you to detox. She is getting rid of all the extra salt and sugar, and caffeine and alcohol, and all the other nasty chemicals you have in your system. You have to be clear of the toxins if you are to receive messages and learn from your experience. The more you purge, the better it is for you.'

'Make it stop, please,' said Jimmy, and he puked again. The last mouthful of vomit remained in his mouth, and he spat it into the bucket. 'There's so much. Where's it all coming from?'

'It's more than just food,' said Amos. 'It's also your anger, your fear, your sadness, your depression, your ego. They are reluctant to leave.'

'My ego? I'm puking up ego? How can you puke up . . . ?' A look of fear crossed Jimmy's face. There was no time to converse with Amos. 'Oh, Jaysus,' he shouted, 'where's the toilet?'

'Out the door and on the right.'

Jimmy darted in the direction indicated by Amos. He ran through the hall towards an open door. He had no time to close the door behind him, and barely enough time to lower his jeans and boxer shorts. He landed on the toilet-seat just as the contents of his bowels exploded into the bowl.

'Oh God!' shouted Jimmy. Another explosion, and another. He feared the bowl would overflow. 'Oh God,' he said again.

'You ate on your way here, didn't you?' said Amos, appearing at the door with a lighted match in his hand.

'Stop looking at me!' roared Jimmy. 'And shut the door!'

The stench from the toilet wafted up through his nostrils, triggering more nausea. For a moment Jimmy was panicked at the prospect of purging from two ends at the same time, and he wondered which he would have to favour.

Fortunately the wash-hand basin was in reach. He grabbed the basin with both hands, raised himself from the toilet-seat, and spewed. Then he lowered himself onto the bowl to work his bowels again, before raising himself to vomit again. It was like a squatting exercise in the gym.

Eventually the vomit was reduced to dry-retching, and the torrential diarrhoea gave way to squirts, and then just gas. It seemed that there was nothing left in Jimmy's digestive tract to purge. He struggled to clean himself, and then used toilet-paper to clean the splash-zone around the toilet-bowl and basin. It was an unpleasant job, especially for someone who was already weak and disorientated, and tired and sweating. He washed his mouth out with tap-water, and cleaned his face.

He emerged from the bathroom but didn't have the energy to make it back to the ceremony-room. Instead, he lay on the tiled floor of the entrance-hall, comforted by the cool sensation on his face.

'Let's try to keep the circle intact, Jimmy,' said Amos, standing above him. 'Let's go back to the room.'

'Leave me alone,' said Jimmy. 'Go away. Please.'

'It's best for the group-energy to keep everyone together.'

'I can't. Just let me be, for a few minutes.'

Amos didn't persist. As he walked away, Jimmy asked: 'And what do you mean by my ego?'

'I looked at your aura and I got a very bad feeling,' said Amos. 'You've a lot of negativity going on.'

'What are you talking about?' asked Jimmy, motionless on the floor.

'There's bad stuff there. You've been nasty to people,' said Amos.

'No I haven't.'

'Yes you have,' Amos insisted quietly.

'No.'

'It looks like you have.'

'Well I haven't.'

'Have you stolen from anyone recently?' asked Amos.

'How do you know about that?' said Jimmy, suddenly fearful that he was being recorded.

'Have you, or haven't you, stolen recently, or been violent to somebody?' asked Amos in a raised voice.

'Maybe,' said Jimmy, raising his voice too, 'but the little fucker deserved it.'

'That's ego for you,' said Amos. 'You assumed your needs were greater than his.'

Jimmy was still panting on the floor. There were no visions now, just exhaustion and nausea – and the disturbance of Amos's judgement. 'Maybe my needs *were* greater.'

'That's an arrogant position,' said Amos.

'Well, needs must, baby,' said Jimmy. 'So is that all you've got for ego?'

'You been mean to your missus?' enquired Amos.

'Ah for fuck sake, she's mean to me.'

'Did you try to shoot her?'

Jimmy hardly had the energy to argue, but became agitated. 'How do you know about this?'

'I just know things,' said Amos calmly.

'Are you recording this?'

'No,' said Amos. 'And this is not about me. This is about you. You are here to investigate yourself, and to heal.'

Jimmy couldn't answer for quite a while. 'She deserved it,' he panted.

'Why?'

'Because she's nasty all the time.'

'So you decided to shoot her.'

'Perhaps,' said Jimmy defiantly.

'That woman who has put up with the shitload of shit that you have brought into both your lives? That woman who has stuck by you when any right-minded person would have run? The only woman to go anywhere near your penis in twenty years – and you decided to shoot her?'

'I wouldn't exactly put it that way.'

'But instead of shooting her, you shot yourself in the balls.'

'How do you know about that?' shouted Jimmy.

'I just know things,' said Amos.

'How? Just tell me. Are you in with the cops, or something?'

'No.'

'Then how?'

'I just know.'

'How?'

'I saw your scarring when you sat on the toilet.'

'That's weird and disgusting,' shouted Jimmy.

'You know what happened that night?' said Amos. 'Karma.'

Jimmy lay on the floor, trying not to listen, but he was powerless.

Amos stood above him in triumph, waving his hands as he spoke. 'You decided that your needs were greater than those of your wife, and worse, the need of your daughter to have a mother. You took your vanity, and your pride, and your ego, and you pointed a bullet at your wife and commanded it to kill her.

Jimmy was silent. He found the retelling of the event painful, and tried to block his ears.

'But that little bullet had more integrity and more courage than you,' said Amos. 'It said: "I will not do it. I will not perform an evil action for this man." It said: "Happiness comes from good actions; suffering comes from evil actions. I will make him suffer for his evil action." I hope you have suffered.'

'I have suffered,' shouted Jimmy.

'That's good,' said Amos.

'No it's not!'

'You erred. You have suffered. And now you are here to heal, and learn.'

Amos returned to the main room, and Jimmy remained on the tiled floor. For how long, he couldn't tell. His perception of time was distorted. It was now dark outside. Inside, the only light came from candles. Their shadows on the high, ornate ceilings gave the hallway an ethereal quality.

He could hear the running and turning of water in another room. He staggered to his feet and followed the sound. He felt guilty because he knew he was supposed to join the others in the ceremony-room, but his feeling of curiosity was greater.

He pushed open a door and saw, inside, a beautiful marble room lit only by candles and their mirrored reflections. Steam rose over an ornate bathtub at the centre of the room, and reclining inside, surrounded by frothing bubbles, was the buckskin lady. Her blonde hair hung wet over her shoulders, and her breasts perked out from her chest, as if curious to see who was entering the room.

Jimmy averted his eyes and turned to leave, but she made no attempt to cover herself. 'Hi,' she said, smiling, while sprinkling water along her arm with a large sponge. She beckoned Jimmy to enter, and he could only glide towards her naked form.

'Hi,' he said. She was so alluring that he was both attracted to and intimidated by her.

'Are you happy you came?' she asked, still smiling.

'Yes,' said Jimmy. 'I'm sorry I was a little rude earlier.'

'That's OK,' she said. 'It's natural to be nervous before your first ceremony.'

A chair stood beside the tub, where she had left her jeans, buckskin top and underwear. 'Mind if I sit down?' asked Jimmy, as he pushed them aside gently.

'Please do.'

Jimmy looked at her blankly. 'I don't know what to say.'

'What would you like to say?' she replied with a smile.

Jimmy's lips moved, but no sound came out. He tried again, and this time spoke, slowly: 'I look at you, and for the first time, I feel I have met Venus. Do you know who I'm talking about when I mention Venus? You are like a goddess of love and beauty and . . . desire.'

She laughed. 'You are funny. I bet you say that to all the girls.'

'No,' said Jimmy quietly. He shook his head. 'I don't.'

Jimmy tried to think of something interesting to say, but nothing seemed appropriate. For a moment, the only sound in the room was the swishing of bath-water. He smiled at her again.

'Do you desire me?' she asked, with a coquettish smile.

'Well . . . yes . . . I suppose so. I think so. Yes.'

'Would you like to kiss me?' she asked.

'Would it be OK?' said Jimmy, sounding like a schoolboy who had been offered a chocolate treat.

'Sure.'

He leaned over towards the bath, inched his head towards hers, and slowly lowered his lips. She pursed her lips at the same time, and they met for a brief, soft kiss.

Jimmy returned to his seat and looked stunned. He was breathless. 'Thank you,' he said softly.

'My pleasure,' she said. 'Did you like?'

'It was wonderful,' said Jimmy, amazed that this was happening to him.

'You can do it again if you want.'

'Are you sure?' Jimmy asked.

'Of course I'm sure; that's why I said it.' Jimmy always liked the directness of the Continentals.

He leaned over, shut his eyes, and met her soft lips with his. Their kiss was like nothing he had ever experienced before. For him, kissing had always been little more than an application to commence a sexual act, but this was an action in its own right. He didn't want it to end.

He kissed her again and again. It felt nourishing. He raised his right hand and stroked her left cheek. She raised a damp arm from the bath, and wrapped it around his neck, to pull him closer. She licked his lips, then licked his tongue, and ran her fingers through his hair.

Jimmy lowered his hand onto her bare shoulder. Everything about her felt seductive; even her shoulder felt sexy. He lowered his hand to her breast. It seemed to have a desire to be caressed, and Jimmy obliged. Her nipple hardened and pressed into his palm. It too wanted attention.

A surge of energy rose from within her body, and passed from her breast into Jimmy's hand and along his arm. All his organs and tissues seemed to illuminate. His body warmed, and parts of him that were beyond her physical reach seemed, nonetheless, to be touched.

He kissed her; not just her lips, but some part of her that was deep down inside. He kissed her spirit. He was intoxicated.

Jimmy broke away slowly, for a rest. He knelt beside the tub and uttered the only words he could think of: 'Thank you.'

She laughed. 'That was very nice.'

'Yes,' he said, beaming. 'It was just lovely. Really, really nice.' He longed for a wider vocabulary.

'Aren't you going to join me in the water?' she asked, matter-of-factly.

Jimmy started to laugh. The moment was so perfect, he hadn't contemplated going further. 'I'd like to,' he said, 'but my personal hygiene isn't the best at the moment.'

'So I heard,' she said, and they both burst out laughing. They laughed for a long time, and kissed some more. Then they held each other. Jimmy pressed his cheek against hers, and held it there and let their heads sway together. She kissed his neck, sending tingles up and down his body.

Their embrace was interrupted by a knock, and Amos entered the room. 'Jimmy,' he said, 'there's someone here I think you should meet.'

'Sure,' said Jimmy, and turned to apologise to his friend in the bath. 'I have to go,' he said. 'Thank you.'

'Thank you, Jimmy,' she said, 'or Jonathan.' She smiled.

'Thank you,' said Jimmy again, realising he didn't know her name. 'Thank you, Venus.' They both laughed again.

Out in the hall, Amos also smiled. 'How are you feeling?' he asked.

'Good. Thanks.'

'OK, follow me,' said Amos, and he led Jimmy through a door at the rear of the house into an orangery. Jimmy looked around, to see a large glass room filled with giant palms and ferns, and other large-leaved ornamental plants. Water trickled down over a rockery, giving the room a restful ambience. It fed a pond, covered by waterlilies, in the middle of the room. For a moment, Jimmy was reminded of Monet's garden in Giverny. It was an enchanting setting.

On a bench beside the pond sat a figure with his back turned. He was looking at what appeared to be a photo-album. The person was familiar, and slowly turned to greet him. It was Jacko.

'Dad!' exclaimed Jimmy. 'Dad? Wh . . . wh . . . what are you doing here?'

'James,' said his father, with a reserved smile, and rising to his feet. 'It's lovely to see you again.' The two men looked at each other and smiled, but stood uneasily. Both seemed ready for an embrace, but neither wanted to initiate it. Hugging had never been a feature of their relationship. Jimmy held out his hand, and the two men shook.

'How is this possible?' asked Jimmy, almost in shock. He looked around for an explanation from Amos, but he had left. 'How could you be here?' he said to his father.

'You called me,' said Jacko.

'Called you? What do you mean?'

'I felt you wanted me here, so I came.'

'But I don't understand. How could I . . . ?'

'Probably your subconscious called me. I felt you calling for me quite a lot over the years, but it's only now that you're . . . open to meeting with me.'

Jimmy struggled for words and looked confused. His father gestured to the seat beside the bench, and both men sat.

'What's a person supposed to say to their dead father?' asked Jimmy, almost laughing, and still in disbelief. 'How . . . how are you?'

'I'm good, thank you. I miss you all, but I'm doing fine.'

'What's it like on the other side?'

'It's good,' said Jacko, 'but not worth dying for.' He laughed, and Jimmy smiled, remembering how his father often enjoyed his own jokes.

'Have you something profound to say to me?' asked Jimmy. 'Have you a message?'

'Not really.'

'Anything at all? People aren't going to believe me when I tell them about this.'

Jacko shrugged. 'That's not important.'

'What about next week's Lotto numbers?'

They both laughed at that prospect. 'No, I don't have the Lotto numbers. Sorry,' said his father. 'It doesn't work that way.'

He paused for a moment to consider what he would say next. 'Well, maybe I do have a message for you. I would like you to know that I'm sorry I wasn't a . . . a . . . warmer father to you. And I'm very proud of you.'

'You're proud of me?' said Jimmy, still not believing what was happening.

'Yes,' said his father. 'I wished I had said it when I was alive – many times. But I didn't, and I'm sorry about that. By the time I realised what mistakes I had made, it seemed too late . . . or too difficult to deal with. So I want you to know now, that I'm very proud of you.'

Jimmy shrugged his shoulders and turned his palms upwards. 'Proud of what? I haven't amounted to very much. I'm not good enough.'

'You have always been good enough,' said Jacko, crossly. 'Always!' He let his comment rest with Jimmy for a moment, and placed his hand on his forearm. 'It just saddens me to hear you put yourself down like that. You got that from me, of course; I admit that. But it's a damaging legacy. You've always been good enough. Always.'

'Have you seen my life lately?' said Jimmy.

'Yes,' said his father, exhaling heavily. 'You stole from that boy, and you nearly murdered your wife. And you've done other stuff as well that is hard to justify. I'm not saying you're perfect. But sometimes circumstances instruct our actions. We do our best under a particular set of circumstances. What's important now is that you undo some of the damage.'

'How?'

'You'll figure that out,' said Jacko. There was a kindness in his tone that Jimmy had not encountered before. 'You have both the brain and the heart to make things better. You're good enough to be a good man.'

Jimmy had rarely been complimented by his father in life, and was warmed by the affirmation coming from him now.

'But that house you want to buy . . . do you really need to put yourself under that pressure?'

'I think it would be nice,' said Jimmy.

'Of course it would, but you've already done well enough in your life. You don't need a new address to confirm that.'

'I thought you would approve of having a son living near Palmerston Park.'

'Why do you allow yourself to be burdened by a dead man's expectations? I'm proud of you, James, just as you are. I will be more proud of you when you have a happier life, and create happiness for people around you.'

'OK,' said Jimmy, 'I'll work on it.'

'Do,' said Jacko.

'Do you . . . Are you . . . are you able to help me out from the other side?'

His father laughed. 'You mean practical stuff? I can try, but my ability to influence your life is far less than your ability to influence your own life. So it's best if you create your own good fortune.'

Jimmy looked down at the book on his father's lap. 'What's in your hand?'

His dad looked down too. 'This is my book of memories. These are my memories of you and me.'

The book was filled with images, some still and others moving. They all featured Jimmy and Jacko, showing the best moments they had had together.

'Look here,' said Jacko, taking a photograph from his book. It was a small 1970s print in faded colour, showing Jimmy as a boy, held up for the camera by his proud, youthful father. His father's hand seemed so large that it almost swallowed Jimmy's. 'This is me and my little buddy,' said Jacko. He smiled at the memory. 'I was so proud of my little boy, my son.'

'I don't remember seeing this before,' said Jimmy, taking the photo from the book. 'Where was it taken?'

'That was our old house in Sandymount,' said Jacko. 'You can't forget that wallpaper.'

Jimmy lowered the photo from his sight. 'What happened to us, dad?' he asked. 'Where did it all go wrong?'

His father shook his head sadly. 'It was a generational thing. My generation was raised in a way that's difficult for you to understand. We were encouraged to be distant, and stubborn, and disciplined. We were to do as we were told. Then you came by with a whole different outlook. You wanted to follow your own path, your own ideas. Maybe you were right, but I . . . I didn't know how to deal with that.'

'We should have had this conversation before.'

'Yes,' said Jacko. 'We should have, but I couldn't. I wanted to. But I didn't know how. When I got sick, there was nobody that I wanted to be with more than my little buddy – or my big buddy, by then – but you didn't come.'

'You didn't want me to come.'

'I did. I just . . . I just couldn't say it. And that was my punishment.'

'Mine too.'

'I died a lonely man.'

'I'm sorry.'

'We both are,' said Jacko, shaking his head sadly. He squeezed Jimmy's forearm. 'I know. But I'm glad we have now.'

'Yes,' said Jimmy.

'And you have to be careful not to repeat my mistakes with your own daughter,' warned Jacko. 'There's a growing distance there that you have to work on.'

Jimmy wanted to contradict his father, but he knew he was right. 'I'll start working on that,' he said.

'Anyway,' said Jacko, 'I know you missed me. But, y'know, someday we'll be together again. It will be all right.'

'Thank you, Dad, it's good to know,' said Jimmy, his eyes softening with tears. Both men welled up. 'So what are we supposed to do now? Tell each other "I love you"?'

'Oh stop,' said his father, laughing. 'That's far too American for me. But we can embrace if you want.' His father raised an arm.

Jimmy leaned in, and for the first time in his adult life, he rested his forehead on his father's shoulder. Jacko extended his arms, and rested his hands on Jimmy's back. Jimmy raised a hand, and put it on his dad's shoulder.

'It's long overdue,' he said.

'I know,' his dad replied, closing his eyes. 'My little buddy, huh? My little buddy.'

The hug lasted a long time. Jimmy didn't recall it ending, but sometime later Rex entered the room, and found him sitting in a chair with his head resting on the back of the bench. He tapped Jimmy on the shoulder, waking him with a start.

'It's time to go outside,' said Rex. 'It's dawn. Brother Amos wants everyone to join him to close out the ceremony.'

Jimmy was disoriented, and unsteady on his feet. Rex took him by the arm and led him through the house to the front door. Outside, the others sat around a crackling fire while Amos played the panpipes. The sky was mostly dark, but a pale strip was emerging over the distant hills to the east.

'Come and join us,' beckoned Amos.

Jimmy became nauseous again, and dizzy. 'I can't. I need to lie down,' he said.

'No, come and join us,' insisted Amos. 'You'll feel better.'

'I can't, I can't,' said Jimmy. 'I'm sorry,' and he broke out of Rex's grip. He found his way back into the main room, and onto his sleeping mat. He pulled his sleeping bag over himself, but caught sight of Rex's disappointed face in the doorway, and felt a sudden pang of guilt.

'I'm sorry, I'm sorry,' he said. 'I know I should be there. I know I should . . . .'

'It's OK, it's OK,' said Rex, trying to reassure him.

'Now, I messed up. I fucked up. I feel really bad,' shouted Jimmy. He started to thrash around in his bedding, and made a vain effort to get up.

'It's OK, I'll look after him, Rex.' It was Amos. He turned and spoke to Jimmy in a calm voice. 'It's OK, Jimmy. I know you're tired. It's nothing to feel bad about.'

'No, I should be there. I know I should. I'm ruining it for everybody. I'm sorry . . . ' shouted Jimmy, still in a state of panic.

'It's OK,' said Amos. 'Just breathe.'

'I *am* breathing!'

'Let's take a few deep breaths – together,' said Amos. 'One, two . . . now hold it.' Rex handed him a lit pipe. While Jimmy continued to hold his breath, Amos exhaled, and then drew deeply on the pipe. He blew the smoke into Jimmy's face, and it seemed to calm him.

'I'm sorry, Malcolm,' said Jimmy quietly. 'Or Brother Amos, I'm sorry.'

'Malcolm, or Amos, it doesn't matter. Call me whatever you like. You've a lot on your mind.'

Jimmy made another vain attempt to rise. His arms and legs couldn't seem to work in unison, and eventually he resigned himself to a peaceful state. Amos waited until he had stopped moving before speaking. 'Y'know, many people misunderstand the role of testosterone because they misunderstand the role of masculinity.'

'Oh,' said Jimmy. He was barely able for a conversation.

'Men who have higher testosterone levels generally die younger,' continued Amos. 'They get involved in more risky activities. They get into conflict. They damage their support-structures. They get into trouble with the law.'

'Now you're telling me,' sighed Jimmy, his eyes closing. 'You're the one who put me on the stuff.'

'I told you to get medical advice, and to be careful with it. I told you to have your bloods checked regularly to make sure you weren't overdosing.'

'You didn't tell me what could happen. A lot of stuff has happened.'

'I know stuff has happened,' said Amos. 'Testosterone makes stuff happen. That's what it's for.

'Testosterone is the life-force that enables everyone – male and female – to impose their will. It helped us kill other animals for food and defend ourselves when attacked. Without it, our species wouldn't have survived.

'Every act of lust; every baby that was ever conceived outside of a test-tube happened because of testosterone. But also every rape. Every murder. Every violent robbery. Every war. Every despicable act of war: testosterone was the enabler.

'Every big business deal: testosterone was at the centre of it. Every race that was ever won; every goal ever scored; every target ever hit: testosterone made it happen.

'You have taken the most powerful substance known to our species, and injected it into your body. You shouldn't be surprised that stuff happened.'

Jimmy struggled with this onslaught of information and wished that Amos would go away. 'So it made me do bad things.'

'You can't blame the hormone,' said Amos. 'Testosterone doesn't make you a bad person. If you're already asshole, it just helps you become a more effective one. But if you are a good person who wants to do good, testosterone will make that path easier for you to follow.' Amos paused, to allow Jimmy to absorb the information.

'You have to decide what kind of man you want to be. If your idea of masculinity is dominance, and aggression, and risk-taking, and revenge, testosterone will help you get there. But do you really want to be that kind of person?'

Jimmy guessed at the answer: 'No.'

'There is another form of masculinity. It calls on you to be a servant to those around you, not a tyrant. A man serves his partner by supporting her. He serves his family by working to provide for their material needs. He is a servant to his friends: always there when they need him. He serves his community through volunteer work.

'If that's the kind of masculinity you choose, your life will be more fulfilling. Some of the people you help, will reciprocate, making your life better. You will have a bigger social circle; more people to support you when you need help. More people will like you and respect you. You will live longer and healthier because, well let's face it, there will be fewer people who want to harm you. Testosterone will help you be that man.'

As he spoke he tucked the sleeping bag under Jimmy's limp body. He made it tight until Jimmy was swaddled in a warm cocoon, and felt safe. 'Remember, for a good life, you must have good relationships.'

'Amos, I really don't think I'm able to concentrate right now,' said Jimmy, almost in a whisper.

'That's OK,' said Amos. 'Let your conscious mind rest. I will talk straight to your subconscious mind.'

'Just leave me,' whispered Jimmy. 'But thank you. I appreci- . . . .' His words fell away.

'You've got to work on your marriage,' said Amos.

'I've tried,' said Jimmy. 'It's a waste of . . . .'

Jimmy's fight against sleep failed. As his eyes shut, the last words he heard from Amos were: 'Show her you care. If she's a good woman, she will respond.'

*

Jimmy was awoken by birdsong. The distinctive *'Teacher, teacher, teacher'* call of a great-tit resonated through an open window, while the trills and warbles of a greenfinch also demonstrated its presence. It was after midday, and light poured through the large panes, reflecting off the bare white walls. Jimmy raised his head and looked around. He was alone. The altar was gone, and so were everyone else's belongings.

He wandered into the hall. It looked smaller now, and dreary. He heard a noise from the kitchen, and found Rex there, sweeping the floor.

'Where is everyone?' he asked.

'All gone,' said Rex, without raising his head.

'Gone? Gone where, like?'

'Gone . . . home, I suppose.'

'I thought we'd all have brunch together, or something,' said Jimmy.

'They tried to wake you,' said Rex. 'But you weren't for stirring.'

Jimmy wandered into the hall again. He found the room where Venus had bathed the night before – or what seemed to be a small, grotty version of it. A bathtub stood apologetically against the wall, with a thick dirty rim indicating several high-water marks.

He made his way to the back door, where he found a small conservatory attached to the house. Some potted plants stood on the floor, near a cheap water feature that had apparently leaked and caused a puddle. There was a bench and a chair, which Jimmy recognised from the night before.

'It was all a dream, wasn't it?' said Jimmy, returning to Rex.

'What?'

'It wasn't real. It was all make-believe.'

Rex shrugged. 'It was whatever you think it was.'

'Is Malcolm coming back?'

'Who?'

'Malc- . . . . I mean Amos, Brother Amos,' said Jimmy.

'No, he's gone.'

'Pity,' said Jimmy. 'I'd like to talk to him about last night.'

'Why don't you gather your stuff? I'll give you a lift back to your car.'

'Sure,' said Jimmy, realising that he was only a distraction to Rex. 'What's his real name, by the way?'

'Who?'

'Brother Amos. What's his real name?'

'Oh,' smiled Rex, resting his hands on his brush. 'His real name is . . . .'

'Actually' – Jimmy raised a hand, to indicate *stop* – 'don't tell me. If I need him, I'm sure I'll find him somehow.'

Outside, Jimmy opened the passenger door of the van, but Rex wouldn't allow him to get in. 'Sorry,' he said, pointing with his thumb to the rear of the van, 'secret location and all that.'

Jimmy closed the sliding door and lay on a beanbag on the floor of the van. He watched through a high window how the trees met at the centre of the road, and how the crest of the Wicklow Mountains rose and fell. He smiled at his memories from the night before. He had no hangover, and felt both relaxed and alert inside.

He needed time to absorb and process all that he had experienced. It all seemed so real at the time, but now it didn't. It was more like a dream; a distortion of reality; a hallucination. Whatever it was, it was a memorable experience, but he needed time to analyse it. He smiled to himself.

At the Glendalough Hotel, Jimmy brushed his teeth and bought a coffee. He grabbed a towel and a change of clothes from his car, and walked through the Monastic City to the Upper Lake.

He threw himself into the cool dark water and remained submerged for as long as the deep breath he had taken allowed. He observed how the bright summer rays penetrated the bog-tinted water, casting a brown hue on the stones below. It felt refreshing. He felt invigorated.

He surfaced, and looked up to see the trees and the steep mountains on both sides, interlocking at the top of the lake. It was a beautiful joyous sight that he had failed to recognise on previous visits there. His only regret was that there was nobody to share the moment with him.

Life is good, he said to himself as he submerged again. Just as the outside of his body felt cleansed by the lake's water, his insides felt cleansed by the happenings of the night before. *Life is good*, he said to himself again.

On the lake's small stony beach, he put on a fresh T-shirt and jeans. As he tossed his stale and soiled clothes from the night before into his bag, something slid out from his shirt pocket. It was a small photograph of himself as a boy, in the arms of his father. A note on the back, in his mother's handwriting, read: 'Daddy & James. Buddies!'

Jimmy had no recollection of seeing that photograph before the previous night. 'Strange,' he said to himself. 'Very strange.'

25

❧❧❧

Resolutions

Driving home through Laragh and Annamoe, Jimmy made several resolutions. He pulled over in Roundwood and sent a text to Milfoth: 'Happy to follow your advice – take house off market & get extension instead. Please come home to discuss. X.' He couldn't remember the last time he had ended a text to her with an 'X', but at this moment it seemed appropriate.

He drove home via Rathmines and looked again at 'Clara'. The 'FOR SALE' sign was still up, and the hospital-consultant neighbour was out washing his Jaguar again. Jimmy looked pitifully at the house. He wondered why anyone would want to buy such a wreck, and indeed, why he had once thought he could take on the burden of such a renovation. He looked again at the neighbour, and wondered why he had recently wanted to live beside someone who made him feel uncomfortable.

Jimmy called the estate agent and told him that he was withdrawing his offer on the house. 'Why?' asked the agent, in a disappointed tone.

'Because . . . .' Part of Jimmy wanted to tell him that he was a shyster who didn't deserve his business, but his mood was far too mellow to insult someone. Instead, he said: 'Because I really think there's someone out there who will love the house more than we would.'

'You don't like the neighbour, do you?' asked the agent, remembering a comment Jimmy had made some weeks before.

'Oh, he too has his story,' said Jimmy, and smiled to himself as he finished the call.

Close to Cork Street, he detoured off his route home, and knocked on the door of the cottage where Davey lived. Samantha answered, and immediately went red with rage.

'What the fuck do you want, ye fuckin' prick, ye?' she roared.

Jimmy was taken aback. His relaxed disposition was no match for Samantha's aggression.

'Get the fuck away from my house,' she shouted.

'Please, Samantha, I just want to talk.'

'I've had enough of your fuckin' talking for one life, now get the fuck away!'

'I'm here because I want to help,' said Jimmy, trying to reassure her. 'I . . . .'

'I've had enough of your help. I don't want any more!' she shouted. 'You're a fuckin' curse, ye are.'

'And that's why I'm here,' pleaded Jimmy. 'I want to put things right.'

'What part of "Fuck off" do you not understand?' she shouted. 'Ye want me to call the cops? I will, ye know. I was going to call them the last time, but Davey wouldn't let me. But I'll call them right now, I will. Just watch.'

Jimmy backed away. 'All right,' he said. He wrote his number on a piece of paper, and handed it to Samantha. 'Please, just give Davey my number. Ask him to call me. I think he'll be glad he did.'

Samantha took the paper, but showed no sign of her attitude softening.

*

When Jimmy got home, he put on a wash: he didn't want Milfoth asking about strange smells from his clothes and the sleeping bag. He returned her possessions to where they had been before the house was put on the market. It meant the house was messy again, but it felt like home.

That evening, as he drew himself a bath, the phone rang. It was Davey.

'What'ya want?' he said.

'Just to talk,' said Jimmy. 'I was thinking of you the last while, and I have an idea that I want to talk to you about.'

'What'ya want?' he asked again.

Jimmy didn't feel like going into detail on the phone. 'Just to talk,' he repeated. 'Can we meet up somewhere?'

'My house, tomorrow, at one o'clock,' said Davey.

The response was so quick and definite that Jimmy was taken aback. 'OK, see you then. Just the two of us, OK?'

'Yeah,' said Davey, and hung up.

*

Jimmy arrived at Davey's house shortly before 1 PM the next day. A large white van was parked in what had become his usual parking place, so he left his car a little way down the street. He worried that the Deveneys might ambush him, but there was no sign of anything untoward.

At one end of the street, a woman and a man stood chatting, but they looked too wholesome to be the sort of people Deveney would hire. At the other end of the street, another woman and man stood talking. They didn't look like Deveney's kind either.

'Anyone else inside?' Jimmy asked, as Davey opened the door.

'No,' Davey replied, and showed him into the familiar front room. 'Are ye here to rob me again?'

Jimmy was taken aback by the suddenness of Davey's question. If he thought this was the case, why would he bring him into his house? 'No,' he replied, 'I want to show you this.'

Jimmy took a leaflet from his pocket and offered it to Davey, but he didn't look at it. 'Just wondering, coz you robbed me the last time. Didn't ye?'

It was a fair point, and Jimmy sighed in resignation. 'I'm sorry,' he said. 'But I want to make things better.'

'Like what, give me back all the money you took?'

Jimmy wasn't just uncomfortable with the subject-matter of Davey's question, but also in his tone, which seemed unnatural – as if he was speaking to a third party. 'I just want to show you this,' said Jimmy. 'It's a course in music production. I think you should do it.'

'Me?' said Davey. 'What the fuck would I do a course for?'

'Because you have a talent for music, and it could help you start a new career.'

Davey was taken aback. 'Me? Talented? I dunno 'bout that.'

Jimmy sat forward and explained: 'I've never met anyone before who taught themselves to read music. Like, I struggled with that for years, and got nowhere. You taught yourself to play the piano. I've heard you from the street, and you are good. You read music and write songs – these are things other people would have liked to do, but just couldn't. You have the talent, and this course will help you develop it.'

'What's in it for you?' asked Davey. 'Last time you were here, ye fuckin' robbed me. Didn't ye? Admit it.'

'I'm sorry,' said Jimmy, struggling to keep the conversation on track. 'If I can help you start a career, that would be worth much more to you.'

'What do you care about me?'

'I do care,' said Jimmy. 'You were kind to me, when Hank and Gunner were tormenting me. And I know you're kind to Coleen, and Samantha. You've got goodness inside you. You're not another Gunner.'

'Did you kill Hank?' asked Davey. 'Ye told me ye did. Didn't ye?'

Jimmy's line of thought was arrested by the abruptness of Davey's question. It didn't seem natural to him. He wondered why Davey wasn't interested in what he was showing him. 'Can we focus on you for a minute?' he asked gently. 'I don't think you're cut out for selling drugs . . . .'

'Are you cut out for selling drugs?' asked Davey.

'No,' said Jimmy. 'But if you . . . .'

'But you're still going to keep selling them, are ye?' asked Davey.

Jimmy was irritated by Davey's diversions. 'Let's just forget about me for a moment,' he said. 'If you keep dealing, the Deveneys, or someone else, are going to ruin your life. And perhaps end it.'

'That's my business,' said Davey.

'Yes, but I've seen you playing with Coleen, and I think you could be a very good dad to her for the rest of her life. But if you keep dealing drugs, she's going to lose a father-figure for the second time. If you love her, you've got to stop dealing.'

'But that's all I know,' protested Davey.

'It's not all you know,' said Jimmy. 'You know music. And you can make money out of it. And you'd have a great backstory.' He moved over to Davey's couch, to point at the leaflet. Davey recoiled slightly.

'I know a fella who teaches on this course,' said Jimmy. 'I've spoken with him, and he'll look out for you. He'll make sure you get your exams, and do OK. So here's the deal: if you agree to go on the course, and stop dealing drugs, I'll fill out the forms, and I will pay your course fees.'

'Yeah, but with my money. The money you stole,' said Davey.

'Can we stop talking about that, please?' said Jimmy, raising his voice. 'I'm trying to help you start a new life for yourself. It will help Samantha and Coleen as well.'

Davey's protests were running out of energy. 'Nobody's ever helped me like this before,' he said. He looked overwhelmed by Jimmy's proposal, but also looked guilty instead of grateful. 'I wasn't expecting this from you.' He seemed to hold the cord-fastener of his hoodie as he spoke, and moved further away from Jimmy.

Jimmy looked at the cord-fastener and it prompted a memory from an episode of *The Redeemables* in which they set up a scam-artist. In order to record the man's bogus business offerings, he had hidden a microphone in the cord-fastener of a potential client's hoodie.

Jimmy reached out to examine the hoodie, but Davie recoiled.

'Can I see that?' asked Jimmy, but Davey blocked the cord-fastener with his hand. 'Is that a microphone?'

Davey looked back at Jimmy in fear, and slowly lowered his hand. 'I didn't want to do it,' he pleaded. 'Samantha called them.'

Jimmy spoke in a whisper. 'You tried to set me up with the cops?'

'I'm sorry,' said Davey. 'I thought you were here to scam me again. I didn't know you were here to help . . . .'

Jimmy rose to his feet, his mouth agape. He shook his head and stared at Davey in disbelief. 'Where are they?' he asked.

Davey pointed to the window. 'Outside,' he said.

Jimmy flew into a rage. He rushed out the door and across the street to the white van. He tried all the locks but nothing opened. He punched the darkened window-panels so hard it seemed they would break, but they were reinforced. He kicked the side panels, and the doors, hard. 'McClean, you fuckin' prick. Come out and face me! Come out and face me!' he shouted, as he kicked the van again.

Jimmy circled the van looking for an entry point. 'Little pigs, little pigs, let me come in!' he sang loudly, as he tried each of the door-handles again. But the van remained still and mute. 'Hey Squeezy, do yer colleagues know you're on the take, huh? Hey everyone, Squeezy is robbing money off crims. Catch that on your fuckin' tape.'

The same woman and man were still at the top of the street. They had stopped their conversation to look at Jimmy's antics. At the bottom of the street, the other woman and man stood watching too. Jimmy shouted at them all: 'He's only a kid! You'd get him killed, pulling a stunt like that!'

Jimmy kicked the van one last time in anger, and stood fuming in the middle of the street. He looked at Davey's house, and saw the younger man looking out the window at him. Davey withdrew from the window when he saw Jimmy approach.

'Davey, Davey!' Jimmy shouted in the window. 'The offer still stands! Forget this bullshit. Call me if you want help. OK?'

Jimmy was still fuming as he drove away. He braked as he passed the woman and man at the top of the street, and shouted out his window: 'Yiz don't even look like Dubs, yiz fuckin' eejits. Yiz just look like thick country Guards trying to blend in.'

The couple looked blankly back at Jimmy.

As Jimmy drove off, he realised they weren't Gardaí; the woman was a teacher in Byron's school.

26

❧❧❧

Trish

Milfoth returned the following day. 'So what's your plan?' she asked. 'Exactly what you suggested. Let's use our money to improve the quality of our lives. Instead of moving house, let's improve the one we're in. Let's knock that wall and let more light in. And extend out that way, to give ourselves a larger kitchen.'

'Why would you want that?' she asked.

'If this would make you happy, then I would like it,' he replied. 'You've put up with a lot, and I'd like to, y'know, make things better.'

'That makes a change.'

Jimmy was about to rise to the bait, but didn't. 'Yes, I'm sorry to say it does. But change is good.'

Milfoth remained non-committal. 'Is that the whole plan?'

'No,' said Jimmy. 'I think we need a holiday: the three of us. Something to bring us together; something to create a happy memory. Together.'

'Like what?' asked Milfoth.

'I was thinking of Greece. Why don't we go back to Santorini; let Byron see where it all began?'

Milfoth smiled in approval. 'That's a nice idea. But none of this resolves the issue of you wanting to live anywhere but Dublin 8.'

'That's resolved,' said Jimmy. 'We live in an interesting area, surrounded by decent people. I've grown to like it; I just wasn't aware of it before. So if you're happy here, and Byron is happy here, then I will be very happy here with you.'

'Are you still going to inject that shit into your body?'

'Yes,' he said. 'But I have a medical need now, and I'm doing it under medical supervision. My doctor will actually do the injecting. And test my bloods regularly, to make sure I'm not overdoing it.'

Milfoth shrugged in a non-committal way.

'I was thinking,' said Jimmy, 'why don't we spend tomorrow celebrating Dublin 8?'

'What do you mean?'

'Just thinkin' of fun ways for you and me to spend time together – like we did once upon a time. We have three breweries in our neighbourhood now, and four distilleries. Let's see how many we can visit in a day.'

Milfoth laughed. 'It would cost a fortune,' she said.

'That's OK – as long as I can pay cash,' said Jimmy. They both laughed.

'Sounds nice,' she said. 'Or go for a bite? Another new restaurant has opened in Rialto. The area is changing.' They both nodded in agreement.

'Or why plan it?' he said. 'Let's just wander out together, and see what happens.'

'OK,' she said, smiling again. 'Let's just wander out together, and see what happens.'

'Together,' said Jimmy.

'Yes,' she said. 'Together.'

They smiled at each other. He moved his hand towards hers, and she moved hers towards his. Their fingers interlocked, like they had when he lay in his hospital bed, as she tended to him. He squeezed hard and she squeezed back with equal pressure. He leaned forward and rested his forehead on hers. She looked into his eyes and smiled.

'Let's try to have a nice life together . . . ' he said, and paused before finishing his sentence with a word that had once tripped off his tongue several times a minute, but in recent years had rarely crossed his mind. He held his grip on her hand, and moved his lips towards hers, and said gently, 'Trish.'